813.5082
P 941
1965 F

PZ
1
O 11
1965

Date Due

APR 1 9 1999			

Demco-293

D1158141

PRIZE STORIES 1965:
THE O. HENRY AWARDS

RAMAKER LIBRARY
Northwestern College
Orange City, Iowa

PRIZE STORIES 1965:
THE O. HENRY AWARDS

Edited by Richard Poirier and William Abrahams

WITH AN INTRODUCTION BY WILLIAM ABRAHAMS

DOUBLEDAY & COMPANY, INC., GARDEN CITY, NEW YORK

1965

29893

Library of Congress Catalog Card Number 21–9372
Copyright © 1965 by Doubleday and Company, Inc.
All Rights Reserved
Printed in the United States of America
First Edition

CONTENTS

PUBLISHER'S NOTE

THE present volume is the forty-fifth in the O. Henry Memorial Award series. No collections appeared in 1952 and 1953, when the continuity of the series was interrupted by the death of Herschel Brickell, who had been the editor for ten years.

In 1918 the Society of Arts and Sciences met to vote upon a monument to the American master of the short story, O. Henry. They decided that this memorial should be in the form of two prizes for the best short stories published by American authors in American magazines during the year 1919. From this beginning, the memorial developed into an annual anthology of the best American short stories, published, with the exception of the years mentioned above, by Doubleday & Company, Inc. Blanche Colton Williams, one of the founders of the awards, was editor from 1919 to 1932; Harry Hansen from 1933 to 1940; Herschel Brickell from 1941 to 1951; Paul Engle from 1954 to 1959 with Hanson Martin co-editor in the years 1954, 1955 and 1956; Mary Stegner in 1960; and Richard Poirier from 1961 until the present, with assistance from William Abrahams last year and this.

Doubleday has also published First-Prize Stories from the O. Henry Memorial Awards 1919–1963.

The stories chosen for this volume were published in the period from the winter of 1963 to the summer of 1964. A list of the magazines consulted appears at the back of the book. The choice of stories and the selection of prize winners are exclusively the responsibility of the editors.

INTRODUCTION

FROM the point of view of the editors the prospect is challenging: a thousand stories to be read, some very short, others formidably long—a year's production (from July 1963 to July 1964) by American writers in American magazines. And, of course, these thousand were the ones accepted for publication—how many thousands of others there must have been that were rejected! One thinks of the countless stories being written for Creative Writing Seminars at the Universities, for Adult Education Classes, for Summer Writers' Conferences, for Mail Order Correspondence Courses: the unknown total is intimidating even to contemplate. Whatever the place of the short story in the affections of American readers, there can be no question that for American writers it is the most attractive and practical form of expression.

Of the thousand published stories, experience has proved and the present instance corroborates, some seven hundred will need only a cursory reading to establish their unsuitability. These are what might be described as "commodity stories," contrived, with varying degrees of awareness, to satisfy the needs of a given market—love, sex, violence, in all their acceptable variations—stories to glance at under the hair-dryer, stories to leaf through while waiting for the TV set to be returned from the repair shop. As they proceed in their stereotyped and all too predictable grooves, falsifying the subjects with which they pretend to be dealing truthfully—even as fantasies they are too conventionalized to be interesting—one suspects that the need they satisfy best is not the reader's to be distracted but the publisher's to fill space. There, doing their job, they recognizably are: month after month in magazine after magazine, the full-packed columns of type that keep the advertisements discreetly apart.

Such stories are contrivances, and no matter how skillfully rearranged or disguised, betray themselves for what they are long before their final paragraphs have been reached. Read in quantity, they prove in spite of their vaunted "entertainment value" progressively tedious; to reread them is a form of self-punishment. Readability, it need hardly be argued, is not the ultimate criterion of merit in a short story; but it is certainly the initial one. Preparing the present collection, where the process of winnowing was continuous and prolonged, the editors found it necessary to read many of the stories several times; invariably, the better ones were felt to have gained. On the other hand, there were those vastly clever constructions whose cleverness would evaporate entirely by a third reading, leaving only commonplace bare bones.

All this is by way of introduction. Our interest, curiosity and affection is given principally to the three hundred stories—let us, for the sake of another category, call them "authentic stories"—that manage to get above the "commodity level," that have been written not to satisfy the presumed needs of a market, but to satisfy the need of the author: essentially, to write a story. Not all of them—alas for honorable intentions—are of uniform excellence; some are downright bad, lamentable in conception and in execution. Yet even in the least successful of them one feels that there has been an attempt to deal with their material honestly: one discerns, however faintly, the signature of an individual writer rather than the trademark of an electronic writing-machine.

Such stories, it is worth noting, have a way of turning up anywhere and everywhere, in the experimental little magazines, in the sober quarterlies, and in a fair number of the magazines of largest circulation, side by side, often, with "commodity stories." (Here perhaps we should also note that even the little magazines have "commodity stories" of their own, falsified to please, all chaotic syntax and ambiguous bawdry; and there are the inordinately solemn and overwritten wee anecdotes that seem "just made" for the quarterlies.) The most remarkable aspect of the "situation" in the contemporary American short story—perhaps even in American life—is that old lines and divisions simply do not apply. One reads, for example, Donald Barthelme's odd, amusing, and disquieting ironies in *The New Yorker*, and also in *Genesis West*; Warren Miller does not amend his manner as he commutes between *The Paris Review* and *The Saturday Evening Post*; Jessamyn West appears equally at home in *The Kenyon Review* and *Good Housekeeping*.

The times are not favorable to generalizations. For those of us brought up to believe in the "typical" *New Yorker* story, the "typical" *Saturday Evening Post* story, or the "typical" *Story* story, anarchy is in the air. Reading, not generalizing, you become aware of a remarkable variety among the stories: something of this is meant to be reflected in the Table of Contents of the present collection.

When one speaks of Action Painting, or Pop Art, or Musique Con-
crète, or Atonalism, or the Theatre of the Absurd, or Beat Poetry,
or the New Novel, one is describing recognizable phenomena. Nothing comparable pertains here: there are no "schools" in the contemporary short story. Of course, there will always be imitations, a
few attaining a life of their own, but more often slavish and infatu-
ated. At present, as for some years past, the baleful Influence is
Faulkner; the once inescapable Hemingway manner has been in
abeyance (but A *Moveable Feast* would seem powerful enough to
invigorate a whole new corps of disciples). Perhaps the most painful imitations to contemplate are those by certain established writers of themselves. This seems a particular pitfall for middle-aged "old
pros" of small imaginative power who pride themselves on their talent
for social observation, their serviceable prose, and their ear for dialogue. In fact, except to devoted contemporaries and to book-review-
ers who have invested in their fame, they appear sadly antiquated,
victims of the age of the tape recorder, which has quite supplanted
them.

On the whole, however, the level of accomplishment is en-
couragingly high, and markedly individual: this holds true, in particular, for the group of stories—thirty-seven this year—from which the
larger than usual final selection has been made. If, even among them,
it is intelligence rather than inspiration that dominates, there is no
cause for regret or alarm. The peculiar balance between intelligence
and inspiration that results in stories on the order of *The Dead*
or *The Lady with the Dog* or *A Simple Heart*, occurs only seldom.
Masterpieces aren't produced to order, or on schedule, nor are they
likely to be recognized as such when they first appear. All the more
reason then to emphasize the high level of accomplishment in
American short stories at present; and one is prepared to enter a
more formidable claim for Miss Flannery O'Connor's prizewinning
story, and for some of the others in this collection. The critic who
announced recently, in a tone of self-congratulation, that he was
giving up reading contemporary short stories (not, however, to the
point of no longer writing about them) presumably because they did
not measure up to his austere standards, might as logically renounce
the contemporary novel (which he did not), since nothing equal to
Anna Karenina or *The Charterhouse of Parma* is being published this
season.

We return for our conclusions to the individuality and variety, the resistance to schools and movements, in the most interesting stories being written at present. Each author goes his own way, flies his own flag—so it would seem. Yet there are signs, if one looks hard enough and takes all these stories together, of what may conceivably prove to be a *tendency*: a fondness for older forms, the fable, the ballad, the legend, the fantasy, the tale, re-created, rather than revived, with intelligence, sophistication, and an undiminished recognition of the complexities of existence. The result is a deliberate externality. The ancestral forms don't allow, very conveniently or plausibly, for introspection: characters are watched from the outside, observed; like dancers, their gestures are made to count for a great deal. Hence the somewhat ritualized, emblematic, and dual nature of many of these stories: they are not only the particular experiences of a set of characters in a fiction, they are also parables of experience in general. Not surprisingly, at the same time as the older forms are being reconstituted, the more recent forms are being gradually discarded: the carefully documented story of social experience has almost disappeared—Miss McCarthy's "The Hounds of Summer" is a notable exception; and the exploration of character in depth, the peeling away of the onion, so to speak, layer by layer, is only seldom encountered. In the "new" short story the lineaments of contemporary mythology are glimpsed close to the realistic surface: a new attempt is being made to give meaning and form to contemporary life.

But here it is necessary to pause: one runs the risk of transforming these stories into confirmations of one's generalizations. They are better discovered on their own terms.

WILLIAM ABRAHAMS

PRIZE STORIES 1965:
THE O. HENRY AWARDS

FLANNERY O'CONNOR's work has appeared several times in O. Henry Prize Story collections. Her 1954 debut with "The Life You May Save May Be Your Own" was followed in 1955 by "A Circle in the Fire," a second-prize winner. In 1957 her story "Greenleaf" was a first prize winner, as was "Everything That Rises Must Converge" in 1963. Miss O'Connor learned that, with "Revelation," she had been awarded the first prize for the third time shortly before her death in Georgia during the summer of 1964.

Revelation

THE doctor's waiting room, which was very small, was almost full when the Turpins entered and Mrs. Turpin, who was very large, made it look even smaller by her presence. She stood looming at the head of the magazine table set in the center of it, a living demonstration that the room was inadequate and ridiculous. Her little bright black eyes took in all the patients as she sized up the seating situation. There was one vacant chair and a place on the sofa occupied by a blond child in a dirty blue romper who should have been told to move over and make room for the lady. He was five or six, but Mrs. Turpin saw at once that no one was going to tell him to move over. He was slumped down in the seat, his arms idle at his sides and his eyes idle in his head; his nose ran unchecked.

Mrs. Turpin put a firm hand on Claud's shoulder and said in a voice that included anyone who wanted to listen, "Claud, you sit in that chair there," and gave him a push down into the vacant one. Claud was florid and bald and sturdy, somewhat shorter than Mrs. Turpin, but he sat down as if he were accustomed to doing what she told him to.

Mrs. Turpin remained standing. The only man in the room besides Claud was a lean stringy old fellow with a rusty hand spread out on each knee, whose eyes were closed as if he were asleep or dead or pretending to be so as not to get up and offer her his seat. Her gaze settled agreeably on a well-dressed grey-haired lady whose eyes met

Copyright © 1964 by The University of the South, Sewanee, Tennessee.

hers and whose expression said: if that child belonged to me, he would have some manners and move over—there's plenty of room there for you and him too.

Claud looked up with a sigh and made as if to rise.

"Sit down," Mrs. Turpin said. "You know you're not supposed to stand on that leg. He has an ulcer on his leg," she explained.

Claud lifted his foot onto the magazine table and rolled his trouser leg up to reveal a purple swelling on a plump marble-white calf.

"My!" the pleasant lady said. "How did you do that?"

"A cow kicked him," Mrs. Turpin said.

"Goodness!" said the lady.

Claud rolled his trouser leg down.

"Maybe the little boy would move over," the lady suggested, but the child did not stir.

"Somebody will be leaving in a minute," Mrs. Turpin said. She could not understand why a doctor—with as much money as they made charging five dollars a day to just stick their head in the hospital door and look at you—couldn't afford a decent-sized waiting room. This one was hardly bigger than a garage. The table was cluttered with limp-looking magazines and at one end of it there was a big green glass ash tray full of cigaret butts and cotton wads with little blood spots on them. If she had had anything to do with the running of the place, that would have been emptied every so often. There were no chairs against the wall at the head of the room. It had a rectangular-shaped panel in it that permitted a view of the office where the nurse came and went and the secretary listened to the radio. A plastic fern in a gold pot sat in the opening and trailed its fronds down almost to the floor. The radio was softly playing gospel music.

Just then the inner door opened and a nurse with the highest stack of yellow hair Mrs. Turpin had ever seen put her face in the crack and called for the next patient. The woman sitting beside Claud grasped the two arms of her chair and hoisted herself up; she pulled her dress free from her legs and lumbered through the door where the nurse had disappeared.

Mrs. Turpin eased into the vacant chair, which held her tight as a corset. "I wish I could reduce," she said, and rolled her eyes and gave a comic sigh.

"Oh, *you* aren't fat," the stylish lady said.

"Ooooo I am too," Mrs. Turpin said. "Claud he eats all he wants to and never weighs over one hundred and seventy-five pounds, but me I just look at something good to eat and I gain some weight," and her stomach and shoulders shook with laughter. "You can eat all you want to, can't you, Claud?" she asked, turning to him.

Claud only grinned.

"Well, as long as you have such a good disposition," the stylish lady said, "I don't think it makes a bit of difference what size you are. You just can't beat a good disposition."

Next to her was a fat girl of eighteen or nineteen, scowling into a thick blue book which Mrs. Turpin saw was entitled *Human Development*. The girl raised her head and directed her scowl at Mrs. Turpin as if she did not like her looks. She appeared annoyed that anyone should speak while she tried to read. The poor girl's face was blue with acne and Mrs. Turpin thought how pitiful it was to have a face like that at that age. She gave the girl a friendly smile but the girl only scowled the harder. Mrs. Turpin herself was fat but she had always had good skin, and, though she was forty-seven years old, there was not a wrinkle in her face except around her eyes from laughing too much.

Next to the ugly girl was the child, still in exactly the same position, and next to him was a thin leathery old woman in a cotton print dress. She and Claud had three sacks of chicken feed in their pump house that was in the same print. She had seen from the first that the child belonged with the old woman. She could tell by the way they sat—kind of vacant and white-trashy, as if they would sit there until Doomsday if nobody called and told them to get up. And at right angles but next to the well-dressed pleasant lady was a lank-faced woman who was certainly the child's mother. She had on a yellow sweat shirt and wine-colored slacks, both gritty-looking, and the rims of her lips were stained with snuff. Her dirty yellow hair was tied behind with a little piece of red paper ribbon. Worse than niggers any day, Mrs. Turpin thought.

The gospel hymn playing was, "When I looked up and He looked down," and Mrs. Turpin, who knew it, supplied the last line mentally, "And wona these days I know I'll we-eara crown."

Without appearing to, Mrs. Turpin always noticed people's feet. The well-dressed lady had on red and grey suede shoes to match her dress. Mrs. Turpin had on her good black patent leather pumps. The ugly girl had on Girl Scout shoes and heavy socks. The old woman had on tennis shoes and the white-trashy mother had on what appeared to be bedroom slippers, black straw with gold braid threaded through them—exactly what you would have expected her to have on.

Sometimes at night when she couldn't go to sleep, Mrs. Turpin would occupy herself with the question of who she would have chosen to be if she couldn't have been herself. If Jesus had said to her before he made her, "There's only two places available for you. You can either be a nigger or white-trash," what would she have said? "Please, Jesus, please," she would have said, "just let me wait until there's another place available," and he would have said, "No, you have to go right now and I have only those two places so make up your mind." She would have wiggled and squirmed and begged and pleaded but it would have been no use and finally she would have said, "All right, make me a nigger then—but that don't mean a trashy one." And he would have made her a neat clean respectable negro woman, herself but black.

Next to the child's mother was a red-headed youngish woman, reading one of the magazines and working on a piece of chewing gun, hell for leather, as Claud would say. Mrs. Turpin could not see the woman's feet. She was not white-trash, just common. Sometimes Mrs. Turpin occupied herself at night naming the classes of people. On the bottom of the heap were most colored people, not the kind she would have been if she had been one, but most of them; then next to them—not above, just away from—were the white-trash; then above them were the home-owners, and above them the home-and-land owners, to which she and Claud belonged. Above she and Claud were people with a lot of money and much bigger houses and much more land. But here the complexity of it would begin to bear in on her, for some of the people with a lot of money were common and ought to be below she and Claud and some of the people who had good blood had lost their money and had to rent and then there were colored people who owned their homes and land as well. There was a colored dentist in town who had two red Lincolns and a swimming pool and a farm with registered white-face cattle on it. Usually by the time she had fallen asleep all the classes of people were moiling and roiling around in her head, and she would dream they were all crammed in together in a box car, being ridden off to be put in a gas oven.

"That's a beautiful clock," she said and nodded to her right. It was a big wall clock, the face encased in a brass sunburst.

"Yes, it's very pretty," the stylish lady said agreeably. "And right on the dot too," she added, glancing at her watch.

The ugly girl beside her cast an eye upward at the clock, smirked, then looked directly at Mrs. Turpin and smirked again. Then she returned her eyes to her book. She was obviously the lady's daughter because, although they didn't look anything alike as to disposition, they both had the same shape of face and the same blue eyes. On the lady they sparkled pleasantly but in the girl's seared face they appeared alternately to smolder and to blaze.

What if Jesus had said, "All right, you can be white-trash or a nigger or ugly"!

Mrs. Turpin felt an awful pity for the girl, though she thought it was one thing to be ugly and another to act ugly.

The woman with the snuff-stained lips turned around in her chair and looked up at the clock. Then she turned back and appeared to look a little to the side of Mrs. Turpin. There was a cast in one of her eyes. "You want to know wher you can get you one of themther clocks?" she asked in a loud voice.

"No, I already have a nice clock," Mrs. Turpin said. Once somebody like her got a leg in the conversation, she would be all over it.

"You can get you one with green stamps," the woman said. "That's most likely wher he got hisn. Save you up enough, you can get you most anythang. I got me some joo'ry."

Ought to have got you a wash rag and some soap, Mrs. Turpin thought.

"I get contour sheets with mine," the pleasant lady said.

The daughter slammed her book shut. She looked straight in front of her, directly through Mrs. Turpin and on through the yellow curtain and the plate glass window which made the wall behind her. The girl's eyes seemed lit all of a sudden with a peculiar light, an unnatural light like night road signs give. Mrs. Turpin turned her head to see if there was anything going on outside that she should see, but she could not see anything. Figures passing cast only a pale shadow through the curtain. There was no reason the girl should single her out for her ugly looks.

"Miss Finley," the nurse said, cracking the door. The gum-chewing woman got up and passed in front of her and Claud and went into the office. She had on red high-heeled shoes.

Directly across the table, the ugly girl's eyes were fixed on Mrs. Turpin as if she had some very special reason for disliking her.

"This is wonderful weather, isn't it?" the girl's mother said.

"It's good weather for cotton if you can get the niggers to pick it," Mrs. Turpin said, "but niggers don't want to pick cotton any more. You can't get the white folks to pick it and now you can't get the niggers—because they got to be right up there with the white folks."

"They gonna *try* anyways," the white-trash woman said, leaning forward.

"Do you have one of those cotton-picking machines?" the pleasant lady asked.

"No," Mrs. Turpin said, "they leave half the cotton in the field. We don't have much cotton anyway. If you want to make it farming now, you have to have a little of everything. We got a couple of acres of cotton and a few hogs and chickens and just enough whiteface that Claud can look after them himself."

"One thang I don't want," the white-trash woman said, wiping her mouth with the back of her hand. "Hogs. Nasty stinking things, a-gruntin and a-rootin all over the place."

Mrs. Turpin gave her the merest edge of her attention. "Our hogs are not dirty and they don't stink," she said. "They're cleaner than some children I've seen. Their feet never touch the ground. We have a pig-parlor—that's where you raise them on concrete," she explained to the pleasant lady, "and Claud scoots them down with the hose every afternoon and washes off the floor." Cleaner by far than that child right there, she thought. Poor nasty little thing. He had not moved except to put the thumb of his dirty hand into his mouth.

The woman turned her face away from Mrs. Turpin. "I know I wouldn't scoot down no hog with no hose," she said to the wall.

You wouldn't have no hog to scoot down, Mrs. Turpin said to herself.

"A-gruntin and a-rootin and a-groanin," the woman muttered.

"We got a little of everything," Mrs. Turpin said to the pleasant lady. "It's no use in having more than you can handle yourself with help like it is. We found enough niggers to pick our cotton this year but Claud he has to go after them and take them home again in the evening. They can't walk that half a mile. No they can't. I tell you," she said and laughed merrily, "I sure am tired of buttering up niggers, but you got to love em if you want em to work for you. When they come in the morning, I run out and I say, 'Hi yawl this morning?' and when Claud drives them off to the field I just wave to beat the band and they just wave back." And she waved her hand rapidly to illustrate.

"Like you read out of the same book," the lady said, showing she understood perfectly.

"Child, yes," Mrs. Turpin said. "And when they come in from the field, I run out with a bucket of icewater. That's the way it's going to be from now on," she said. "You may as well face it."

"One thang I know," the white-trash woman said. "Two thangs I ain't going to do: love no niggers or scoot down no hog with no hose." And she let out a bark of contempt.

The look that Mrs. Turpin and the pleasant lady exchanged indicated they both understood that you had to *have* certain things before you could *know* certain things. But every time Mrs. Turpin exchanged a look with the lady, she was aware that the ugly girl's peculiar eyes were still on her, and she had trouble bringing her attention back to the conversation.

"When you got something," she said, "you got to look after it." And when you ain't got a thing but breath and britches, she added to herself, you can afford to come to town every morning and just sit on the Court House coping and spit.

A grotesque revolving shadow passed across the curtain behind her and was thrown palely on the opposite wall. Then a bicycle clattered down against the outside of the building. The door opened and a colored boy glided in with a tray from the drug store. It had two large red and white paper cups on it with tops on them. He was a tall, very black boy in discolored white pants and a green nylon shirt. He was chewing gum slowly, as if to music. He set the tray down in the office opening next to the fern and stuck his head through to look for the secretary. She was not in there. He rested his arms on the ledge and waited, his narrow bottom stuck out, swaying slowly to the left and right. He raised a hand over his head and scratched the base of his skull.

"You see that button there, boy?" Mrs. Turpin said. "You can punch that and she'll come. She's probably in the back somewhere."

"Is thas right?" the boy said agreeably, as if he had never seen the button before. He leaned to the right and put his finger on it. "She sometime out," he said and twisted around to face his audience, his elbows behind him on the counter. The nurse appeared and he twisted back again. She handed him a dollar and he rooted in his pocket and made the change and counted it out to her. She gave him fifteen cents for a tip and he went out with the empty tray. The heavy door swung to slowly and closed at length with the sound of suction. For a moment no one spoke.

"They ought to send all them niggers back to Africa," the white-trash woman said. "That's wher they come from in the first place."

"Oh, I couldn't do without my good colored friends," the pleasant lady said.

"There's a heap of things worse than a nigger," Mrs. Turpin agreed. "It's all kinds of them just like it's all kinds of us."

"Yes, and it takes all kinds to make the world go round," the lady said in her musical voice.

As she said it, the raw-complexioned girl snapped her teeth together. Her lower lip turned downwards and inside out, revealing the pale pink inside of her mouth. After a second it rolled back up. It was the ugliest face Mrs. Turpin had ever seen anyone make and for a moment she was certain that the girl had made it at her. She was look-ing at her as if she had known and disliked her all her life—all of Mrs. Turpin's life, it seemed too, not just all the girl's life. Why, girl, I don't even know you, Mrs. Turpin said silently.

She forced her attention back to the discussion. "It wouldn't be practical to send them back to Africa," she said. "They wouldn't want to go. They got it too good here."

"Wouldn't be what they wanted—if I had anythang to do with it," the woman said.

"It wouldn't be a way in the world you could get all the niggers back over there," Mrs. Turpin said. "They'd be hiding out and lying down and turning sick on you and wailing and hollering and raring and pitching. It wouldn't be a way in the world to get them over there."

"They got over here," the trashy woman said. "Get back like they got over."

"It wasn't so many of them then," Mrs. Turpin explained.

The woman looked at Mrs. Turpin as if here was an idiot indeed but Mrs. Turpin was not bothered by the look, considering where it came from.

"Nooo," she said, "they're going to stay here where they can go to New York and marry white folks and improve their color. That's what they all want to do, every one of them, improve their color."

"You know what comes of that, don't you?" Claud asked.

"No, Claud, what?" Mrs. Turpin said.

Claud's eyes twinkled. "White-faced niggers," he said with never a smile.

Everybody in the office laughed except the white-trash and the ugly girl. The girl gripped the book in her lap with white fingers. The trashy woman looked around her from face to face as if she thought they were all idiots. The old woman in the feed sack dress continued to gaze expressionless across the floor at the high-top shoes of the man opposite her, the one who had been pretending to be asleep when the Turpins came in. He was laughing heartily, his hands still spread out on his knees. The child had fallen to the side and was lying now almost face down in the old woman's lap.

While they recovered from their laughter, the nasal chorus on the radio kept the room from silence.

> *"You go to blank blank*
> *And I'll go to mine*
> *But we'll all blank along*
> *To-geth-ther,*
>
> *And all along the blank*
> *We'll hep eachother out*
> *Smile-ling in any kind of*
> *Weath-ther!"*

Mrs. Turpin didn't catch every word but she caught enough to agree with the spirit of the song and it turned her thoughts sober. To help anybody out that needed it was her philosophy of life. She never spared herself when she found somebody in need, whether they were white or black, trash or decent. And of all she had to be thankful for, she was most thankful that this was so. If Jesus had said, "You can be high society and have all the money you want and be thin and svelte-like, but you can't be a good woman with it," she would have had to say, "Well don't make me that then. Make me a good woman and it don't matter what else, how fat or how ugly or how poor!" Her heart rose. He had not made her a nigger or white-trash or ugly! He had made her herself and given her a little of everything. Jesus, thank you! she said. Thank you thank you thank you! Whenever she counted her blessings she felt as buoyant as if she weighed one hundred and twenty-five pounds instead of one hundred and eighty.

"What's wrong with your little boy?" the pleasant lady asked the white-trashy woman.

"He has a ulcer," the woman said proudly. "He ain't give me a minute's peace since he was born. Him and her are just alike," she said, nodding at the old woman, who was running her leathery fingers through the child's pale hair. "Look like I can't get nothing down them two but Co' Cola and candy."

That's all you try to get down em, Mrs. Turpin said to herself. Too lazy to light the fire. There was nothing you could tell her about people like them that she didn't know already. And it was not just that they didn't have anything. Because if you gave them everything, in two weeks it would all be broken or filthy or they would have chopped it up for lightwood. She knew all this from her own experience. Help them you must, but help them you couldn't.

All at once the ugly girl turned her lips inside out again. Her eyes were fixed like two drills on Mrs. Turpin. This time there was no mistaking that there was something urgent behind them.

Girl, Mrs. Turpin exclaimed silently, I haven't done a thing to you! The girl might be confusing her with somebody else. There was no need to sit by and let herself be intimidated. "You must be in college," she said boldly, looking directly at the girl. "I see you reading a book there."

The girl continued to stare and pointedly did not answer.

Her mother blushed at this rudeness. "The lady asked you a question, Mary Grace," she said under her breath.

"I have ears," Mary Grace said.

The poor mother blushed again. "Mary Grace goes to Wellesley College," she explained. She twisted one of the buttons on her dress. "In Massachusetts," she added with a grimace. "And in the summer she just keeps right on studying. Just reads all the time, a real book worm. She's done real well at Wellesley; she's taking English and Math and History and Psychology and Social Studies," she rattled on, "and I think it's too much. I think she ought to get out and have fun."

The girl looked as if she would like to hurl them all through the plate glass window.

"Way up north," Mrs. Turpin murmured and thought, well, it hasn't done much for her manners.

"I'd almost rather to have him sick," the white-trash woman said, wrenching the attention back to herself. "He's so mean when he ain't. Look like some children just take natural to meanness. It's some gets bad when they get sick but he was the opposite. Took sick and turned

good. He don't give me no trouble now. It's me waitin to see the
doctor," she said.

If I was going to send anybody back to Africa, Mrs. Turpin thought,
it would be your kind, woman. "Yes, indeed," she said aloud, but
looking up at the ceiling, "it's a heap of things worse than a nigger."
And dirtier than a hog, she added to herself.

"I think people with bad dispositions are more to be pitied than
anyone on earth," the pleasant lady said in a voice that was decidedly
thin.

"I thank the Lord he has blessed me with a good one," Mrs. Turpin
said. "The day has never dawned that I couldn't find something to
laugh at."

"Not since she married me anyways," Claud said with a comical
straight face.

Everybody laughed except the girl and the white-trash.

Mrs. Turpin's stomach shook. "He's such a caution," she said, "that
I can't help but laugh at him."

The girl made a loud ugly noise through her teeth.

Her mother's mouth grew thin and tight. "I think the worst thing
in the world," she said, "is an ungrateful person. To have everything
and not appreciate it. I know a girl," she said, "who has parents who
would give her anything, a little brother who loves her dearly, who is
getting a good education, who wears the best clothes, but who can
never say a kind word to anyone, who never smiles, who just criticises
and complains all day long."

"Is she too old to paddle?" Claud asked.

The girl's face was almost purple.

"Yes," the lady said, "I'm afraid there's nothing to do but leave
her to her folly. Some day she'll wake up and it'll be too late."

"It never hurt anyone to smile," Mrs. Turpin said. "It just makes
you feel better all over."

"Of course," the lady said sadly, "but there are just some people
you can't tell anything to. They can't take criticism."

"If it's one thing I am," Mrs. Turpin said with feeling, "it's grateful.
When I think who all I could have been besides myself and what all
I got, a little of everything, and a good disposition besides, I just feel
like shouting, 'Thank you, Jesus, for making everything the way it is!'
It could have been different!" For one thing, somebody else could
have got Claud. At the thought of this, she was flooded with gratitude

and a terrible pang of joy ran through her. "Oh thank you, Jesus, thank you!" she cried aloud.

The book struck her directly over her left eye. It struck almost at the same instant that she realized the girl was about to hurl it. Before she could utter a sound, the raw face came crashing across the table toward her, howling. The girl's fingers sank like clamps into the soft flesh of her neck. She heard the mother cry out and Claud shout, "Whoa!" There was an instant when she was certain that she was about to be in an earthquake.

All at once her vision narrowed and she saw everything as if it were happening in a small room far away, or as if she were looking at it through the wrong end of a telescope. Claud's face crumpled and fell out of sight. The nurse ran in, then out, then in again. Then the gangling figure of the doctor rushed out of the inner door. Magazines flew this way and that as the table turned over. The girl fell with a thud and Mrs. Turpin's vision suddenly reversed itself and she saw everything large instead of small. The eyes of the white-trashy woman were staring hugely at the floor. There the girl, held down on one side by the nurse and on the other by her mother, was wrenching and turning in their grasp. The doctor was kneeling astride her, trying to hold her arm down. He managed after a second to sink a long needle into it.

Mrs. Turpin felt entirely hollow except for her heart which swung from side to side as if it were agitated in a great empty drum of flesh.

"Somebody that's not busy call for the ambulance," the doctor said in the off-hand voice young doctors adopt for terrible occasions.

Mrs. Turpin could not have moved a finger. The old man who had been sitting next to her skipped nimbly into the office and made the call, for the secretary still seemed to be gone.

"Claud!" Mrs. Turpin called.

He was not in his chair. She knew she must jump up and find him but she felt like some one trying to catch a train in a dream, when everything moves in slow motion and the faster you try to run the slower you go.

"Here I am," a suffocated voice, very unlike Claud's, said.

He was doubled up in the corner on the floor, pale as paper, holding his leg. She wanted to get up and go to him but she could not move. Instead, her gaze was drawn slowly downward to the churning face on the floor, which she could see over the doctor's shoulder.

The girl's eyes stopped rolling and focussed on her. They seemed a much lighter blue than before, as if a door that had been tightly closed behind them was now open to admit light and air.

Mrs. Turpin's head cleared and her power of motion returned. She leaned forward until she was looking directly into the fierce brilliant eyes. There was no doubt in her mind that the girl did know her, knew her in some intense and personal way, beyond time and place and condition. "What you got to say to me?" she asked hoarsely and held her breath, waiting, as for a revelation.

The girl raised her head. Her gaze locked with Mrs. Turpin's. "Go back to hell where you came from, you old wart hog," she whispered. Her voice was low but clear. Her eyes burned for a moment as if she saw with pleasure that her message had struck its target.

Mrs. Turpin sank back in her chair.

After a moment the girl's eyes closed and she turned her head wearily to the side.

The doctor rose and handed the nurse the empty syringe. He leaned over and put both hands for a moment on the mother's shoulders, which were shaking. She was sitting on the floor, her lips pressed together, holding Mary Grace's hand in her lap. The girl's fingers were gripped like a baby's around her thumb. "Go on to the hospital," he said. "I'll call and make the arrangements.

"Now let's see that neck," he said in a jovial voice to Mrs. Turpin. He began to inspect her neck with his first two fingers. Two little moon-shaped lines like pink fish bones were indented over her windpipe. There was the beginning of an angry red swelling above her eye. His fingers passed over this also.

"Lea' me be," she said thickly and shook him off. "See about Claud. She kicked him."

"I'll see about him in a minute," he said and felt her pulse. He was a thin grey-haired young man, given to pleasantries. "Go home and have yourself a vacation the rest of the day," he said and patted her on the shoulder.

Quit your pattin me, Mrs. Turpin growled to herself.

"And put an ice pack over that eye," he said. Then he went and squatted down beside Claud and looked at his leg. After a moment he pulled him up and Claud limped after him into the office.

Until the ambulance came, the only sounds in the room were the tremulous moans of the girl's mother, who continued to sit on the floor. The white-trash woman did not take her eyes off the girl. Mrs. Turpin looked straight ahead at nothing. Presently the ambulance drew up, a long dark shadow, behind the curtain. The attendants came in and set the stretcher down beside the girl and lifted her expertly onto it and carried her out. The nurse helped the mother gather up her things. The shadow of the ambulance moved silently away and the nurse came back in the office.

"That ther girl is going to be a lunatic, ain't she?" the white-trash woman asked the nurse, but the nurse kept on to the back and never answered her.

"Yes, she's going to be a lunatic," the white-trash woman said to the rest of them.

"Po' critter," the old woman murmured. The child's face was still in her lap. His eyes looked idly out over her knees. He had not moved during the disturbance except to draw one leg up under him.

"I thank Gawd," the white-trash woman said fervently, "I ain't a lunatic."

Claud came limping out and the Turpins went home.

As their pick-up truck turned into their own dirt road and made the crest of the hill, Mrs. Turpin gripped the window ledge and looked out suspiciously. The land sloped gracefully down through a field dotted with lavender weeds and at the start of the rise their small yellow frame house, with its little flower beds spread out around it like a fancy apron, sat primly in its accustomed place between two giant hickory trees. She would not have been startled to see a burnt wound between two blackened chimneys.

Neither of them felt like eating so they put on their house clothes and lowered the shade in the bedroom and lay down, Claud with his leg on a pillow and herself with a damp washcloth over her eye. The instant she was flat on her back, the image of a razor-backed hog with warts on its face and horns coming out behind its ears snorted into her head. She moaned, a low quiet moan.

"I am not," she said tearfully, "a wart hog. From hell." But the denial had no force. The girl's eyes and her words, even the tone of her voice, low but clear, directed only to her, brooked no repudiation. She had been singled out for the message, though there was trash in the room to whom it might justly have been applied. The full force of this fact struck her only now. There was a woman there who was neglecting her own child but she had been overlooked. The message had been given to Ruby Turpin, a respectable, hard-working, church-going woman. The tears dried. Her eyes began to burn instead with wrath.

She rose on her elbow and the washcloth fell into her hand. Claud was lying on his back, snoring. She wanted to tell him what the girl had said. At the same time, she did not wish to put the image of herself as a wart hog from hell into his mind.

"Hey, Claud," she muttered and pushed his shoulder.

Claud opened one pale baby blue eye.

She looked into it warily. He did not think about anything. He just went his way.

"Wha, whasit?" he said and closed the eye again.

"Nothing," she said. "Does your leg pain you?"

"Hurts like hell," Claud said.

"It'll quit terreckly," she said and lay back down. In a moment Claud was snoring again. For the rest of the afternoon they lay there. Claud slept. She scowled at the ceiling. Occasionally she raised her fist and made a small stabbing motion over her chest as if she were defending her innocence to invisible guests who were like the comforters of Job, reasonable-seeming but wrong.

About five-thirty Claud stirred. "Got to go after those niggers," he sighed, not moving.

She was looking straight up as if there were unintelligible handwriting on the ceiling. The protuberance over her eye had turned a greenish-blue. "Listen here," she said.

"What?"

"Kiss me."

Claud leaned over and kissed her loudly on the mouth. He pinched her side and their hands interlocked. Her expression of ferocious concentration did not change. Claud got up, groaning and growling, and limped off. She continued to study the ceiling.

She did not get up until she heard the pick-up truck coming back with the negroes. Then she rose and thrust her feet in her brown oxfords, which she did not bother to lace, and stumped out onto the back porch and got her red plastic bucket. She emptied a tray of ice cubes into it and filled it half full of water and went out into the back yard. Every afternoon after Claud brought the hands in, one of the boys helped him put out hay and the rest waited in the back of the truck until he was ready to take them home. The truck was parked in the shade under one of the hickory trees.

"Hi yawl this evening?" Mrs. Turpin asked grimly, appearing with the bucket and the dipper. There were three women and a boy in the truck.

"Us doin nicely," the oldest woman said. "Hi you doin?" and her gaze stuck immediately on the dark lump on Mrs. Turpin's forehead. "You done fell down, ain't you?" she asked in a solicitous voice. The old woman was dark and almost toothless. She had on an old felt hat of Claud's set back on her head. The other two women were younger and lighter and they both had new bright green sun hats. One of them had hers on her head; the other had taken hers off and the boy was grinning beneath it.

Mrs. Turpin set the bucket down on the floor of the truck. "Yawl hep yourselves," she said. She looked around to make sure Claud had gone. "No. I didn't fall down," she said, folding her arms. "It was something worse than that."

"Ain't nothing bad happen to you!" the old woman said. She said it as if they all knew that Mrs. Turpin was protected in some special way by Divine Providence. "You just had you a little fall."

"We were in town at the doctor's office for where the cow kicked Mr. Turpin," Mrs. Turpin said in a flat tone that indicated they could leave off their foolishness. "And there was this girl there. A big fat girl with her face all broke out. I could look at that girl and tell she was peculiar but I couldn't tell how. And me and her mama were just talking and going along and all of a sudden WHAM! She throws this big book she was reading at me and . . ."

"Naw!" the old woman cried out.

"And then she jumps over the table and commences to choke me."

"Naw!" they all exclaimed, "naw!"

"Hi come she do that?" the old woman asked. "What ail her?"

Mrs. Turpin only glared in front of her.

"Somethin ail her," the old woman said.

"They carried her off in an ambulance," Mrs. Turpin continued, "but before she went she was rolling on the floor and they were trying to hold her down to give her a shot and she said something to me." She paused. "You know what she said to me?"

"What she say?" they asked.

"She said," Mrs. Turpin began, and stopped, her face very dark and heavy. The sun was getting whiter and whiter, blanching the sky overhead so that the leaves of the hickory tree were black in the face of it. She could not bring forth the words. "Something real ugly," she muttered.

"She sho shouldn't said nothin ugly to you," the old woman said. "You so sweet. You the sweetest lady I know."

"She pretty too," the one with the hat on said.

"And stout," the other one said. "I never knowed no sweeter white lady."

"That's the truth befo' Jesus," the old woman said. "Amen! You des as sweet and pretty as you can be."

Mrs. Turpin knew just exactly how much negro flattery was worth and it added to her rage. "She said," she began again and finished this time with a fierce rush of breath, "that I was an old wart hog from hell."

There was an astounded silence.

"Where she at!" the youngest woman cried in a piercing voice. "Lemme see her. I'll kill her!"

"I'll kill her with you!" the other one cried.

"She b'long in the sylum," the old woman said emphatically. "You the sweetest white lady I know."

"She pretty too," the other two said. "Stout as she can be and sweet. Jesus satisfied with her!"

"Deed he is," the old woman declared.

Idiots! Mrs. Turpin growled to herself. You could never say anything intelligent to a nigger. You could talk at them but not with them. "Yawl ain't drunk your water," she said shortly. "Leave the bucket in the truck when you're finished with it. I got more to do than just stand around and pass the time of day," and she moved off and into the house.

She stood for a moment in the middle of the kitchen. The dark protuberance over her eye looked like a miniature tornado cloud which might any moment sweep across the horizon of her brow. Her lower lip protruded dangerously. She squared her massive shoulders. Then she marched into the front of the house and out the side door and started down the road to the pig parlor. She had the look of a woman going single-handed, weaponless, into battle.

The sun was a deep yellow now like a harvest moon and was riding westward very fast over the far tree line as if it meant to reach the hogs before she did. The road was rutted and she kicked several good-sized stones out of her path as she strode along. The pig parlor was on a little knoll at the end of a lane that ran off from the side of the barn. It was a square of concrete as large as a small room, with a board fence about four feet high around it. The concrete floor sloped slightly so that the hog wash could drain off into a trench where it was carried to the field for fertilizer. Claud was standing on the outside, on the edge of the concrete, hanging onto the top board, hosing down the floor inside. The hose was connected to the faucet of a water trough nearby.

Mrs. Turpin climbed up beside him and glowered down at the hogs inside. There were seven long-snouted bristly shoats in it—tan with liver-colored spots—and an old sow a few weeks off from farrowing. She was lying on her side grunting. The shoats were running about shaking themselves like idiot children, their little slit pig eyes searching the floor for anything left. She had read that pigs were the most intelligent animal. She doubted it. They were supposed to be smarter than dogs. There had even been a pig astronaut. He had performed his assignment perfectly but died of a heart attack afterwards because they left him in his electric suit, sitting upright throughout his examination when naturally a hog should be on all fours.

A-gruntin and a-rootin and a-groanin.

"Gimme that hose," she said, yanking it away from Claud. "Go on and carry them niggers home and then get off that leg."

"You look like you might have swallowed a mad dog," Claud observed, but he got down and limped off. He paid no attention to her humors.

Until he was out of earshot, Mrs. Turpin stood on the side of the pen, holding the hose and pointing the stream of water at the hind quarters of any shoat that looked as if it might try to lie down. When he had had time to get over the hill, she turned her head slightly and wrathful eyes scanned the path. He was nowhere in sight. She turned back again and seemed to gather herself up. Her shoulders rose and she drew in her breath.

"What do you send me a message like that for?" she said in a low fierce voice, barely above a whisper but with the force of a shout in its concentrated fury. "How am I a hog and me both? How am I saved and from hell too?" Her free fist was knotted and with the other she gripped the hose, blindly pointing the stream of water in and out of the eye of the old sow whose outraged squeal she did not hear.

The pig parlor commanded a view of the back pasture where their twenty beef cows were gathered around the hay-bales Claud and the boy had put out. The freshly cut pasture sloped down to the highway. Across it was their cotton field and beyond that a dark green dusty wood which they owned as well. The sun was behind the wood, very red, looking over the paling of trees like a farmer inspecting his own hogs.

"Why me?" she rumbled. "It's no trash around here, black or white, that I haven't given to. And break my back to the bone every day working. And do for the church."

She appeared to be the right size woman to command the arena before her. "How am I a hog?" she demanded. "Exactly how am I like them?" and she jabbed the stream of water at the shoats. "There was plenty of trash there. It didn't have to be me.

"If you like trash better, go get yourself some trash then," she railed. "You could have made me trash. Or a nigger. If trash is what you wanted why didn't you make me trash?" She shook her fist with the hose in it and a watery snake appeared momentarily in the air. "I could quit working and take it easy and be filthy," she growled. "Lounge about the sidewalks all day drinking root beer. Dip snuff and spit in every puddle and have it all over my face. I could be nasty.

"Or you could have made me a nigger. It's too late for me to be a nigger," she said with deep sarcasm, "but I could act like one. Lay down in the middle of the road and stop traffic. Roll on the ground."

In the deepening light everything was taking on a mysterious hue. The pasture was growing a peculiar glassy green and the streak of highway had turned lavender. She braced herself for a final assault and this time her voice rolled out over the pasture. "Go on," she yelled, "call me a hog! Call me a hog again. From hell. Call me a wart hog from hell. Put the bottom rail on top. There'll still be a top and bottom!"

A garbled echo returned to her.

A final surge of fury shook her and she roared, "Who do you think you are?"

The color of everything, field and crimson sky, burned for a moment with a transparent intensity. The question carried over the pasture and across the highway and the cotton field and returned to her clearly like an answer from beyond the wood.

She opened her mouth but no sound came out of it.

A tiny truck, Claud's, appeared on the highway, heading rapidly out of sight. Its gears scraped thinly. It looked like a child's toy. At any moment a bigger truck might smash into it and scatter Claud's and the niggers' brains all over the road.

Mrs. Turpin stood there, her gaze fixed on the highway, all her muscles rigid, until in five or six minutes the truck reappeared, returning. She waited until it had had time to turn into their own road. Then like a monumental statue coming to life, she bent her head slowly and gazed, as if through the very heart of mystery, down into the pig parlor at the hogs. They had settled all in one corner around the old sow who was grunting softly. A red glow suffused them. They appeared to pant with a secret life.

Until the sun slipped finally behind the tree line, Mrs. Turpin remained there with her gaze bent to them as if she were absorbing some abysmal life-giving knowledge. At last she lifted her head. There was only a purple streak in the sky, cutting through a field of crimson and leading, like an extension of the highway, into the descending dusk. She raised her hands from the side of the pen in a gesture hieratic and profound. A visionary light settled in her eyes. She saw the streak as a vast swinging bridge extending upward from the earth through a field of living fire. Upon it a vast horde of souls were rumbling toward heaven. There were whole companies of white-trash, clean for the first time in their lives, and bands of black niggers in white robes, and battalions of freaks and lunatics shouting and clapping and leaping like frogs. And bringing up the end of the procession was a tribe of people whom she recognized at once as those who, like herself and Claud, had always had a little of everything and the God-given wit to use it right. She leaned forward to observe them closer. They were marching behind the others with great dignity, accountable as they had always been for good order and common sense and respectable behavior. They alone were on key. Yet she could see by their shocked and altered faces that even their virtues were being burned away. She lowered her hands and gripped the rail of the hog pen, her eyes small but fixed unblinkingly on what lay ahead. In a moment the vision faded but she remained where she was, immobile.

At length she got down and turned off the faucet and made her slow way on the darkening path to the house. In the woods around her the invisible cricket choruses had struck up, but what she heard were the voices of the souls climbing upward into the starry field and shouting hallelujah.

SANFORD FRIEDMAN was born in New York, went to Carnegie Institute of Technology (Pittsburgh) where he majored in acting and playwriting. He has written seven full-length plays, the first of which, *Dawn from an Unknown Ocean*, was produced when he was nineteen at the University Playhouse on Cape Cod. The last, *The Abolitionist*, describes John Brown's raid at Harpers Ferry. After his discharge from the Army in 1953 he, with several associates, leased and renovated the Carnegie Hall Playhouse where they co-produced, among other plays, Morgan's *The River Line*, Ionesco's *The Bald Soprano*, Beckett's *All That Fall*. In 1958 he co-produced Behan's *The Quare Fellow* at the Circle-in-the-Square, New York. Originally published in *Partisan Review*, "Ocean" is a section of his first novel *Totempole* which will be published in 1965 by E. P. Dutton. He is now living in New York City and at work on a second novel.

Ocean

THE center of Seaside's social life was not the public beach, but the Casino on Ocean Avenue. There, on top of the low clay cliffs that lined the Jersey coast for miles, the summer residents pursued their pleasures as if the beach and ocean did not exist. The Casino's facilities included bathhouses, a restaurant, a lounge, a card room, an outdoor dance floor and bandstand, and a fifty foot pool.

Stephen had received his first swimming lessons in the pool when he was three, but now, at the age of six, he had very mixed and complicated feelings about it. On the one hand, he adored the pool just because it was made of water. That in itself was saying a lot since Stephen loved the water more than almost anything—not more than Clarry, of course, and not more than his marine collection, but more than Mommy sometimes, and more than Daddy at others, and certainly a whole lot more than his brother, Roggie. The other thing he liked about the pool was the fact that you could jump into it whenever you liked, providing of course you had waited an hour after lunch. There was always someone around to keep an eye on you—

Copyright © 1964 by Partisan Review.

like Mommy right this minute: "Three bam."—that was its one advantage over the ocean.

But whatever its advantages, the swimming pool just didn't compare with the ocean. In the first place the ocean, salty or not, wasn't
filled with this irritating chemical that burned your eyes. In the second place there weren't all these grown-ups eating and knitting and
gossiping and playing Mah Jong and Michigan rummy and backgam-
mon and bridge, and whispering about the Lindbergh baby—at the
ocean you could get off on your own. In the third place there weren't
all these older children—including Roggie—showing off by plunging
into the water an inch away from your nose, trying so hard to blind
and drown you. The ocean didn't need to be churned up artificially,
it had a way of churning itself up—of making its own stir, its own
splash and spray and waves, wilder than any kicking children.

And yet, for some reason, the ocean's wildness—the feature that
attracted Stephen most—made the grown-ups nervous, and they for-
bade him to go into the water alone. That hateful rule created awful
problems for Stephen, not only because no one trusted Bruce, the
lifeguard, to rescue him if he should drown, but also because Mommy
was suffering from something a little bit like chicken pox called neurasthenia that made her skin break out and itch terribly, and she
wasn't supposed to set foot in salt water. Stephen had a theory of his
own that the water would wash away the sores and scabs that covered Mommy's back (and stained her sheets and nightgowns), but
Mommy had explained that brine was an irritant. Clarry had a problem, too, about going into the ocean: she claimed she couldn't swim.
But Stephen knew it wasn't all *that* simple because once, when he
asked her why she stayed in her uniform instead of putting on a bathing suit when they went down to the beach, Clarry laughed and said,
"'cause they don't make 'em big enough for me"; and another time,
when Stephen asked her why she refused even to wade, Clarry said,
"What's the matter with you, sugar? These folks don't want my kind
messin' up their water." That left only Daddy, but Daddy had to work
in New York five days a week and could take Stephen into the ocean
only on week-ends and Friday afternoons when, like today, he came
back from the City early, at four-fifteen . . . Stephen looked up at
the big clock on the white wall outside the members' lounge: 2:00.
. . . It would be hours and hours and hours before Daddy's train
arrived.

. . . But even so, even though he was not allowed to go into the ocean except on week-ends, Stephen preferred the sea to the pool, the beach to the casino—at least there was the sand. Not only could you embrace the sand and eat the sand and drool your saliva into it, and punch and pat it, and roll and run and turn somersaults on it, and flop and jump and stand on your head on it, and let it trickle through your fingers, and dribble it between your daddy's toes, and throw it into your brother's eyes and pick it out of your belly-button; but also, down by the water's edge, when the tide was low, you could dig pits and pools and caves and caverns in the sand, you could build bridges, moats, canals, towers, temples, castles, kingdoms in the sand.

As a matter of fact, Stephen Wolfe had quite a reputation for his sand creations on the Seaside public beach. Grown-ups and children alike admired his patience and imagination, and stood enthralled while Stephen patty-caked pies and cones and domes in the sand, let the sand drip from his fingers like paraffin, creating pagodas and minarets, mounded and moulded the sand into Pueblo huts and Moroccan hovels, amassed great piles of sand and made them into ziggurats, sliced through others with a stave from an orange-crate and produced Assyrian palaces, Egyptian pyramids and Rockefeller Center, transformed the stave into London Bridge, scooped out giant reservoirs and filled them with water piped from the sea, engineered a system of canals and water-ways through a city the size of Bruges, and spent entire days reconstructing Babylon, Jerusalem and Carcassonne.

And yet, no matter how arduously he labored, how deep he dug his moats, how high he flung his bulwarks, how much he reinforced his walls, at some point in the night the sea came in and stole his castles from him. At first Stephen had thought Daddy was the culprit, and then he decided that it was Roggie who sneaked down to the beach and trampled his creations, until one day Clarry made it clear to him. "There's a war goin' on between them two—between the ocean and the land. Has been since the beginnin' of creation. That old ocean's on the warpath 'cause it come first and the land come after. It jealous now 'cause the land is so much larger. Jealous 'cause the land has got itself collected—sittin' cool and pretty—while's the ocean, it always on the go, restless and rampagin'. Sort of like the difference between a man and woman. Yes sir," Clarry chuckled, "that what it remind *me* of: the natural, born-in difference between a man and woman. Why that old ocean's like a starvin' animal, lappin' at the land. Ain't nothin' gonna satisfy it 'til it's licked us all way." Stephen agreed. The trouble with the ocean—its only drawback—was that it wanted to gobble up everything in sight. But on the other hand, it gave things back. It gave back all those treasures that he had been collecting now for three successive summers—his great marine collection that was resting right this minute safe and sound at home on the radiator box in front of his bedroom window . . .

"Stevie, kitten," Mommy called.

Quickly, not in answer to his mother's call but in order to escape it, Stephen submerged, swam under water and came up on the other side of the pool. Holding onto the tiled conduit, Stephen hugged the side of the pool and held his breath, hidden from sight—or so he thought—listening to Mommy and the girls playing Mah Jong.

". . . Two bam. One crack. Six dots. Pung! Flower. East wind. Soap. Kong!"

"Come on, kitten," Mommy called again. "I can see you there. You've been in for over an hour."

"Green. Four bam. Four dots. South. Red. Flower. Five crack. Mah Jong!"

Stephen peeked over the side of the pool and saw Mrs. Tishman press her jeweled fingers down and move the rest of her row of tiles up like linotype onto the top of her rack.

"I tell you she's been to the stable today," Aunt Ida remarked.

"She stepped in it good!" Aunt Fanny corroborated.

"Up to her knees!" Mrs. Kanig added.

As always, this puzzling commentary was followed by a din as familiar to Stephen as the sound of the milkman loading the empties into his wagon: the ladies were mixing the Mah Jong tiles. "Excuse me, girls," Harriet said. "I'm going to get that child out of the water before he turns into a fish." Hearing this, Stephen pushed off from the side and swam toward the center of the pool. "Come on, Stevie, come out now. I'm not fooling with you anymore."

"Oh, Mommy," Stephen pleaded.

"Come on now."

"Just five more minutes?"

"No! You heard me: out!"

"But Roggie's—"

"I don't want to hear about Roger. If you expect to go in the ocean with Daddy later on, you'll come out now—right this minute!"

"Oh, Mommy," Stephen complained, ascending the semi-circular steps at the shallow end of the pool.

"Look at you! Look at your eyes, they're bloodshot. You won't be happy until you turn into a fish. Come on now," Mommy said, taking Stephen's hand and leading him towards the Mah Jong table. "I want you to go inside and change your suit. Come; I'll give you the bathhouse key."

"There he is! There's my angel," Aunt Ida glowed. *"Unbeschreiblich,* Hattie, is that a doll!"

"Stevie," Mommy coached, "give Aunt Ida a kiss."

"Hello, Aunt Ida," Stephen said. Kiss! "Hello, Aunt Fanny." Kiss.

"Huhwo, wuffie," Aunt Fanny gabbled, her mouth, as always, packed with pralines.

"What about *me?*" Mrs. Tishman asked. "Don't *I* get a kiss?"

"Hello, Mrs. Tishman." Kiss. "Hello, Mrs. Kanig." Kiss.

"All right, darling," Mommy said. "Here's the key. Now go and change your suit."

Stephen did as he was told: took the key and trotted around the pool towards the bathhouses. As he did so, Aunt Ida repeated the word *unbeschreiblich,* and Stephen thought: there are just too many words like that—like pung and kong and Mah Jong—that don't make any sense . . . As he entered Row A of the bathhouses, Stephen slowed down to a walk to protect his bare feet from the splintery boards. He loved this part of the Casino. Its long, narrow, east-west streets, intersected by shorter, broader avenues, constituted a city for him—a city in which he could explore and hide and chase around for hours without ever really getting lost or run over. Occasionally, among the million, identical, gray wooden doors (each with its six-inch diamond cut way above the level of a grown-up's eyes) Stephen would discover one that wasn't locked—a bathhouse that had not been rented for the summer!—and appropriate it for himself, turning it into a tower or dungeon, a place in which to think his private thoughts, hold dialogues with imaginary friends, store treasures and eavesdrop on his neighbors. It was in one of these dark cells that he had first overheard the words: "Hauptman," "F. D. R.," "tits" and "excruciate," before some officious attendant evicted him and made sure the door was locked for the remainder of the season.

When Stephen reached the end of Row A, he turned right briskly, padded past B and C and D Streets, took a left at E Street, until he reached the door marked 97, and inserted the key. Once inside, he ignored the two turkish towels hanging on separate hooks on the right hand wall, ignored the first one on the left and pulled down the

second. After locking the door behind him, he walked to the end of E
Street, turned left and meandered towards the men's shower. On
the way, between E and D Streets, he came to the wall marked
WOMEN. As always, as he passed, Stephen tried surreptitiously to
catch a glimpse of the women inside, but the barrier obstructed his
view. He knew what lay beyond was identical to what lay beyond the
wall marked MEN: one enormous room without a ceiling, one long,
green wooden bench, one clothes wringer and three unpartitioned
showers with rusty chains. After the showers came a little house with
a cement floor, two white sinks, two silver mirrors, two white urinals,
three gray booths and three white toilets. Long ago, when he was
little, Stephen had gone behind the wall marked WOMEN almost
every day with Mommy, except when Roggie took him behind the
wall marked MEN. On week-ends, of course, he had always gone behind the wall marked MEN with Daddy and that's the way it had
been for years and years until one summer when Mommy announced
he had grown too big to continue coming with her anymore. When
Stephen had asked her to come, instead, with *him*, Mommy only
laughed and said she couldn't. That had left him slightly confused.
Not only had he grown accustomed to going to the Women's, he considered it his proper place—until, that is, Daddy explained that it
was much more fun and natural "for the boys to get off on their own"
and "keep the girls out of their hair." After that, the whole thing had
seemed much more reasonable, and Stephen didn't mind being re-
stricted to the area behind the wall marked MEN—as a matter of fact,
he considered it a privilege. The only thing that bothered him about
the women and made him try to peer beyond the barrier every time
he passed, was that Stephen didn't know exactly what it was he had
seen when he was little that he was supposed to have forgotten now
that he was big . . .

After crossing D Street, he came to the wall marked MEN, casually
tossed his towel over his shoulder and strolled around the barrier. Inside there was an old, old, fat man, standing in front of the long
green bench, taking off his bathing suit. As Stephen approached, the
old, old, fat man said hello. Stephen said hello in return and sat down
in the sunshine to watch the man disrobe. As always with grown-ups,
under his bathing suit, the old, old man wore one of those silvery
pouches that looked like a horse's feed-bag over his peepee-er. Stephen had not yet figured out the purpose of those pouches . . . did
they keep the grown-ups warm? Or were they more like Mommy's

hairnet—that awful brown web she wove around her head at night before she went to bed. Was that the reason little boys didn't have to wear them, because they didn't have any hair to keep in place? . . . Stephen watched the old man roll down over his enormous belly the elastic, supporting the silvery pouch, until the whole thing— elastic and pouch together—turned into a figure 8 around his blood- less ankles and he stepped out of it clumsily. When he bent over to pick up both his bathing suit and the figure 8, the old man's belly sagged like the underside of the hammock when Daddy was lying in it. Also, the old man's peepee-er looked like the neck of a dead chicken, and Stephen had to chuckle.

"What's the matter with you, sonny?" the old man asked "Ain't you ever seen your father? What are you doing anyway, sitting there like that? This ain't a peep-show." Stephen could tell from the harsh- ness of his voice that the old man was angry and he turned away guiltily. A moment later he heard the old man exclaim, "Oooisch!" and Stephen turned around again, only to be confronted by the chicken neck bobbing up and down as the old man cowered and cavorted under the icy shower. "Look here, sonny," he grumbled, re- leasing the rusty chain and stopping the flow of water, "ain't you got anything better to do than sit there staring at me?"

"Can I run your bathing suit through the wringer for you?" Stephen asked.

"No, you can't," the old man answered curtly, donning his terry- cloth robe to protect his modesty. "You're Sol Wolfe's son, ain't you?" he asked, collecting his belongings. "The younger," he added sardonically, as he moved towards the exit—his clogs clattering over the floor boards—and disappeared.

The ambiguity of these last words left Stephen puzzled and staring after the old man, but his concern was only momentary. A second later he hopped off the bench, pulled down his bathing suit and ran to the first shower. Standing on tip-toe, stretching his left arm until the muscles ached, Stephen was just able to reach the rusty ring and pull it down. Taking pains to keep the freezing water from spattering his shoulders, he doused his bathing suit, released the chain and skipped over to the wringer. Carefully, he inserted a corner of his bloated, blue wool bathing suit—black now from the water—between the ivory-colored rubber rollers and began to turn the crank. Almost as if they were synchronized, Stephen's tongue emerged from his mouth at the same rate of speed as his bathing suit from between the rollers, so that by the time the garment was completely wrung-out, flat and dry and blue again—some of the surface hairs even silver in the sunlight—Stephen was licking his nose. Indeed, he loved the clothes wringer so much that when he was finished with his bathing suit, he repeated the entire process with his turkish towel from dousing through cranking. As a little boy, Stephen had tried, without success, to run his fingers and even his tongue between the rollers, and he still looked forward to the day when he would be tall enough to experiment with his peepee-er.

When he was finished, Stephen wrapped his damp towel around his waist, wandered back to E 97, changed into his red wool bathing suit, put on his orange water wings and waited impatiently for Daddy to come.

By the time Saul arrived, an unpleasant wind was blowing out of the south-east and the sky was overcast. The ocean didn't look the least bit tempting—after all, it was September 7th, the summer was over and this was to be their last week-end before moving back to New York—but Saul knew how disappointed the boys would be if he cancelled their dip, and he got into his bathing suit. "Come on, kids," he said. "We better hurry. There's going to be a storm."

"In that case, Dad, let's go down by the wooden steps," Roggie suggested.

Before Saul could answer, Stephen exclaimed, "No!"

"But Roggie's right, *kleine* dear. Look how much time we could save."

"No!"

"All right. We'll go the way we always do."

"No fair!" Roggie objected. "Why do we always have to go *his* way?"

"I'll tell you what, sweetheart, why don't *you* go down the wooden steps, and Stevie and I'll go down the main one, and then we'll all meet on the beach."

"Why can't you come with me and let him go by himself, if he's so stubborn?"

"Because he's too little. You know he can't go by himself."

"Why can't Mommy take him?"

"Because Mommy's playing Mah Jong."

The question settled, Stephen turned to his brother and made a nefarious face like Dr. Fu Manchu about to pull the switch that would annihilate the whole white race.

"Look at him! Look at him!" Roggie shouted. "Stinker!"

"I'm *not* a stinker!"

"Listen, kids," Daddy intervened, "either we go this minute or we don't go at all. Come on now, Roggie. Let's see who'll get there first."

"Are you kidding, Dad?" Roggie scoffed.

"All right. On your mark, get set—" Even before Daddy had a chance to say go, Roggie tore away across the dance floor, around the bandstand, toward the narrow wooden stairs that scaled the cliffs from the beach to the Casino. At the same moment Stephen took hold of Daddy's hand and tugged him in the opposite direction: out of the Casino, down the gravel driveway, onto Ocean Avenue, toward Seaside's stellar attraction: the promenade and Grand Stairway, two blocks south.

Construction of the Grand Stairway was begun in 1888 and completed in 1891, at a time when Seaside had hopes of contending with Newport and Southampton for favor as the foremost resort on the Eastern Seaboard. Built of red sandstone in the shape of an "X," the stairway could be approached from either the north or south—it made no difference which, since its two broad descending flights were symmetrical and converged onto a central landing halfway down the side of the cliff before they branched off toward the beach in opposite directions. But in the forty-six summers that had passed since the ribbon-cutting ceremony, the elements—the merciless wind and spray—the bathers' clogs, and toy tin shovels had taken their toll of the stately stone newels and Victorian bas reliefs, the ornately carved balusters and rails, and had left the stairway a ruin, just as the years had ruined its earliest users—lovely young ladies with pink and yellow parasols—who sat, now, gray and withered dowagers, all bundled-up on stiff-backed benches along the promenade. And yet to Stephen the Stairway still retained its former grandeur. He considered it the most splendid in the world—except, perhaps, for the one in Central Park leading down to the fountain and the rowboat pond—and always insisted on using it.

When they reached the stairhead, Stephen saw the red flag flapping on Bruce's lifeguard pole, he saw the waves and whitecaps and the darkness gathering in the south-east. Instead of deterring him, these signs of storm only excited and spurred Stephen on, and he practically dragged Daddy after him, down the two long flights. At the foot of the south flight, stretched out on the sand, his head of curly black hair pillowed on his palms, was Roggie, trying for all the world to look completely casual, despite his heaving chest. "What took you so long, slowpoke?"

"I am not a slowpoke!"

"I've been waiting here an hour."

"You couldn't have. We only—"

"Come on, kids," Daddy interrupted. "Let's go in right away, before it gets too cold."

There were very few people left on the beach. Even those who had not been scared away by the on-coming storm, were leaving now because of the hour, straggling toward the Stairway, dragging their towels and umbrellas, toys and thermos bottles, backrests and inner-tubes across the littered sand. As Stephen ran toward the water, he spotted the old, old fat man he had seen in the shower earlier that afternoon, and he slowed down and waited for Daddy.

When their paths crossed, Daddy stopped and greeted the old man cheerfully. "Hello, Max."

"Hello, Sol."

"Boys, say hello to Mr. Strauss, the toughest pinochle player in New Jersey."

"Hello, Mr. Strauss," Roggie said, shaking hands.

"That's Roger, Max, my older boy," Daddy explained with pride. "And this is Stevie, the younger one. *Kleine,* say hello to Mr. Strauss."

"There's no need, Sol. The youngster and I have met," Mr. Strauss said insinuatingly. "Ain't we, sonny?"

Stephen looked blank.

"Have you, Max? Where was that?"

"In the shower room, this afternoon. I must say, Sol, the boy has got a most peculiar habit."

"Peculiar, Max?" Daddy asked defensively. "What do you mean?"

"Come, Sol," Mr. Strauss suggested, taking hold of Daddy's arm. "Walk me to the stairs a minute."

"Boys, you stay here and play, but don't go in 'til I come back. And no roughhouse."

"Okay, Dad," Roggie said, wrapping his arm around his brother protectively, "I'll take care of him."

When the grown-ups were out of earshot, Stephen whispered, "Roggie, what exactly does peculiar mean?"

"Peculiar! Well now, let's see. . . . Peculiar. That means kind of . . . oh, you know . . . kind of—I think I could tell you better by saying it in a sentence. Let's see now: 'the old lady . . . the old lady was very, very peculiar.' You understand?"

"Not exactly."

"Wait a minute. I'll think up another one. 'Ickes is a most peculiar name.' "

"Who's Ickes?"

"What's the matter with you? Don't you know *anything?*"

Suddenly startled by the breaking of a very large wave, Stephen exclaimed, "Gosh! Did you see that one? Let's go down and see what it's brought us."

"That's all you think the ocean's there for—don't you, Stevie?—to bring *you* presents." Stephen raced down to the tide line and waited impatiently for the leisurely surf to recede from the shore and reveal its store of treasures. "You heard what Daddy said: you can't go in 'til he comes back."

"I'm not going in," Stephen answered, ankle-deep in water. "I'm just looking," he explained, feeling the wave's ebb tow at his heels, eroding the sand under his feet—his feet sinking deeper and deeper into the softness as he watched the stampede of stones and shells and sea wrack rush headlong back into the ocean. "Ohh!" he gasped, suddenly seeing a piece of green glass among the rubble and snatching it up before the next wave broke. "Look, Roggie. Look! An emerald!"

"You act like it's the first green you ever found. You must have two hundred greens by now."

"No I don't. I have thirty-six—thirty-seven now."

Suddenly, despite the noise of the surf, despite the fact that Daddy was well over a hundred yards away and the wind blowing in his direction, the boys recognized their father's voice, roaring in the distance. Together they turned and saw him standing at the bottom of the stairs that led to the Casino, shaking his fist at Mr. Strauss who was hurriedly mounting the steps. Automatically, Stephen began to gnaw at the cuticle of his thumb. "What is Daddy mad about?"

"Don't ask me," Roggie said, sucking his lower lip and turning away discreetly.

Taking the cue from his brother, Stephen turned away, too, and began to examine the emerald, but his ears remained fixed on his father's voice. None of the words, only the anger was intelligible to Stephen. Listening intently, he looked up from the piece of glass at the ocean. A comber was moving toward the shore, mounting steadily: ten, twelve, twenty-five feet high—or so it seemed to Stephen—a tidal wave like Daddy's voice, looming up, crashing down, splashing his thighs with stinging brine, spattering his face with foam, dragging, dragging at his ankles. But Stephen stood his ground.

"Look! A zeppelin!" Roggie exclaimed. Stephen looked up and smiled at the silver cucumber, floating through the sky. "Some day I'm going to fly in one of those."

"Can I come, too?"

"I don't know. We'll see."

"Oh, Roggie, please, please let me come, too."

"We'll see, I said. We'll see how good you are from now on."

"I'll be good. I promise."

"Here comes Daddy."

"Look, Daddy, look," Stephen shouted, pointing at the zeppelin, but Daddy didn't look.

"Come on, kids," Daddy said, putting his arms around the shoulders of both his sons. "Let's go in. It's getting late."

"Wait a second, Daddy," Stephen said, storing the emerald inside his bathing suit for safe-keeping.

"No one criticizes *my* boys and gets away with it," Daddy went on. "Not while *I'm* alive, they don't . . . careful now, it's kind of rough. Come on, *kleine*, take my hand . . . that-a-boy. Roggie, don't go out too far; better stick near us."

"I'm okay, Dad. It's not *that* rough," Roggie said, stroking and kicking with all his might, trying for Daddy's sake to demonstrate his best form. "Watch me! Watch me!"

"That's very good, Rog. Very good. Just be careful," Daddy said, lifting Stephen in his hands and holding him for one thrilling moment above the crest of a wave.

"Yipeeee!" Stephen screamed. When they got beyond the breakers, Daddy let go of Stephen. With his water wings on, Stephen floated like a bob, and Daddy's head and shoulders broke the surface like a bust resting on a mantel. "Is it over my head?"

"Sure it is."

"Is it over yours?"

"No, sweetheart. I can still touch bottom here. Let's see how well you swim." Stephen lay back lackadaisically, kicked his left leg and flung his right arm out perpendicular to his body. "Come on now, you can do better than that. That's not the way you were taught. Look at Roggie. You remember," Daddy coached. "Stroke, kick, breathe. Stroke, kick, breathe. Just like in the swimming pool."

. . . But the ocean *wasn't* like the swimming pool—everyone knew that!—What made Daddy always say it was? The swimming pool was nothing but a great big box—eight feet deep at one end, two feet at the other—whose water was piped in through a spout and drained off at the sides, whose only sign of life was what you, the swimmer, brought to it. *That* was the all-important difference! In the ocean you didn't need to bother swimming, the ocean did it *for* you. The ocean was alive! . . . "Daddy."

"What, *kleine?*"

"Let's play zeppelin."

"Zeppelin?"

"You know, instead of playing boat."

"All right," Daddy said, and he submerged obligingly.

Stephen scrambled onto Daddy's broad back and wrapped his arms around Daddy's neck and his legs around his tummy. The contact of their lubricated flesh reminded Stephen of Clarry's soapy hands in the bathtub, and he deliberately wriggled and squirmed and coiled his limbs around Daddy's body. "Mmmmmmmmmmmm!" Stephen imitated the motor of a zeppelin, as Daddy did the breast-stroke. "Faster!" he commanded, and Daddy obeyed, swimming parallel to the shore. In his excitement Stephen forgot about the zeppelin and began to jog up and down on Daddy's back. "Giddyap!"

"Hey! I thought I was a zeppelin," Daddy said, spitting out a mouthful of water.

"No, a horse! A horse!" Stephen squealed, sitting upright and straddling his daddy, holding on to Daddy's bald head with both hands like a stirrup, moving it from right to left, manipulating it like a joystick, like a rudder, like a steering wheel. There, now, between Stephen's thighs, Daddy had become his horse, his plane, his boat, his car, his engine, steaming through the ocean. Almost in a state of rapture, Stephen vised his mount and pounded on its back, as if it were nighttime and he were squeezing and pummeling his pillow.

"Easy, fellow, easy," Daddy cautioned.

Stephen was too enthralled to pay attention. "Mmmmmmmmmm-uh!" he exclaimed. The sound articulated and released all the energy and tension, all the exaltation in Stephen's body, but in his delirium he accidentally ducked his father's head. All of a sudden Daddy reared. At the same moment a huge wave swept Stephen off Daddy's back, lifted him up to a dizzying height, dashed him down into the depths, pulled him under and pounced on him with all its weight, winding him and flooding his lungs, rolling him along the bottom, heaving him over stones and cutting shells, dragging him toward drowning death, engulfing him in heavy, hurling, airless, black-death black . . .

When, at last, Stephen recovered consciousness, even before he opened his eyes, he felt someone's hand holding his head, someone's fingers stroking his cheek, and he heard Daddy saying, "Don't be silly, Rog, he isn't dead, he's only winded. There's nothing to cry about. Look! Look! He's opening his eyes. What did I tell you. . . . Hello, sweetheart. How do you feel?"

Daddy's face was white as milk; his eyes were big and red and bulging, and his brows were raised. Roggie was crying. The sky was very, very dark. "What time is it?"

"Ten past five."

"I thought it was night."

"That was some mean wave, huh, sweetheart? Thank God you had your water wings on."

"Why did you do that, Daddy?" Stephen asked, blinking his blood-shot eyes.

"What?"

"Drown me."

"Drown you! Me? It was the wave, sweetheart. The wave! It rolled you—all of us! Roggie, too. It's a lucky thing any of us are still alive."

"Hello, Stevie," Roggie snivelled. "How do you feel?"

"Hello, Roggie."

"He's all right," Daddy reassured himself and Roggie. "Aren't you, fellow? Imagine thinking it was *me!*" Stephen reached inside his bathing suit. "What's the matter? What is it, darling? Does something hurt you?" Almost immediately Stephen found what he was looking for—the emerald!—and he smiled and clutched it in his fist. "What is that?"

Stephen was not, as yet, convinced that Daddy *hadn't* tried to drown him, and he didn't feel like revealing his treasure. "Nothing."

"All right, then. Let's go back to the Casino. Mommy'll be worried. You think you can make it, *kleine?*"

"Sure."

Mommy was terribly upset when Stephen reported what had happened. After thanking God it was the last week-end of the summer, she asked Daddy a lot of questions about himself and Bruce, and criticized them both severely. That made Daddy furious, and he began to shout about Mommy playing Mah Jong all the time instead of looking after her children, and Mommy shouted back something about her neurasthenia, and Daddy said he didn't give a good goddamn, it was her responsibility to keep the *kinder* out of trouble, and did she know what had happened with Mr. Strauss that very afternoon, whereupon Mommy screamed that Mr. Strauss was a bum, and Daddy screamed that *Mrs.* Strauss was a tramp, and they went on fighting all the way home in the car, until Mommy began to sob, and Stephen squeezed the piece of green glass so tightly it almost cut his palm.

When they reached the house, the first thing Stephen did, as always, was to run to the kitchen to show Clarry the treasure he had found. "My, that's a pretty one, sugar," Clarry smiled. "Lemme see, that makes thirty-six, don't it?"

"Thirty-seven, Clar."

"Thirty-seven! My, my: thirty-seven emeralds. What we need more of now is some sapphires, ain't it, sugar?"

"I know, Clar. But they're awful hard to find."

"Course they hard to find. You don't find precious gems lyin' in the gutter. That's what makes 'em precious. Now, I tell you what, sugar: before we go back to the City next week, you and Clarry is gonna go down to that there beach and scour it until—" Suddenly, hearing Mr. and Mrs. Wolfe upstairs, continuing their fight, Clarry interrupted herself and asked, "What's the matter with your eyes, sugar? You been cryin'?"

"My eyes?"

"They's all bloodshot," Clarry said, and she stopped sprinkling the calves' liver, and wiped her big floury hands on her apron.

"Oh, I forgot," Stephen exclaimed. "I was drowned."

"What do you mean?" Clarry chuckled. "You was drowned."

"I'm not kidding, Clarry."

"If you was drowned, sugar, you wouldn't be standing here right now."

"I mean it, Clar," Stephen stated earnestly. "Daddy drowned me in the ocean and I was dead for a long time."

Clarry laughed jovially. "Listen, sugar, once you dead, you *stay* dead. They're ain't no comin' back."

"I'm telling you I *was*," Stephen insisted. "Ask Roggie if you don't believe me. Ask anybody!"

"All right, sugar, have it your way. Tell me, how do it feel, bein' dead?"

"It was horrible. I was so scared, Clar," Stephen reported weakly, his face contracting with pain. "I don't ever want to die again."

Clara lifted Stephen up and set him down on the sturdy, unpolished, marble-topped table. Now Stephen was on a level with Clarry's compassionate eyes, and he could feel her warm breath against his cheek. "Course not, sugar. And you don't have to. You don't have to. Not whiles Clarry's around. You don't have to worry, sugar," she said, drawing Stephen's head to her shoulder, nestling her soft cheek against his forehead and stroking his hair. "Clarry'll look after you."

Though he could no longer see her eyes, Stephen heard the catch in Clarry's throat, he felt her bosom heave, her strong arms hug him tightly, and he knew that she was crying. "What's the matter, Clar?"

"Nothin', sugar. Nothin'. Clarry'll look after you."

"Is Rosie dead?"

"Rosie! What's the matter with you, sugar? You know Rosie's in Chicago. I've told you that a hundred times: my baby's in Chicago."

"But if you never see her, isn't that like being dead?"

"Course it ain't. It seem like that sometime," Clarry said, staring straight ahead of her, looking right through Stephen just as if he wasn't there, "like Rosie gone forever, but it ain't. It ain't like that. I dassen't let it be. Come on, now," she continued in her normal tone of voice, returning Stephen to the floor. "You better put that emerald away 'fore it time for dinner."

Stephen ran upstairs. For a moment he stopped to listen outside of Mommy's and Daddy's door, but there wasn't a sound. Realizing that their fight was over, he hurried along to the radiator box in his own room where, much to Mommy's chagrin, Stephen had succeeded in recreating the seashore's smell and sound and texture. Scarcely an inch of the cream-colored radiator lid was left exposed by his multifarious marine collection. Among its many treasures were a dessicated starfish, a perfect pear whelk, the feather of a tern, a piece of driftwood the color of smoke, two withered skate egg cases, the spoored carapace of a calico crab, a blue crab claw, a silver-streaked horse mussel embossed with several barnacles, a kidney-shaped piece of coral, fourteen periwinkles, five ashtray-size clam shells, three rough limpets, scallop shells, slipper shells, cockle shells, blue mussels, razor clams and the immaculate remains of a broken sand dollar which had been one of Stephen's most prized possessions before his curiosity got the best of it. Crowded next to these, like the minerals and gems in the Morgan collection at the Museum of Natural History, were the hundred-fifty-odd pieces of surf-sanded colored glass that Stephen had collected over the years—: sapphires from Vicks and Noxzema jars, emeralds, zircons and aquamarines from ale, beer and coca-cola bottles, moonstones from baby oil jars, rose quartz from an unknown source and one rare piece of onyx from a bottle of My Sin.

Before adding it to his collection, Stephen studied the newly-found emerald. Now that it was dry, it began to show tiny deposits of salt in its pores, and its surface felt pleasantly powdery. Held one way, it looked like a piece of candy corn, held another, it became the head of a tomahawk. Compared with the other emeralds, it had a poster-paint quality; it was greener, gaudier, the color of a lime. Placing it was no simple matter. Like a master jeweler creating a lavaliere, Stephen moved it here and there, seeking an aesthetic balance, studying its form and color in relation to the other gems.

As he was doing this, a gust of wind came through the screen and blew the tern feather onto the floor. Stephen picked it up, smoothed its barbs and returned it to its proper place, between the teeth of the blue crab claw. The dogwood tree on the front lawn was being bent to the right so violently, it looked as if it was about to snap. The wind tore off some of its leaves and whirled them upwards. Stephen watched them ascend into the menacing gray-black sky, and wondered when the storm would break. He feared lightning and thunder more than Mommy and Daddy's fights or his own semi-annual visits to Dr. Rosenstrock, the dentist. Almost the first thing he ever did upon entering a stranger's house was to inquire about its lightning rod. The image of the skewered onion planted on a gabled roof was as meaningful to Stephen as the crucifix on her church was to Clarry. He understood nothing about their workings except for the one vital fact that lightning rods kept the fire-bolts away from his body by conducting them into the cellar. What fiendish fires ensued down there, Stephen preferred not to think about.

For some reason the storm held off all through dinner and through his bath, so that by the time Stephen was ready for bed he had almost forgotten about it. After Mommy had kissed him goodnight, and the soft but monumental security of Clarry's bosom relinquished him to the dark, Stephen lay in bed musing, as always, over the ocean. He listened to the pounding surf, smelled the brine, and searched for the grains of sand that invariably materialized in his hair, his bellybutton, his bed. He did not question how they came to be there; Stephen knew—knew that he was part of them, the sea and sand, mixed with them, a blend of them the way green is a blend of yellow and blue. As on every other night, before he was able to fall asleep, he had to get out of bed, tip-toe to the radiator and examine his marine collection one more time. He had to seize the whelk and take it back to bed with him and hold it to his ear, uncertain in his somnambulation whether the roaring-rush he listened to emanated from the shell, the ocean or his heart.

At some point in the middle of the night a lightning-crack awakened Stephen to tears. Even without looking, he knew the house had been struck and rent in two. Someone had taken the lightning rod off the roof and stuck it through his open window; some evil executioner, armed with electric currents, was standing in his bedroom, trying to electrocute him. The whole house quaked as the bolts flashed and crackled before his hand-covered eyes and the thunder detonated inside his eardrums and the rain deluged his marine collection. . . . But it wasn't only the rain, it was the ocean, too. The ocean was angry. It had come onto the land, exactly as Clarry had predicted it would. It was just outside his window there, trying to get in, trying to reclaim all the treasures he had stolen—all the shells and gems and creatures. The only way to save them was to shut the window. He had to shut the window! . . . And yet Stephen knew that if he did, if he got out of bed, the evil executioner would spy him and hurl a bolt of fire smack into his face, so he helmeted his head in his pillow and dived under the covers, where, lumped together like a pull of toffee, he eventually cried himself to sleep.

The next morning, when the family came down to breakfast, Clara greeted them with a barrage of communiqués. "Miz Wolfe! Miz Wolfe! Disaster! Catastrophe! Worst ever! Five hundred drowned: women 'n children. Right down here, here in our own backyard, right off Seaside! Ocean liner, comin' home from Trinidad: burnin' and drownin'—flames a hundred foot high—"

"The *Conte di Savoia*?" Mommy exclaimed, clapping her hand to her breathless bosom.

"Now, Hattie, don't get hysterical. Your father isn't due back from

Europe for another week. Anyway, she said it was coming from Trinidad, not Naples." Daddy turned back to Clarry. "What's its name?"

"Name, Mr. Wolfe?"

"The name of the ship."

"I think the radio man say it called *Tomorrow's Castle*."

. . . I knew it! Stephen thought. *Tomorrow's Castle* struck by lightning in the night and burning on the beach. Flames a hundred feet high, burning women and children, burning the wall marked WOMEN with children inside: burning—but not the MEN . . . *Tomorrow's Castle* battered by the waves, wearing-it-away waves, washing-it-away waves—all of my constructions drowning and burning in the waves of MEN with children inside . . . "I knew it!" Stephen exclaimed intensely.

"You don't know anything, stupid!" Roggie said in his most superior manner. "As usual, Clara's got it wrong. The name of the ship is the *Morro Castle*, capital M-o-r-r-o, not t-o-m-o-r-r-"

"That's my little professor," Daddy said proudly.

"Oh, I've heard of that! It goes on Caribbean cruises. Thank God it's not the *Savoia*," Mommy sighed.

"The number of dead is estimated at two hundred-fifty, not five hundred," Roggie continued. "It was coming back from Havana, not Trinidad, and it's anchored off a place called Shark River Inlet, not Seaside. May I have my eggs now?"

"How do you happen to know all that, Roger dear?" Mommy asked, as a deflated Clarry slunk from the room.

"I heard it on the radio before the rest of you were up. Did you think I was telepathetic?" Roggie's insolence made Daddy chuckle.

"Don't be fresh, Roger! And don't you encourage him, Saul."

"Who's encouraging him? I was laughing at his mistake," Saul lied.

"The word is telepathic, darling," Mommy said icily.

"I am *not* stupid!" Stephen growled, making a bulldog face and landing a brutal kick on his brother's shin.

"Damn you!" Roggie shouted, hurling his napkin ring at Stephen's face.

"Roger, don't you dare curse like that in front of me!" Mommy admonished him.

"Stephen, stop that! Put down that napkin ring!" Daddy said.

"But he threw it at *me!*"

"I saw you kick him first," Daddy said.

"He called me stupid."

"Sticks and stones will break my bones—" Roggie chanted.

"Damn you, too!" Stephen yelled, slinging back the napkin ring.

"Did everybody see that?" Roggie asked threateningly, sliding back his chair. "No one can say I started it *this* time!"

"Mommy!" Stephen cried, as Roggie turned the corner of the table, his fist prepared to inflict a series of eggies.

"Sit down, Roger. Roger, sit down!" Mommy shouted, leaping up herself and grabbing Roggie's arm. "Sit down, I said!"

"Here we are," Clarry said, smiling as she pivoted her big body through the swinging door and found herself in the middle of the tug-of-war and spilled the platter of eggs all over the carpet. This made Stephen laugh hysterically, and Clarry's eyes bulged from their sockets like a French bulldog's.

"God damn it!" Daddy roared. "Why the hell don't you watch where you're going?"

Stephen stopped laughing and clenched his fists. "It wasn't Clarry's fault," he said timidly.

"Who asked you? The whole thing's *your* fault in the first place!"

After the eggs were wiped up and a new batch cooked and eaten, Daddy and Roggie retired to the front lawn to have a catch, and Stephen went upstairs to play with his marine collection. He was standing in front of the window holding the whelk to his ear, thinking about the destruction of *Tomorrow's Castle*, and watching Daddy throw the hardball—projecting his arm its full length instead of throwing it from the wrist the way he, Stephen, did—when Mommy entered the room.

"What are you doing, sweetheart?" she inquired tenderly.

"Playing."

"You know, my love, we have to think about packing soon. We're going home on Wednesday—remember? You ought to start sorting out your collection."

"Sorting?"

"I mean, for instance, you don't want to take something like this, this old mussel, back to New York, do you?"

"Yes."

"But it smells. So do these devil's purses. Don't you want to leave them here?"

"No."

"All right, darling, do as you like, but find a box to put them in." Harriet smoothed down Stephen's golden hair. "You know, my love, no matter what anyone says, Mommy knows you aren't stupid." Stephen squeezed his mother's hand between his cheek and shoulder, as they watched Roggie dash across the lawn to catch a high throw. But just as the ball was about to nest into his mitt, Clarry appeared on the front steps and he fumbled it.

"'Scuse me, gentlemens. I just thought his royal highness would like to know the burnin' hulk of the *M-o-r-r-o Castle* is bein' towed toward Sandy Hook."

"What did Clarry say?" Stephen asked.

"Saul, what did Clara just say?" Mommy called through the window.

"I don't know. Something about the *Morro Castle*."

"Pay no attention. She was only taking revenge on me," Roggie said, tossing the retrieved ball back to Daddy.

In the course of the day interest in the fate of the burning vessel intensified. By noon the Seaside Ladies Conservation Committee had rallied its forces and was making a door-to-door collection of roughwear for the victims of the disaster. Emergency first-aid stations were set up at Point Pleasant and Sea Girt for the care of the survivors suffering from shock. In the afternoon a fisherman in Belmar discovered the body of a drowned woman floating near the shore. All along the Jersey coast solemn crowds gathered in hopes of catching a glimpse of the burning luxury liner or any of its passengers—dead or alive. While the Coast Guard combed the sea for casualties and the merchant marine responded to the *Morro Castle's* repeated distress calls, the Governor surveyed the scene from the cockpit of an airplane.

By three o'clock Stephen had finally convinced Mommy to let Clarry take him down to the beach. When they reached the balustrade of the Grand Stairway, Stephen gasped. "Look, Clarry! Look!"

The ocean was like an enormous cauldron of boiling rice: as far as the eye could see, its surface was covered with churning foam. Closer to shore huge walls of dirty green water rose to the height of trees, before crashing onto the beach. The beach itself looked brand new, swept clean, without a sign of human traffic; there wasn't a footprint or a piece of paper anywhere, only the unbroken sandcrust, looking as it must have looked before life became amphibious.

"Mean," Clarry muttered.

"Let's go down!" Stephen urged excitedly.

"Uh-uh, sugar. It too dangerous down there. You get swept away like the *Morro Castle*."

"Where is it, Clar? Where *is* it?"

"Where's what, sugar?"

"*Tomorrow's Castle.*"

"It in someplace called Sandy Hook."

"Where is that?"

"Got me, sugar."

"But I have to see it, Clar. I *have* to."

"Maybe we can see it tomorrow, sugar, when it clears. Come on now, let's go back. It ain't nice down here."

Stephen acquiesced reluctantly. Hand in hand they lagged the long blocks home. On the way he confided to Clarry how the ocean had tried to break into his room the night before.

By five o'clock the flaming *Morro Castle* had broken away from its tow. After drifting several hours, the surf grounded it on a sandbar off Asbury Park. When Stephen heard the news, he refused to go to sleep until he had wrested a promise from Mommy to take him to Asbury the very next day. "And can we play miniature golf?"

"Yes, darling, yes. Now go to sleep."

As if it were Christmas or his birthday, on Sunday morning Stephen awakened at 5:55, restless with anticipation and excitement: eager to get under way. His room was filled with a fugue of birdsounds and, gradually, as the day began to dawn, lovely bright sunlight; every trace of Friday night's storm was gone. But by the time the family piled into the Chevrolet—Stephen in the back seat next to Mommy, Roggie up front next to Daddy—it was 11:25 and everyone's nerves were slightly frayed. Because it was Sunday and the weather so good, every car, truck, trailer, bus, motorcycle, bicycle, beach and station wagon within a radius of two hundred miles was on the road, heading for Asbury Park.

For a while, as the Chevy moved along unimpeded by the traffic, the brothers played a lively game of license plates. Stephen spotted one from Tennessee—his favorite state, not because it counted more than any other but because the plate itself was visually onomatopoetic—and one from California which counted fifteen points, and gave him a comfortable lead, until Roggie claimed he saw a foreign plate from a country called British Columbia, which, according to the rules, counted twenty-five. Since Stephen did not see the plate himself and had never heard of the country, he accused his brother of cheating, and the game ended in a fray that required the intervention of both parents.

As they approached Allenhurst the traffic began to jam, making Daddy slow down and stop and stall and start again every other second—something which always angered him. "You and your bright ideas," he grumbled, glaring at Mommy in the rear-view mirror. "I said we should have left right after breakfast. I said—"

"We couldn't leave Clara stranded in church."

"Then we shouldn't've come."

"But we promised the children." Mommy smiled and petted Stephen's head.

"At this rate we'll be lucky if we get there in time to come back." Daddy wrapped his right arm around Roggie's shoulder. "Another one of your mother's brainstorms!"

Stephen studied Daddy's pinky. The straight black hairs looked like mermaid's hair matted under his chunky gold signet ring. "Sit back, darling," Mommy said, laying her hand on Stephen's shoulder. Suddenly her fingers clamped his flesh painfully and Mommy gasped. "That's a red light, Saul!" The abrupt stop nauseated Stephen.

"Who's driving this buggy, you or me?"

"You are, Saul."

"Then just sit back and keep quiet—unless you want to walk."

Now that they were standing still, the smoke from Daddy's cigar, mixed with the smell of gasoline and the exhaust from other cars, was sickening. Stephen tried to roll his window lower, but the rear wheel prevented it. Honk! Honk! Honk! He turned around and saw the man in the car behind, honking his horn impatiently. "Roggie, look! It's a Pierce Arrow."

"What's the matter with *you*, you bastard!" Stephen heard Daddy shout. "Can't you see it's red?"

"It's green, Saul," Mommy corrected.

"God damn it! Whose side are you on?" Daddy demanded, as he pulled his head back into the car and stepped on the gas. "That imbecile began to honk before it changed. Or didn't you notice? It's always *my* fault, isn't it? Never the other guy—always me! No matter what happens—"

"I didn't say—"

"Could you get us there any better, brain trust?"

"Don't call me—"

"Then shut up, damn it, just shut up!"

"Don't you dare—"

Stephen sat forward on the seat in an effort to get more air. He watched the orange signs go by and tried to read their message. On the first and second he made out the words *she, the* and *by*. On the third and fourth he was able to read *She . . . it was her. . . .* The fifth, of course, he knew at sight: BURMA SHAVE.

"—any more of your god damn lip!" Daddy roared.

Turning away from the window, Stephen saw Mommy squeezed into the opposite corner. She was watching the scenery. At the same time, her white-gloved hand groped blindly for her beaded bag, located it and fished out an embroidered handkerchief. For a moment Stephen smelled her strong gardenia perfume until the heavy cigar smoke overwhelmed its sweet aroma.

"What are you crying about, anyway?" Daddy asked.

"Nothing," Mommy answered, almost voicelessly, her shoulders quivering as she raised the handkerchief to her nose. Empathically, Stephen reached towards Mommy's bare, freckled arm and stroked her vaccination. In response Mommy turned around, pressed Stephen's hand endearingly and tried to force a smile, but her chin was as flat and pocked as a cooking pancake, and her mascara trickled down the sides of her nose, silently staining her cheeks.

"Then stop it!" Daddy said.

Mommy turned back toward the window. Stephen could hear her muted whimpering, and the tears welled up in his own eyes. Suddenly Daddy stopped short again, and Stephen gagged, his mouth flooding with saliva. "Daddy!"

"Stop it, I said," Daddy repeated, driving on, "before I really give you something to cry about."

"Daddy!"

"What is it, *kleine?*"

"Will you stop a second? I'm car-sick."

By the time they reached Asbury it was one o'clock. There were seventy-five thousand people there looking at the liner and Daddy had to park eleven blocks away from Sixth Avenue and the Boardwalk, off which the *Morro Castle* was grounded. Because Stephen had been car-sick, Harriet thought he should have some chicken broth, but no one else agreed, so they gulped down hot dogs and pressed toward the Boardwalk. Daddy, running interference for the family, had several verbal battles with strangers along the way but managed by a combination of height and brawn, charm and tyranny, to get within a quarter of a mile of the disabled vessel.

"There it is! There it is!" he shouted. "Will you look at that: still smoking."

"Where? Where? I can't see!" Roggie and Stephen cried in unison.

"Come on, fellow, up you go," Daddy said, hoisting Roggie onto his shoulders.

"Tut! Tut! Tut!" Mommy clucked, seeing the wreck and straining to lift up Stephen by his waist.

"Higher, Mommy! Higher!" Stephen pleaded. "The man's hat's in . . ." But suddenly it was there: the gigantic, red-streaked hulk swerving in the lively surf as if it were on a pivot, its broadside parallel to shore but listing slightly toward the sea, its lifeboats all scorched and askew, dangling from their davits, and other fallen rigging hanging down across the rows and rows of portholes, charred and smoking still after thirty hours. . . . *Tomorrow's Castle*: bigger than the whale in the Museum of Natural History, bigger than an apartment house and stronger than an armory, but dying now, lying on its side, coughing smoke and bleeding lead, destroyed and dying in the ocean . . . awful, awful ocean . . . Stephen reached out his hand to console the ship, but Mommy, unable to support his weight any longer, lowered him into the forest of trousered legs.

The next day Stephen begged Mommy to take him back to Asbury Park, but she refused. "You know how car-sick you got yesterday. You know how bad the traffic was. I'll take you to the beach, sweetheart. Maybe you'll be able to see the *Morro Castle* from there."

When they reached the stairhead Stephen looked toward Asbury, and down on the beach below he looked again, but from neither place could he see *Tomorrow's Castle*. To ease his disappointment, Mommy suggested he build something big—a fortress or a castle—so the beach would have something to remember him by when he went away for the winter. Stephen thought Mommy's idea a good one and decided to build the biggest castle in history. He surveyed the sand and chose a spot ten yards from the water's edge. He cleared the site of stones and shells, and set to work carrying handfuls of wet sand up from the water and mixing them with the drier sand, creating a kind of cement. By noon, when Mommy came to take him to lunch, he had amassed a solid block of sand the size of a steamer trunk.

"Oh Mommy, I can't stop now. Can't you bring me back a sandwich?"

"But isn't it finished, darling? It looks finished to me."

"Oh no! I have to put the turrets on. I have to build the wall. I have to dig the moat."

When Mommy returned with his lunch, Stephen was still working feverishly, setting jagged fragments of shells around the perimeter of his castle's roof. He could scarcely spare the time to gobble down his sandwich before he began to build the walls. Harriet turned her backrest toward the sun and watched Stephen as he scurried to and from the waterfront, carrying scoops of dripping sand—doing in a single day and alone the labor an army of Egyptians at Giza had taken several generations to complete. Had it been earlier in the summer, he would by now have attracted an audience of envious children and grown-ups to watch him consummate his colossus, but on this September afternoon there was almost no one on the beach. Stephen was glad. He didn't need or even want an audience to urge him on. He wasn't building it for *them*. He was building it for himself, this mausoleum—for himself and those women and children who had died aboard *Tomorrow's Castle*; he was building it as a monument to them and as a resurrection of the ship itself, to stand against the ocean. No wave in all the Atlantic was big enough or brave enough to trespass this far up the sand; even if there were, he would see to it his walls were thick enough to repulse the worst assault. . . . I must make them higher, I must reinforce them, he thought, anxiously glancing at the sun to see how much time he had left.

At half-past four, long after Mommy had called to say they must be going soon, Stephen was down at the water's edge on one of his countless missions to collect wet sand, when something in the water distracted him. At first he couldn't even distinguish the shape as it floated there a foot or two beneath the surface. The only fact he felt fairly certain about was that the thing was white. A fish, he thought, but dead and floating on its back. He watched with fascination as the tide brought the fish's underbelly closer to the shore. No, it's like that thing underneath a cow where the milk comes out, he thought, as he began to discern four inflated upright fingers. Fingers! All of a sudden his heart beat uncontrollably, his flesh tingled, and he lost his sense of hearing as he breathed the one word "hand." . . . It's a hand, he thought, unable to move. A hand! A hand! A woman's hand, and he plunged into the ocean.

"Stevie! Stevie! What are you doing? It's much too cold!" Harriet shouted, leaving her backrest and hurrying toward her son. "What's the matter with you? Have you taken leave of your senses? Come out of there before you catch pneumonia!" she scolded.

"Ohhh, Mommy—"

"You heard what I said, come out of there this instant!"

"Ohhh, Mommy—"

"I'm going to tell your father on you and you know what'll happen then."

"But Mommy," Stephen conspired, "I found a hand."

"What? What on earth are you talking about? Come out of there, I said!" This time Stephen obeyed and began to emerge from the ocean, holding the white hand by its wrist. When Mommy saw it she shrieked and covered her eyes.

"Shhh, shhh," Stephen said, not wanting anyone to overhear or see them.

"What is it?" she asked in pain.

"A hand," he confided, still holding the dripping thing.

"Oh you're awful! Simply awful!" Mommy said, after she uncovered her eyes. "You're worse than your brother, to play a trick like that on me! Throw that stupid glove away!" she said, more annoyed than relieved.

"It's a hand."

"It is *not* a hand! It's a glove. And I'll thank you not to scare me like that ever again."

At last Stephen examined his catch. . . . Mommy was right, it *was* a glove, a woman's white cotton glove exactly like the ones Mommy wore. Anyone could see that, now that the water had drained out of it, leaving it hanging there, limp, between his fingertips. But what in the world was a woman's glove doing in the ocean?

Harriet was just as troubled by the question as Stephen. She thought about the Lindbergh baby. She thought about the dirigible— what was its name?—that had crashed a couple of years ago, killing seventy-five boys—the *Akron!*—off this very coast. "Oh how silly of me," she said, ejecting her pent-up breath as she realized the truth of the matter. "It's from the *Morro Castle.*"

. . . *Tomorrow's Castle* . . . Stephen hurriedly turned to look at his construction. It was still intact, untouched by the tide.

"It must have belonged to one of the passengers. How terrible . . . terrible," Harriet said, wondering whether she ought not to keep the glove and turn it in to the authorities. "No. Throw it back, dear, throw it back, and let's go home. We're late enough as is."

With all his strength Stephen hurled the glove back into the ocean, but it didn't travel very far. As he watched it sink out of sight, it turned into a hand again.

The following day, the last Stephen spent in Seaside, Mommy and Clarry were up at dawn. He could hear them clattering in the kitchen. After breakfast Mommy said, "Clara and I have a lot of work to do today. Do you think you can play by yourself? . . . Or with your brother?" she added as an afterthought.

"But I have to go down to the beach and say goodbye to my castle," Stephen said.

"That's all right, if Roger'll go with you. Otherwise, I want you to stay around the house. Oh! and find a shoebox for those shells and things. I don't want to have to be worrying about them at the last minute."

Stephen knew, before he asked, that Roggie would refuse to take him to the beach, so he put on his bathing suit, sneaked out of the house, and went by himself, running all the way. When he got to the stairhead, he looked for his castle, but he couldn't see it. He rushed down the steps toward the spot where he had worked all the previous day, but the spot had disappeared. Both the castle and the sand on which it stood had disappeared. Half the beach in fact had disappeared, and Stephen was frantic. He knew he had built it to the right of the stairhead, and he searched farther and farther south but found nothing. He retraced his steps and ran toward the cliffs—back and forth between the ocean and the cliffs—but found nothing. Finally, at the water's edge, he discovered the ocean lapping at a little gray amorphous mound of sand and recognized the bits of seashell he had used for turrets. He sat down beside the shapeless ruin, supporting his chin in his hands, but he couldn't cry. It demanded something more than that, the ocean, more than tears, he thought. . . . Maybe once a woman wept the ocean and then it turned into a man. . . .

Suddenly, not five feet from his toes, creeping up the pebbles, he saw that hand again, the hand of the woman who had drowned aboard *Tomorrow's Castle*. . . . So it wasn't a glove after all. It couldn't be! It was still alive, trying again and again to crawl out of the ocean, but the tide refused to let it. That was the trouble with the ocean: it wouldn't let go of your hand—even after it had eaten your entire body.

Stephen raised his head and gazed out to sea, where the ocean

seemed to overflow into the horizon. He looked at the shifting whitecaps. He singled out a special wave and tried to observe its progress
as it traveled toward the shore, but half way in it drowned or got
mixed up with another wave, and he lost sight of it. He tried again,
but the same thing happened, until finally he settled for watching the
general movement of the incoming tide. He watched it crash on the
beach in front of him and eat away the sand beyond the spot on
which he sat. He watched it ebb back into itself, taking with it yet
another portion of his already unrecognizable castle. . . . Tomorrow
there won't even be a trace of it, he thought. By tomorrow the ocean
will have taken all of it, even the turrets, giving me back in exchange
a broken shell, a blue crab claw, a little piece of coral—all sorts of un-
fair things! Nothing like a seahorse or an ocean liner. No! That would
be too valuable. The most I can expect is a dead or dying fish . . . a
woman's hand. . . . "But where's her body?" Stephen cried aloud.
"What have you done with her body?"

The tide had reached its flow now, and Stephen was sitting up to
his waist in water. Feeling it caress his limbs, Stephen had to weewee.
Cautiously he glanced up and down the beach. There wasn't
a soul in sight, not even Bruce; the summer was over. As it flooded
out of him, his weewee hot against his thighs, Stephen felt a great release. He loved the idea of sitting there in his own water, mixing his
own water with the ocean's, mixing the ocean with himself. How
many times had Mommy said "You'll turn into a fish"? Well, now at
last the time had come. . . . Who cares? he thought, lying back and
letting the tide tow him into the sea. Who cares about the things on
shore? . . . As if he were going to sleep, Stephen shut his eyes deliberately. Deliberately he abandoned his resistance. He longed to be
unconscious now, longed to leave the world behind and turn into a
fish. More than anything, he longed for the ocean to work its will and
ravage him the way it had ravaged *Tomorrow's Castle* until there was
nothing left of him but a little brittle fingernail lying on the sand.
. . . Who cares about those dead and broken things when there is this
—the turbulence, the touching! . . . "Goodbye, Clarry! Goodbye,
Mommy!" Stephen cried as he drifted out to sea. "I love you, ocean,
love you!" he confessed, feeling the water under him.

Stephen's lover responded vigorously, pulling him down, rolling
him over, spilling him out onto the sand. Stephen paid no attention.
As soon as he had wiped his eyes, he scrambled to his feet again and
ran back into the water, abandoning himself like something inert un-

til his lover tossed him out a second time. . . . It's like a game, he
thought, lying on the cold soft sand. . . . No matter how many times
the ocean kicks you out, the sand is always there to welcome you,
dead or alive, and to give you back again, until the ocean's had a
chance to tear you into little pieces and turn the pieces into sand—
until the sand itself is eaten by the ocean, and the land becomes
the sand, and there are no more houses anywhere, and no more people
left on earth . . .

After surrendering himself for the third time, Stephen staggered
to his feet and stumbled out of the water. He was exhausted and
exhilarated. He filled his lungs with the clean sharp air. He stood and
stared up at the Casino perched on top of the cliffs. For a moment
he remembered the wall marked MEN and the wall marked
WOMEN. He almost toppled over as he threw back his head and
gazed into the sky. . . . Mommy is the land, he thought, Daddy is
the ocean. "No, that's not right," he said aloud. "*I'm* the land and
Roggie's the ocean." No, somehow that wasn't right either, and
Stephen mulled it over in his head and made it into jingles as he
straggled home:

> *"Daddy is the ocean,*
> *Mommy is the land.*
> *Roggie is the ocean,*
> *Stevie is the sand.*
> *Stevie is the ocean,*
> *Daddy is the land.*
> *Mommy is the ocean,*
> *Roggie is the sand . . ."*

That night, before he went to sleep, Mommy questioned Stephen
about his marine collection. "What's the matter with you darling? I
thought I asked you to pack these awful shells and things. That's not
like you, to disobey me."

Stephen propped himself on his elbow and deliberated for a moment. "I don't think I'll take them with me."

"What?"

"I think I'll leave them here."

"Oh, thank goodness! That's my angel child," Mommy said, switch-
ing off the light and leaving the room.

In the dark, Stephen lay down in bed and lullabied himself to
sleep:

"Daddy is the ocean,
Mommy is the land.
Roggie is the ocean,
Stevie is the sand . . ."

WILLIAM HUMPHREY is the author of two books, *The Last Husband and Other Stories* and *Home from the Hill*. His third book, *The Ordways*, was published in early 1965.

The Ballad of Jesse Neighbours

FEW marriages were being made in Oklahoma in 1934 and Jesse Neighbours didn't have a pot, nor a window to throw it out of, but Jesse just couldn't wait. Things might never get any better! He had to have her—Naomi Childress, that is. What were they going to live on, love? Well, they would have each other and they would scrape by somehow. Things couldn't go on like this much longer. Meanwhile, two can live cheaper than one. And Naomi didn't expect any diamond rings.

Jesse was just twenty, though he looked older, and Naomi just eighteen. In the road of their courtship there had been one bad bump. It was the old story: poor boy, heiress, and her father. Jesse's people had never owned one red acre to sit back now and watch being blown away in dust. Will Neighbours had raised, rather was raising, seven children, Jesse the eldest, as a sharecropper. And so from the first Jesse had had to come to the Childresses hat in hand. For Old Bull Childress had a house and clear title to twenty-seven acres of hardscrabble. The deed was unencumbered through no fault of Bull's. He had tried, but nobody would loan him anything on that patch of jimsonweeds and cockleburs.

Bull's consent to the marriage had been given only on condition that the bride be taken to a home of her own, and not to live with her in-laws. And indeed to have got another into Will's place they would have had to hang her on a nail at night. Bull's provision might have proved an insuperable obstacle. But fortunately Jesse was the son of a man known for hard work and honesty; and though only twenty, Jesse himself, after some ten years now, was beginning to earn a name as a steady worker. And so Mr. Buttrell, Will's landlord, agreed to try Jesse on shares on a place that he happened to have standing vacant.

Copyright © 1963 by Esquire, Inc.

Not a very big place, and maybe not the best thirty acres left in Oklahoma, but a place of his own and land which a strong young fellow not afraid of a little work could make out on—always barring Acts of God, of course—with a two-room dog-run cabin, a well, a barn, a tool shed and a chicken house. Jesse had a heifer due to freshen around September and Naomi was raising a dozen layers that she had incubated underneath the kitchen range. There would be a pair of shoats as a wedding present from Will. The two of them were spending every spare moment fixing the place up. It would have curtains made from the pretty flowered prints that chicken feed came sacked in, and all that winter a quilt on a quilting frame had hung above the dining table in the Childress' parlor, and the neighbor women came over every Thursday afternoon and quilted on it, and made jokes about it that made Naomi's round and sweetly fuzzy cheeks glow like a ripe Elberta peach. And she was canning all that previous summer and fall as if she had three hands. If nothing else they would be able to live on cucumber pickles. Jesse had an old car. Something was always going wrong with it, but luckily Jesse had a second one exactly like the first, except for the lack of wheels, which squatted out in the front yard, a sort of personal parts department, very handy. He had given up smoking and instead was putting his tobacco money in a jar, and by fall he hoped to have enough to make a down payment on a mule. He was the saving kind, saved tinfoil, twine, saved rubber bands, making large balls of all three items which he stored in cigar boxes.

Naomi knew what a catch she had made. She had first taken serious notice of Jesse Neighbours one night at a country dance for which he supplied the music. He hired out around the section as a one-man band. He had a rig which he was buying on installment from the mail-order catalog. Once in it he looked like a monkey in a cage. With his hands he played guitar while with his feet he worked two pedals on which were drumsticks that banged a pair of snare drums; one stick was bare wood, the other was covered like a swab with bright orange lamb's wool. A French harp was held in his mouth on a wire frame with earpieces. The boy was a musical fool. In his pockets he always carried some kind of musical instrument: a Jew's harp, a French harp, an ocarina. He played the musical saw, the washboard, water glasses, blew a jug. He could draw music out of anything. And on the guitar or the banjo or the mandolin he picked notes, not just chords but whole tunes. His singing voice was like a bee in a bottle, a melodious, slightly adenoidal whine, wavering, full of sobs and breaks, and of a pitch like a boy's before the change of voice. That night when he laid aside the French harp and sang:

> I don't want your greenback dollar;
> I don't want your watch and chain;
> All I want is you, my darling;
> Won't you take me back again?

it seemed to Naomi that he was singing to her alone. And when with his next number he showed the other, light shade of his nature with *Sal, Sal, Sal, oh, Sal, Sal, let me chaw yore rozin some,* then Naomi was hooked. And Naomi was not the only one, as she very well knew.

But the music he courted her with was none of his lovesick ballads. Seated on her front porch on a Sunday afternoon, in his fresh-ironed khakis so stiff they squeaked, his chauffeur's black leather bow tie fluttering on his Adam's apple as he sang like a black butterfly, he would throw back his head and bawl:

> I heard the crash on the highway.
> I knew what it was from the start.
> I rushed to the scene of destruction.
> The picture was stamped on my heart.
>
> I didn't hear nobody pray, dear brethren,
> I didn't hear nobody pray.
> The blood lay thick on the highway,
> But I didn't hear nobody pray.

For it was bad enough already, him being landless. If on top of that he had come around strumming and crooning ballads and ditties Old Bull Childress would have shooed him out of the yard like a stray dog. Bull would think, any fellow that played all that well, not just chords but notes, must have spent a lot of time sitting in the shade learning to pick them out, and that was not the kind of a man he wanted for a son-in-law. The truth was, Jesse had spent very little time learning; it just came naturally. But of course he could not say that. The pious wail of *The Crash on the Highway* was meant to overcome a prospective father-in-law's misgivings.

And Jesse was not shiftless. He was a most unusual combination of music and prudence. His music meant a little extra money. He liked to play and sing, and in fact his foot was always tapping to some tune running in his head, but he liked to be paid for it too. He was ambitious. He meant to get ahead. He was already thinking of a family of his own, thinking of it with a passion beyond his years, and notwithstanding her blushes he broached the subject very early with Naomi. He spoke of it with such earnestness that she had to say at last, she hoped he was not thinking of quite as big a one as his own. It had not occurred to her that, however many there were, he meant to bring them up in a very different way from the way he and his brothers and sisters had been brought up.

Though it might be hard to understand why a young fellow should want to follow in his father's footsteps when his father's only followed in those of a mule, and why he should want to do it in order to own something which the wind blew away in clouds of red dust before your eyes, Jesse Neighbours meant to own land of his own one day. Not that he couldn't wait. Not that his longing made him discontent with what he was starting out with. But stumbling along behind the plow among the blocks of dirt like chunks of concrete paving, straining against the handles, grunting, his face caked with dust, he would let himself think of the future. He was of an age and a seriousness to have a place in the councils of family men, farmers, and on the corner of the street in town on Saturday afternoon Jesse had heard it said time and time again that this land was cottoned out. Well, he meant to rotate his crops. He would have a margin of land over what he needed in order to just get by, enough to quarter his acreage and leave one quarter to lie fallow by turns each year. Then there was the weather. A man might have a good year, but then one of drought could wipe out all that he had saved. The weather, they said, was one thing you could do nothing about. But there was one thing you could do. You could grow one crop that did not depend so heavily on the weather. Jesse had heard those same men say that this land, once the range of the buffalo, was best suited to grazing. He meant to have a little herd of beef cattle some day. He knew already what breed. Bramers. Funny looking things they were, with that white hide like a scalded hog, that hump on the back like a camel, and those great flopping ears. And mean! But they were from India and could stand this Oklahoma heat and dryness like no others, and fever ticks never bothered them. Jesse didn't fool himself: he would never own any big herd. That was for men with capital, not for the likes of him. He would always be a dirt farmer. But a few he would have; then in a year when there came a drought or a hailstorm, or worst of all, when the crop was so good the bottom fell out of the market prices, then you wouldn't have to go crawling to the bank and lick spit and put yourself in hock right up to your very eyeballs.

And though he would be a clodhopper all his days, if he started a little herd his sons wouldn't have to slave like this, daylight to dark, seven days a week, just to keep body and soul together; they would be cattlemen, breeders. Patience, he would need patience to save and then save more, until he could buy good stock, blooded, purebred, pedigreed—it paid off in the long run. And, sweat pouring from his face like rainwater off a hat brim as he hunched himself, he drove the plowshare back into the stony ground and swore at the wheezing mule, thinking as he lurched down the row, if a man started out with one heifer, bred her and was lucky and she had twins and they were both heifers, and each of them had a heifer. . . . So that he never heard his little sister until she was at his back, though all the way down from the house she had been screaming at the top of her lungs that they'd struck oil on the Childress' place.

Oil-well derricks on those Oklahoma plains were a commoner sight than trees. New ones sprang up, old ones were drilled deeper, with every fresh discovery of oil anywhere within a hundred miles. Bad times and bad soil bred them like weeds, where no edible plant would grow. The lucky ones struck water, and the derrick was converted into a windmill. Even Bull Childress had long since given up hope for anything from that one down behind his house. Jesse had forgotten it so completely that for a moment he hardly knew what his little sister was talking about.

"They claim it's a real gusher, Jess," she said. "The Childresses are rich! Naomi's going to be one of them millionairesses, like you read about in the newspapers."

Even as she spoke her voice ran down like a phonograph, seeing the look in her brother's eyes, blank holes in the terra-cotta mask of his face. Her mouth gaped, snaggle-toothed, as it dawned on her that the news she had brought might not be good news, after all.

Jesse leaned for a moment on the plow handles, breathing hard, his head sagging between his shoulder blades, sweat dripping from the tip of his nose. He spat thinly and of the color of blood and wiped the back of his gritty hand across his lips. Then he straightened, and settling the reins about his neck, grasping the handles and pointing the plowshare downward again, he said in a dry husky voice, "Come up, mule."

The story told was that the well blew in while Old Bull was in the outhouse looking at the pictures in the unused pages of the mail-order catalog, and that when she let go he shot off the hole and out the door with his flap hanging open and his britches down around his knees, tripped and sprawled flat on his face, rolled over, looked up, and then lay there moaning with joy and letting the slimy, thick, foul-smelling black rain spatter in his face and into his open mouth like sweet California wine. The roar was a steady explosion and the stink enough to make you gag. Air to breathe there was none and the sky turned black as in a dust storm. And as he lay there Bull's moaning turned insensibly into a whimper, a sob, as he thought of the years of his life that had gone into that hard, unyielding soil, the sweat from his hanging brow that had watered every inch of it, of the furrows he had broken, the cotton sacks he had dragged across it bent double beneath the broiling sun, the seed he had sown in it and which had rotted there, never sprouting. Of this dry red dirt he had eaten his alloted peck, and more. His head was bent to it like an ear on an undernourished stalk; his skin had taken on its very color like a stain. And all this while deep underground lay this black treasure. And rolling over he commenced to beat the earth with his fists for having hidden its riches from him all his life until now. Then when he had exhausted himself beating it, he flung his arms wide in an embrace and kissed the ground again and again.

In the house he found his daughter trying to pull down the windows and his wife cursing over her wash that had been hanging on the line and which now looked like a heap of mechanic's rags. Aghast at her blasphemous complaints, Bull roared, "You'll wear silks and laces from now on, you old fool! Shut your mouth and thank the good Lord! Don't let him hear you grumbling!" And grabbing up the laundry he flung it to the floor and danced on it with his bare black feet, bellowing jubilantly.

All afternoon it rained down and Bull hopped from one window to the next, crowing, "Spew, baby, spew! Oh, honey, don't never stop! Flood us! Drown us in it! Oh, Godawmighty, blow her sky high! Let it come down for forty days and forty nights!" Three times in the course of the afternoon he dashed outdoors like a boy in a summer shower and baptized himself anew, letting it dance in his open palms and blacken his upturned face, and in that state he would return, tracking up the floors, and demand a hug and kiss from each of his women, chasing them screaming through the house.

All night long it fell like a spring rain on the noisy sheet-iron roof, and the stench grew hellish. But Bull lay unsleeping in his bed, smacking his old woman's flat bony behind whenever he suspected her of dozing off, listening to the patter overhead and crooning, "Oh, keep it up, sweet Jesus. Oh, pour it down. Don't never stop till I tell you."

Toward daybreak the next morning the crew succeeded in capping the well, and they ventured out to have a look around. The world looked burnt, smelled burnt too. From the eaves of buildings, from the handles of tools long abandoned about the yard, from the limp leaves of trees and plants the black syrup hung in long slow-swelling drops. From the sagging fence wires they were strung in ropes like beads and amid the leaves of bushes they resembled small poisonous black berries. From every blade of grass, like a viscous black dew, hung a single unfalling drop. A dying songbird staggered about the yard, his wings heavy and useless. Upon the pool in the bottom of the cast-iron washpot lay insects in a thick, still crust.

"Won't nothing ever grow here ever again," Mrs. Childress wailed, seeing her dead peonies and the earth around them that looked as if it had been tarred and asphalted.

"I hope to God not!" cried Bull. "I done raised all the crops I ever aim to off of it!"

Breakfast (oily biscuits, coffee that tasted like it had been drained from a crankcase) was hardly over when Bull said, "Well, gals, y'awl take off your aprons and paint your faces. The Childresses are headed for the big city. Don't bother packing nothing. We won't need none of this trash—" the sweep of his arm comprehended the sum of their previous life—"never no more."

So they piled into the cab of the truck (a pickup, cut down from a La Salle sedan) and took off. In town they stopped just long enough for Bull to go to the bank, from which he returned carrying two bulging canvas sacks, and after that they never even slowed down for Idabel, nor even Paris, but drove straight to Dallas, with Old Bull sitting on that horn all the way. And when they got there they drove straight to the Adolphus, pulled up out front, and though they had not brought one piece of luggage with them, sat there honking until the whole corps of bellhops and porters had been sent out to receive them. When they got out, so did the broody hen who had made the trip with them unbeknownst. She staggered off her nest among the corn shucks and cracker sacks in the trunk bed, and out into the street, and there she died, in a shower of feathers and with a bloodcurdling squawk, underneath the wheels of a new red Ford V-8, right on the corner of Commerce and Akard.

Without turning his head, jerking his thumb over his shoulder at the old jitney, Bull said to the head greeter, "Get shut of that for me, will you? Maybe you know some poor devil that can use it."

They were not turned away. They were welcomed like royalty. After Corsicana, after Spindletop, after Kilgore, Dallas had developed a keen collective nose for crude oil, and rolled out the red carpet for their kind of barefoot millionaire. Bull drew his X on the register as big as a level-crossing sign.

And at Neiman-Marcus that same afternoon they seemed to have been expecting Naomi. To her request for a permanent wave and "a beauty treatment," they smiled, and showed her in. She was undressed and popped into a box with her head sticking out like a turkey's at a turkey shoot, parboiled, removed feeling as if she had been peeled and her quick exposed, stretched out on a white table and kneaded like dough until her bones jellied and her brain melted and ran. She was put into a white gown and whisked into a second chamber, seated in a dentist's chair, and mud, or what certainly seemed like mud, piled on her face. To soft music wafted sourcelessly in, a bevy of sibilant attendants busied themselves about her, one to each foot, one to each hand, plying, chafing, clipping. The mud was removed, then came lotions icy and astringent, a brisk facial massage, a shampoo. The head beautician materialized, a gorgeous young sorcerer of intermediate sex with bangs and plucked brows, a pout, fluttering hands smaller and whiter and far softer than Naomi's own, a voice like molasses in January and a pettish toss of the head. From a palette of rosy tints he chose, and with brushes and swabs applied them to Naomi's cheeks, frowning, standing back from time to time to squint at her like an artist before his easel. Her head was anointed with the contents of various vials, her hair cut and curled.

At last it was finished and she was permitted to look. One glimpse and she looked about for confirmation. They nodded. She looked again, sidelong, scared. She reached out a hand (once, or rather always, red and cracked from lye soap, cold water, broom handles, the bails of buckets—now white, soft, a row of small pointed flames burning at the fingertips) and shyly touched the vision in the glass. Her lips parted in wonder, her lips that had blossomed, sweetly sullen, moist, quivering. Wonder, not self-infatuation, was what she felt, for that was not her, it was a creature from another world, out of the pages of *Silver Screen*, beautiful as a dummy in a store window. Her hair was a platinum cloud. Her eyes had doubled in size. Beneath lids elongated and shaded with blue, the whites sparkled, the pupils swooned with themselves, liquid with promise and cruel caprice. Her brows had been resettled; they arched of themselves. Sophistication had been shadowed into her hitherto round and girlish cheeks.

To maintain this new beauty of hers, regular and frequent return visits would be necessary. Meanwhile there were certain ointments and extracts of which she herself was to make nightly application. This cream, from the beestings of wild Mongolian sheasses. This, with ambergris secreted by afflicted whales and found floating upon tropical seas. A hair rinse of champagne and plover's eggs. This jelly rich in the hormones of queen bees fed on the nectar of Alpine wildflowers. This lotion, to prevent dry skin, containing morning dew from the Sahara. Miracles of modern science and ancient recipes, the guarded secrets of Cleopatra and the Queen of Sheba, precious as virgin's milk, reserved for the world's privileged few fair women.

In a mirrored room carpeted like spring grass haughty models paraded for her private pleasure. Naked ones—no, not naked, clothed in lingerie so diaphanous as to seem to be. Then dressed in spidery lace, silk as fine as smoke, scratchy tweeds to tickle the skin and suave satins to soothe it. Leathers supple and scaly, of reptiles and birds and unborn calves. Furs from every corner of the globe, Andean chinchilla that shrank shyly from the touch as if still alive, sleek otter, marten, mink and sable, ermine fluffy as thistledown, velvety clipped beaver, smooth leopard, kinky karakul. Around their svelte necks they wore ropes of pearls, chains of icy green emeralds, around their thin wrists that had never wrung out a mop, bracelets of diamonds and rubies and gold, tiny watches that imprisoned time and kept them eternally young. The bills were to be sent to her daddy, Mr. O. B. Childress, care of the Adolphus Hotel.

"The Hotel Adolphus?" said the lady.

"That's right," said Naomi; and that night she was able to correct her mother's pronunciation: the accent in *hotel* fell on the second syllable.

They stayed a week, saw the zoo, the aquarium, went to a nightclub, and took all their meals in restaurants.

The new Packard was delivered to the door at the hour of departure. It was mustard-colored; the seats, upholstered in red leather, looked like davenports. And though it was as long as a hearse, when the porters had brought down all the hatboxes and shoeboxes and boxed dresses and coats and suits and piled them on the sidewalk and started packing the car, it was evident that they would never get it all in. So Bull telephoned the dealer and another Packard, identical twin to the first, was brought over. As he was the only one in the family who could drive, Bull turned to the manager who had come out to bid them good-bye and said, pointing to one of the porters, "What'll you take for that boy there? And throw in his uniform?" The porter couldn't drive either. He could steer, though, and that was how the Childresses returned home, one car hitched behind the other.

Jesse did not expect any word from Naomi, and it was not just that he believed her father would forbid her to send him any. The lore of his class, the songs he sang, were rich in cynical commentaries on such situations as his. He cursed her and dismissed her from his mind. Or told himself he had. But the first time he saw her on the street, and she passed him by as if afraid of dirtying herself by looking at him, though he tried to despise her new clothes they frightened him instead, and her new hairdo and those little refinements of carriage that she was already exhibiting all made her so beautiful that he was smitten as never before. The scent she left behind her in the street broke his heart. And he might have been dead for all she cared. Not a word. Not a glance. Not even for old times' sake.

Meanwhile, following Bull Childress' strike, the oil fever hit the section and it seemed to poor Jesse that everybody except his folks had a piece of ground big enough to drill a hole and sink a pipe; only they had none. Land prices began to skyrocket, and there went the other dream of Jesse's life. Land that always, until now, had gone begging at twenty dollars an acre, land that had sold for unpaid taxes and gone unsold even for that, was suddenly fetching thousands and thousands of dollars. He alone owned none. Now he never would.

Clyde Barrow and Bonnie Parker were dead, the Texas badman and his gun moll. The town, one Saturday just past noon when Jesse joined his gang of buddies on Main Street, pullulated with the news. Dead. Clyde Barrow and Bonnie Parker. It had happened some days before (the previous Wednesday, in fact), but it was news, for if like Jesse and most of the others on the streets you spent Monday through Saturday morning behind a plow talking only to a mule, it was in town on Saturday afternoon that you caught up on the week's events.

Clyde and Bonnie. Dead. The groups of men collected on the corners were both subdued and excited, with an air at once conspirational and challenging, as if defying a ban on public gatherings; and like the people of an occupied country, when a partisan hero (and heroine) one of their own has been caught and executed by the authorities, the flag of their traditional, classless, blood-sympathy with the outlaw flew at half-mast.

The folk hero, in yet another avatar, was dead, and already the prose of their lament was growing cadenced and incantatory, half on its way to being verse, and soon would be music, and then, in the cotton fields, to the rhythm of the chopping of a hoe, on records in café nickelodeons, on street corners sung by blind, legless veterans to the whang of a steel guitar, young men would be adjured to take warning and listen to me, and told his story. How he was a poor boy— and thus already, even before his first recorded infraction (which had been to defend his sister's honor against a rich lecher, or the theft from hunger of a dime loaf of bread, or through impatience with the law's delay in righting a wrong which he, a poor boy, had suffered), on the outs with the law. A poor boy, alone, against the world, and orphaned. Orphaned of a father, that is; for a mother there would be, old and ailing, to visit whom in her illness he regularly slipped through the cordon of deputies and marshals posted around the family homestead with the loose insolent ease of a nocturnal panther. A poor boy who died young; handsome it went without saying, with women by the score ready to die for him, and one who gained immortality by dying with him. And a man (already in the barbershops and around the marble machines in the cafés they were wondering how the law could have known Clyde would come down that road at that hour of the day; he whose every move had been as stealthy and as sly as a hunted coyote; they who for two years he had made look like monkeys), a bosom friend, the one man he had ever taken into his confidence, whose life perhaps, which is to say undoubtedly, he had saved, ready to kiss his cheek in public for a handful of silver.

The actual place it had happened was in Louisiana, where, as their car passed through a narrow and bushy defile, they had been jumped, ambushed, by a party of local and out-of-state lawmen who opened fire with shotguns, pistols and automatic rifles. The car in the picture looked like a collander and the bodies of a thin, undersized young man and a thin young woman, who even in death retained the lean and sinewy wariness of an alley cat, looked like wild game, the lawmen standing over them with their guns, posing with stiff proud smiles, as in those photographs of hunting parties with the days's trophies lying at their feet. "I hated to bust a cap on a woman," the gallant leader of the posse was quoted as saying. "Especially when she was sitting down. But if it wouldn't of been her it would of been us."

And so at last it had come: the end of a reign of terror throughout the whole Southwest of some two years, as the newspapers put it. The end which had been expected daily (he would go out blazing, would take as many with him as he could, if they gave him a chance, which they didn't, and her too, old cigar-smoking Bonnie too, would never surrender, not Clyde, but would, should it come to that, save one last cartridge, or rather two, for themselves) had been foreseen and almost already lived through, yet never for one moment believed in, and secretly prayed against, even by those holding what they considered the sure number in the betting pools that had been made on the date.

And already, in the barbers' chairs beneath the turbaned mounds of towels, on the shoeshine stands, to the click of snooker balls, in the otherwise unused, except as a kind of local Salvation Army shelter for the town's two incorrigible and homeless drunks, waiting room of the depot, hanging around waiting for old 88 to howl through and fling off the mail sack, they were saying: a dozen of them, and after two years of being made to look like a pack of fools, against one man and a girl! And without even giving them a chance to surrender (when what they meant was, without giving them a fighting chance to return fire). And saying that when the bodies were taken from the car (he had been at the wheel) she was found to have died in the act of drawing her pistol—not no lady's purse popgun but a real sonofa-bitch honest to by God old .45 government-issue Colt automatic—from the glove compartment. And maybe her kind was what had led that poor boy astray in the first place, but she had stuck by her man, I God, through thick and thin, you had to say that for Bonnie Parker, she had stuck by her man.

And then—a note of state pride in the voice then, and a dry cackle of a snort, "I God, they ain't caught Purty Boy yit!" Meaning Oklahoma's own Pretty Boy Floyd. And how there was a man—not mentioning no names, but if you was to, why, it wouldn't be the first time they ever heard it, and he lived not so very far away—that answered a knock on the farmhouse door late one cold and rainy winter night and called, *Who's there?* and got back for answer, *A friend,* and opened the door and held the lamp up to a handsome young face that he had never seen before except on the wall alongside the rental boxes in the post office, but had said, *Come in, friend,* for he had been honored by the title, been proud to give him the night's lodging he asked for, and had turned the kids out despite his protests and made them down a pallet on the floor, and next morning had found, or his wife had, pinned to the blanket a one-hundred-dollar bill. And that man was not the only man in Oklahoma that such a tale might tell. Not none of these biggety new oil-rich that up to six months ago had always wiped on a cob and now tried to look as if they never wiped at all, but them that still knew what it was to be a poor boy and on the outs with the law—which two things came to the same.

And someone wondered, for sooner or later someone was bound to, if it really was Clyde and Bonnie in that car. For the law shot first and asked questions later, and never confessed afterward to any little mistakes of theirs. And they had been made to look mighty foolish for a long time. And they could use the bodies of a young man and a young woman, too shot up to be really identified, for public consumption. And that led to talk of the greatest badman of them all. How a man, an old-timer, had turned up in Oklahoma City, or maybe it was Tulsa, not so very long ago, claiming he was Jesse James and could prove it, and that the dirty little coward who, in the song, had shot Mr. Howard and laid poor Jesse in his grave, had done no such thing, only it had been convenient at the time to let it be thought so. —And our Jesse listened, smiling bashfully, the black leather bow tie riding up his Adam's apple as he ducked his chin, reddening a little, as one must when a hero is being spoken of who shares one's name.

And they talked of other storied outlaws past and present, of Baby Face Nelson and Dillinger, of Sam Bass and Billy the Kid, and always, here among Jesse's crowd in particular, the word poreboy, a poreboy, sounded, like the bass string which the hand must always strum no matter what the chord, on a guitar. A poreboy who had got himself into a little trouble, and was maltreated and made mean by the law because he was a poreboy with nothing and nobody to buy them off, whom they might club and rubber-hose with impunity, a poreboy with no one to go his bail. For the gang that Jesse squatted and whittled and spat with in town on Saturday afternoon was different now from his former companions. Instead of the older, steadier (and as he now thought of them, cowed and beaten) family men, he hung out now with a group of young men of all ages, bachelors married and unmarried, hired hands and tenant farmers' sons and young mechanics and day laborers from the town and those without any fixed address nor visible means of support nor any traceable origins who spent the days between Saturdays sitting along the loading platform of the cotton compress or in the domino parlor, those left out of the current oil boom, who made vague threats every now and then of running off and joining the Navy. And always in their telling there was a woman in it too, at the root of it always some woman, one for whose sake a poreboy had gone wrong, and who, if she had not actually sold him out, had deserted him when the chips were down. As in the ballad, merely one of the most popular of hundreds on the theme, which had become Jesse's favorite among his repertoire:

> *I got no use for the women.*
> *A true one can never be found.*
> *They'll stick by a man while he's winning;*
> *When he's losing they turn him down.*

Except for passing showers lasting half an hour, and leaving upon the parched soil a crust like dried blood, it was six weeks since rain had fallen. The sun swooped lower by the day, singeing the stunted cotton like feathers in a flame. There was not even dew by night to settle the dust that choked the air. Men's heads were commencing to shake. It looked as if they were headed into another summer like the last, and the one before that.

In all of Oklahoma there was probably just one farmer whose mood this weather exactly suited, and that was Jesse Neighbours. He was spoiling for something, he himself did not know what. Now that he had nothing and no one to work for he was working harder than ever, in the field before daybreak and out till after nightfall, unable to straighten his back, stalking down the rows (it was cotton-chopping time) with his hoe rising and falling as though motor driven, neither speaking nor spoken to for twelve to fourteen hours at a stretch, so that his mind was furrowed by his thoughts as regular as a tractored field, throbbed to a beat as insistent as the rise and fall of his hoe. You chopped three acres a day and what did it get you? A plate of greens at night, enough to just keep you going tomorrow. You picked two hundred pounds, dragging the heavy sack after you like a wounded animal its entrails, bent double, blinded by your own salt sweat, no time to mop your brow, other hands quick to pick whatever you missed, half a cent a pound, take it or leave it, and at the end of the season what did you have? Enough to not quite pay your bills at the company store. Convinced now that farming was for fools—fools like him—Jesse delighted in every affliction that beset the crops: the fitful blossoming of the cotton, as if discouraged by the price it was fetching on the market, the coming of the boll weevils and the leaf hoppers and the corn smut, the blackbirds in clouds, the dust storms, the scorching sun that wrung a man out like a rag. He despised his condition and despised himself for acquiescing in it. And it was not long before that talk of desperadoes which had been dropped like refuse in a corner of his heated and airless brain burst aflame through spontaneous combustion.

People were robbing banks again, now that they had reopened following their little holiday. In town every Saturday there was talk of some bold new stickup. Then on Monday back to the fields, up and down the long weary rows, swinging a hoe or dragging a sack, and Jesse dreamed of fast cars, a new one stolen every week, always on the move, always in the money, spend it fast before it burned a hole in your pocket, plenty more where it came from, of living by the gun, quick on the trigger, feared and adored by multitudes, your exploits followed in the daily newspapers, good-looking women at your feet, fancy clothes, fast company. And when his name was on everybody's lips, then wouldn't Naomi feel sorry! Suppose you got caught? That was the risk you ran. Suppose you got killed? Suppose you did. Death by gunfire, quick, clean, a pistol bucking in your hand, at the end of a few glorious years, going out in a blaze, dying young and leaving a handsome corpse—compared with that was long life, spent in a cotton field, such a precious thing? Before long Jesse had begun to save up his money.

His earnings at picking went to the support of the family, but what he picked up playing Saturday night dances was his. After being jilted he had recklessly gone back to smoking; now he quit again and once more began putting his tobacco money in a jar. It was no mule this time that he was saving for. He had to have a pistol; and before she would be reliable as a getaway car the old buggy needed a set of rings and at least one new tire to replace the one on the right rear with the boot and the slow leak around the valve.

Which bank Mr. O. B. Childress kept his money in Jesse did not know, but he wanted to be sure not to rob that one. Not that Jesse had any love for Bull. But Bull's money was, or would be, Naomi's; and if it should come to pass that having robbed just one bank and got away

with it he decided not to make a career of it but came back home rich
and they got married after all, he would not want it on his conscience
that some part of his money was his wife's. The surest way to avoid
it was to go outside the state.

Across the river over in Texas, in the county seat of Clarksville
some forty miles away, was a bank which had been the object not long
since of a spectacularly unsuccessful robbery attempt. The three rob-
bers had been shot down like fish in a barrel as they emerged from
the bank by lawmen posted on the adjacent rooftops. That gang had
failed because they were too many—including a fourth who had informed the law of their plans. No one would be able to tip them off
on him; and according to Jesse's calculations, swollen with self-con-
ceit, the Clarksville sheriffs would be incapable of imagining that their
bank might be struck again. And when things had blown over and he
returned home in the chips, he would explain how he came into it by
saying he had gone wildcatting in Texas and struck oil. And if he got
caught? He was not aiming to get caught. And if he got killed? Who
was there to care if he did?

The old buggy turned out to need more than a new tire or two, as
Jesse found when, cotton picking over, he went to work on her. He
gave her a valve job, up to his elbows in grinding compound, cleaned
the plugs, put in points, regulated the timer. Then came the crowning
touch, installation of a second carburetor, taken from the companion
car, the adapter engineered by himself. The result was pickup that left
new model cars sitting, as he proved on the road to Tishomingo where
he went one day in October in quest of that pistol.

And on a subsequent trip shortly thereafter, thanks to that carburetor, she hit seventy, shaking like a shimmy dancer but she did it.
That was a practice run down to Clarksville, where under an assumed
name he opened a savings account at the bank with that fruit jar full
of pennies and nickels and dimes, which took the teller a long time
to sort out and count, giving Jesse a chance to study the layout.

He chose Halloween. You could wear a mask then and be just one
among many, and the noise of firing, should it come to that, would be
lost among the firecrackers and torpedoes. The night before Jesse
wrote a letter to his folks, to be mailed from somewhere when the
job was finished (it was found on him afterward) explaining that he
had left home to seek his fortune and would come back when he had
made good, that he had left without saying good-bye so as to avoid
tears, and not to worry about him.

He left the car in a side street in back of the bank, as planned, engine running, a thing that attracted no notice in those days when old cars were often left running at the curb for fear of their not starting again. In an alleyway he slipped on his witch's mask. The square was filled with masked revelers and there was noise of fireworks. At the door of the bank Jesse faltered for just a moment, then boldly stepped in.

It was all over in seconds. Jesse went to one of the cages, pulled his pistol and said, "This is a stickup." The teller ducked, bells clanged, Jesse panicked and ran, straight into the arms of a bank guard, who held him in a bear hug while a second guard slugged him senseless with a blackjack.

A young man who identified himself as his attorney, appointed by the court, came round a few days later to visit Jesse in his cell. He was still new to his trade and nervous as a young intern with his first cancer patient. In exasperation he said at last, "Fool! If you just had to rob a bank, why didn't you pick one near home? Or don't you even know that here in Texas armed bank robbery is a capital offense?"

No, Jesse said, he never knew that.

At the trial the lawyer pled his client's youth and previous good character and lack of criminal record. But there had been a rash of bank robberies of late, and it was felt that an example must be made. Being from out of state went against the defendant also. The jury was out one hour and returned a verdict of guilty, and the judge sentenced Jesse Neighbours to die in the electric chair.

Appeal was denied, and in answer to their letter to the Governor of Texas Jesse's father and mother received a form reply regretting that nothing could be done, the law must take its course.

Execution was fixed for a day in February. Will and Vera went down to Huntsville the day before to bid the boy good-bye. They were given an hour together, but three-fourths of it passed in silence. They spoke of things going on around home, as they agreed beforehand they would. Once or twice they laughed over something, and once started all three laughed loudly. All through the interview his mother kept glancing nervously at her boy's hair despite herself, thinking of it being shaved off, as she had heard was done. Nothing was said about Naomi Childress. When the time was about up Jesse said he was sorry for the troubles he had brought on them, and they said not to think about that. He said tell his little brothers, and especially Doak, not to be proud of their outlaw brother and want to follow in his footsteps, but to be sensible boys and stick to farming, as crime did not pay. His mother would have liked to ask if he had made his peace with the Lord but was afraid of embarrassing him. When it came time to say good-bye they kissed and she managed to stay dry-eyed, as Will had admonished her that she must. It was he whose eyes filled with tears as he and Jesse shook hands.

They were told they could come for him anytime after seven the next morning. Money being a little tight, and neither of them feeling much like sleep, they passed the night sitting in the waiting room at the depot. They did not know the exact hour of execution. But when at shortly past five the lights in the station dimmed they reached for one another's hand and sat holding them until, after about four minutes by the clock on the wall, the lights brightened again. At seven at the penitentiary gate they found a truck waiting with a casket on the bed. They were given Jesse's effects, his guitar, his clothes, and a bale of tinfoil from the inner wrappings of ready-rolled cigarettes, each sheet rubbed out smooth as a mirror, at the sight of which his mother could not keep back a tear.

They were given a ride back to the depot in the cab of the truck. There the casket was put on the scales and weighed and Will paid the loading charges. Then it was put on a cart and rolled out to the end of the platform. They went back to their seats in the waiting room. There remained in the shoebox which Vera had put up for their trip some biscuits and meat but neither felt hungry. When the train came in they watched the casket loaded into a freight car. Their seats were in a coach in the rear. The overhead rack being too narrow for it, the guitar rode across their laps. And still though they sat, in two hundred and fifty miles it happened now and again that one or the other would brush the strings, drawing from them a low chord like a sob.

TOM MAYER's work has appeared in *The New Yorker, Harper's,* and *Sports Illustrated*. His story "Just Fine" was chosen by *Story* magazine in 1963, while he was at Harvard, as the best college work of short fiction. He is attending Stanford University, from which he has received a Creative Writing Fellowship, and is working on a novel to be published by Viking.

Homecoming

WE CAME up the long rise to the top of the Galisteo shelf at about sixty, which was all the car would do, and then we could see the whole northern end of the Estancia Valley. The steel of the railroad tracks below glinted in the afternoon sun, and we could see the steeple of the church at Lamy behind the rolls in the plain. I could tell there wasn't much wind, which was unusual, because there weren't any twisters. Sometimes you can see seven or eight separate twisters from the top of the shelf.

I was driving and my mother was sitting in the front seat with me, her eyes inflamed and pinkish from a week of crying. I glanced over at her, and I could see her holding herself erect, almost as if she were sitting at attention, but the left corner of her mouth kept twitching, the way it does when she is upset.

As we started down the grade I let up on the gas, and the old Hudson began backfiring. "We really ought to trade this thing in," I said. "It's gone 106,000 miles and it has a perfect right to blow up anytime."

"It was your father's car," my mother said, "and, besides, we don't have enough money for a new one. We'll just have to make do."

The part about money was a lie, but I didn't answer, because I didn't want to start an argument with her. I had only been trying to start a conversation.

The Galisteo shelf, under one name or another, runs all the way from the Sangre de Cristo Mountains to the Jemez. In the west, on

From *Bubble Gum and Kipling* by Tom Mayer. Copyright © 1963, 1964 by Tom Mayer. First appeared in *Harper's Magazine*. By permission of The Viking Press, Inc.

the other side of the Ortiz, it is called La Bajada. At its base is Lamy, the railroad depot for Santa Fe, and, as I said, from the top you can see the whole northern end of the Estancia Valley. The valley is usually brown in summer, from overgrazing and the sun, and it stretches all the way to Texas. I know the northern end of it well. I have ridden over most of it many times, and it became a habit with me to pick out the most important places from the top of the shelf. I do it every time I drive down.

We were at the bottom of the grade, almost to the overpass where the road goes over the tracks, when my brother Johnny, who was sitting in back, said, "Do you think it's gonna rain this afternoon?" He was only thirteen, and my father's death was very hard on him.

"No," I said. "What makes you think that?"

"There's some clouds over the Ortiz, so I thought it might rain."

"You know rain never comes from the west," I said. I wasn't mad, just stating a fact.

"No, I didn't know," Johnny said.

"Yes you did. Come on now and think of once when it's rained from the west."

Johnny thought for a minute. Then he said, "I guess I can't."

"Damn right you can't," I said. "You know rain clouds always start from the Sangres."

"Don't pick on Johnny like that," my mother said. "He didn't mean anything."

"I know."

"Well then why were you picking on him? He didn't do anything."

"I wasn't picking on him," I said.

"You were too."

"Oh for Chrissake," I said. "I was not."

Mother started to cry. "Shut up, will you, Mother?" I said. "You've done nothing but cry all week." Of course that only made her cry all the more, so after a minute I said, "Mother, I'm sorry. I didn't mean that. Please don't cry. Please."

That calmed her down a little bit, but I didn't look over at her, because I knew the corner of her mouth would be twitching.

I turned left toward Lamy just before the overpass. When we got to town I parked behind the station. Lamy is a very small town. It has an old adobe church, a few adobe houses, mostly unplastered and crumbling, the station, a general store, a Gulf filling station, the

Pink Garter saloon, and five or six of those yellow-board railroad shacks. There are yellow shacks like those in every town along the Santa Fe, and the railroad even paints A T & S F on some of them.

There was a redcap sitting on one of the baggage carts when I got out, and he said, "You need help?"

"Yeah," I said. "I gotta coffin coming in on the baggage car."

"Which train?"

"Eastbound Chief."

"O.K." he said. "It's on time. Three twenty. Westbound comes through at four was why I asked."

"Fine," I said.

It was five past three by my watch and I walked around to the platform. There were a couple of people I had never seen before and Donal McNally. Donal McNally was my father's best friend, and whenever anything went wrong we knew we could count on Donal. He and my father had been in the Australian army together in the first world war, and my father brought Donal out to New Mexico to work on his ranch. Donal didn't stay on the ranch, but got into political writing, and now he is syndicated in sixteen newspapers. Sometimes we didn't see Donal for a long time, but whenever anything went wrong we could always count on him.

"Hello Jerry," he said.

"Hello," I said. Johnny came walking over and Donal ruffled his hair. Donal is a big man, getting fat, and Johnny hardly came to his waist.

"How you figure to get the coffin to the mortuary?" Donal asked.

"Hudson, I guess." I hadn't really thought about it.

"It might be a tight fit. I got to thinking about that so I hired a hearse to take it up in for you. Also it might upset your mother pretty bad if she had to ride all the way back with it in the car."

"You're right about it upsetting her," I said. "And about the rest of it, too. Where did you park the hearse?" I hadn't seen it when we drove in.

"Over at the filling station. Driver had to get some gas."

"Thank you very much," I said, "for thinking of it."

"That's all right. . . . How is she?"

"Mother?"

"Yes."

"Pretty shaky, I guess. She's been crying a lot."

"She's upset."

"I know."

"Well, you can't blame her for it."

"No you can't."

"Johnny," he said. "Come on. Let's go cheer up your Mommy."

They walked off and left me standing by myself. Donal had his hand on Johnny's head. I looked down at the overpass, and the semaphore was down and the signal light red. You can see the overpass, which is several miles away, from the platform, though at the eastern end of the station the tracks twist off out of sight into the Glorieta Canyon.

On an impulse I started to walk one of the rails. I was out of practice, but I didn't slip too much. I learned to walk rails when I was five or six. Whenever we'd load sheep, my father would want me out of the way. Loading sheep is a very touchy business, and he didn't want to have a little boy around to spook the animals. You got to have a goat to lead them up the ramp, and if you panic them they bunch up and crush each other. You lose 2 per cent to crushing anyway, but no more if you are careful. My father was a very careful loader and he didn't want to take chances by having me around. "Jerry," he used to say, "why don't you go down and practice rail-walking? I'll come down later and we'll have a contest. Be sure you stay on the siding and don't get on the main line." Sometimes I would have to practice rail-walking by myself for three or four hours or even half a day while the *borregueros* and my father loaded. Loading is dirty work, but no matter how tired he was my father would always have a rail-walking contest with me after he was finished. He would be covered with caked dust and manure, and even so he usually beat me.

By the time I was eight, though, I stopped walking rails and learned to use a sheep counter. Not that it was hard work, but it is very important. Later I learned to help with the herding itself, and then I would be tireder and dirtier than my father when we finished.

When we were loading animals from the Peele place, a ranch my father bought in the 'twenties, we used the Lamy pens, which are on the other side of the overpass from the station. The sheep from the old Torreon ranch, which belonged to my great-grandfather, we loaded at Vaughn on the southern route of the Santa Fe. We sold the Peele place after my father had his first heart attack three years ago, but I imagine we'll hold onto the Torreon as long as we can.

I slipped off the rail once and turned around to come back. I guess thinking about loading, and the rail-walking, had started me off, because I remembered the time Dinah had puppies in the lobby of the old Harvey House at Lamy. They tore the Harvey House down in the summer of 1950 and this was the winter before. The Harvey House was a big California-Spanish hotel like the ones in Gallup and Flagstaff, and they tore it down because nobody even used the dining room any more. My father told me that in the old days when he was a kid it was a very swanky place. There were lace vines growing all over the archways, and in the courtyard was a goldfish pond. Except for stock tanks, that goldfish pond was the only pond I saw until I was seven or eight. I remembered I'd always wanted to go wading in it and try to catch a goldfish.

We stopped there often coming home from the Torreon. We have always lived in Santa Fe in my mother's house as well as on the Torreon. Her father was a Supreme Court justice, and we kept the house in Santa Fe partly so that Johnny and I could go to school in town, but also because mother doesn't like to live on the ranch all year round.

When we stopped at the Harvey House in winter we would sit around in front of the big fireplace in the lobby and drink hot chocolate, and if it was summer we would go into the bar. The bar was very dark and cool, and my parents would have Tom Collinses while I drank ginger ale.

The time that Dinah had puppies we were driving north on a very cold day. It was snowing a little, and the wind was blowing so strong it swayed even the heavy Hudson. My parents and I were sitting in the front seat, and Old Mike and Dinah, my father's Airedales, were in back. My father had kept Airedales ever since the 'thirties when he ran sheep in the Jemez summers and needed bear dogs. Old Mike had been a bear dog, and one of his ears was missing.

Dinah had been whimpering for quite a while, and my mother said she thought maybe her time was coming. Suddenly Dinah snarled and bit Old Mike on the shoulder very badly. Old Mike didn't make a sound. My mother turned around and said, "Oh my God, Ned. She's whelping." Sure enough Dinah had Old Mike's shoulder clenched in her teeth and the first pup was about halfway out. My father said, "Jesus H. Christ," which is what he always said when he was annoyed, and stopped the car.

He got out and got into the back seat. Very carefully he pried Dinah's teeth loose, and then he snapped his fingers so that Old Mike jumped over into the front seat with us. His shoulder was bleeding a lot, and my father said, "Jerry, take this handkerchief and hold it on Old Mike's shoulder to stop the bleeding. You drive, Agnes. I'll stay back here." Dinah snarled again, but my father petted her, and she quieted down. He was wonderful with all kinds of animals.

My mother said, "We can't drive all the way home like this. We'll have to stop somewhere."

"I know," my father said. "We'll stop at Lamy."

We were only about five miles from Lamy and we drove on in with me holding the handkerchief on Old Mike's shoulder, and my father in the back seat petting Dinah. My father was the only one who said anything, and he talked to Dinah. "Easy little girl," he said. "Easy darlin' little girl. Everythin's all right and nothin's gonna hurt my darlin' little girl so easy little girl easy." Dinah lay down on her side and put her head in my father's lap. When she had finished with the first pup my father leaned across her very carefully and cut the cord with his pocket knife. He sterilized the knife every morning, because sometimes he had to puncture bloated sheep with it. If a lot of sheep are badly bloated you don't have time to give them all bloat medicine, so you puncture their stomachs. My father could usually save two out of three if that happened. He took the pup in his hand and said, "It's dead. She must have crushed it." Then he put the dead pup on the floor and kept talking to Dinah.

When we got to Lamy my father said, "Stop in front of the Harvey House." He picked Dinah up and carried her into the hotel.

The clerk was a young man named Silvo Torres. His father was old Reginaldo, one of our best *borregueros*, and Silvo had been born on the Torreon. He saw the situation right away and he said to my father in Spanish, "Take her over by the fireplace. I'll get some blankets."

There was a big Navaho rug in front of the fireplace, and my father sat down on it with Dinah. Just then she whined, and cried, and the second pup had started. Silvo came back with the blankets, and my father covered her with them.

The second pup took about fifteen minutes, but it was alive. It looked exactly like a rat—Airedales are ugly puppies until they are almost a month old—and my mother put it in her sheepskin to keep it warm. Old Mike and I sat away at a respectful distance and watched.

Dinah had five more pups in three hours. At one point a lady in a fur coat came in to wait for her train, and, when she saw what was going on, she said, "Oh how repulsive." My father didn't look up, but my mother was mad. I could tell because her cheeks got red. Old Mike snarled at the lady. She waited for a minute or two and then she went out.

Silvo fixed up a whelping box from old boards, and brought it in. My father put Dinah in it with the pups, and covered them with blankets. We stayed at the Harvey House overnight, and Old Mike slept in my room. We were probably its last guests. The next morning we drove home with eight Airedales instead of two.

I slipped off the rail again, while I was trying to turn around, and I looked at my watch. Three fifteen. I went over and sat on a baggage cart in the shade. I looked toward the east end of the station where the Glorieta Canyon starts. The only important train I'd ever met before was a westbound. That was when Mother came back from Chicago after she had my little sister Janet, who died when she was less than a year old. All of us were cesareans, and my mother went to Chicago because she didn't have much confidence in the local hospital.

Janet was born December sixth, and my mother came home Christmas afternoon on the Super Chief. My father and I met them. My father brought half-a-dozen roses down to the train, and I remember he looked a little funny standing there on the platform in his dirty old ranch sheepskin holding half-a-dozen roses. The train was late and both my father and I thought we heard it several times before we did. I put my ear down to the track, which was very cold, to listen.

When the train did come, my mother was the only person who got off. She was carrying Janet in her arms, and she cried when she saw the roses. She let me hold Janet while she kissed my father, and she cried some more.

Thinking about her standing there crying, I heard the whistle of the train. I looked toward the overpass, and I could see the headlight of the diesel.

Donal came up, and I jumped off the baggage cart. "Where's the redcap?" he asked.

I looked around and saw the redcap pulling another cart up toward where the baggage car would stop.

"There," I said, and pointed. Donal and I started after him.

I turned to watch the train come by. I love to watch the big five-unit diesels the Santa Fe uses, and usually I wave to the engineer. That day, though, I thought I probably shouldn't. The engine passed us with a huge rush, even though it wasn't going very fast, and the baggage car stopped exactly in front of the redcap. The door of it opened and the brakeman lifted two mail sacks onto the cart.

"Got a coffin?" asked the redcap.

"Yes," the brakeman said. "As a matter of fact I've got three. Phelps, Huevelle, and Gordon."

The redcap looked at me. "Gordon," I said. "Edmund Gordon."

The brakeman said, "Your father?"

"Yes. He died of a heart attack. At a stock growers' convention in San Francisco."

"I'm sorry."

"Thanks. He's had a bad heart for a long time."

The redcap climbed into the car and they slid the coffin onto the cart. Donal looked at the tag and said, "This is the one." Then he put his arm around my shoulders for a moment. The redcap pulled the cart away down the platform, and my mother and Johnny were standing by the station. "Take it over to the hearse," Donal said. A Cadillac hearse was pulled up by the buses. Donal turned to me. "I'll tip him. You get your mother on home. This is awfully hard on her, and she needs you. She needs you and rest. I'll look after everything at the mortuary; you just get your mother on home."

"Thank you very much for everything," I said. He put his hand on my shoulder again, and walked off after the redcap.

Johnny was crying when we got in the car, though my mother had stopped. "Shouldn't we look inside and see if it's Daddy?" Johnny asked.

Mother smiled. It was the first time she had smiled all week. Johnny was sitting in front with us this time, and she put her arms around him. "No Johnny, we can't look inside. Not here. I wanted to too, but it's not Daddy any more. It wouldn't do any good to look."

"Why not?" Johnny asked.

"I don't know," my mother said. "It just wouldn't do any good."

I was afraid she was going to start crying again, so I said, "Donal's going to ride up to the mortuary with the coffin. It'll be better that way."

"I know," my mother said. "He told me he was. It's very nice of him."

I backed the car out as the hearse pulled around us. I let the clutch in, and the motor almost died. It backfired loudly, and I said, "Jesus H. Christ." I said it again. "Jesus H. Christ." I felt like slamming my fist into the dashboard as hard as I could, but the motor caught and I put the car in second gear.

EVA MANOFF was born in New York in 1941, lived in the Bronx until 1958 when she entered Antioch College in Yellow Springs, Ohio. After graduation in 1963 she spent some time in California, and is now a copy research assistant in an advertising agency. She wrote her first novel at the age of seven but "it wasn't until my last year of college that I was able to produce anything resembling a short story." In 1962 the *Antioch Magazine* printed "Echoes of Love and Sorrow" and a year later they accepted "Something Beautiful in Growing." "Mama and the Spy" is her third published story.

Mama and the Spy

My MOTHER is afraid of many things. But the day she faced that spy, right in our own house, she was full of a wild courage. I guess in a way it was love that got the best of her fear. Because when someone you love is in danger it can make you so mad that you will spit right in the eye of your most feared enemy.

My sister, Emily, was seventeen, and she was looking for trouble. She called it truth, that thing she was looking for, but my mother said it was trouble, and she shivered and clutched me to her bosom.

"I know," she said to Emily, "what will happen to you. You'll sign your name on a paper and they'll put you in jail—you'll see."

Her eyes burning behind her plain glasses, she appealed to my father, who sat in his big chair calmly smoking his pipe.

"Don't let her do it, David," my mother pleaded. "It's not the way it used to be. This time, I ask you, use your head."

My father was torn. Emily was following the path of his own convictions, much as I, his son, would have done had I been a few years older. He was proud of Emily, but he hated to see Mama suffering.

"This is America," he said, "a free country. Emily is a citizen and she is committing no crime." He puffed on his pipe and leaned forward in his chair.

"Besides," he continued, "you're exaggerating. In the first place,

Copyright © 1963 by The Condé Nast Publications, Inc.

she won't be asked to give her last name. In the second place, the Government isn't interested. She's not joining the Communist Party. The rest they don't care about."

Emily stood before our parents, her feet planted solidly on the flowered carpet. She was a pretty girl, and when she was excited, as she was then, her face flushed and her eyes sparkling, she was almost beautiful.

Under that dark hair, there was a brain that gave no rest. She wanted something, my sister, and it wasn't just to learn. She wanted to fight and be as strong as any man who ever died for a cause. She wanted to prove to herself that my father was right about the world and mankind. Maybe even more important at that time she needed to show herself, her friends, her teachers in school, and the whole damn country that she was neither afraid nor ashamed of sticking to her beliefs. I think she would have been glad to go to jail. I envied her.

"It's hysteria," she said to my mother, "it's panic. They want you to be afraid. Don't you understand that?"

My mother understood very well. "All the same," she said, "it's not a good time. Why make trouble?"

"Because," said Emily grandly, "nobody has the right to tell me what to think. Not even Senator McCarthy."

"He's a pig," I said from behind my mother's elbow, "a weasel, a rat!"

My mother spoke sharply, "Paul, that's enough from you. He's not a Hitler after all." She believed in America, my mother, even though she was afraid.

"In that case," said Emily quickly, "I don't have to worry. Besides, the whole thing is completely ridiculous. You're making a mountain out of a molehill."

My mother sighed. She looked once more at my father. He was gazing thoughtfully at Emily, his balding head shining in the lamplight.

Mama sighed again, "I don't like you to go on the subway late at night," she said. "It's a terrible neighborhood down there."

Emily had covered that possibility. "You remember Louise," she asked, "from camp last summer? She's going, too. Her parents already gave her permission. I could meet her at Fordham Road, and we could ride down and back together. The school is right near the station."

And that was how it started. My mother consented reluctantly, and my father pulled some crumpled bills from his wallet. The next Thursday, the first Thursday in October, my sister and her friend Louise, a chubby girl with braces on her teeth, took the subway downtown and joined an introductory class in Marxist theory.

The classes were held in the large loft of a dingy building in lower Manhattan. There was a small registration fee, which went toward the rent and the teachers' salaries. Every night of the week there was a different class. If there was any money left over, it went to the latest urgent cause. Aid to Southern Negroes maybe, or lawyer's fees for a Smith Act victim.

This establishment had been in existence since before World War II. My father, and even my mother, had attended classes in the Forties. It was kept going by a few dedicated individuals who hired the teachers, solicited students, and sold pamphlets at the door as you came in.

There were twelve students in Emily's class. On Friday night, the night after the first meeting, she sat in our living room and gave a description of her classmates to my father and me.

"Mostly," she said, "they're old people. Louise's uncle who lives in Brooklyn, he goes. There's one really old lady."

"What does he do?" my father asked.

"I said an old *lady*."

"I mean the uncle," my father explained patiently. "Maybe I know him."

"I don't think so," said Emily. "He works in a drugstore in Brooklyn."

My father was in a printing shop, a few blocks from our house. They made all kinds of engraved invitations and cards.

"Maybe I met him somewhere, who knows?" said my father, undaunted. "Where does he go in the summer?" He was convinced he knew not only every Jew in the city but also everyone connected in some way with the progressive movement.

"I don't know," Emily said impatiently, "listen to the rest. The teacher is great. He's a big tall guy with white hair."

"What's his name?" my father interrupted again.

"John," Emily said and continued, "there's also a few younger people, about thirty years old or so. And guess what?"

"What?" I asked eagerly. I had been lying on the carpet at my sister's feet, listening intently and wishing that I, too, could attend the class.

Emily looked toward the kitchen where my mother was preparing supper and listening to the six-o'clock news on the radio.

"What?" I asked again.

Emily leaned forward, closer to my father's chair, and I strained to hear from my position on the floor. "There's a spy in my class," she whispered proudly, "an FBI man."

"How do you know?" I breathed.

"Yes," said my father, "how do you know?"

"Louise's uncle told us," Emily said, "after class. He spotted him right away. He says there's one in every class."

"Well," said my father, seeming unperturbed, "maybe he'll learn something."

"What does he look like?" I asked. "Does he carry a gun?"

"That's what Louise's uncle said," Emily told my father. "He says maybe the spy will learn something. Also, he thinks it's funny, because everyone pays for the course. He says the Government is keeping the school from going bankrupt."

My father chuckled and lit his pipe.

"What does he look like?" I persisted.

"Who?" Emily was enjoying it. She looked as if she didn't know what I was talking about.

"The spy," I said, exasperated.

"Shsh," Emily put a finger to her lips and glanced in the direction of the kitchen. "He's young," she said, "cleancut, and he wears a suit. Also he has a notebook. Nobody else takes notes. And," she finished, "he's kind of cute."

My mother came into the room, drying her hands on her apron.

"Emily," she said, "you set the table. And Paul," pointing to me, "wash your hands and comb your hair. And please," she said anxiously, looking at the three of us, "when Grandma and Grandpa get here, there are two things we will not discuss."

"Number one," I said, having been warned in private, "is my Bar Mizvah. I never bring it up anyway. Grandpa looks at me and says pretty soon it will be time to start Hebrew lessons, and Grandma thanks God and she knocks on the table. And every time I try to tell them I don't *want* a Bar Mizvah, you give me a terrible look and . . ."

"Number two," my mother said firmly, "is Emily's class." She drew herself up and sucked in her plump belly. "Spy included," she said and marched out of the room.

My father grinned. Emily threw up her hands. "The walls have ears," she groaned.

"Mama's no dope," I said, getting up from the carpet.

"Thank you," my mother called from the kitchen, "now go and wash."

The next morning, when Emily was still asleep, my mother trembled in the kitchen and told her menfolk that those classes would surely bring us trouble.

The apartment building where we lived at that time was in a newly built section of the west Bronx. We had two elevators in our wing, one for the odd floors and one for the even. The building was looped around a large courtyard, with a narrow concrete pathway and a flower garden in the middle. In the afternoon it was very noisy in the court, with children running and laughing on the concrete and their mothers yelling at them from the windows above.

Often when I came home from school my mother would watch for me from behind our living room curtain. In that way she was able to meet me at the elevator, give me a dish or pot to take to my grandmother, who lived around the corner, or shove some money in my hand and tell me what to buy at the store. She would manage to do all this before the elevator doors could close, and she would even have time to grab my school books and answer my objections.

Plunging downward in the odd elevator, I would brood on my martyred condition. "Suppose I had to go to the bathroom," I would grumble to myself, and then I would be in the noisy, crowded court-yard, tripping over some misplaced tricycle.

On my way home once again, I would be almost certain to meet Emily, loitering home from high school with Charlie Cohen from next door. Cursing, I would rush past them, for the satisfaction of letting the elevator door close in Emily's face. She never even seemed to notice.

Once my sister's classes started, Thursdays became the most bitter. I had to run all the afternoon errands, plus doing all of Emily's table-clearing and dishwashing after supper. Added to this was the resentful memory of the time I had asked to go to one of Emily's classes. Emily and my father had laughed, and Mama had called me her baby. That was the worst of all.

All through the meal on those Thursday evenings there would be talk about the class, what the teacher had said last week, what Louise's uncle had said, and later on, what Emily had said in front of all the students and the teacher, too. The spy had faded into the background, mainly because, as Emily informed us, he never said anything. He only took notes.

"He's probably dumb," my father would say when the questions about the spy met with no juicy answer.

"He can write," I would point out. "He's saving it all up for the Attorney General." Mama would usually shiver at that.

I was beginning to wish Emily *would* go to jail. She was getting in my hair with her Marxist theory. I had to admit, though, that Mr. Spy had turned into a real dud. We wouldn't get any action from him, I was sure of that. Even my mother began to relax.

It turned out, though, that I was wrong. The spy started action in November, a week or so after Election Day. What he did first was to start sitting next to Emily in class.

"He watches me," she told my father.

"So?" he said, not anxious yet. "You're a pretty girl."

Emily blushed, "That's not the point. He's not a human being, he's a spy. He probably thinks I belong to the Labor Youth League."

The next week she came home with a slightly more unsettling story.

"He asked Louise what my last name was. Doesn't he know that none of us will give him the time of day, let alone our right names? Everybody knows what he is. Even the old lady won't look at him."

My father was disturbed at last. "Has he bothered to talk to anyone else?" he questioned. "What did Louise tell him?"

"He hasn't been annoying anybody else as far as I know," Emily said, and then added triumphantly, "Louise told him my last name was Smith."

Oh, Louise, she was real clever. A regular orthodontured Mata Hari. Smith! What an imagination.

My father had a hard time calming my mother, who alternately gave anxious warnings and pressed her hand to her heart. Papa gave Emily instructions on how to make evasive statements and went over his own past, searching for incrimination. He found plenty. Union meetings, various demonstrations, petitions signed. We all worried.

The spy got more persistent. He accosted Emily at the door one evening and asked her to have coffee with him after class.

"What did you tell him?" I gulped, excited.

"I told him," said my sister, "that I had to go straight home. And then, when class was over, Louise and I walked to the BMT subway with Louise's uncle, so the spy would think we lived in Brooklyn."

"That was brilliant," I said, wishing I had thought of it myself. "Louise's idea no doubt?"

"No," said Emily, glowing, "it was mine. What do you think of that?"

"I think," I said spitefully, "that he isn't a spy at all, and you're wasting your time giving him the runaround."

"And *I* think," said my mother, "that it is time for you, Emily, to give up the class. No more fooling around with something that could blow up on you any minute."

But we were all against her, my father, my sister, and I, in spite of our growing apprehension. Somewhere inside we didn't believe that anything could really happen. And if it did . . . well . . . innocent people had been crucified before. You didn't have to go far back in history to find them, either.

I have been half-joking about all we went through over that spy. But it wasn't funny then. We were struggling, my family, for something, even if it was just the right to sign our names where we would and to go to any function we wished to attend. And although we laughed at the spy, we held him in great contempt. Because what kind of a human being is it, after all, who makes his living hunting down his own innocent countrymen?

It is true that we were guilty of some things. We were guilty of idealism and of a secret wish to become heroes, perhaps even martyrs. More grievous, perhaps, we were guilty of fear. But that kind of guilt belongs in a person's private world and is not to be dragged out in the streets or written up in a stranger's notebook.

We hated that spy and all he stood for. And there were times when we walked our own familiar streets in fear.

Emily's ruse didn't work. The spy found us out. He found out our last name and where we lived. Maybe he even knew what my father did for a living. A spy's job, after all, is to uncover whatever he can. He arrived on our doorstep one Wednesday afternoon in early December. The first snow had already fallen, only to vanish in a last day of feeble sunshine. It was cold and windy, and I struggled home from school, my ears red and numb. I had left my winter cap at home that morning in a general rebellion.

The courtyard was quiet, more quiet than usual. A few bundled toddlers in front of my entrance were shooting each other with woolen fingers and muffled "bang-bangs." I stepped over a small corpse and went inside.

A young man was standing beside the elevators. He was wearing a luxurious camel's hair coat, a woolen scarf, and a brown hat with a small feather in the band. He turned a pale-blue gaze on me as I pressed the button of the odd elevator. The close-cut hair, just visible around his ears, was reddish. I had never seen him before.

He spoke to me in a voice devoid of all Bronx inflection. "Does a girl named Emily Stein live in this building?"

I knew in a flash who he was. I was taken by surprise, and all my rehearsed orations flew out of my head. There was no point in lying. Our name and apartment number were on the mailbox. It would only be a matter of time before he would ring our doorbell and ask Mrs. Stein if she had a daughter named Emily. Besides, I knew perjury was a criminal offense. Anything I said would be held against me, just like in the movies.

"Who wants to know?" I asked. I couldn't look at him.

"A friend," he said.

Still playing innocent, I thought. Doesn't he realize that we know who he is? But then I remembered he couldn't have an idea yet of who *I* was.

"Well if you're a friend," I managed to mumble, "you should know where your friends live."

The elevator had come down, and I rushed into it, slamming the door in his surprised face. He could have wrenched the door open quickly, but he didn't. He was probably still processing my information. I pressed the button marked "5," my fingers shaking.

My mother was waiting at the elevator door, my cap and a coin in her hand. I rushed out and grabbed her by the wrist.

"The spy, the spy," I gasped, trying to drag her toward our apartment door.

She seemed bewildered for a moment and resisted my tugging. "What are you talking about?"

The door slammed, and the elevator started to go down.

"Hurry, Mama," I said in a panic. "He's coming up!"

She caught on. Swiftly now, she hurried down the hall, pushing

me ahead of her. We reached our open door and slipped inside. My
mother fixed the double lock in place. We stood in the foyer,
trembling.

"If only Papa was here," my mother wailed. Then she started to
collect herself. She smoothed her hair and stepped back from the
door.

"How do you know it's him?" she asked in a whisper.

"He asked if Emily Stein lived here. He said he was a friend. I didn't
tell him. I slammed the elevator door in his face. I know it was him."
It was hard to breathe.

In terror, we heard the elevator door closing down at the end of
the hall. Footsteps sounded.

"All right," my mother whispered, "go take your jacket off and
don't worry."

Then the doorbell rang, shrill, and scaring us all over again. There
was a minute of terrible silence. Then Mama spoke.

"Who's there?" she said.

A voice came from behind the door, but we couldn't make out the
words. Fumbling with the lock, my mother managed to get the door
open just a crack. She thrust her face out.

"What is it?" she asked in a voice cold with forced steadiness.

"Mrs. Stein?" came the voice.

Mama nodded wordlessly.

"May I come in?"

"What do you want?" she asked, not budging from that door.

"I'd like to have a word with you in private."

A door slammed down the hall, and shuffling footsteps approached. A curious neighbor, no doubt. Mama opened the door
quickly and let the young man squeeze into the narrow foyer.

He looked past her solid figure and recognized me. His eyes
looked into mine for a second, and his mouth opened slightly. I
stood, twisting a jacket button, forcing my eyes to remain on his
face.

"I'd like to have a word with you in private," he repeated, changing the direction of his glance.

Mama looked around distractedly, but didn't order me to leave.
"Say what you have to say here," she said to the spy.

The young man cleared his throat. "Do you have a daughter named
Emily?" he asked with a polite smile.

Mama drew herself up. "Who's asking?" she said sharply.

The spy's smile faded. He took a wallet from his pocket and opened it to a badge that was pinned inside. "My name is Joseph Grant," he said briskly. "Central Intelligence. I'm a Government representative."

So now the cards were on the table. All was lost. I prayed silently that Emily would be later than usual in coming home.

"My husband isn't here right now," said Mama desperately. "Come back another time."

"Madam," he said, "don't be afraid. I'm not here on official business."

My mother recovered, straightened her glasses, and looked at him steadily. "I'm not afraid," she said. "If you didn't come on business, what is this then with the badge? A social call?"

I looked at her, astounded. Her eyes were blazing, and her curved figure suddenly seemed hard as stone. I took heart.

"You heard her, Mister," I said defiantly. "We're not afraid of you."

He seemed to waver for a minute. Almost pleadingly, he asked once again to speak to my mother in private. This time she gave him a definite refusal. I glowed, a man at last.

"All right," he said. He unwound his scarf and opened the top button of his coat.

"Since you're making yourself comfortable," said my mother, "you might have enough manners to take off your hat."

I couldn't believe my ears. In a daze, I watched him take off his hat, his red head exposed before us.

"Mrs. Stein," he began, "I told you who I was because I wanted to be honest with you. I know your kind of people are suspicious of my profession." He was speaking rapidly, earnestly enough, but his words rankled.

"What kind of people would that be?" asked Mama belligerently.

"I mean people who think the way you do," he hastened to add, "the way Emily thinks. What I mean is, people who go to the kind of classes Emily goes to."

"They go to learn," said Mama quickly. "Why do you go?"

He pretended he hadn't heard that. He went right on talking. "They all know who I am," he said plaintively, "and they don't like me."

This was very peculiar. What did he want of us, for God's sake? Sympathy? Bewildered, Mama said nothing.

"Emily," the spy continued, red in the face as well as the head, "won't talk to me at all. I went to a lot of trouble to find out who she was and where she lived only because . . ." he stopped and looked at me again.

"Because," he repeated, as if he were reciting a poem he had learned by heart, "I'm very much impressed with her. I want to go out with her." His voice had risen, and he was flushed up to the ears. Some spy!

"You want . . . you want to take Emily out?" Mama asked almost timidly.

"I thought," he finished, "that you could bring her to her senses. You could tell her that I mean no harm."

For a moment nobody said anything. Then slowly, almost ominously, my mother began to speak. "I can't believe you," she said and shook her head back and forth. "I can't believe that you mean no harm. Either you are a very good actor, or . . ." she shook her head again, "or you are a fool."

"I went to a lot of trouble," he said again. "Emily is a beautiful girl, intelligent . . ."

Mama suddenly exploded, "From *your* mouth, I don't need to hear that!" Suddenly it was as if all the weeks of bottled up terror, the moments of panic as she stood behind her locked door, were at last released in a tremendous flood of blessed anger.

"Nobody," she said, practically choking over her own words, "nobody who does what you do, taking down the names of innocent people, and, and . . . bringing fear and hate under the name of democracy, nobody like you is fit to scrub my daughter's feet!"

Joseph Grant was stung. "I'm in the service of my country," he declared, "and the free world."

"Then God help this country," Mama retorted. "God help us if this is how we get our freedom."

He started to speak, but she held up her hand. Her whole body was shaking.

"You listen to me, Mr. Graham," his lips silently formed the name "Grant," but she went on, oblivious, "my parents crossed an ocean for your freedom. I'm an American, and I want to be proud of it. You make me ashamed. You fill me with shame," she repeated, her voice shrill, "not for my daughter and not for all the people who will lose their jobs because of your notebook, but for you. You and the people who teach you what to do!"

"Tell that," I said, inspired, "to McCarthy."

"Now," said my mother, winded but firm, "you will please leave my house." She opened the door and the redheaded spy, mute and clutching his hat, departed from our lives forever.

He never did come back to the class. After a month or two, we couldn't even remember his face.

When my sister came home, a few minutes after the spy's exit, she found us, Mama and me, in the kitchen. We were clutching each other and laughing, only Mama was half-crying, too.

"Joseph Grant," I howled, "All-American Spy, was here to see you, Emily. He wanted to take you on a date."

Emily stared at me, "You're crazy," she said and turned to our mother. "What's going on?"

We continued to laugh, the two of us, like a pair of maniacs. I waltzed my mother around the linoleum floor.

"And Mama," I shouted at my dumbfounded sister, "told him to get lost. Right, Mama?"

"Of course," said my mother, giggling. Then she saw Emily's dismayed face and stopped. "I did the wrong thing?" she said incredulously.

"No," Emily said fiercely, "no. Only why wasn't I here to tell him a thing or two?"

"Mama did great!" I said. "Wait till we tell Pop."

Emily's face softened, and she smiled, a big delightful smile. "How did you do it, Mama? How did you have the nerve to send him away?"

"Well," said my mother, her hands on her hips, and the tears still rolling happily down her cheeks, "I took a look at him and I saw he wasn't a Jewish boy. So of course the whole thing was out of the question."

NANCY A. J. POTTER was born in New York City and attended Tufts and Boston Universities. She has published short stories in the *Yale Review*, the *Kenyon Review*, and the *Colorado Quarterly*. She now teaches at the University of Rhode Island.

Sunday's Children

AT 3:15 on the last Sunday afternoon of October, Virginia Scanlan parked her car outside a fun house on the boardwalk at Point of Firs. The fun house, properly named the Jungle of Horrors, was boarded up—had been boarded up for ten years. Ginny put down the sun visor and began reading an old issue of the *Digest* she kept in the glove compartment and had been reading off and on for several months. Before she got through two paragraphs of the condensed novel, all three hands of her watch crossed each other at 3:19. That might be a sign, but she couldn't act on only one of them. She looked around for another test. If the old gull squatting on the boardwalk flew toward her, she would start the car and drive past Steve Cleary's house. If the gull flew toward the beach, she would go back home and wash some blouses. It took the gull a long time to decide to move and then it only hopped around in a big circle cocking its head. Finally it half ran toward Ginny's car and looked affronted as she started the car and ground the gears.

When she reached Steve's street, she considered the possible tactics. She could crawl along at the lowest possible speed, not turning her head but shifting her eyes toward the porch where he might be sitting. Or she could speed along as if her life depended on getting off that street and then, with great surprise at seeing him, jam on the brakes and back to his front walk.

She arranged her face for the indifferent rush, but a hundred tics wrecked her mask. And naturally her plan to roar the length of the street crumbled. At that moment, she hoped he wouldn't be there at all, and then she could go home to the unwashed blouses and the long nap. But it was too late for that; Steve Cleary was taken, surprised, raking leaves in his front yard. Although she had been plot-

Copyright © 1963 by La Salle College.

ting this moment all day, she saw him as a stranger, guarding his lawn with a bamboo rake. His mother made him wear glasses at home. The weight of them seemed to make the rest of his face sag down to his big chin.

"Well, hello." He could not pretend to be happy at seeing Ginny.

The open smile she'd practiced on the street fell away, and she gave her face over entirely to the tics. She concentrated all her energy on getting an offhand tone into her voice, but all that came out was a squeak: "Could you come out with me for a little while now?"

He dug the bamboo rake into the grass. "I'd like to. I would. But my mother has this leaf project lined up. She wants them burned."

"Oh. Well, it doesn't matter. I just thought it was a nice day, and I happened to be driving by. That's all."

Somewhere Mrs. Cleary listened behind the screen door, from the garage, from the back porch. She would be standing, her shaking head stretched in front of her body on a rigid neck. She could not give Ginny Scanlan the satisfaction of seeing her raking leaves. Mrs. Cleary sharpened her dislike for Ginny at breakfast every morning, and by afternoon it was very well polished.

"Perhaps later. I'll get done in an hour or so and then we can go to a movie or something. Could you meet me downstreet at five?"

His voice at home was a little above a whisper. It was as if he were giving a lesson in lip reading, to which she was to respond with the appropriate sign. She nodded and drove away from the enemy castle before the wicked witch came out on her rake.

She was no Gretel, by a damn sight, not at thirty-five. And he was no Hansel either, not at forty on his last birthday. Nor did Mrs. Cleary make a very good witch. Her sin and sorrow lay in living too long, which she knew well but denied hourly by making great promises of what she would do next week, next year, when she got on her feet again and settled a few things, when the buyer arrived for the house, when she moved into a little place of her own. In her seventy-fifth year she talked of a fresh start, saying you're as young as you feel. So she kept surprising the day by getting up earlier and earlier, scratching in the pantry and kitchen in the thin hours before dawn, eating a second breakfast on the stove fender a few hours later when Steve came downstairs at six. Each morning he searched for signs of new decay, which might be told with horror and satisfaction, in the dropping of a dish or a fit of tears. But every year she reckoned on more weakness and shrewdly studied ways to lean her chin on her hand to hide the shaking, to conceal the liver spots on her hands by wearing gloves, to change the subject when she forgot names. Steve patched the weak spots in the dike, bought her new glasses with built-in hearing aids and space shoes and tranquilizers before Mame Cleary knew they made such things and before she'd studied how to avoid them. Most of the time when Steve was around she sat hidden behind the stove, often in the dark to save the electricity, watching the plain clock with Roman numbers until it was exactly the hour or the half-hour. Then she listened to five minutes of the news. When he was not there, she probably sneaked around the house the way women do, but still listened to the news or worried about whether the clock was right. She was cheerful, except on the subject of Virginia Scanlan, and if you asked how she felt, she always said, "A hundred percent."

About old age, Ginny knew a few things too. She had buried two grandmothers, one miserable and fat who got eaten with cancer, the other gentle and thin who died at Ginny's high school graduation. After the grandmothers, came great aunts and uncles who didn't count because they sickened and decayed elsewhere. The present source of information was her own mother, who spent the nights crying out names and imperative sentences from behind the door of the bedroom she no longer shared with Mr. Scanlan, who could not climb stairs after his last stroke. It took him a long time to scuff from the living room sofa that was his bed to the kitchen table, but once there, he ate like a horse and he listened to all the Red Sox games and he always knew who Ginny was. It could have been much worse.

She drove back to the fun house, parked again, and tried to read the condensed novel. But she found herself reading the wrong words. This kept happening. On the table of contents "Snore Cures" became "Snake Crews." Something called "Are We Picking the Right President" was "Are We Pickling the Night Residue." Too tired, she supposed. Even the newspapers were too hard. She would really have liked to go back home and sleep away the afternoon. But her suburb was almost on the other side of the city, and now that she'd made so much a fool of herself, she deserved to sit there.

The town Steve had always lived in was on the shore. Once the city had pushed itself that far, it gave up and left behind its pretenses: strings of bungalows with scrawny gardens behind them. But the city had never been able to convert Point of Firs to urban ways.

One defense against that was the amusement park, never really successful. Even in its best years it had been shabby. Then as fires and bankruptcies made bigger gaps along the boardwalk, the season became shorter and the rides fewer. The roller coaster finally sagged and stopped running. The Democrats and the P.T.A. held state conventions in the Grand Typee ballroom with the revolving stained glass chandelier. They did not use the chandelier, of course, but Steve remembered Saturday night dances in the 1930's—when girls with long black hair swung their accordion-pleated skirts toward and away from thin sailor suits of the coast guardmen from the lighthouse station. And over them flickered little spectrum rainbows as the chandelier turned and the Hawaiian guitar rippled. Steve had stood sucking softly on the straws of his coke on the edge of the floor concentrating on these pleasures of the future before wheeling home.

The last dance in the Grand Typee ballroom, which was really moderate sized and without a single similarity to a wigwam, had been in the summer of 1947. Steve, freshly out of the Air Force, had taken a young war widow from the South who was waiting to find out what to do next. He couldn't remember her face now, but she had had a very good time at the dance and, wanting to repay him, she stroked his neck and shoulders fiercely as he drove her home to her apartment. He never became a very good driver and that night was a clumsy memory. After the summer, the war widow found out what to do and moved away from the sea where her husband's body had disappeared. With her went her little girl—Steve had liked the kid—and they never had another dance in the Grand Typee ballroom.

"It's the kind of town," he often said to Ginny, "you wish you didn't live in, so you could visit it. When you're born into it, where's there to go?"

She nodded. What else could you say? And in five years of almost every Wednesday and some Sundays, they'd improvised on what they had to say until the topics were threadbare and no new skein of talk could lighten the pattern or patch the holes. Perhaps they had not talked that much and had only had so much chance to think before and during conversations and so much time to review them afterwards, a dialogue went on in their heads day after day. She knew the name of Steve's third grade teacher—Elaine Grassi Igoe—and about the Christmas his father had gotten five watches at one time and wore all of them and the grand doings of his service buddy, Fish Dunlop, who still drank a fifth of Old Crow every day and a half and the way his grandfather, a union organizer, had looked when the heart attack grabbed him—about to push a company truck loaded with cotton bales into the Merrimack in February of 1934. He had all her stories, her relatives, her failures, in his head, and except that the silences were too hard to take, they would have walked speechless through their Wednesday and Sunday nights.

"What do you talk about with Tim?" she asked her sister one night over the dishes. But her sister, long married, had looked up from scrubbing the broiler and waited for her to smile as if it were a joke. No answer. After that, she took to listening for a few weeks to the conversations of her married friends. Not all of them talked all the time, but what they said was about their children and their children's sicknesses or teachers or cars and vacations. They seldom mentioned their youth, which was mostly what she talked about with Steve. Ginny supposed that marriage gave them new topics—enough to last ten years or so and new things to do when the conversation wouldn't run.

Wednesday nights had fewer silences. At five o'clock she went into the relief room and put on new lipstick and her suede pumps and then waited in the parking lot. This avoided his going through the reception line in her living room. Her father thwacking his evening *Traveler* with his one good hand and croaking, "You look like a damn Christmas tree on stilts." Her mother's "Have a nice time, dear," as if they were all caught up in an Andy Hardy movie or maybe one of those comic strips where for twenty years nobody gets a day older.

Anyway, the living room, more than the rest of that house, was an old battlefield, and it could never mean the same thing to a sightseer, even the veteran of an almost identical one. So they met in the neutral scene of the company parking lot and drove back slowly to the Stop and Shop in Beale Square, where they got out. Anybody seeing them would have thought they were late shoppers, getting a bottle of milk for morning coffee. For Steve, who had managed the Beale Square Supermarket for six years, closing time was very much like church.

He stood beside the door unlocking it as each stacker and checker took off his apron, hung it on a hook in the back closet, and shrugged himself into the unfamiliar coat. "Night, Joe, Ed, Frank, Bud. Night, Mr. Cote." Steve would never be on first name basis with the butcher, Mr. Cote, a long-faced aristocrat. Most butchers are prima donnas, and good ones like Cote deserved respect. The door was automatic, but Steve held it open anyway for Cote, who, like a captain, waited for everyone else to leave.

Behind, the music now silent, Ginny walked up and down between towers of cans under the faint whine of neon lights. The raw materials of eating mystified her, the choices of size and substance and color, the casual tone of cookbooks, no comfort in a frenzied kitchen. She had never made a whole meal in her life; the kitchen was her mother's as clearly as if the range were padlocked against intruders. Any interest in cooking that Ginny might have owned had withered and died. Once in the summer at a beach picnic for the store, she sat watching Steve confidently season and broil a mound of steaks. She had been frozen by the fear someone would ask her to toss a salad, and she would drop the lettuce in the sand. But no one asked her to do anything, and their not asking made her sick. She was often sick. "You get your bad stomach from your father," her mother said. The only kind of food she liked was what you got at drugstore counters.

Steve drove the scattered pushcarts into each other. He was pleased with their two neat rows, not so happy about the clumps of unsold bread and the fat African violets that refused to bloom and sell themselves. Until the last he saved the rolls of sales slips from the cash registers. He lifted them carefully off the machines and locked them into the safe in the glassed-in square he called his office to look at first thing in the morning. Then he remembered Ginny and found her staring into a bin of frozen turkey pies.

"Have you ever had one?" she asked.

"Never." He was shocked she thought his mother capable of that.

"How can they be sure that 25 minutes at 350 degrees does the trick?"

"It's all worked out. Somebody in a big kitchen in St. Paul or Grand Rapids decides all the frozen turkey pies in America need 25 minutes. Like the cake mixes."

There were a good many Wednesday nights when she would rather have gone right home from work and he would rather have stayed in the store adding up the sales slips, but they always went to the Miter for drinks and dinner. They had three martinis and listened to Honey Holman, a nice girl with a long neck, play "When the Red, Red Robin Comes Bob, Bob, Bobbing Along," on the Hammond organ. The Miter served hot hors d'oeuvres which tasted exactly like the dinner, so it was hard to know when the dinner began or ended. They knew everybody at the Miter—the waitresses, Sam Rosten, who owned it, Honey Holman, and a lot of the salesmen who stayed in the hotel above. Steve usually invited some of them to have a cordial at his table after dinner, so there was plenty of talk there and enough afterward in the car going home.

The rest of the week after work she went bowling and took her nieces and nephews to get new shoes, or wrote letters, or found relatives for her mother to visit. He played the drums in a very good marching band that rehearsed twice a week and made a number of appearances on weekends. One of the big network shows had them on TV, and *Life* had done a piece on them.

On Sundays, usually, they went to the movies and had dinner at the Four Elms, skipping the drinks. Without mentioning where they were going, but with everyone knowing, they edged out of their houses on discreet excuses about meeting friends, ransoming the evening with elaborate promises of being back soon, which they would be. Sundays were never as good as Wednesdays. On the crest of the week of work, they rolled through Wednesdays. On Sundays they met like strangers, kept their masks glued on, and left gratefully when the time was up. Sometimes when there were band concerts or leaves to be raked, they skipped the Sundays entirely. On a couple of those nights, one of them might drive across the city and peek through the window at the other, sitting in the living room in front of the TV set, and return home.

So this October Sunday she had thrown a wrench into the schedule by coming in the middle of the leaf raking. But the cost of driving up to his house seemed to her to offset her intrusion.

When he got out of his car, she saw that he had changed. At a certain age, people stop wearing their clothes and allow the clothes to take over. Ginny knew his suits all hung in his closet with his shape still in them, as the arms of her dresses rested against the stiff arms of others.

They walked along the boardwalk, she on tiptoe to keep her heels from being caught in the holes; he thought women on Sunday wore heels. She was careful to hold her arm rigid so that the charm bracelet wouldn't rattle. They had given each other every gift they could think of, and he had settled on the bracelet to which he kept adding charms. It was a very heavy bracelet. It had a motorcycle with movable wheels, a telephone with moving dial, a tennis racket, a Christmas tree, a replica of the Miss America statue, and one each of most of the animals in the Ark.

The movie theater had been built at the same time as the Grand Typee ballroom. Its ceiling wore irregular rows of bulbs between other rows of thick-necked cherubs. On both side walls, paintings of tall austere women who might have been Indian or Greek raised orange torches.

"This is supposed to be good," Steve said. "It got four stars. The *Post* had an article about it. They filmed it in Spain, but it really happened in Nebraska."

"Who goes to find out how many stars to give it?" She was looking around the shattered and scuffed seats before the lights went out. They were the two oldest people there. Everybody else was the child of somebody Steve had gone to high school with. Ginny watched them attempting to knot their supple arms around each other and noticed how they lost hold and slipped away and then wrestled back trying to find a comfortable embrace. The lights went out.

The movie was about two couples who spent a great deal of time in the kitchen of one set. The two couples were learning they had married the wrong people. One husband and the other wife could have managed very well, but the second wife, miserable with her husband's silence and their bills and his drinking, went crying into the night and was blinded by a speeding car and killed in the rain. Her husband, guilty and unshaven, sat with the other couple in their kitchen patching things up. This is where the movie left them, over a large meal, in the dark kitchen, their children growing up around them.

"I don't know why they have to be like that," Steve said on the way out.

"Like what?" Ginny asked, although she had wondered too.

"All full of misery. God knows, the people I know aren't like that."

"Probably. It all works out in the end anyway, doesn't it?"

"I suppose."

Without two cars they would never have managed the five years of twice a week. Now he solemnly opened her door and helped her in and patted her on the shoulder; then like a little parade, they drove away toward dinner.

The Four Elms had once been a speakeasy. Then it became a family restaurant. Behind it was a pond in which a family of ducks swam waiting for a dinner. In front of it were the two remaining elms and a parking lot full of Buicks. All day Sunday, families waited in line for free tables, all the men turning their hat brims round and round in their hands, their wives, who wore little furs over their silk dresses, talking to each other. The children and grandchildren threw stones at the ducks. When the tables were free, they took off their overcoats and hung up their furs, read through the menu, and ordered the day's special, which for Sunday was veal cutlets and spaghetti. It was, as Steve often said, a place that gave you a good value for your money. And these people were good eaters; they had all been to church that morning and had taken the whole family for a drive up to Point of Firs. They had put on their best clothes, listened with worry to the sermon, given enough to the two collections, observed the speed laws, bought frozen custard for the children, and now they were eating the day's special.

Steve and Ginny pushed themselves up the waiting bench, speaking to men from the store and women from her office. When the waiter asked, "What'll it be, Steve?" he answered, "Two cutlets and bring me a beer and the little lady a coke." Which he did. They ate slowly, talking about the movie, remaking the lives of the characters so that they would not have been killed and orphaned. Their benches were set back to back with other couples. Behind Steve's, Ginny saw an almost identical head, gray in the same spots, heavy jawed. At her back she heard a voice encouraging children to eat everything on their plates and a bracelet jangling as it rose and fell.

Always when it was over, they waited after the dessert as if something was going to happen. Then Steve collected his change and they said goodnight to everybody they would see in the morning. In the parking lot he unlocked her car, held the door open, and patted her shoulder again.

"Wednesday, huh," he said.

She hesitated a moment and said, "Sure—Wednesday."

DONALD BARTHELME was born in Philadelphia in 1931, grew up in Houston, and attended the University of Houston where he was the editor of the student newspaper, and later on the staff. He is presently associated with the new quarterly magazine published by Longview Foundation, *Location*, New York. He has been published in *Harper's*, *New World Writing*, *Contact*, *The Reporter*, *New Yorker*, *Art and Literature*, *Harper's Bazaar*. His collection of stories *Come Back, Dr. Caligari* was published by Little Brown in 1964.

Margins

EDWARD was explaining to Carl about margins. "The *width* of the margin shows culture, aestheticism, and a sense of values or the lack of them," he said. "A very wide left margin shows an impractical person of culture and refinement with a deep appreciation for the best in art and music. Whereas"—Edward quoted his handwriting-analysis book—"whereas a narrow left margin shows the opposite. No left margin at all shows a practical nature, a wholesome economy, and a general lack of good taste in the arts. A very wide *right* margin shows a person afraid to face reality, oversensitive to the future and generally a poor mixer."

"I don't believe in it," Carl said.

"Now," Edward continued, "with reference to your sign there, you have an *all-round wide margin*, which shows a person of extremely delicate sensibilities with love of color and form—one who holds aloof from the multitude and lives in his own dream world of beauty and good taste."

"Are you sure you got that right?"

"I'm communicating with you," Edward said, "across a vast gulf of ignorance and darkness."

"I brought the darkness, is that the idea?" Carl asked.

"You brought the darkness, black man," Edward said. "Funky, man."

"Edward," Carl said, "for God's sake."

Copyright © 1964 by The New Yorker Magazine, Inc.

"Why did you write all that jazz on your sign, Carl? Why? It's not true, is it? Is it?"

"It's kind of true," Carl said. He looked down at his brown sandwich board, which said:

I Was Put In Jail In Shelby County Alabama For Five Years For Stealing A Dollar And A Half Which I Did Not Do. While I Was In Jail My Brother Was Killed & My Mother Ran Away When I Was Little. In Jail I Began Preaching & I Preach To People Wherever I Can Bearing the Witness of Eschatological Love. I Have Filled Out Papers For Jobs But Nobody Will Give Me A Job Because I Have Been In Jail & The Whole Scene Is Very Dreary. I Need Your Offerings To Get Food. Patent Applied For & Deliver Us From Evil.

"It's true," Carl said, "with a kind of dismal inner truth, which shines forth as the objective correlative of what actually did happen, back home."

"Now, look at the way you made that 'm' and that 'n' there," Edward said. "The tops are pointed, rather than rounded. That indicates aggressiveness and energy. The fact that they're also pointed, rather than rounded, at the bottom indicates a sarcastic, stubborn, and irritable nature. See what I mean?"

"If you say so," Carl said.

"Your capitals are very small," Edward said, "indicating humility."

"My mother would be pleased," Carl said, "if she knew."

"On the other hand, the excessive size of the loops in your 'y' and your 'g' displays exaggeration and egotism."

"That's always been one of my problems," Carl answered.

"What's your whole name?" Edward asked, leaning against a building. They were on Fourteenth Street, near Broadway.

"Carl Maria von Weber," Carl said.

"Are you a drug addict?" Edward asked.

"Edward," Carl said, "you *are* a swinger."

"Are you a Muslim?"

Carl felt his long hair. "Have you read 'The Mystery of Being,' by Gabriel Marcel? I really liked that one. I thought that one was fine."

"No, c'mon, Carl, answer the question," Edward insisted. "There's got to be frankness and honesty between the races. Are you one?"

"I think an accommodation can be reached and the government is doing all it can at the moment," Carl said. "I think there's something to be said on all sides of the question. This is not such a good place to hustle, you know that? I haven't got but two offerings all morning."

"People like people who look neat," Edward said. "You look kind of crummy, if you don't mind my saying so."

"You think it's too long?" Carl asked, feeling his hair again.

"Do you think I'm a pretty color?" Edward asked. "Are you envious?"

"No," Carl said. "Not envious."

"See? Exaggeration and egotism. Just like I said."

"You're slightly boring, Edward. To tell the truth."

Edward thought about this for a moment. Then he said, "But I'm white."

"It's the color of choice," Carl said. "I'm tired of talking about color, though. Let's talk about values or something."

"Carl, I'm a fool," Edward said suddenly.

"Yes," Carl said.

"But I'm a *white* fool," Edward said. "That's what's so lovely about me."

"You *are* lovely, Edward," Carl said. "It's true. You have a nice look. Your aspect is good."

"Oh, hell," Edward said despondently. "You're very well-spoken, Carl. I've noticed that."

"The reason for that is," Carl said, "I read. Did you read 'The Cannibal,' by John Hawkes? I thought that was a hell of a book."

"What's your cranial capacity, Carl?"

"Oh, like three or four pounds. I don't know."

"Get a haircut, Carl," Edward said. "Get a new suit. Maybe one of those new Italian suits with the tight coats. You could be upwardly mobile, you know, if you just put your back into it."

"Why are you worried, Edward? Why does my situation distress you? Why don't you just walk away and talk to someone else?"

"You bother me," Edward confessed. "I keep trying to penetrate your inner reality, to find out what it is. Isn't that curious?"

"John Hawkes also wrote 'The Beetle Leg' and a couple of other books whose titles escape me at the moment," Carl said. "I think he's one of the best of our younger American writers."

"Carl," Edward said, "what *is* your inner reality? Blurt it out, baby."

"It's mine," Carl said quietly. He gazed down at his shoes, which resembled a pair of large dead brownish birds.

"Are you sure you didn't steal that dollar and a half mentioned on your sign?"

"Edward, I *told* you I didn't steal that dollar and a half." Carl stamped up and down in his sandwich boards. "It sure is *cold* here on Fourteenth Street."

"That's your imagination, Carl," Edward said. "This street isn't any colder than Fifth or Lex. Your feeling that it's colder here probably just arises from your marginal status as a despised person in our society."

"Probably," Carl said. There was a peculiar look on his face. "You know, I went to the government and asked them to give me a job in the Marine Band, and they wouldn't do it?"

"Do you blow good, man? Where's your axe?"

"They wouldn't give me that cotton-pickin' job," Carl said. "What do you think of that?"

"This 'eschatological love,'" Edward said. "What kind of love is that?"

"That is later love," Carl said. "That's what I call it, anyhow. That's love on the other side of the Jordan. The term refers to a set of conditions which . . . It's kind of a story we black people tell to ourselves to make ourselves happy."

"Oh me," Edward said. "Ignorance and darkness."

"Edward," Carl said, "you don't *like* me."

"I do too like you, Carl," Edward said. "I find you very interesting to have a conversation with. Where do you steal your books, mostly?"

"Mostly in drugstores," Carl said. "Drugstores are good, because mostly they're long and narrow and the clerks tend to stay near the prescription counters at the back of the store, whereas the books are usually in those little revolving racks near the front of the store. It's normally pretty easy to slip a couple in your overcoat pocket, if you're wearing an overcoat."

"But—"

"Yes," Carl said, "I know what you're thinking. If I'll steal books I'll steal other things. But stealing books is metaphysically different from stealing like money. Villon has something pretty good to say on the subject, I believe."

"Is that in 'If I Were King'?"

"Besides," Carl added, "haven't *you* ever stolen anything? At some point in your life?"

"My life," Edward said. "Why did you remind me of it?"

"Edward, you're not satisfied with your life! I thought white lives were *nice!*" Carl said, surprised. "I love that word 'nice.' It makes me so happy."

"Listen, Carl," Edward said, "why don't you just concentrate on improving your handwriting?"

"My character, you mean."

"No," Edward said, "don't bother improving your character. You haven't got time. Just improve your handwriting. Make larger capitals. Make smaller loops in your 'y' and your 'g.' Watch your word spacing so as not to display disorientation. Watch your margins."

"It's an idea. But isn't that kind of a superficial approach to the problem?"

"Be careful about the space between the lines," Edward went on. "Spacing of lines shows clearness of thought. Pay attention to your finals. There are twenty-two different kinds of finals, and each one tells a lot about a person. I'll lend you the book. Good handwriting is the key to advancement, or if not *the* key, at least *a* key. You could be the first man of your race to be Vice-President."

"That's something to shoot for, all right."

"Would you like me to go get the book?"

"I don't think so," Carl said, "no, thanks. It's not that I don't have faith in your solutions. What I *would* like is to go in this store and get warm. Would you mind holding my sandwich boards for a minute?"

"Not at all," Edward said, and in a moment he had slipped Carl's sandwich boards over his own slight shoulders. "Boy, they're kind of heavy, aren't they?"

"They cut you a bit," Carl said with a malicious smile. "I'll just go into this men's store here. Be right back."

When Carl returned, the two men slapped each other sharply in the face with the back of the hand—that beautiful part of the hand where the knuckles grow.

LEON ROOKE lives in Chapel Hill, North Carolina. His short novel "The Line of Fire" was published in *The Noble Savage* and his short stories have appeared recently in *The Free South Review, Epoch, Reflections,* and *Red Clay Reader.* He is at work on a novel.

If Lost Return to the Swiss Arms

He LINGERED a long time but when the sun was at three o'clock the old man left his place on the park bench and headed for his hotel because by that hour the final mail would have been delivered.

The distance from the park to the hotel was not great but there were some things along the way which the old man took pleasure in watching and today there were some children playing too and because he stood among them until the last one ran home, by the time he reached the Swiss Arms the dinner hour was almost over.

The desk clerk, a young man and his friend, told him the girl was saving his place in the dining room but that he would have to hurry. This surprised the old man and from his vest pocket he lifted the gold watch, examined it, and with a slow deep breath returned it to his pocket.

"Time certainly flies, doesn't it, son?" he said.

"Yes sir."

"There you go: humoring me because I'm an old man. I know what you're thinking: so young, that you've got all the time in the world."

"You'd best go on in now and eat your soup, sir."

"Bah! Soup! It's the only thing I can stand and I can't stand it."

He was not hungry but went anyway to his regular table in the corner and sat until he was the last person at the tables, with a cup of tea before him that he did not touch except for his cold fingers on the warm outside of the cup.

The girl did not come to tell him it was time to close but a short while after that time the old man took the napkin from his lap, gave it a small shake, and returned it to his spot beside the plate. From his change purse he took the dime, placing it on the table with its edge showing from beneath the napkin so that when the girl came to

Copyright © 1963 by Carolina Quarterly.

clear the table she would be certain to see it—although the precaution was not necessary since the girl had long since come to expect it there. Of all her tips she valued his dime the most.

Quietly as he had entered he thought to leave the dining hall, to walk swiftly as he could out of the place because he knew that if the girl saw him she would ask why he had not drunk his hot tea or eaten his soup. But this time too she caught him before he got to the door:

"Oh, sir! Sir! You didn't touch your soup and your tea is cold. Why don't you let me bring a tray up to your room later on when your appetite is better? I'd love to do that, if you'll let me."

This she always did. The old man, as he had done so often in the past, told her not to bother, that he felt somewhat tired now and would just like to rest a while.

"Yes, I understand, but I'll just peek in later to see how you feel."

Despite his protests she always brought the tray anyway and sat by it until he ate at least a portion of the food which at one time he would have liked so well but for which he had no taste now.

"Why do you bother with me, an old man?" he asked. "You ought to be giving your attention to that young man out at the desk."

"Oh, he isn't interested in me."

Her eyes flirting with him, she brushed a speck from his coat, gave him a brief, mischievous glance, and left him to clear his table. Such a nice girl, he thought, and watched her until she passed through the swinging doors into the kitchen.

The old man had had intentions of inquiring of the mail when first he returned to the hotel from the park but because the clerk had mentioned nothing about it and because already he had kept them waiting with his dinner he had not asked if a letter by chance had arrived for him. But now he thought he might ascertain the matter and with this in mind he approached the desk.

"Son, did I by any chance—"

The young clerk, smiling warmly, immediately stood and said:

"I'm sorry, sir. I forgot earlier but we're in luck today. A letter came for you."

The old man, who almost never received any mail, told the boy thank you in an apprehensive but eager voice, and watched with some degree of wonder the boy's swift movement as he turned and reached behind him into the narrow box to withdraw the letter. From the clerk's manner the old man knew that he too was happy that a letter finally had come. The clerk passed him the letter then turned away so the old man might regard it with the privacy he desired.

But the old man was perplexed.

"It's typewritten. My name and address, it's typewritten, see here?"

"Yes sir, it certainly is."

Although he didn't say so the old man knew from this that it was highly unlikely that the letter was from any close or personal friend or that it was either of the two letters he had, for such a long time now, been expecting.

"There's no return address. Why is that?"

"I don't know, sir. Why don't you open it?"

"What's your hurry? That's what's wrong with you young scamps. Always in a hurry."

"Yes sir."

The old man peered at the envelope a moment longer, then with his pen knife he carefully sliced along the end of it. He up-ended the envelope that its contents might slide down but his fingers, cold and crippled, missed the inside letter which slid free and fell to the floor. A second sheet, folded, remained inside.

"I'll pick it up, sir."

But the old man, on guard against that, picked up the letter himself before the boy could pass around the desk. He thought he recognized the letter now, the one which had fallen, and he laid it on the desk and stared at it while fumbling at his breast pocket for his glasses. It was, he knew, his own letter, one which he had composed with great care some time ago and mailed to a lady-friend in another state. But, placing the glasses over his nose, he held the letter at arm's length and, for several moments, studied it.

"She sent it back," he said. "She sent back my letter. Look how ragged it is there where she opened it."

"Yes sir."

"That isn't like her. She must be getting careless in her old age. Wonder why she sent it back?"

"Maybe there's an explanation in the other letter."

"Hmmm. Maybe so, maybe so."

He put that letter aside and picked up the original envelope and blew into it. It puffed open and he pulled from it a folded sheet of white paper.

"Would you like me to read it for you, sir? The light down here isn't too good."

"Yes, yes, that's good of you. I would."

The sheet bore a printed head, proclaiming it to be from the office of the public executor. Below this was the date, the old man's name and address and the words: Dear Sir, Miss Beaumont is—but the boy didn't want to read them.

"Yes, go on, what does it say?"

"It says: 'Dear Sir. Miss Beaumont is dead. She died July 1 of a heart ailment, after a long period of illness. I am hereby returning your letter which was turned over to me with the remainder of her personal belongings.'"

After some time the old man took off his glasses and fumbled at his breast pocket for his handkerchief. He wanted to wipe the windows of his glasses. But he had forgotten the handkerchief that morning while dressing himself and preparing for his walk to the park. Probably the handkerchief was there now, on the dresser beside the tie clasp which he had also forgotten, and the dozen or so peanuts the counterman at the cafe had given him days before to feed the squirrels that ran about his feet as he sat on his place on the bench in the park.

"But it doesn't say how she died," he said. "It doesn't say if she suffered. It says nothing."

"I'm sorry, sir. Maybe you could write a relative for details."

"Relatives? No. Miss Beaumont was all alone, she had no one."

"Why not go to your room now and get some rest?"

"Rest? Yes, I'll do that, thank you, son."

"You'll feel much better afterwards, I'm sure. I'll have the girl bring you hot soup and—"

"What? Soup? Yes, that would be nice."

The boy ushered him to the foot of the stairs and the old man slowly took them, the letter held loosely open in one hand, his other touching upon the rail. Half-way up he turned: "But she's younger than I am, in perfect health. There must be a mistake."

"Get some rest, sir. You've been out all day."

When the old man had gone safely up the stairs the young clerk went into the dining room to ask the girl if the old man had eaten properly, and when she said the old man had hardly eaten a bite he said to her that later on if she wished she might take him a little soup and hot tea, that the old man was not feeling well.

"You don't need to tell me," she said, "I was going to do it anyway," and stared at him a moment, not hiding her resentment of his unnecessary suggestion. Abruptly, she whirled and walked away, leaving the boy stranded there wondering why she, mere kitchen help, should always be so huffy with him.

In his room the old man pulled the string that lit the naked bulb above his bed, with one extended hand shielding his eyes from the strong light. He sat on the bed but very soon arose and went to the sink in the corner of the room. He turned on the cold water thinking he might wash his face and rinse the glasses but for several seconds he stood there staring at the running water, his purpose forgotten. He didn't remember to turn off the water but crossed back to the edge of his bed and again sat down. With his finger-tips he kneaded the skin around the sunken bridge of his nose, his eyes closed, his head sagging into his shoulders. He rested. He sat a long time that way, then removed the envelope from his pocket, took the executor's note from it, lay the sheet flat on his knees, and read again *Miss Beaumont is dead*. He read the letter-head, the date and salutation and body and complimentary close, this done, he read it again. With a sigh he stretched out over the bed, his hand over his stomach, the letter on his chest. The light bothered his eyes and he pulled the string and closed his eyes to the comfortable darkness. He became aware however of the water pouring from the pipe in the corner and turned his head that way, wondering how long it had been running and if he had turned it on himself. He felt terrible, his body ached throughout, but, shaking his head as though to say that this was only another now expected barrier thrown up between himself and peace, he rose and walked in his stocking feet to the faucet in the corner.

Once before he fell asleep or as a dream within that sleep he thought of going to the town where Ann Beaumont all her life had lived and where, for a time, they had been the best of friends, to ask of her and to see the grave which claimed her, but that city was a long way and he would not know where to begin and was an old man anyway with only enough money to quietly live out the remainder of his days. Another time, also as if in a dream, he thought he heard the voice of the girl from the dining room and soon after that the boy from the desk, both of them telling him that here now was his soup and hot tea and that these he should eat and drink if he thought to recover his strength. But then they were gone and he woke up and there was no one, neither the girl nor the boy, nor soup nor tea either to prove that they had been there, and he was alone. "I feel sorry for them," he thought, "for those two, both of them such fine young people," and thought of them as he dropped off again into sleep, himself hurt in some way he did not understand because although they showed every kindness in the world to him they showed no concern or friendship for one another but a kind of enmity instead which always appeared to grow stronger in his presence.

He did not go to the park the next day but lay stricken in the bed with a great unresolved weight spreading through him, cheered only by the diligent attention of the boy and girl from downstairs.

"I've got to get up from here," he said to the girl that second day. "I can't just lie here and go down like the sun, I've got to get up, get out of this room, go on with my life."

"Then eat your soup," she said, "and be quiet. You fuss a lot to be so young."

"I'm past seventy," he said, "too late to be taking advice from you. What do you know anyway?"

"Nothing, perhaps. Except how to cook, how to serve, how to keep an old man from killing himself before he's ready to go."

"That's not enough," he said. "To survive in any kind of style you'll need more."

She removed his dishes, drew the cover up to his nose, and sat a moment holding him in queer regard, squinting, her cheek angled in the palm of her hand. Her elbow rested in her lap, that lively thoughtful expression emerging and receding on her face; she looked, the old man thought, perfectly lovely, bewitching even, strange too, he thought, because he could remember the time when she looked to him like any ordinary girl one might expect to find working on tables in a restaurant.

"You're remarkable," he said, "a remarkable girl. You deserve something more than a job in a restaurant. Keeping tabs on an old man who didn't have the good sense to look after his health. You need a home, a husband and children."

"No thanks," she said, and patted his hand. "Anyway, my job, like my age, is only temporary. I've got to be off now." She rose, straightening from her lap the folds of her clean white uniform.

"You ought to be out chasing after men," he said. "Show that fool downstairs a thing or two." She left, treating him to such a wink and smile that he felt truly cheered, could feel it spreading through him like an instant fluid.

The boy brought the evening newspaper and sat down to read to him.

"Ah, yes," he said, "I know without listening. Some one has called for an end to nuclear testing in the atmosphere, another has called for resumption of testing underground, negotiations lag. In the old days we only flew from New York to Paris and the whole world rejoiced. It was a step forward, a step in the right direction. But what went wrong? Now . . . you ought to pay more attention to that girl, son, she's all you got."

"We're not interested in one another, sir. I wish you would forget all that."

"She's all you've got, and enough too. They've taken the world from you, it's out of your hands now. Listen to this: walk with your good clothes into the poor sections of town and it's only right that they smack you down; walk into the ghettos and if those living there hate you or knock you down that's only right too: a young man, no older than you, told me that only last week, sitting beside me in the park with his dark glasses and beard."

"I don't feel that way."

"You don't? No, I didn't think you did."

"Don't worry about it. You—"

"A man gets my age, you'd think he would know what it's all about . . . Turn to page twelve. I want to hear what Amy has to say today to BESIEGED, to AT MY WIT'S END."

"I hope you'll feel better soon, sir."

For days the old man lay in convalescence, protesting all the while that he felt no sickness now, that there was no need for this attention, wishing between times for their visits but then telling them when they came they should not trouble themselves so much with him, asking: but what have I to give you? . . . troubled that the companionship he got from them was so much more rewarding than he, old and dull and of no use, could give to them.

"Oh, don't be silly," the girl said, or, teasing, wrinkled her nose at him and said: "Now we don't believe that, do we?" as she ran in on her lunch hour with bright tidy curtains that she had made herself to dress his window; as she dropped in "just for a second" to dust his bureau or with new flowers for his bedside; to freshen his bed or clean the eyeglasses he somehow always misplaced or forgot to wear.

Occasionally, by accident and never by design but just the opposite since the boy and girl tried deliberately to avoid any such encounter, one would arrive while the other also was there, and he would rebuke them with such words as: "I don't know which of you are worse, both of you such nice young people, you could try to find a little happiness in one another," embarrassing each of them to such degree that one or the other would flee down the corridor.

But then one day she came in and said, "Now, look, you've been playing sick long enough, you can get up now," and he got out of bed and took the chair which she had pulled up by the window with the curtains drawn back, and with the morning sunlight streaming through the window he sat with his head back and the hot bright sun on his face, falling asleep there and sleeping until he woke with lather on his face and the boy asking if he'd like a shave.

"Looks like it's too late now for me to object," the old man said.

"That's right," the boy said, and smiled.

The old man, though saddened by the death of Miss Beaumont and his own failing health, was happy because his young friends treated him so well and began thinking again about getting back into his old routine, the walk to the park that was rich with the sight of familiar people and the loud play of children. After perhaps a week in his room he dressed and went down the stairs. He walked without stopping to see the things he liked normally to watch but went directly to the park, afraid that those in the park might have forgotten him after his long absence. When he had taken his place on the bench they came, the pigeons and the squirrels, but after a while they went elsewhere because the old man had nothing to give them except his time. He felt, despite himself, that things were no longer the same.

"Good morning, Mrs. Knox."

"Good morning, sir. Did you get a good night's rest?"

"Not too well. You see a friend of mind passed on and I—"

"Oh, I'm sorry to hear that, well toodle ooo."

"—passed on and . . ."

He was not hungry and did not remember when lunch time came and passed but was content with sitting and watching the people pass down the paths of the park and the birds drifting from bench to bench where others, old like himself, sat pitching them crumbs.

In the afternoon when the sun was at three o'clock and a shadow half upon the old man's brow he left the park for his hotel, stopping several times on the way to see all that he had missed in those days he had not walked his way to the park. Children were on their knees playing with marbles but the old man's attention was drawn to one in particular and he stopped beside her, fumbling in his pocket for the penny he thought to be there.

"Hello."

"My mommie says I'm not to talk to people I don't know."

The old man watched the young girl streak away from him and a stout woman in blue jeans snatch the child up into her arms at the corner and hurry away with her. The children played on, taking no notice of him. He continued on his way to the Swiss Arms but once within sight of it his spirits began to lift and he was happy to see the clerk coming through the lobby towards him and pleased as the boy lightly touched his elbow and led him into his place in the dining room.

"I'll sit with you a moment if you don't mind," the boy said, and sat down opposite the old man at the small table. "How was your day, your strength coming back?"

"Fine, fine," the old man said, meticulously spreading the napkin over his lap, embarrassed then and resisting the desire to advise the boy he should not snap his fingers that way and stare off so impatiently at the girl busy at another table, that there was no hurry, she would get to them when she could.

"There's no reason for this," the boy said, waiting a moment longer, and the old man, watching the boy, began to see that the enmity between the two was stronger now and puzzled over the cause.

"She has instructions to serve you immediately when you enter," the boy said, "I told her so myself."

"That wasn't necessary," the old man began, "she—"

"I know she's your friend," the boy said, "but she doesn't take her job seriously, she thinks she can sing her way through anything, she doesn't do what she's told, she isn't even nice."

The old man thought this all so absurdly untrue that a smile grabbed at the corners of his mouth and he looked off apologetically at the girl. Catching his eye, the girl smiled too which the old man acknowledged with a slight dip of his head, but with his back to the girl the boy was unaware of the exchange.

"Excuse me," the boy said, "I'll see what I can do," and he angrily rose from the table.

"Please," the old man said, "there's no need, no need to get upset."

But the boy already was going, trailing after the girl who now was hurrying through the swinging doors of the kitchen with a tray of soiled dishes in her hands.

"Don't, please," the old man said but by the time he got up both were out of sight. He followed to the swinging doors but stood there perplexed, debating whether he should intrude, if already he had not intruded too much into their affairs. From where he stood he could hear them, their voices crossing one another's in an angry unfamiliar cadence, interrupting one another's speech, their imposed hush intensifying that anger all the more, among their words his own name, not his name either but *the old man*, the girl saying *you've been waiting for this a long time haven't you?* to which the boy was replying *That's a lie, not me but you*, and more of it until at once it struck the old man that in no uncertain way he as much as anything was the cause of their animosity, that odd as it was one was angry at the other for the attention that other was showing him, that they were jealous of this attention but he couldn't believe this and stood as before debating whether he should intervene, stop their argument, tell them how it pained him to see them this way.

if only he knew you as you really are, the boy was saying

which way? the girl answered, *how would you know how I really am or anything about me, why are you such a fool?*

Me!

Yes, you! a fool!

and the sharp crossfire continuing as the old man turned away and with his slow stiff steps left the room.

Later when the girl climbed the stairs with his hot soup and tea she found his door locked and no answer to her call and later still when the boy tapped on the door and said that he was going off duty now and was there anything he could do before he left he got no reply either although both had the feeling that he was in the room and deliberately refusing them.

The next day the old man was up early and out of the hotel before the boy gained his station behind the desk and neither saw him until evening when he took his seat well within the dining room hour. He said nothing when the girl told him that she had missed him and commented that he seemed a little tired, and although it pained him to treat her with such indifference, confused over what he ought to do, shortly thereafter he replaced the napkin on the table and left the room.

"That man," the girl thought when she came to clear his table, "he eats nothing, how does he live?" and she thought of him with much concern and even love, like a father he was, a *dear* old man, but when she lifted the napkin and reached for the customary dime it wasn't there. No, she thought, of course it's here, and she pushed aside the plate but it wasn't there and she opened the napkin thinking the dime might have caught in a fold but it wasn't there. He had not left it.

She ran to the desk and told the clerk: "Something is wrong, he always leaves it," but the clerk was insistent: "No, it probably slipped his mind."

"That isn't the case," she said, "I know it isn't, something is wrong."

The clerk himself went into the dining hall to look but found nothing and returned to find her standing at the foot of the stairs looking up towards the old man's room.

"He's been acting strangely since yesterday," the girl said, "did you say something to upset him?"

"Me? No, why should I?"

"Because you're so ignorant," she said, "you wouldn't know even if you had," and at that the boy stared hard at her, frustrated by her reasoning and hating her for her arrogance.

"If you're so smart," he said, "why don't you do something to help him, why don't you leave him alone?" and the girl opened her mouth in a kind of amazement and gazed at the boy and he gazed back until she said, "Oh, you're so silly, so very silly," and turned her back to him and escaped into the dining room.

In his room the old man lay on the bed, his hands clasped over his stomach, his eyes closed before the glare of the naked swinging light above. He felt in his breast pocket for his handkerchief, thinking to use this as a shield for his eyes, but his pocket was empty. He fingered his vest pockets too but found in one only his gold watch and in another the hard remains of bread crumbs saved from a lunch he did not recall. If he had remembered he could have tossed these to the pigeons but he had forgotten them as so often he had forgotten the electric light and the water faucet and the names of the boy and girl downstairs who had been and still were so nice to him. He didn't notice the handkerchief on the bedside table nor did he at first think to pull the string that would turn off the bulb. When finally he did the room was pitched into such breathtaking darkness that the old man felt a strange feebleness, worse than his sickness; he felt his own loneliness and inefficacy. He longed for the quick impulsive smile of the girl, the serious, sulking figure of the boy. He pulled on the light again and lay staring up at the bright dusty bulb. Without turning his head he could see cobwebs in each corner of the room and the broken plaster in the ceiling. "It's a clean hotel," he thought, "how did they get there? Every minute of your life you're pushing one way and something else is pushing another, and how is it that you know when to stop pushing? It's such an effort," he thought, "such an effort to get along"—but this was self-indulgence, he felt, an old man's effort to reconcile his sad ending with his ill achievements, and to avoid such thoughts he rolled on his side and held that position until the wall fell away and he found sleep.

Later on the boy knocked on the door and, getting no answer, let himself in. "Just like a girl," he thought, "to think the worst. The old man is fine, he's sleeping," and quietly he closed the door and went downstairs.

But the girl was worried and afraid and when she came with his tray of food and got no answer she stood a long time outside the door with her legs apart and her head down, much as if she could feel through the door the great fatigue which she fancied he must be feeling.

When the light of the morning sun broke through the curtains the old man awoke. He scolded himself for having left the electric light burning through the night and for having gone to sleep in his clothes. Now they would have to be pressed, another expense. He wondered what time it was and why he had done such foolish things and he stared a long time at the dust particles suspended and turning in the funnel of sunlight that flooded the window before he remembered that his long-ago friend was no longer alive. He wondered too what the cause was and was touched with the fear that not knowing the cause was somehow his own fault and he felt guilty too to recall that there had been times in the last few years when he had envied her, thinking surely that she, being so charming and so *good* a person, would have more than an abundance of friends and diversions.

He sat throughout the morning in his room, remembering Miss Beaumont, considering himself, as he stared at the dust particles treadmilling up from the floor along that bright beam of sunlight, realizing too that the dust existed outside of that beam as well, that all over the room, unseen, the dust was moving, wondering why in a room so still this should be so.

He left his room and went down the stairs and through the lobby and walked outside and gained a chair on the lawn, turning it away from the sun. Although he expected no more letters he thought to wait for the postman who might after all bring a circular or two. No, no letters. All his old friends were gone, forgotten, had drifted beyond all knowledge of him; he sat on, rocking, waiting. He wanted to walk to the park, there to sit and feed and watch the birds and squirrels but he had nothing to give them and not the strength to get there. A mother with her two boys and a girl crossed by him on the sidewalk and he gazed at them but they walked on, chatting, taking no notice.

Somehow he missed the postman. He woke, with a snap of his head from his shoulders, and knew that it was late. Cold. He arose from his chair and entered the hotel and began climbing the stairs to his room. But he had forgotten his key. Standing before his door, fumbling idly in his pockets, he tried to recall where he had left it, the key attached to the small diamond-shaped plastic holder which had impressed on it the words IF LOST RETURN TO THE SWISS ARMS. He was about to return to the lobby to ask for the duplicate when he saw the clerk bounding up the stairs, bringing it.

"Lost it again, huh?" the clerk said, and smiled. He opened the door and stepped aside for the old man to enter and then he entered himself. Once again the boy was struck by the peculiar odor and order and particular shade of everything in the old man's room that pastel curtains alone could not dispel. The overhead light was burning and he reached up and quietly pulled the string that put it out. The old man, dropping into the chair by the window, didn't notice.

"I think I'd like a little taste of something to eat later on. Will the girl be coming up?"

"Yes sir, I'll see about that, you just take it easy."

"She's a nice girl."

"Sir?"

"A pretty little thing."

"Yes sir."

"Such a nice girl."

"She likes you too, sir."

The boy could see that the conversation tired the old man, that he was pale and had no strength, and suggested that he go to bed but the old man sat on, gazing out of the window, hardly aware that he had been spoken to. Leaving, the boy silently closed the door.

A great pain struck the old man soon after the boy had gone and he struggled to the bed and sat on its edge waiting for the pain to quit but the pain remained and the old man lay down, watching the ceiling and thinking that this pain, with a life of its own, might reach out and touch him anywhere.

In the evening the girl brought the tea and the soup and sat with him urging him to eat it, that he must, falling silent when the old man could not.

"I'll be all right," he said, "you go on back to your young man."

"He isn't my young man," she said.

"Go on back to him."

"But I'm not interested—"

"*Listen to me!*" he said, and she fell silent, sensing the urgency in his voice, waiting for him to continue, but finding just that urgency there, nothing more, as the old man blinked his eyes and rolled his head from side to side, blinking his eyes as the pain rolled with him.

"Do something," he said, "don't let it slip away like this," and in the corridor outside his door a few minutes later the girl thought about and tried to scramble some sense into his words: that vague *something* and *it*, he had said, but of what it was he speaking? Life? Probably so but if so whose had he meant: his own? hers, the young man's? But the question was passed over quickly by the weight of her remorse: the old man was suffering, he would need a doctor.

The doctor after much persuasion came and examined the old man in his room and after a brief probing told them all that there was nothing wrong, that the old man had another ten or fifteen good years left in him, that he should rest and sleep and avoid any excitement and the doctor was paid and he left.

"See, I told you," the boy said to the girl, "there was nothing to worry about."

But the girl was not convinced.

Much later that evening a taxi stopped before the hotel and the girl emerged from it and told the driver to wait and she went into the hotel. She wore street clothes, the lamb's wool sweater and the stylish skirt on which she had spent a large portion of her salary; she wore heels and brought in her purse the present for the old man which she had got from the drugstore. In his room the old man was at a loss for the words by which to express his thanks or his regrets but at the same time he felt a heavy impatience; the girl's face reflected her own doubts but the old man read determination and understanding there too and he tried bravely to stifle his pain until she had gone and when she bent over and kissed his brow and said she was leaving now he told her that her lips were warm like the sun, which brought the trace of a smile into her eyes and when he said that she must get back to her young man now she said yes, I'm going and like that she left his room.

Downstairs, she paused at the dining room entrance and looked in and stood a moment undecided before she entered and went directly to the old man's table and removed the RESERVED sign from it and walked out and got into her taxi and was taken away from the Swiss Arms hotel.

In the night the old man died. He died quietly, with his hands across his chest, the overhead light burning and the water running in the faucet at the corner.

PETER TAYLOR has published four volumes of short stories, the most recent "Miss Leonora When Last Seen and Fifteen Other Stories" in 1964; a novel and a play. He teaches creative writing at the University of North Carolina at Greensboro. He was the first prize winner of the 1959 O. Henry Prize Stories for his story "Venus, Cupid, Folly and Time."

There

"LET me tell you something about the Busbys," the old gentleman said to me. "The Busbys don't wash themselves—not adequately. And especially not as they grow older."

That was how he opened our last conversation. It was our last meeting aboard ship, and the last he and I will be likely to have in this world. He was the kind of shipboard acquaintance you make who never seems real afterward. You remember him more distinctly than you do someone you have met on a plane or a train, but it is only because you were with him for a longer time. Nowadays particularly, there seems something unreal about people you have known on a sea voyage. To me, at least, it is nearly always as though I have met some character out of the past or out of a novel. And I never know whether it seems stranger when they *do* or when they *don't* explain why they are traveling by ship instead of by plane. In any case, the odd thing was that this man was a shipboard acquaintance who had come originally from my own hometown, and it was of people back *there* he was speaking, not of our fellow passengers. We two had grown up in the same inland city, and we came more or less from the same stock there; yet the thirty or forty years that separated us made us strangers to one another as no distance across the surface of the earth nowadays, and no difference in nationality, could possibly have. . . . At least so it seemed to me at the time. And nothing could have amused me more than his assumption that I would be acquainted with the same families that had once so absorbed his interest.

"Those Busbys! Those Busbys!" said he, thumping on the smoking

Copyright © 1964 by Kenyon College.

table between us with his long lean middle finger. "It all comes to one thing: such people have no imagination about themselves!" At first he resorted to this finger thumping and those exclamations to make sure he got my full attention. But finally, seeing me comfortably fixed in my chair, my academic pipe lighted, and my whole attention directed to his discourse, he spoke without bothering to look at me. "That's what made the Busbys a laughingstock. Lack of imagination about themselves. Of course the Busbys were not alone in this lack of theirs, but, despite all the good company they were in, it was no less damaging to them. There was a Busby boy named David, for instance, about the age of two young-lady cousins of mine. They used to visit us every summer when I was a small boy, and David Busby would try to court the younger girl. But she, being an out-of-town girl and not impressed by the Busby money, mocked him behind his back. Whenever he had been especially attentive to her, she and her sister had a little parody they would recite. It began, 'David, David, dirty but true . . .' Moreover, when there was a series of parties, they used to count the times that David appeared wearing the same shirt with the same soiled spots on it. He would change his collar, so they said, for any little old chafing-dish party (his detachable collar, you know—the kind Americans never wear any more), but it took an affair of the first magnitude to bring him out in a clean shirt. . . . Poor fellow, I guess he never knew what a little fresh linen might have done for him with the girls."

As the old gentleman spoke he gazed off across the public room, as though trying to see out of first one porthole and then another. He was a strikingly handsome old man, with a decidedly clean and well-scrubbed look, and he had described himself to me as a retired career man from the diplomatic service, which I see no reason to doubt he was. I'd judge that he was well past seventy, but his figure was very slender still and straight, and by day he was given to wearing a beige or a checked waistcoat under a close-fitted tweed jacket. Or sometimes he wore a double-breasted navy jacket with brass buttons. There was always a handkerchief in the breast pocket of his jacket, and he owned at least one pair of brown suede shoes. Though his hair was white it was quite thick, and always perfectly groomed of course. His face was almost incredibly youthful looking. There were neat little wrinkles about his eyes and at the corners of his mouth, but otherwise his skin was as smooth and pink as a little child's. Somehow this had the effect of making me think a good deal about his age and about how he must have appeared when he was younger. I am confident that he had been a beautiful, towheaded child, that his hair became black in young manhood, that after forty his temples turned becomingly gray, and that finally his entire panache had gone snow white in his sixty-fifth year or thereabouts.

He impressed me from the beginning as someone with great personal reserve and reticence. And until that last day on shipboard he had never revealed to me anything about himself—not even inadvertently. But as people of genuine reserve very often are, he was voluble enough on other subjects—particularly on the subject of *other* people. . . . He had a way of making you feel that he couldn't say what he was saying to anyone but you. From the outset I observed in him what seemed a mixture of masculine frankness and almost feminine gossipiness. It was this mixture which must always have constituted his charm for people. Yet at that time I imagined he could only speak to me as he did because we came originally from the same place and because we had both asserted, right away, that we would never under any circumstances go back *there* to live. "Our hometown is a cultural desert, as I'm sure you'll agree," he had said to me when he learned that I was an academic. "Most people there haven't even the imagination to see how urgent it is that they get away from the place if they are going to stay alive."

Though he had not himself really lived at home since he went East to college in 1906, the old man's voice still retained a flavor that I recognized even before we had introduced ourselves. I had sat eavesdropping in the bar one night—the night of our second day out—and heard how his voice contrasted with those of the other passengers with whom he associated, an assortment of Englishmen and Eastern seaboard types. That was really what made me distinguish him from the others in the first place. And soon after we began our nightly talks he and I discovered that he had known—ever so slightly—an uncle of mine who had died before I was born. And it turned out that I knew a girl—ever so slightly—who had married the son of one of his boyhood friends. That's how it went. At no point did we discover a mutual acquaintance. We missed completely when it came to individuals, but there was no mistaking the city that he and I had in mind or the kind of people there about whom Mr. Charles Varnell and I knew most.

During that last session of ours we were alone in the first-class smoking lounge. Though there was little likelihood of anyone's wishing to join us, Mr. Varnell had deliberately selected two chairs that were set well apart from all others. Our ship had docked that afternoon at Cherbourg and was resting in port while the Continental passengers were let off and others were received on board for the return voyage to New York. During the night ahead the ship would cross over to Southampton, and in the morning Mr. Varnell and I would say our brief goodbyes before going down the gangplank. Actually I did catch another glimpse of him in customs, and I even spotted him again, at a considerable distance, after we had detrained at Waterloo Station an hour later. He and his wife were being greeted there by some old-fashioned, rather toney-looking English friends. As a matter of fact, I recalled his having told me, when with mere perfunctory politeness I suggested we might run into each other in London, that he and his wife were stopping with friends for only a few hours. They would be in London "almost no time at all." They had been "out to New York" for six weeks, and now they had to rush down to Surrey and put their house there in order before going up to Scotland for a month ("We're going up to Scotland to shoot"—or some such elegant and wonderfully dated remark). I never knew whether his wife was English or American or of some other nationality. As for her appearance, it is sufficient to say that she looked the way *his* wife *should* look. I was never introduced to her, not even that morning at the gangplank when he and I shook hands and parted. Our leavetaking was so brief and casual that the other passengers, and perhaps even his own wife, may have supposed that neither of us was sure of when, during the voyage, he had talked to the other. But our real farewell had already taken place—in the dead stillness of the Port of Cherbourg. It was he who did the talking on that occasion, and I imagine that what he said to me then had had to wait until he knew that he and I would not talk again.

I laughed outright of course when he said the sort of thing he did about the Busbys' not washing themselves. I suppose he expected me to. But he didn't laugh. "It is no small matter," he insisted, "for people not to wash—regardless of how rich or well-to-do they are. It kept all the Busbys from ever amounting to anything outside their own little bailiwick. Let me tell you. I used to sit behind that same David Busby's grandfather in church—Mr. Lionel Busby. I was just a little fellow at the time, and what I chiefly remember about him are the deep creases and wrinkles in the back of his neck. I have never seen anything to equal it on a man of his position in the world—the visi-

ble dirt, that is to say, caked in those creases on the neck of that extremely rich old man. The Busbys were *very* wealthy at that time. I
used to hear it debated at home whether Mr. Lionel was our second
or third richest citizen. And he was no self-made man. If I am not mistaken, they had owned downtown real estate since before the Civil
War. Mr. Lionel himself went East somewhere to college. But even
up there they couldn't teach a Busby to wash his neck properly. And
after college he came back, the way most of those people do, and
married somebody at home—some girl who, I suppose, didn't care
about or was willing to overlook the peculiar characteristics of the
Busbys.

"Now, a man *can* be careless about his personal cleanliness. I understand that. A man *can* be somewhat slovenly in his dress. Some of
my closest friends are so—to a certain degree. But what I found most
revolting was its being the trait of a whole family, and a trait that the
community regarded with a tolerance beyond all comprehension.
Further, whereas it is possible for a gentleman to have such a weakness, it is not possible for a lady. And yet there were two Busby
maiden ladies of my mother's generation, aunts to said David Busby,
daughters to old Mr. Lionel; and *they* managed it, and *they*, by the
community at large, were forgiven. They were a laughingstock, yes;
but the point is that their defect *was* regarded as a laughing matter. I
remember them as two old creatures with dyed black hair and reeking
of perfume. Their fondness for personal finery, their tendency to be
always overdressed, was proverbial. But the state and condition of
their clothing was generally a scandal. My mother used to speak of a
certain black lace mantilla that one of them wore. It slipped from the
lady's shoulder one day when Mother was sitting beside her on our
parlor settee, and when Mother helped her retrieve it she found the
thing as stiff with old spillage as though it had been freshly starched.
Those two ladies were renowned also for the jewels they possessed
and for the number they ornamented themselves with on all occasions. They were not averse to telling the history and value of every
brooch, bracelet, or pendant earring they had on. They spoke of their
jewels always as their 'stones,' and some rustic wit out there once remarked that the Busby ladies ought to put fewer precious stones on
their fingers and more pumice stone on their elbows.

"But the prize story about the two Busby ladies is a very old and
familiar sort of story. It is that of the burglar and the two old maids.
. . . The Misses Busby came in from a party one evening and heard

the intruder moving about upstairs. He was after some of their 'stones' of course, and of course they were wearing most of what he was after. The two intrepid ladies didn't even call in the servants or the neighbors or send out for help of any kind. With an ice pick and an ax they hunted down their man, who, as it fortunately happened, was unarmed. . . . There were several versions to the story, all of them ending with the man stretched out—in a dead faint—on the floor of one of the upstairs bedrooms. One version, probably the correct one, had it that the fellow was such a coward that he passed out cold at the sight of the ice pick and the ax. And then there was a pornographic version, of course, which I shall spare you. And there was also a third version, in its way as indelicate as the second, being the version which found favor amongst people most intimately acquainted with the Busby family. It seems the man had hidden himself in an old-fashioned clothespress, and the condition of the garments stored therein was so strong that when the old maids found their man he was already overcome by the rank and musty emanations. They dragged him out into the room, but he did not recover consciousness until after the police had finally been summoned and had removed him from the scene of the crime. His own version of what happened will never be known. He maintained through his trial and ultimate conviction that he could remember nothing. He may only have been possuming, of course, but it is possible on the other hand that the fellow had suffered an awful shock—of one kind or another."

Mr. Varnell told these anecdotes about the Busbys with never a smile and with but little discernible relish for the details he brought forth. He seemed to know the stories so well that it was not really necessary for him to think of what he was saying or how he would say it. One felt, even, that most of his phrases had been used in the exact context before. What made it interesting, though, was that one got the impression it had been such a long, long time before. There were moments when he seemed to listen to his own voice with a certain detachment and wonder. He was like a man delving into a trunk he had packed away years ago and who did not know, himself, what he would come upon next. His transition from the Busbys to the Jenkinses was quite abrupt and at the same time seemed very natural and easy, too. It was as though he had put down one old photograph or letter and picked up another. "The astonishing thing to me was always that the Busbys, like the Jenkinses and other families with equally marked peculiarities, remained in the very cream of society *there*. Nobody there minded them as they were, and so why need they change themselves? *Anything* was forgivable. If you ever met a Jenkins, for instance—as I am sure you have—you simply expected to meet a fat man, or, worse, a fat woman. It was entirely because the Jenkinses wouldn't stop eating. Jenkins apologists liked to put out that their trouble was glandular, just as the Busbys were all supposed to be nearsighted, or farsighted, or whichever it is that would excuse their not knowing that the backs of their necks were dirty. But once I saw Alice Jenkins eat eight pieces of fried chicken, three servings of potato salad, and a whole half of a watermelon in one sitting. It was on a picnic at Riverview Mills. Alice, you see, was the only Jenkins of my generation, but she was a plenty. That day at Riverview Mills we all went out on the pond in rowboats. The couples paired off, sitting side by side in the boats—in general they did. But there was never any pairing off on Alice's part. Without any companion she occupied the entire poop seat in her boat. There was a great deal of merriment over the fact, and she joined right in with it. But there was something repulsive to me about the way the boat sank down under her weight; and somehow it was worse because the image of all the other Jenkinses, all her fat relations, rose up in my mind.

"A couple of years later Alice was a debutante, and during the summer before her coming out she starved herself until she got to be quite decent looking. In fact, she appeared that fall looking a very handsome woman and with quite elegant manners. She got engaged soon after Christmas, however, and by the time she married in May she was a full-size Jenkins again. In the years just after that I used to see her when I would be back home on a visit. It would be at the Sunday night buffet supper at the country club; and not many years passed before she was surrounded there by a tribe of little Jenkins elephants (I forget now what her married name was). They occupied a long table that the Jenkinses had been occupying every Sunday night for years, and Alice's parents would still be there with them, as well as some of her enormous cousins and uncles and aunts. How they all heaped up the food on their plates! I can see them now trooping back to the buffet for second and third helpings. The food at the country club was the best in town in those days, and the Sunday night buffet supper was surely the best bargain ever offered anywhere. Probably it was only this combination that could bring the Jenkinses out in full force, because they were great homebodies really, and the men in the family as well as the women were said to be splendid cooks. On his first trip to the buffet Alice's father used to take a tiny serving of every dish, even a pinch of each relish and a few drops of every sauce. Back at his table you would see him tasting away very thoughtfully. He had a high, rounded-out stomach, wonderfully symmetrical (like a giant tureen), and almost no chest. He wore a little gray, two-pronged imperial that stuck down like a meat fork over the white napkin which was tucked under his collar. While eating, he eyed his food intently, though, if some passerby happened to catch his eye, he would throw back his head and laugh aloud at himself and wave one corner of the napkin at the spectator. On his second trip to the buffet he narrowed his choice to four or five of the principal dishes. He became even more selective on his third trip. And the highest compliment he could pay the club chef was to go back for a fourth serving of some single dish.

"After supper, on a hot summer evening, the whole herd of elephantine Jenkinses would repair to the capacious wicker chairs out on the terrace beside the golf course. A special chair was reserved there for old Mrs. Jenkins, who outweighed her husband by at least 50 pounds and whose wide posterior could not be accommodated between the arms of any ordinary chair. Once they were all seated out there, they didn't rise until it was time to leave. Friends passing along the terrace, or seated in other groups nearby, would call out to them, asking how they had enjoyed their supper. They would reply in an enthusiastic chorus: 'Marvelously! Enormously!' Frequently, when it was time to go home, or if a little shower had come up, it would be discovered that Mrs. Jenkins had fallen into a deep sleep in her chair. There would be a great stir and commotion with even the grandchildren joining in the effort to wake the sleeper and prize her out of her chair. All over the club grounds people would hear them and would smile at each other and say, 'It's only the Jenkinses trying to wake Miss Nanny.'

"Not a very edifying picture, is it?" said Mr. Varnell, looking altogether serious, and disregarding my audible signs of amusement. "And let me tell you," he continued, "the Busbys and the Jenkinses were not very exceptional people in our hometown. It used to seem to me that every family there had some awful deficiency—I might almost say affliction—that marked them as a family. It wasn't so, of course. Or it was nearly always only something they might have overcome if they hadn't been so self-satisfied and so mutually indulgent.

You and I know what it was they needed to do, of course. But why was it those people with so much money and so much leisure couldn't understand what their next step ought to be? More often than not they were people of genuine capability. The men were actually men of imagination when it came to business and money matters. The women, though you could not say they were cultivated, were not without charm and manners of a kind. But they stuck themselves off there and lived their sort of tribal life. Of course some of them would pick up and leave for a while. Even the Lionel Busbys did, I think. But they couldn't stick it out long enough. They always came back saying that 'people in Europe' or 'people up East' were condescending to them. Naturally! What else can you do but condescend to people until they have learned to wash themselves and eat with moderation. Some of them even enlarged their fortunes by taking their capital with them and investing it in bigger things than we had there. But still they came back at last, singing that false old tune that there's no place like home.

"Even when I was an adolescent I used to wonder how I could ever really fall in love with any girl who came from one of those families. And I never developed a genuine romantic interest in one of them till after I was in college. She was a Morris—Laura Nell Morris. I won't bore you by telling you what a beautiful creature Laura Nell was. Suffice it to say that it was love at first sight for me. And suffice it to say, on another score, that she bore only the very slightest family resemblance to her brothers and sisters and to her parents. She was a silly, harum-scarum kind of girl. I won't pretend otherwise. She had *no* conversation, and yet at a party she would never stop talking. She recited limericks, and riddles, and shaggy-dog stories, and she remembered and would make us listen to every poor joke she had ever heard at vaudeville and minstrel shows. Further, she was the sort of person who prided herself on always taking a dare, no matter how foolish it was. You couldn't afford to speak the word in her presence. It is a wonder she never got into serious trouble, whereas actually the most punishment I think she ever took was one night when somebody dared her to keep silent for fifteen minutes. She succeeded all right. But I was her escort on that occasion and afterward when I was taking her home I saw Laura Nell Morris, for the only time ever, in what I would call low spirits.

"There is even worse to be said about Laura Nell, however, and I might as well get the worst over with. She had a passion for playing elaborate practical jokes, not on her friends and contemporaries but on members of her own family—particularly on the older members. The odium of this was somewhat mitigated, perhaps, by the happy fact that the family did not mind her jokes so much as they might have done. They thought it childish of her, and they were baffled by her willingness to take such pains as she did in the preparation of her jokes. But it was their view that if Laura Nell derived real satisfaction and amusement from the practice, then they must not absolutely forbid her continuing and must not resent being, themselves, her objects. That was what the Morrises were like. If such extreme tolerance and disinterested regard for one another made them seem ridiculous, it was at the same time a most appealing quality for a family to have. And among its consequences, I am perfectly convinced, was the measure of individuality which all its members developed.

"I have already said how little the Morrises looked alike. There was a redheaded grandfather whose coloring did turn up in two of the older children. And Laura Nell, who was the youngest of the five, had just a suggestion of red in her dark hair. Perhaps there was something about the eyes of all the children to remind you of the father, if you noticed carefully. And there was a gentleness of speech general amongst them—even in the case of Laura Nell—that made you know they had been brought up by the same mother. But surely they had nothing more in common. There was a very tall brother, a short brother, and one of medium height. The middle-sized one was athletic, the tall one bookish, and the short one socially inclined. Laura Nell's only sister was the eldest child, and she was known for her quiet and responsive disposition, for her way of drawing out other people in conversation so that they would appear to best advantage.

"Part of Laura Nell's attraction for me—need I say it even?—was the very absence of any strong family marking. At our first meeting I didn't realize that she was at all related to the other Morrises. She was three years younger than I, and she had grown into a young lady since I went away to school. I was convinced that I had never laid eyes on her or on any of her family before. It turned out that I had in fact been acquainted with two of her brothers but had always supposed that they were, at most, distant cousins to each other. I found the very idea of such a family intriguing, and I find it so even to this day. Their mere unlikeness to one another, alone, would not of course have accounted for the impression they gave. It was their dissimilarity plus, in every case, without exception, a very strong and attractive personality. It was inconceivable to me that such a family should be content, generation after generation, to waste themselves on a town like ours. Mr. Morris was a lawyer with a national reputation in his profession. A good proportion of his clients were in New York and Philadelphia, not to mention Chicago and other cities nearer by. It would have been a very natural thing for him to have moved his family to New York. With such connections as he had, with Mrs. Morris' considerable fortune, and with all their natural social graces and intellectual capabilities, what interesting lives they might have had, what *serious* careers they might have made for themselves, if only they had got away from there. For the Morrises there would have been no handicaps, no bars of any kind.

"Once when I was talking to Mr. Morris about Laura Nell I made a point of telling him what an interesting and admirable family I thought they were. I even went into some detail as to why I found them so. 'Well,' he said to me, 'you *are* in love with my daughter if you think she and we are as different from the rest of the world as all that. In fact, you have about the worst case I've ever encountered. Laura Nell is a fortunate young lady. I wish you success with her. Sincerely I do.' But he treated the matter casually and even lightly. He made no objection to my suit. But he did not offer to speak in my favor to Laura Nell. If he had, the matter might have come out differently. I am not sure, though. At any rate, it couldn't have come out worse.

"Laura Nell's mother did not take such a disinterested view of my suit. She was a most amiable and sympathetic woman, and she told me that she could not imagine a more satisfactory son-in-law than I was certain to make. Still, she would not try to influence Laura Nell. In our conversations she spoke of Laura Nell almost as if she were someone else's daughter and spoke as if I were a son whom she was comforting and encouraging. There was always *some* of that in Mr. Morris' tone, too. If my own parents had lived until I was a grown man, I think they might have talked to me as Mr. and Mrs. Morris did. I like to think so. But I had no very near relative of any kind after I was in my teens, and the elderly banker and old bachelor who was my guardian and who had controlled my trust fund till I came of age was not anybody to turn to. My real confidants were Mr. and Mrs. Morris.

"Soon after Laura Nell refused me the first time, I came to call one day when she wasn't at home. It was during the last week of September, and Mrs. Morris took me down to the end of the garden to show me her chrysanthemums. The late summer and fall flowers were a specialty with her, and she was certain that there was going to be a killing frost that night. There were splendid arrays of asters and dahlias on either side of the garden walk, but we had to go to the very end of the garden and climb to the top of a little terrace there in order to look back toward the house and have a proper view of the chrysanthemums. It was a chilly late-afternoon, with the air bright and dry. I stood beside Mrs. Morris on the brick terrace and was able for a moment to admire the beds of russet and gold just below where we were standing. But it was only for a moment. At the other end of the garden I saw the great neo-Georgian house with its Palladian windows upstairs and its wide porch below. The muscular wisteria vines on the trellis of the porch were already leafless at that season. Suddenly I said to Mrs. Morris, 'Laura Nell has refused me. . . . I am convinced now that there is no hope for my cause.'

"I was not really convinced of it—sad to relate. The passing of nearly two years and a considerably more drastic gesture on Laura Nell's part would be required for that. But Mrs. Morris herself was, there can be little doubt, convinced even then. She did not tell me to give Laura Nell time, or anything of that kind. When I withdrew my gaze from the house and looked at her, there was the sweetest, gentlest look in her gray eyes that I believe I have ever beheld in human eyes. And when she spoke it was not encouragement but consolation she offered me.

"The consolation came in a strange form. Laura Nell's practical jokes on her family were something that the family kept very much to themselves. I mean to say, they often referred to the fact that she had such a weakness, and on some occasions they were cautious in their behavior for fear of being led into one of her traps. But they would never oblige you with an account of any particular joke. If pressed, they would only laugh and say, 'It's much too grim. For Laura Nell's own sake it can't be told.' And since Laura Nell would not discuss the subject herself, I had never had any clue to what her jokes were like until that afternoon when I was out there at the end of the garden with Mrs. Morris. What she revealed to me is all I know to this day of Laura Nell's jokes.

" 'My dear,' she began, 'I can't blame you for being so in love with Laura Nell. She's an enchanting little person. But I want to tell you about two pranks that a certain young lady played on members of her own family. It may amuse you, and you may want to reflect on what caprices such a girl might some day treat her lawful husband to.' With no more preface than that and with no further explanation of her reason for doing so, she then told me about a joke that the certain young lady had once played on her father and about another she had played on her maternal grandmother only a year before the old lady died. . . . It seems that the grandmother had a great fondness for attending funerals, and especially the funerals of indigent relations and friends and even slight acquaintances who were not so well-to-do as herself. The measure of her sympathy for the bereaved and the strength of her determination to be present at the funeral depended in each case on how straitened the family's circumstances were. Well, the old lady's granddaughter did a terrible thing. She arranged that she herself should accompany her grandmother to one of these funerals, and then when the hour came she got them into the wrong funeral. And she did it on purpose, as a joke. The poor acquaintance who was dead was one that the old lady had not seen in many years and that she probably would not have recognized had she met her on the street. Whereas the funeral they attended was that of a wealthy neighbor whom she had been seeing with some regularity in recent years but whose death did not seem to touch her at all.

"Since the grandmother's hearing and sight were not what they had once been, she managed to sit through the funeral service without discovering the trick that was being played on her. It was only at the end when they had gone up to view the remains and she had looked down into the face of her dead neighbor that she understood whose funeral it was. The shock was such that she had to lean on her granddaughter's arm all the way to the carriage, but by the time the driver, whom she reprimanded for having taken them to the Presbyterian instead of to the Methodist Church—by the time the driver had helped them inside the carriage and closed the door she had realized that the 'mistake' was all her granddaughter's doing. The girl didn't deny her guilt for a moment, and she only restrained her merriment until they had got out of the sight and hearing of the mourners. 'It's only what you deserve, Grandma,' she said to the old lady, who sat staring at her incredulously, 'for being so unsympathetic to your own kind.'

"The practical joke that the girl played on her father was not so bad as that, but it had a similar theme. The father prided himself on the tradition that his ancestors back in Virginia, 100 years before, had been ruined by the 'cult of hospitality.' In fact, he kept in touch with a host of distant kin in Virginia; furthermore, new and seemingly ever more distant members of the connection were continually being made known to him. It was not uncommon for them to come and put up at his house overnight when they were (ostensibly) passing through town on their way to the West Coast or to the Deep South; and they did not scruple to write to him from time to time for small loans or free legal advice. He spoke of them censoriously as 'broken down aristocrats,' but still he was proud of them as living proof of the old family tradition. . . . A telephone call came on a Saturday night, purportedly from a relative that had never been heard from before. The male voice said that the speaker was 'having certain difficulties with the law' and that he, along with his wife and their seven children, were stranded 'temporarily' at a downtown rooming house without the means of buying their Sunday dinner next day. The desired invitation to dinner was obtained, of course, and at 1.00 o'clock the next day the host and his family had assembled in the front drawing room to welcome their troubled cousins. Instead of their cousins, however, there arrived at precisely 1.00 o'clock another family quite well known to all present. It was a Mr. and Mrs. Herman Miller, their two married sons, their daughters-in-law, and their grandchildren. Mr. Miller's investment and brokerage company had recently collapsed, he had been indicted by the grand jury, and it was generally conceded that in the end he would not avoid a jail sentence. The Millers' home had already been foreclosed on, and they were preparing to move from it the following Monday morning. For a number of years they had been living in very fine style, and by their host that Sunday noon they had always been regarded as parvenues and fourflushers. They were received for dinner that day, however, in a most cordial and hospitable manner by a family who grasped at once whose work the whole business had been.

"I can only account for Laura Nell's practical jokes and for her overbearing, chatterbox ways by attributing it all to an excess of vitality. She had a store of energy that she didn't know what to do with. She ought to have found some sensible use to put it to, but somehow she couldn't. She remained a silly, harum-scarum girl when she ought to have been maturing into the wonderful young woman that she might have been. And yet her very vitality and animation were what attracted me first. I fell in love with her on first sight almost, and when I discovered that, though she would listen to no one else, she *would* listen to me, it seemed to me that I had only then begun to live and I was sure for the first time that I was going to be able to make something of my life.

"I suppose she was in love with me, at first. During the first weeks and months of our acquaintance she gave every sign of being so— every sign that a young lady of that day could give. And during that period I had but one object in life. It was finding moments when I could be alone with her. Laura Nell seemed as eager as I for those moments, and by the time we had known each other a year we had discoursed upon every subject that a young lady and a young gentleman of that day were permitted to discourse upon. I was no longer living there at home even then. I had begun training for my career immediately after college (I was one of the first to have any formal training in the field). But I took every opportunity to go back home and see Laura Nell. I was confident that she would someday be my wife, and I could already imagine her as a brilliant hostess and as the heroine of a thousand drawing rooms from St. Petersburg to Buenos Aires. I was sure of how swiftly she would be transformed into a really serious person once I got her away from *there*.

"From the very earliest days of my courting Laura Nell I found myself talking to her about the other families that moved in our own circle—that is, about the other people whom we both had more or less grown up with. At the beginning she was greatly amused by all I had to say about those people. I can hear her pretty laughter now and hear her urging me to continue and say more. 'What else?' she would say. 'What else? Go on.' The truth is, I wonder now if she understood that all my criticism of others implied a favorable comparison of them to herself, and wonder if she realized that while I was giving my true opinion of those people and the life they lived and while I had a genuine interest in the whole subject, I was also using it to pay her the most direct compliment that good taste and the proprieties of that age permitted—permitted at that stage of our courtship. Perhaps she did understand, but, as time passed, my talk itself—particularly my talk about the peculiar traits those families had—became even more interesting to her and ceased altogether to be a matter of amusement. And finally she came to reject all my complaints and strictures against those people, who were so unlike herself and her own family, and she even became their staunch defender and apologist. It is hard for me to remember accurately how long a time was required for this transition. Sometimes it seems to me that the entire course of our friendship lasted but one brief summer. Other times it seems to me that it must have consumed half my youth. I know in fact, of course, that it was a period of three years—three years when I was making the final break back there and committing myself once and for all to another life.

"It was not until the second summer after I had met Laura Nell that I felt myself in a position to speak of marriage. By then I felt I could give her some concrete image of the life I was offering her. But by then Laura Nell was no longer in love with me. I can say that now, though I could not have said it at the time. I believed there to be certain difficulties in her mind about the life that I proposed for us, certain imaginary obstacles to our happiness, but I thought that with time she—or I—would overcome such doubts as she had. It was not, you see, as though she were any less fond of my company than she had been formerly or any less interested in the career I was bent upon or in my ideas about the place and the people that she and I knew best. No, despite the serious way she had listened to all I had ever said to her, she was very much the same silly girl that I had met a year and a half before. I was not in the least surprised that she burst out laughing when I made my formal proposal or even that she should treat it as a joke and tease me about it before her parents and other members of her family. 'He's too serious for me, much too critical,' she would say when we were all assembled in the drawing room before dinner on a Sunday (I would be visiting back home, taking most of my meals at their house). 'You should hear the way he analyzes other people. Within a month he'd know what I'm really like, and then there would be the devil to pay.'

"'What she's saying,' her oldest brother said on one occasion, 'is that you're too good for her. I'd take heart from that. There couldn't be a better omen.'

"But the trouble was, Laura Nell said the same things to me in private. And she said, in effect, that she was too simple and artless a person to be taken out into the great world that I wanted to live in. She would be nothing but an embarrassment to a man who was as 'serious' and 'critical' as I was. At last I began to feel that it truly was all those things I said about such people as the Jenkinses and the Busbys that disquieted her so. I came to realize that no one was readier than Laura Nell to overlook those people's limitations and forgive their failure to find a way out of that little pond in which they were such big fish. She was prepared to forgive them *everything*. When

I ridiculed those who went away only to come back with their tails between their legs, she said she couldn't blame them for wanting to live amongst friends. When I talked about what wonderful experiences might be in store for her family if they got away from there, she replied that it would be the same with them as with 'everybody like us.' To me it was amazing to hear her equating herself and her remarkable family with those other, unattractive, unimaginative, provincial people. But that was what she did. 'I know how it would be,' she said. 'We'd do very well for a while, like the others. Then the truth would dawn on us suddenly.'

" 'What truth?' I asked. 'What is it that would dawn on you? I don't think you really know, yourself, what you mean.'

"She laughed at me, as if to say I was much too stupid. 'Why, it's easy: Dawn on us that we'd gone too far from home and that we'd better get back before it was too late.'

"It is hard to remember, after so many years, precisely the things she said. I do remember certain things, though. Once when I went home for a few days in February I had the happiness, for some moments, of believing that she might be coming round. We had attended a large reception together which turned out to be an announcement party for two of our friends. When we returned from the party to her house we went, for some reason, into a little card room that opened off the drawing room. We sat down in two little gilded chairs, facing each other across the card table's polished surface of inlaid woods. She was still wearing her furs, her gloves, and even her hat and veil. The hat was of brown velvet with a very high crown and little, cream-colored bows pinned all over it. It was the most becoming hat I ever saw her wear; somehow it made you want to reach out your hand and take hold of her tiny pointed chin, or even lift the veil and kiss that tight little mouth. When she first spoke, it even crossed my mind that in another moment I might be holding her in my arms. 'Would it make you miserable,' she began, 'to think you were going to end your days here where you grew up?' Through her veil I could not quite make out the expression in her eyes. I imagined that she was giving me an opening, that in my absence she had missed me, that she was now willing to debate with me how and where we might make a life together. I imagined that this was our critical hour and that I must be firm.

" 'I am only made miserable,' I said, 'by the thought that you may end *your* life here in a kind of misery you can't foresee.'

"But as usual, she laughed at me. 'I was not thinking about *us*,' she said. 'I was thinking about *them*'—the engaged couple, she meant, whom we had seen that afternoon. 'You know very well there is no chance for us. And please don't be so silly as to worry about me. Don't ever, ever worry about me. I was not made for misery of any kind.' . . . It is the sentence she wound up with that I remember most distinctly, of course: 'I was not made for misery of any kind.' As she spoke those words, her voice carried an impossible mixture of utter frivolity and total despair. And her eyes seemed to shine through her face veil with a luminosity that could not be explained and that cannot be described—a light both bright and dim, warm and cold, both shimmering and glassy.

"That was in February, and I went out to see Laura Nell again in April of that year. She never seemed more radiant to me than she did that spring. But the real reason for my visit was that during the month of March she had ceased to answer my letters and—in addition—I had learned from a mutual friend that Laura Nell Morris had made a March trip to New York to buy her spring and summer wardrobe— had done so, you understand, without letting me know she was in that part of the country. Her Easter outfit was a coatsuit of cerulian blue! I went to church with her and her family on Easter morning, and as I sat beside her in the family pew—and knelt beside her and rose with her to sing the old hymns—I think I was conscious in a way I had never been before of the glory of Laura Nell's physical beauty, frankly conscious, that is to say, of the wonderfully womanly figure beneath the snug-fitting coatsuit. When the congregation sang the hymns and spoke the words of the psalm, it was only Laura Nell's voice that I heard, and when I heard her I felt sure there had never been one of God's creatures more thoroughly alive or so full of the joy of being so. . . . On her head she wore a hat made entirely of feathers dyed the same shade as that of her suit. What a perfect hat it was for her—designed to complement the smooth texture of her skin as well as the reddish tints in her hair. Her eyes, which often seemed a gray-green, were pure blue that morning. Now and then during the service she turned to me and smiled. Each time she did so, I had the illusion immediately afterward that she had actually spoken to me and said what she could not possibly have said there.

"But I had come home that time with a suspicion, and now that I had seen her I believed that my suspicion was bound to be con-firmed. Even on my February visit I had observed that she was more attentive to her dress and to her appearance in general than she had ever been in the past. The brown velvet hat with cream-colored bows was not something she would have worn a year earlier. And since then there had been her trip to New York, and now the evidence of the satisfaction and pleasure she had taken in her shopping presented itself each time she appeared. There was a question in my mind that I could not go away without asking. I wanted to know who my rival was.

"On Easter afternoon we went for a drive in her father's trap. The little vehicle was spanking new, and drawn by a pretty bay mare that stepped along smartly. I drove the mare of course, and as we rode along Laura Nell took to counting the automobiles—the 'machines,' we called them—that were on the streets. She counted seven, and I suspect that represented the total number owned in the city at that time. It was a warm day for mid-April, but the sky was gray and overcast, and when finally we turned and headed for home I commented on what a dreary sky it was. 'I don't think it's dreary at all,' Laura Nell said. 'It is a lovely shade of gray.' When I looked at her with a skeptical smile, she said, 'Is there any real reason why a gray sky cannot be thought as beautiful as a blue one?'

"It seemed to me that she was *trying* to make a quarrel between us. Suddenly I asked: 'Why have you stopped answering my letters?'

"She looked straight ahead and gave a little shrug. 'Letters are no good any more,' she said. 'I'll always be glad to see you when you come, but let's give up letters.'

" 'Is there someone else, Laura Nell?' I asked.

"She didn't answer until we had driven half a block. I watched her face, and what I felt most was pity. I could see it was going to be so hard for her to tell me. It *was* hard for her, and I can't ever forget how she said it. 'No, there is no one,' she said. It was as though she wished with all her heart and soul that that had not been the answer she had to give me. After a moment she laughed, and actually slipped her arm through mine. A futile gesture and a meaningless laugh. There was no concealing the emptiness in her heart. There was nothing more I could say.

"I didn't see her again until she was taken ill in the summer of 1911, more than a year later. . . . But I must tell you about something she had said to me long before that Easter. It was after she had already listened to me many a time on the subject of people like the Jenkinses and the Busbys. She had at first, you remember, found it very amusing to hear me describe how their family traits got on my nerves and how it annoyed me that they took refuge in a place that seemed willing to forgive them everything. Then, after a period during which she found it merely interesting or curious, she came to reject my criticism and showed that in her mind she associated herself and her own family with those people! It was while so disposed that she once said to me: 'Since you are so critical of everyone else, and so intolerant, I wonder that you're willing to forgive the terrible trait all we Morrises have in common.'

" 'There is no such trait,' I said. We were alone in the family parlor in the back of the house, and we were seated together in one of those wicker conversation chairs that are considered antiques nowadays but which were then merely hopelessly out of fashion and mid-Victorian and so, quite naturally, relegated to the back parlor. 'There is no such trait in this family,' I said, letting my eyes skip about the parlor walls from one gilt-framed studio-portrait to another.

"She tossed her head and laughed, and then looking me squarely in the eye she said, 'Ours is worse than obesity or dirtiness. My red-headed grandfather used to point it out whenever someone said how unlike we all were, or whenever we bragged on ourselves in any way.'

" 'Some of you have his red in your hair . . .'

" 'Oh, it's nothing like that,' she said. 'It is an unpardonable trait.' She went on at great length, saying she supposed it was what kept them from ever wanting to leave home and that it made her feel very close to the very people that I was so 'unsympathetic' with. 'I tell you what!' she said at last, bringing her hand down on the wicker arm between us. 'I'll make a bargain with you. If ever you can guess what it is without asking anybody—without getting any hints even —then I'll forgive you everything. Do you understand what I mean?'

"I thought I understood what she meant, but I told her that I wanted no such bargain. If she could not accept me because she loved me, then I wouldn't try to win her in a bargaining. I put it down as more of her silliness—as another of her jokes, and whenever she brought it up again I changed the subject.

"After she was taken sick I used to go out to see her every three or four weeks—as often as I could get away from my work. They took her all about the country to different kinds of specialists, just trying to get a diagnosis, if nothing more. I have come to suppose that it must have been some kind of cancer that she had, but in those days one didn't so much as breathe the word. . . . When I would see her between her journeyings about the country to visit doctors, she enjoyed pointing out to me that doctors were quite as ignorant in other places as they were *there*. During the year that we did not see each other, Laura Nell had written to me occasionally, and I had always answered her letters, but in our letters and when I saw her afterward during her illness we wrote and spoke as old friends reminiscing about old, old times that had little relation to our present and future. Her mother, overhearing us once, took me aside and said that it broke her heart to hear Laura Nell talking that way—as though her youth, and even her life itself, were something in the past. I expressed my regret at having led her into that kind of conversation, but Mrs. Morris quickly reassured me, saying that it was not just with me that Laura Nell talked so. She confided in me that the doctors everywhere were as disturbed by her indifference to finding the cause and cure of her suffering as they were by her physical symptoms. Now, I am not going to tell you that Laura Nell Morris died because she lacked a will to live. I have no doubt that had she lived today the nature of her illness might have been better understood and that some means might have been found at least to retard the work of her disease. I am convinced that today we should not have had to watch her strength ebb away month after month without respite or restitution even for the briefest period. And, even as it was, the poor girl took a certain joy from the life that went on around her till the end. Her indifference was not to life but to illness. In fact, as illness drew those she loved closer about her she seemed almost to relish the condition. And, silly girl that she was, she would not think of what the final consequence might be. Or would not think of it in a serious way. If the worst should come, she told her mother, she could not imagine a 'better worst' than hers would be—with everybody she 'cared about' being so 'darling' to her and so 'close at hand.'

It was after this and other similar remarks had been reported to me that I asked Mrs. Morris to walk out into her garden with me one afternoon. We went to the very spot where she had tried to console me, nearly two years before, with her accounts of Laura Nell's practical jokes. It was in the late spring, this time, that we stood on the low terrace and looked back toward the house. Pink and white peonies were in bloom on the borders of the center path. There were red and white roses in the big square rose bed just below us. Jonquils and narcissuses had already gone, and the summer flowers were not in yet. There was no other color at all except the fresh verdure of the trees all around and the new foliage of the wisteria on the porch trellises. While we eyed the garden (both of us wishing, I believe, that we had the heart to speak of its beauty, or wishing that it were not so beautiful), I began to say mechanically the thing I had brought Mrs. Morris out there to hear. I cannot remember the words I used, but I told her that Laura Nell had once tried to tease me with the idea that there was some terrible family trait they all shared. I wondered if she knew what it was Laura Nell had in mind and, if so, would she be willing to tell me.

"She gazed at me at first without comprehension. And so then I went on to say that it was something her grandfather used to mention when anyone pointed out how different they all were from each other. Mrs. Morris' mouth fell open, and she stared at me as though I had spoken an obscenity. I believe I suffered more during the seconds that that lady's eyes were so fixed on me than I did at any other time. But the pain was of short duration. Mrs. Morris suddenly turned away, and I could see that she had brought her hands up to her face and that she was pressing her finger tips against her eyes as if to force back tears. I stepped toward her and put one arm about her. I half expected her to draw away, but when she didn't I took her in my arms and began trying to comfort her. That she permitted me to comfort her was the deepest consolation I could possibly have known. It was perhaps the most consoling moment of my adult life. It was as though my own parents had not been taken from me when I was only a boy really, as though I had had a sort of second chance that everyone wishes for with his mother. And presently she looked up at me and said, 'I can tell you what Laura Nell meant.' She was smiling now, and I knew from her voice that there would be no more tears. 'It was only a grim little joke that Laura Nell's grandfather used to make,' she said, 'and it is just like Laura Nell to have remembered it. He used to say that the Morrises were all alike in at least one respect: they all had to die some time or other. . . . A fairly trite kind of joke, I used to think—and still think. I do apologize for having given way so just now.'

"We stayed in the garden a few minutes longer. Then we walked back between the peonies to the house, and I went away without going up to see Laura Nell again. Next morning I took the train back East.

"But ten days later I was there again. And now I resolved to carry through my original purpose. Seated at her bedside, I told Laura Nell that I had discovered what the Morrises' dreadful failing was, and I gave proof of my knowledge. She lay with her eyes closed, and without making any sign that she understood me. But I continued. 'I must remind you of your promise,' I said. 'Now you must get well so that you can keep your end of the bargain and marry me.'

"She opened her eyes and smiled at me. I was filled with hope, for I actually believed—had believed from the start—that my scheme might work. I had thought that the very fatuousness of what I was attempting might appeal to Laura Nell, and I believed that even while she lay there already so near death she still possessed resources that would enable her to respond to a challenge of that kind. It was impossible for me to believe otherwise. When I was persuading her parents and her doctors to grant me that last quarter-hour alone with her I concealed my purpose from them, but I think that they too believed I might work a magic with her.

"I took the frail hand that lay on the coverlet and was about to say more when she asked in a whisper, 'Did I make you such a promise?'

" 'You did,' I said. 'Or that was how I understood you.'

" 'You did not want to make the bargain, though.'

" 'I had no choice.'

" 'But the condition—' she whispered. 'I made a condition.'

"I knew what she meant, and she saw at once that I did. And also at once I saw that she knew I had not met her condition.

" 'You asked someone what it was,' she said.

"I nodded and bent down and kissed her hand in an effort to hide my face.

" 'Well, I forgive you anyway,' she said. 'I think I understand you better than in the old days. . . . It *is* a little frightening even at best. . . . Probably it is just as well always to run away from it.' Until that moment I had never understood what our differences were or realized how close we were to each other. But when I raised my head, her eyes were already closed, and I never saw them open again. . . . The doctors could not predict how long she might linger, and so I was not there at the end. The telegram saying that she had died came on the third of July. I went out to the funeral, of course, and when I returned to Washington my first assignment to a foreign post was awaiting me.

"For a number of years I corresponded with Mrs. Morris, and of course I always called on the family on the rare occasions when some matter of my property took me back there. This was not often, though, and I eventually got rid of all my interests that made the trips necessary. Gradually over the years I have lost touch with everyone there. None of them ever comes over here for any length of time except an occasional stray lamb like yourself. When they come, they come only as tourists or—nowadays—on flying business trips; and invariably the first question they have to ask a person like myself is, don't I ever get 'the least bit' homesick. What rot. What utter rot! It's something more than home *they're* sick for, if only they knew. *She* knew at the last. And knew it was no better to welcome and want the inevitable than to turn your back on it and let it overtake you when and wherever it will. I say they'd do better to stay at home altogether than to come the way they do. Their little tours abroad must be as painful to them as my little excursions back home were to me after Laura Nell was dead. But, anyhow, I seldom see them when they do come. In the profession that I followed, I learned at last not to complicate my life with entertaining the tourists."

PETER S. BEAGLE was born in New York City, and graduated from the University of Pittsburgh in 1959. His novel, A *Fine and Private Place* was published by the Viking Press in 1960, and a nonfiction book called I *See By My Outfit* is scheduled for 1965. He has also published poetry in *The Texas Quarterly*. He lives in Santa Cruz, California, with his wife and three children.

Come Lady Death

THIS all happened in England a long time ago, when that George who spoke English with a heavy German accent and hated his sons was King. At that time there lived in London a lady who had nothing to do but give parties. Her name was Flora, Lady Neville, and she was a widow and very old. She lived in a great house not far from Buckingham Palace, and she had so many servants that she could not possibly remember all their names; indeed, there were some she had never even seen. She had more food than she could eat, more gowns than she could ever wear; she had wine in her cellars that no one would drink in her lifetime, and her private vaults were filled with great works of art that she did not know she owned. She spent the last years of her life giving parties and balls to which the greatest lords of England—and sometimes the King himself—came, and she was known as the wisest and wittiest woman in all London.

But in time her own parties began to bore her, and though she invited the most famous people in the land and hired the greatest jugglers and acrobats and dancers and magicians to entertain them, still she found her parties duller and duller. Listening to court gossip, which she had always loved, made her yawn. The most marvelous music, the most exciting feats of magic put her to sleep. Watching a beautiful young couple dance by her made her feel sad, and she hated to feel sad.

And so, one summer afternoon she called her closest friends around her and said to them, "More and more I find that my parties entertain everyone but me. The secret of my long life is that nothing has

Copyright © 1963 by The Atlantic Monthly Company, Boston 16, Massachusetts.

ever been dull for me. For all my life, I have been interested in everything I saw and been anxious to see more. But I cannot stand to be bored, and I will not go to parties at which I expect to be bored, especially if they are my own. Therefore, to my next ball I shall invite the one guest I am sure no one, not even myself, could possibly find boring. My friends, the guest of honor at my next party shall be Death himself!"

A young poet thought that this was a wonderful idea, but the rest of her friends were terrified and drew back from her. They did not want to die, they pleaded with her. Death would come for them when he was ready; why should she invite him before the appointed hour, which would arrive soon enough? But Lady Neville said, "Precisely. If Death has planned to take any of us on the night of my party, he will come whether he is invited or not. But if none of us are to die, then I think it would be charming to have Death among us—perhaps even to perform some little trick if he is in a good humor. And think of being able to say that we had been to a party with Death! All of London will envy us, all of England!"

The idea began to please her friends, but a young lord, very new to London, suggested timidly, "Death is so busy. Suppose he has work to do and cannot accept your invitation?"

"No one has ever refused an invitation of mine," said Lady Neville, "not even the King." And the young lord was not invited to her party.

She sat down then and there and wrote out the invitation. There was some dispute among her friends as to how they should address Death. "His Lordship Death" seemed to place him only on the level of a viscount or a baron. "His Grace Death" met with more acceptance, but Lady Neville said it sounded hypocritical. And to refer to Death as "His Majesty" was to make him the equal of the King of England, which even Lady Neville would not dare to do. It was finally decided that all should speak of him as "His Eminence Death," which pleased nearly everyone.

Captain Compson, known both as England's most dashing cavalry officer and most elegant rake, remarked next, "That's all very well, but how is the invitation to reach Death? Does anyone here know where he lives?"

"Death undoubtedly lives in London," said Lady Neville, "like everyone else of any importance, though he probably goes to Deauville for the summer. Actually, Death must live fairly near my own house. This is much the best section of London, and you could hardly expect a person of Death's importance to live anywhere else. When I stop to think of it, it's really rather strange that we haven't met before now, on the street."

Most of her friends agreed with her, but the poet, whose name was David Lorimond, cried out, "No, my lady, you are wrong! Death lives among the poor. Death lives in the foulest, darkest alleys of this city, in some vile, rat-ridden hovel that smells of—" He stopped here, partly because Lady Neville had indicated her displeasure, and partly because he had never been inside such a hut or thought of wondering what it smelled like. "Death lives among the poor," he went on, "and comes to visit them every day, for he is their only friend."

Lady Neville answered him as coldly as she had spoken to the young lord. "He may be forced to deal with them, David, but I hardly think that he seeks them out as companions. I am certain that it is as difficult for him to think of the poor as individuals as it is for me. Death is, after all, a nobleman."

There was no real argument among the lords and ladies that Death lived in a neighborhood at least as good as their own, but none of them seemed to know the name of Death's street, and no one had ever seen Death's house.

"If there were a war," Captain Compson said, "Death would be easy to find. I have seen him, you know, even spoken to him, but he has never answered me."

"Quite proper," said Lady Neville. "Death must always speak first. You are not a very correct person, Captain." But she smiled at him, as all women did.

Then an idea came to her. "My hairdresser has a sick child, I understand," she said. "He was telling me about it yesterday, sounding most dull and hopeless. I will send for him and give him the invitation, and he in his turn can give it to Death when he comes to take the brat. A bit unconventional, I admit, but I see no other way."

"If he refuses?" asked a lord who had just been married.

"Why should he?" asked Lady Neville.

Again it was the poet who exclaimed amidst the general approval that this was a cruel and wicked thing to do. But he fell silent when Lady Neville innocently asked him, "Why, David?"

So the hairdresser was sent for, and when he stood before them, smiling nervously and twisting his hands to be in the same room with

so many great lords, Lady Neville told him the errand that was required of him. And she was right, as she usually was, for he made no
refusal. He merely took the invitation in his hand and asked to be
excused.

He did not return for two days, but when he did he presented himself to Lady Neville without being sent for and handed her a small
white envelope. Saying, "How very nice of you, thank you very much,"
she opened it and found therein a plain calling card with nothing on
it except these words: *Death will be pleased to attend Lady Neville's
ball.*

"Death gave you this?" she asked the hairdresser eagerly. "What was
he like?" But the hairdresser stood still, looking past her, and said
nothing, and she, not really waiting for an answer, called a dozen
servants to her and told them to run and summon her friends. As
she paced up and down the room waiting for them, she asked again,
"What is Death like?" The hairdresser did not reply.

When her friends came they passed the little card excitedly from
hand to hand, until it had gotten quite smudged and bent from their
fingers. But they all admitted that, beyond its message, there was
nothing particularly unusual about it. It was neither hot nor cold to
the touch, and what little odor clung to it was rather pleasant. Everyone said that it was a very familiar smell, but no one could give it a
name. The poet said that it reminded him of lilacs but not exactly.

It was Captain Compson, however, who pointed out the one thing
that no one else had noticed. "Look at the handwriting itself," he
said. "Have you ever seen anything more graceful? The letters seem as
light as birds. I think we have wasted our time speaking of Death as
His This and His That. A woman wrote this note."

Then there was an uproar and a great babble, and the card had
to be handed around again so that everyone could exclaim, "Yes, by
God!" over it. The voice of the poet rose out of the hubbub saying,
"It is very natural, when you come to think of it. After all, the French
say *la mort*. Lady Death. I should much prefer Death to be a woman."

"Death rides a great black horse," said Captain Compson firmly,
"and wears armor of the same color. Death is very tall, taller than
anyone. It was no woman I saw on the battlefield, striking right and
left like any soldier. Perhaps the hairdresser wrote it himself, or the
hairdresser's wife."

But the hairdresser refused to speak, though they gathered around
him and begged him to say who had given him the note. At first

they promised him all sorts of rewards, and later they threatened to do terrible things to him. "Did you write this card?" he was asked, and "Who wrote it, then? Was it a living woman? Was it really Death? Did Death say anything to you? How did you know it was Death? Is Death a woman? Are you trying to make fools of us all?"

Not a word from the hairdresser, not one word, and finally Lady Neville called her servants to have him whipped and thrown into the street. He did not look at her as they took him away, or utter a sound.

Silencing her friends with a wave of her hand, Lady Neville said, "The ball will take place two weeks from tonight. Let Death come as Death pleases, whether as man or woman or strange, sexless creature." She smiled calmly. "Death may well be a woman," she said. "I am less certain of Death's form than I was, but I am also less frightened of Death. I am too old to be afraid of anything that can use a quill pen to write me a letter. Go home now, and as you make your preparations for the ball see that you speak of it to your servants, that they may spread the news all over London. Let it be known that on this one night no one in the world will die, for Death will be dancing at Lady Neville's ball."

For the next two weeks Lady Neville's great house shook and groaned and creaked like an old tree in a gale as the servants hammered and scrubbed, polished and painted, making ready for the ball. Lady Neville had always been very proud of her house, but as the ball drew near she began to be afraid that it would not be nearly grand enough for Death, who was surely accustomed to visiting in the homes of richer, mightier people than herself. Fearing the scorn of Death, she worked night and day supervising her servants' preparations. Curtains and carpets had to be cleaned, goldwork and silverware polished until they gleamed by themselves in the dark. The grand staircase that rushed down into the ballroom like a waterfall was washed and rubbed so often that it was almost impossible to walk on it without slipping. As for the ballroom itself, it took thirty-two servants working at once to clean it properly, not counting those who were polishing the glass chandelier that was taller than a man and the fourteen smaller lamps. And when they were done she made them do it all over, not because she saw any dust or dirt anywhere, but because she was sure that Death would.

As for herself, she chose her finest gown and saw to its laundering personally. She called in another hairdresser and had him put up her hair in the style of an earlier time, wanting to show Death that she was a woman who enjoyed her age and did not find it necessary to ape the young and beautiful. All the day of the ball she sat before her mirror, not making herself up much beyond the normal touches of rouge and eye shadow and fine rice powder, but staring at the lean old face she had been born with, wondering how it would appear to Death. Her steward asked her to approve his wine selection, but she sent him away and stayed at her mirror until it was time to dress and go downstairs to meet her guests.

Everyone arrived early. When she looked out of a window, Lady Neville saw that the driveway of her home was choked with carriages and fine horses. "It all looks like a great funeral procession," she said. The footman cried the names of her guests to the echoing ballroom. "Captain Henry Compson, His Majesty's Household Cavalry! Mr. David Lorimond! Lord and Lady Torrance!" (They were the youngest couple there, having been married only three months before.) "Sir Roger Harbison! The Contessa della Candini!" Lady Neville permitted them all to kiss her hand and made them welcome.

She had engaged the finest musicians she could find to play for the dancing, but though they began to play at her signal not one couple stepped out on the floor, nor did one young lord approach her to request the honor of the first dance, as was proper. They milled together, shining and murmuring, their eyes fixed on the ballroom door. Every time they heard a carriage clatter up the driveway they seemed to flinch a little and draw closer together; every time the footman announced the arrival of another guest, they all sighed softly and swayed a little on their feet with relief.

"Why did they come to my party if they were afraid?" Lady Neville muttered scornfully to herself. "I am not afraid of meeting Death. I ask only that Death may be impressed by the magnificence of my house and the flavor of my wines. I will die sooner than anyone here, but I am not afraid."

Certain that Death would not arrive until midnight, she moved among her guests, attempting to calm them, not with her words, which she knew they would not hear, but with the tone of her voice, as if they were so many frightened horses. But little by little, she herself was infected by their nervousness: whenever she sat down she stood up again immediately, she tasted a dozen glasses of wine without finishing any of them, and she glanced constantly at her jeweled watch, at first wanting to hurry the midnight along and end the waiting, later scratching at the watch face with her forefinger, as if she would push away the night and drag the sun backward into the sky. When midnight came, she was standing with the rest of them, breathing through her mouth, shifting from foot to foot, listening for the sound of carriage wheels turning in gravel.

When the clock began to strike midnight, everyone, even Lady Neville and the brave Captain Compson, gave one startled little cry and then was silent again, listening to the tolling of the clock. The smaller clocks upstairs began to chime. Lady Neville's ears hurt. She caught sight of herself in the ballroom mirror, one gray face turned up toward the ceiling as if she were gasping for air, and she thought, "Death will be a woman, a hideous, filthy old crone as tall and strong as a man. And the most terrible thing of all will be that she will have my face." All the clocks stopped striking, and Lady Neville closed her eyes.

She opened them again only when she heard the whispering around her take on a different tone, one in which fear was fused with relief and a certain chagrin. For no new carriage stood in the driveway. Death had not come.

The noise grew slowly louder; here and there people were beginning to laugh. Near her, Lady Neville heard young Lord Torrance say to his wife, "There, my darling, I told you there was nothing to be afraid of. It was all a joke."

"I am ruined," Lady Neville thought. The laughter was increasing; it pounded against her ears in strokes, like the chiming of the clocks. "I wanted to give a ball so grand that those who were not invited would be shamed in front of the whole city, and this is my reward. I am ruined, and I deserve it."

Turning to the poet Lorimond, she said, "Dance with me, David." She signaled to the musicians, who at once began to play. When Lorimond hesitated, she said, "Dance with me now. You will not have another chance. I shall never give a party again."

Lorimond bowed and led her out onto the dance floor. The guests parted for them, and the laughter died down for a moment, but Lady Neville knew that it would soon begin again. "Well, let them laugh," she thought. "I did not fear Death when they were all trembling. Why should I fear their laughter?" But she could feel a stinging at the thin lids of her eyes, and she closed them once more as she began to dance with Lorimond.

And then, quite suddenly, all the carriage horses outside the house whinnied loudly, just once, as the guests had cried out at midnight. There were a great many horses, and their one salute was so loud that everyone in the room became instantly silent. They heard the heavy steps of the footman as he went to open the door, and they shivered as if they felt the cool breeze that drifted into the house. Then they heard a light voice saying, "Am I late? Oh, I am so sorry. The horses were tired," and before the footman could re-enter to announce her, a lovely young girl in a white dress stepped gracefully into the ballroom doorway and stood there smiling.

She could not have been more than nineteen. Her hair was yellow, and she wore it long. It fell thickly upon her bare shoulders that gleamed warmly through it, two limestone islands rising out of a dark golden sea. Her face was wide at the forehead and cheekbones, and narrow at the chin, and her skin was so clear that many of the ladies there—Lady Neville among them—touched their own faces wonderingly, and instantly drew their hands away as though their own skin had rasped their fingers. Her mouth was pale, where the mouths of the other women were red and orange and even purple. Her eyebrows, thicker and straighter than was fashionable, met over dark, calm eyes that were set so deep in her young face and were so black, so uncompromisingly black, that the middle-aged wife of a middle-aged lord murmured, "Touch of the gypsy there, I think."

"Or something worse," suggested her husband's mistress.

"Be silent!" Lady Neville spoke louder than she had intended, and the girl turned to look at her. She smiled, and Lady Neville tried to smile back, but her mouth seemed very stiff. "Welcome," she said. "Welcome, my lady Death."

A sigh rustled among the lords and ladies as the girl took the old woman's hand and curtsied to her, sinking and rising in one motion, like a wave. "You are Lady Neville," she said. "Thank you so much for inviting me." Her accent was as faint and as almost familiar as her perfume.

"Please excuse me for being late," she said earnestly. "I had to come from a long way off, and my horses are so tired."

"The groom will rub them down," Lady Neville said, "and feed them if you wish."

"Oh, no," the girl answered quickly. "Tell him not to go near the horses, please. They are not really horses, and they are very fierce."

She accepted a glass of wine from a servant and drank it slowly, sighing softly and contentedly. "What good wine," she said. "And what a beautiful house you have."

"Thank you," said Lady Neville. Without turning, she could feel every woman in the room envying her, sensing it as she could always sense the approach of rain.

"I wish I lived here," Death said in her low, sweet voice. "I will, one day."

Then, seeing Lady Neville become as still as if she had turned to ice, she put her hand on the old woman's arm and said, "Oh, I'm sorry, I'm so sorry. I am so cruel, but I never mean to be. Please forgive me, Lady Neville. I am not used to company, and I do such stupid things. Please forgive me."

Her hand felt as light and warm on Lady Neville's arm as the hand of any other young girl, and her eyes were so appealing that Lady Neville replied, "You have said nothing wrong. While you are my guest, my house is yours."

"Thank you," said Death, and she smiled so radiantly that the musicians began to play quite by themselves, with no sign from Lady Neville. She would have stopped them, but Death said, "Oh, what lovely music! Let them play, please."

So the musicians played a gavotte, and Death, unabashed by eyes that stared at her in greedy terror, sang softly to herself without words, lifted her white gown slightly with both hands, and made hesitant little patting steps with her small feet. "I have not danced in so long," she said wistfully. "I'm quite sure I've forgotten how."

She was shy; she would not look up to embarrass the young lords, not one of whom stepped forward to dance with her. Lady Neville felt a flood of shame and sympathy, emotions she thought had withered in her years ago. "Is she to be humiliated at my own ball?" she thought angrily. "It is because she is Death; if she were the ugliest, foulest hag in all the world they would clamor to dance with her, because they are gentlemen and they know what is expected of them. But no gentleman will dance with Death, no matter how beautiful she is." She glanced sideways at David Lorimond. His face was flushed, and his hands were clasped so tightly as he stared at Death that his fingers were like glass, but when Lady Neville touched his arm he did not turn, and when she hissed, "David!", he pretended not to hear her.

Then Captain Compson, gray-haired and handsome in his uniform, stepped out of the crowd and bowed gracefully before Death. "If I may have the honor," he said.

"Captain Compson," said Death, smiling. She put her arm in his. "I was hoping you would ask me."

This brought a frown from the older women, who did not consider it a proper thing to say, but for that Death cared not a rap. Captain Compson led her to the center of the floor, and there they danced. Death was curiously graceless at first—she was too anxious to please her partner, and she seemed to have no notion of rhythm. The Captain himself moved with the mixture of dignity and humor that Lady Neville had never seen in another man, but when he looked at her over Death's shoulder, she saw something that no one else appeared to notice: that his face and eyes were immobile with fear, and that, though he offered Death his hand with easy gallantry, he flinched slightly when she took it. And yet he danced as well as Lady Neville had ever seen him.

"Ah, that's what comes of having a reputation to maintain," she thought. "Captain Compson too must do what is expected of him. I hope someone else will dance with her soon."

But no one did. Little by little, other couples overcame their fear and slipped hurriedly out on the floor when Death was looking the other way, but nobody sought to relieve Captain Compson of his beautiful partner. They danced every dance together. In time, some of the men present began to look at her with more appreciation than terror, but when she returned their glances and smiled at them, they clung to their partners as if a cold wind were threatening to blow them away.

One of the few who stared at her frankly and with pleasure was young Lord Torrance, who usually danced only with his wife. Another was the poet Lorimond. Dancing with Lady Neville, he remarked to her, "If she is Death, what do these frightened fools think they are? If she is ugliness, what must they be? I hate their fear. It is obscene."

Death and the Captain danced past them at that moment, and they heard him say to her, "But if that was truly you that I saw in the battle, how can you have changed so? How can you have become so lovely?"

Death's laughter was gay and soft. "I thought that among so many beautiful people it might be better to be beautiful. I was afraid of frightening everyone and spoiling the party."

"They all thought she would be ugly," said Lorimond to Lady Neville. "I—*I* knew she would be beautiful."

"Then why have you not danced with her?" Lady Neville asked him. "Are you also afraid?"

"No, oh, no," the poet answered quickly and passionately. "I will ask her to dance very soon. I only want to look at her a little longer."

The musicians played on and on. The dancing wore away the night as slowly as falling water wears down a cliff. It seemed to Lady Neville that no night had ever endured longer, and yet she was neither tired nor bored. She danced with every man there, except with Lord Torrance, who was dancing with his wife as if they had just met that night, and, of course, with Captain Compson. Once he lifted his hand and touched Death's golden hair very lightly. He was a striking man still, a fit partner for so beautiful a girl, but Lady Neville looked at his face each time she passed him and realized that he was older than anyone knew.

Death herself seemed younger than the youngest there. No woman at the ball danced better than she now, though it was hard for Lady Neville to remember at what point her awkwardness had given way to the liquid sweetness of her movements. She smiled and called to everyone who caught her eye—and she knew them all by name; she sang constantly, making up words to the dance tunes, nonsense words, sounds without meaning, and yet everyone strained to hear her soft voice without knowing why. And when, during a waltz, she caught up the trailing end of her gown to give her more freedom as she danced, she seemed to Lady Neville to move like a little sailing boat over a still evening sea.

Lady Neville heard Lady Torrance arguing angrily with the Contessa della Candini. "I don't care if she is Death, she's no older than I am, she can't be!"

"Nonsense," said the Contessa, who could not afford to be generous to any other woman. "She is twenty-eight, thirty, if she is an hour. And that dress, that bridal gown she wears—really!"

"Vile," said the woman who had come to the ball as Captain Compson's freely acknowledged mistress. "Tasteless. But one should know better than to expect taste from Death, I suppose." Lady Torrance looked as if she were going to cry.

"They are jealous of Death," Lady Neville said to herself. "How strange. I am not jealous of her, not in the least. And I do not fear her at all." She was very proud of herself.

Then, as unbiddenly as they had begun to play, the musicians stopped. They began to put away their instruments. In the sudden shrill silence, Death pulled away from Captain Compson and ran to look out of one of the tall windows, pushing the curtains apart with both hands. "Look!" she said, with her back turned to them. "Come and look. The night is almost gone."

The summer sky was still dark, and the eastern horizon was only a shade lighter than the rest of the sky, but the stars had vanished and the trees near the house were gradually becoming distinct. Death pressed her face against the window and said, so softly that the other guests could barely hear her, "I must go now."

"No," Lady Neville said, and was not immediately aware that she had spoken. "You must stay a while longer. The ball was in your honor. Please stay."

Death held out both hands to her, and Lady Neville came and took them in her own. "I've had a wonderful time," she said gently. "You cannot possibly imagine how it feels to be actually invited to such a ball as this, because you have given them and gone to them all your life. One is like another to you, but for me it is different. Do you understand me?" Lady Neville nodded silently. "I will remember this night forever," Death said.

"Stay," Captain Compson said. "Stay just a little longer." He put his hand on Death's shoulder, and she smiled and leaned her cheek against it. "Dear Captain Compson," she said. "My first real gallant. Aren't you tired of me yet?"

"Never," he said. "Please stay."

"Stay," said Lorimond, and he too seemed about to touch her. "Stay. I want to talk to you. I want to look at you. I will dance with you if you stay."

"How many followers I have," Death said in wonder. She stretched one hand toward Lorimond, but he drew back from her and then flushed in shame. "A soldier and a poet. How wonderful it is to be a woman. But why did you not speak to me earlier, both of you? Now it is too late. I must go."

"Please stay," Lady Torrance whispered. She held on to her husband's hand for courage. "We think you are so beautiful, both of us do."

"Gracious Lady Torrance," the girl said kindly. She turned back to the window, touched it lightly, and it flew open. The cool dawn air rushed into the ballroom, fresh with rain but already smelling faintly of the London streets over which it had passed. They heard birdsong and the strange, harsh nickering of Death's horses.

"Do you want me to stay?" she asked. The question was put, not to Lady Neville, nor to Captain Compson, nor to any of her admirers, but to the Contessa della Candini, who stood well back from them all, hugging her flowers to herself and humming a little song of irritation. She did not in the least want Death to stay, but she was afraid that all the other women would think her envious of Death's beauty, and so she said, "Yes. Of course I do."

"Ah," said Death. She was almost whispering. "And you," she said to another woman, "do you want me to stay? Do you want me to be one of your friends?"

"Yes," said the woman, "because you are beautiful and a true lady."

"And you," said Death to a man, "and you," to a woman, "and you," to another man, "do you want me to stay?" And they all answered, "Yes, Lady Death, we do."

"Do you want me, then?" she cried at last to all of them. "Do you want me to live among you and to be one of you, and not to be Death anymore? Do you want me to visit your houses and come to all your parties? Do you want me to ride horses like yours instead of mine, do you want me to wear the kind of dresses you wear, and say the things you would say? Would one of you marry me, and would the rest of you dance at my wedding and bring gifts to my children? Is that what you want?"

"Yes," said Lady Neville. "Stay here, stay with me, stay with us."

Death's voice, without becoming louder, had become clearer and older; too old a voice, thought Lady Neville, for such a young girl. "Be sure," said Death. "Be sure of what you want, be very sure. Do all of you want me to stay? For if one of you says to me, no, go away, then I must leave at once and never return. Be sure. Do you all want me?"

And everyone there cried with one voice, "Yes! Yes, you must stay with us. You are so beautiful that we cannot let you go."

"We are tired," said Captain Compson.

"We are blind," said Lorimond, adding, "especially to poetry."

"We are afraid," said Lord Torrance quietly, and his wife took his arm and said, "Both of us."

"We are dull and stupid," said Lady Neville, "and growing old uselessly. Stay with us, Lady Death."

And then Death smiled sweetly and radiantly and took a step forward, and it was as though she had come down among them from a great height. "Very well," she said. "I will stay with you. I will be Death no more. I will be a woman."

The room was full of a deep sigh, although no one was seen to open his mouth. No one moved, for the golden-haired girl was Death still, and her horses still whinnied for her outside. No one could look at her for long, although she was the most beautiful girl anyone there had ever seen.

"There is a price to pay," she said. "There is always a price. Some one of you must become Death in my place, for there must forever be Death in the world. Will anyone choose? Will anyone here become Death of his own free will? For only thus can I become a human girl."

No one spoke, no one spoke at all. But they backed slowly away from her, like waves slipping back down a beach to the sea when you try to catch them. The Contessa della Candini and her friends would have crept quietly out of the door, but Death smiled at them and they stood where they were. Captain Compson opened his mouth as though he were going to declare himself, but he said nothing. Lady Neville did not move.

"No one," said Death. She touched a flower with her finger, and it seemed to crouch and flex itself like a pleased cat. "No one at all," she said. "Then I must choose, and that is just, for that is the way that I became Death. I never wanted to be Death, and it makes me so happy that you want me to become one of yourselves. I have searched a long time for people who would want me. Now I have only to choose someone to replace me and it is done. I will choose very carefully."

"Oh, we were so foolish," Lady Neville said to herself. "We were so foolish." But she said nothing aloud; she merely clasped her hands and stared at the young girl, thinking vaguely that if she had had a daughter she would have been greatly pleased if she resembled the lady Death.

"The Contessa della Candini," said Death thoughtfully, and that woman gave a little squeak of terror because she could not draw her breath for a scream. But Death laughed and said, "No, that would be silly." She said nothing more, but for a long time after that the Contessa burned with humiliation at not having been chosen to be Death.

"Not Captain Compson," murmured Death, "because he is too kind to become Death, and because it would be too cruel to him. He wants to die so badly." The expression on the Captain's face did not change, but his hands began to tremble.

"Not Lorimond," the girl continued, "because he knows so little about life, and because I like him." The poet flushed, and turned white, and then turned pink again. He made as if to kneel clumsily on one knee, but instead he pulled himself erect and stood as much like Captain Compson as he could.

"Not the Torrances," said Death, "never Lord and Lady Torrance, for both of them care too much about another person to take any pride in being Death." But she hesitated over Lady Torrance for a while, staring at her out of her dark and curious eyes. "I was your age when I became Death," she said at last. "I wonder what it will be like to be your age again. I have been Death for so long." Lady Torrance shivered and did not speak.

And at last Death said quietly, "Lady Neville."

"I am here," Lady Neville answered.

"I think you are the only one," said Death. "I choose you, Lady Neville."

Again Lady Neville heard every guest sigh softly, and although her back was to them all she knew that they were sighing in relief that neither themselves nor anyone dear to themselves had been chosen. Lady Torrance gave a little cry of protest, but Lady Neville knew that she would have cried out at whatever choice Death made. She heard herself say calmly, "I am honored. But was there no one more worthy than I?"

"Not one," said Death. "There is no one quite so weary of being human, no one who knows better how meaningless it is to be alive. And there is no one else here with the power to treat life"—and she smiled sweetly and cruelly—"the life of your hairdresser's child, for instance, as the meaningless thing it is. Death has a heart, but it is forever an empty heart, and I think, Lady Neville, that your heart is like a dry riverbed, like a seashell. You will be very content as Death, more so than I, for I was very young when I became Death."

She came toward Lady Neville, light and swaying, her deep eyes wide and full of the light of the red morning sun that was beginning to rise. The guests at the ball moved back from her, although she did not look at them, but Lady Neville clenched her hands tightly and watched Death come toward her with her little dancing steps. "We must kiss each other," Death said. "That is the way I became Death." She shook her head delightedly, so that her soft hair swirled about her shoulders. "Quickly, quickly," she said. "Oh, I cannot wait to be human again."

"You may not like it," Lady Neville said. She felt very calm, though she could hear her old heart pounding in her chest and feel it in the tips of her fingers. "You may not like it after a while," she said.

"Perhaps not." Death's smile was very close to her now. "I will not be as beautiful as I am, and perhaps people will not love me as much as they do now. But I will be human for a while, and at last I will die. I have done my penance."

"What penance?" the old woman asked the beautiful girl. "What was it you did? Why did you become Death?"

"I don't remember," said the lady Death. "And you too will forget in time." She was smaller than Lady Neville, and so much younger. In her white dress she might have been the daughter that Lady Neville had never had, who would have been with her always and held her mother's head lightly in the crook of her arm when she felt old and sad. Now she lifted her head to kiss Lady Neville's cheek, and as she did so she whispered in her ear, "You will still be beautiful when I am ugly. Be kind to me then."

Behind Lady Neville the handsome gentlemen and ladies murmured and sighed, fluttering like moths in their evening dress, in their elegant gowns. "I promise," she said, and then she pursed her dry lips to kiss the soft, sweet-smelling cheek of the young lady Death.

J. C. OATES, who is on the faculty of the University of Detroit, has published fiction in many American magazines. Her collection of stories *By the North Gate* was published in 1963 and her first novel *With Shuddering Fall* in 1964. Previous stories by Mrs. Oates have appeared in *The Best American Short Stories* and in *Prize Stories: The O. Henry Awards* for 1963 and 1964.

First Views of the Enemy

Just around the turn the road was alive. First to assault the eye was a profusion of heads, black-haired, bobbing, and a number of straw hats that looked oddly professional—like straw hats in a documentary film; and shirts and overalls and dresses, red, yellow, beflowered, dotted, striped, some bleached by the sun, some stiff and brilliant, just bought and worn proudly out of the store. The bus in which they were traveling—a dead dark blue, colored yet without any color—was parked half on the clay road and half in the prickly high grass by the ditch. Its old-fashioned hood was open, yanked cruelly up and doubled on itself, and staring into its greasy, dust-flecked tangle of parts was the driver, the only fair, brown-haired one of the bunch. Annette remembered, later, that as her station wagon moved in astonishment toward them the driver looked up and straight at her: a big indifferent face, curious without interest, smeared with grease as if deliberately, to disguise himself. No kin of yours, lady, no kin! he warned contemptuously.

Breaking from a group of children, running with arms out for a mock embrace, a boy of about seven darted right toward Annette's car. The boy's thick black hair, curled with sweat, plastered onto his forehead, framed a delicate, cruelly tanned face, a face obviously dead white beneath its tan: great dark eyes, expanded out of proportion, neat little brows like angels' brows—that unbelievable and in-

Copyright © 1964 by The University of Nebraska.
The first book by J. C. OATES, *a collection of stories called* By the North Gate, *was published by Vanguard in 1963. Stories have appeared in* Epoch, Mademoiselle, Literary Review, *and in both the* O. Henry *and* Martha Foley *anthology selections for 1963.*

decent beauty of children exploited for art—a pouting mouth, still
purple at the corners from the raspberries picked and hidden for the
long bus ride, these lips now turning as Annette stared into a hilarious
grin and crying out at her and the stricken child who cringed beside
her, legs already drawn up fatly at the knees——

In agony the brakes cried, held: the scene, dizzy with color, rocked
with the car, down a little, back up, giddily, helplessly, while dust exploded up on all sides. "Mommy!" Timmy screamed, fascinated by
the violence, yet his wail was oddly still and drawn out, and his eyes
never once turned to his mother. The little Mexican boy had disappeared in front of the car. Still the red dust arose, the faces at the
bus jerked around together, white eyes, white teeth, faces were pro-
pelled toward the windows of the bus, empty a second before. "God,
God," Annette murmured; she had not yet released the steering
wheel, and on it her fingers began to tighten as if they might tear the
wheel off, hold it up to defend her and her child, perhaps even to
attack.

A woman in a colorless dress pushed out of the crowd, barefooted
in the red clay, pointed her finger at Annette and shouted something
—gleefully. She shook her fist, grinning, others grinned behind her;
the bus driver turned back to his bus. Annette saw now the little boy
on the other side of the road, popping up safe in the ditch, and jumping frantically—though the sharp weeds must have hurt his feet—and
laughing, yelling, shouting as if he were insane. The air rang with
shouts, with laughter. A good joke. What was the joke? Annette's
brain reeled with shock, sucked for air as if drowning. Beside her
Timmy wailed softly, but his eyes were fastened on the boy in the
ditch. "He's safe, he's safe," Annette whispered. But others ran toward her now—big boys, tall but skinny, without shirts. How their
ribs seemed to run with them, sliding up and down inside the dark
tanned flesh with the effort of their legs! Even a few girls approached,
hard dark faces, already aged, black hair matted and torn about their
thin shoulders. They waved and cried, "Missus! Missus!" Someone
even shouted, "Cadillac!" though her station wagon, already a year
old, was far from being a Cadillac. As if to regain attention the little
boy in the ditch picked up something, a handful of pebbles, and
threw it at the car, right beneath Timmy's pale gaping face. A babble
of Spanish followed, more laughter, the barefoot woman who must
have been the boy's mother strode mightily across the road, grabbed
the boy, shook him in an extravagant mockery of punishment: sucked

her lips at him, made spitting motions, rubbed his head hard with the palm of her hand—this hurt, Annette saw with satisfaction, for the child winced in spite of his bravado. At the bus the American man's back swelled damply and without concern beneath his shirt; he did not even glance around.

Annette leaned to the window, managed a smile. "Please let me through," she called. Her voice surprised her; it sounded like a voice without body or identity, channelled in over a radio.

The boys made odd gestures with their hands, not clenching them into fists, but instead striking with the edges of their hands, knife-like, into the air. Their teeth grinned and now, with them so close (the bravest were at her fender), Annette could see how discolored their teeth were, though they had seemed white before. They must have been eating dirt! she thought vaguely. "Please let me through," she said. Beside her Timmy sat in terror. She wanted to reach over and put her hand over his eyes, hide this sight from him—this mob of dirty people, so hungry their tongues seemed to writhe in their mouths, their exhaustion turned to frenzy. "Missus! Missus! Si, si, Cadillac!" the boys yelled, pounding on the front of the car. The women, men, even very old people—with frail white hair—watched, surprised and pleased at being entertained.

"Please. Please." Suddenly Annette pressed on the horn: what confidence that sound inspired! The boys hesitated, moved back. She toyed with the accelerator, wanting to slam down on it, to escape. But suppose one of them were in the way. . . . The horror of that falling thud, the vision of blood sucked into red clay, stilled her nervousness, made her inch the big car forward slowly, slowly. And in the back those unmistakable bags of groceries, what would be showing at the tops? Maybe tomatoes, pears, strawberries—perhaps picked by these people a few days ago—maybe bread, maybe meat—Annette's face burned with something more than shame. But when she spoke her voice showed nothing. "Let me through, please. Let me through." She sounded cool and still.

Then she was past. The station wagon picked up speed. Behind her were yells, cries no longer gleeful, now insulting, vicious: in the mirror fists, shouting faces, the little boy running madly into the cloud of dust behind the car. He jerked something back behind his head, his skinny elbow swung, and with his entire body he sent a mud-rock after the car which hit the back window square, hard, and

exploded. With her fingers still frozen to the steering wheel Annette
sped home.

Beside her the child, fascinated, watched the familiar road as if seeing it for the first time. That tender smile was something strange; Annette did not like it. Annette herself, twitching with fear, always a
nervous woman, electric as the harassed or the insanely ill are, saw
with shock that her face in the mirror was warm and possessed. That
was she, then, and not this wild, heart-thumping woman, afraid of
those poor children in the road. . . . Her eyes leaped home; her mind
anticipated its haven. Already, straightening out of a turn, she could
see it: the long, low, orange-brick home, trees behind the house not
yet big enough for shade, young trees, a young house, a young family. Cleared out of the acres of wheat and wood and grass fields on
either side, a surprise to someone driving by, looking for all the world
as if it and its fine light-green grass, so thin as to look unreal, and its
Hercules fence had been picked up somewhere far away and dropped
down here. Two miles away, on the highway which paralleled this
road, there were homes something like this, but on this road there
were only, a half-mile ahead, a few farmhouses, typical, some shacks
deserted and not deserted, and even a gas station and store; otherwise nothing. Annette felt for the first time the insane danger of this
location, and heard with magical accuracy her first question when her
husband had suggested it: "But so far out. . . . Why do you want it
so far out?" City children, both of them, the hot rich smell of sunlight
and these soundless distances had never been forbidding, isolating.
Instead each random glance at the land strengthened in them a sense
of their own cleverness. Children of fortune, to withdraw from their
comfortable pasts, to raise a child in such safety! ——It was fifteen
miles to the nearest town, where Annette did her shopping and
Timmy went to school, and forty miles to the city where her husband
worked.

Annette turned into the driveway, drove slowly into the garage.
Still in a trance, angry at herself, she got out of the car but stood with
her hand still lingering on the steering wheel. A thin, fashionably
thin young woman, for years more woman than girl, in a white dress
she stood with a remote, vague smile, hand lightly on the wheel, mind
enticed by something she could not name. Perplexed, incredulous: in
spite of the enormity of what threatened (the migrant workers were
hardly a mile away) she felt slowed and meaningless. Her inertia
touched even Timmy, who usually jumped out of the car and slammed

the door. If only he would do this, and she could cry, "Timmy! *Please!*" calm might be restored. But no, he climbed down on his side like a little old man; he pushed the door back indifferently so that it gave a feeble click and did not even close all the way. For a while mother and son stood on opposite sides of the car; Annette could tell that Timmy did not move and was not even looking at her. Then his footsteps began. He ran out of the garage.

Annette was angry. Only six, he understood her, he knew what was to come next: he was to help her with the packages, with the doors, open the cupboards in the kitchen, he would be in charge of putting things into the refrigerator. As if stricken by a sudden bad memory Annette stood in the garage, waiting for her mind to clear. What was there in Timmy's running out? For an instant she felt betrayed—as if he cherished the memory of that strange little boy, and ran out to keep it from her. She remembered the early days of her motherhood, how contemptuous she had been of herself, of what she had accomplished—a baby she refused to look at, a husband neurotic with worry, a waiting life of motherhood so oppressive that she felt nausea contemplating it: Is this what I have become? What is this baby to me? Where am I? Where am *I?* Impassioned, a month out of college and fearful, in spite of her attractiveness, that she would never be married, Annette had taken the dangerous gamble of tearing aside her former life, rejecting the familiar possessions and patterns that had defined her, and had plunged, with that intense confident sharp-voiced young man, into a new life she was never quite sure had not betrayed the old, stricken the old: her parents, her lovely mother, now people to write to, send greeting cards to, hint vaguely at visiting. . . .

Sighing, she began to move. She took the packages out of the car, went outside (the heat was now brilliant), put them down and, with deft angry motions in case Timmy was secretly watching, pulled down the garage door and locked it. "There!" But when she turned, her confidence was distracted. She stared at the house. Shrubbery hiding the concrete slab—basements were not necessary this far south—rosebushes bobbing roses, vulnerable, insanely gaudy, the great picture window that made her think, always, someone was slyly watching her, even the faint professional sweep of grass out to the road—all these in their elaborate planned splendor shouted mockery at her, mockery at themselves, as if they were safe from destruction! Annette fought off the inertia again; it passed close by her, a whiff of something like

death, the same darkness that had bothered her in the hospital, delivered of her child. She left the packages against the garage (though
the ice cream in its special package might be melting) and, awkward
in her high heels, hurried out the drive. She shielded her eyes: nothing in sight down the road. It was a red clay road, a country road that
would never be paved, and she and her husband had at first taken
perverse pride in it. But it turned so, she had never noticed that before, and great bankings of foliage hid it, disguised its twistings, so
that she could see not more than a quarter mile away. Never before
had the land seemed so *flat*.

She hurried. At the gate the sun caught up with her, without ceremony. She struggled to swing the gate around (a few rusty, loosened
prongs had caught in the grass); she felt perspiration breaking out
on her body, itching and prickling her, under her arms, on her back.
The white dress must have hung damp and wrinkled about her legs.
Panting with the exertion, she managed to get the gate loose and
drag it around; it tilted down at a jocose angle, scraping the gravel;
then she saw that there was no lock, she would need a padlock, there
was one in the garage somewhere, and in the same instant, marvelling
at her stamina, she turned back.

Hurrying up the drive she thought again of the little Mexican boy.
She saw his luxurious face, that strange unhealthy grin inside his embracing arms—it sped toward her. Cheeks drawn in as if by age, eyes
protruding with—it must have been hunger—dirty hands like claws
reaching out, grabbing, demanding what? What would they demand
of her? If they were to come and shout for her out in the road, if she
were to offer them—something—milk, maybe, the chocolate cookies
Timmy loved so, maybe even money? would they go away, then,
would they thank her and run back to their people? Would they
continue their trip north, headed for Oregon and Washington? What
would happen? Violence worried the look of the house, dizzied Annette: there were the yellow roses she tended so fondly, rich and
sprawling against the orange brick. In the sunlight their petals, locked
intricately inside one another, were vivid, glaringly detailed, as if their
secret life were swelling up in rage at her for having so endangered
their beauty.

There the packages lay against the garage, and seeing them Annette forgot about the padlock. She stooped and picked them up.
When she turned again she saw Timmy standing just inside the
screen door. "Timmy, open the—" she said, vexed, but he had already

disappeared. Inside the kitchen she slammed the bags down, fought back the impulse to cry, stamped one heel on the linoleum so hard that her foot buzzed with pain. "Timmy," she said, her eyes shut tight, "come out in this kitchen."

He appeared, carrying a comic book. That was for the look of it, of course; he had not been reading. His face was wary. Fair like his mother, blond-toned, smart for his age, he had still about his quiet plump face something that belonged to field animals, wood animals, shrewd, secret creatures that have little to say for themselves. He read the newspaper like his father, cultivated the same thoughtful expression; encouraged, he talked critically about his schoolteacher with a precocity that delighted his father, frightened Annette (to her, even now, teachers were somehow *different* from other people); he had known the days of the week, months of the year, continents of the world, planets of the solar system, major star groupings of the universe, at an astonishing age—as a child he approached professional perfection. But Annette, staring at him, was not sure, now, that she could trust him. What if, when the shouting began outside, when "Missus! Missus!" demanded her, Timmy ran out to them, joined them, stared back at her in the midst of their white eyes and dirty arms? They stared at each other as if this question had been voiced.

"You almost killed him," Timmy said.

His voice was soft. Its innocence showed that he knew how daring he was; his eyes as well, neatly fringed by pale lashes, trembled slightly in their gaze. "What?" said Annette. "What?"

The electric clock, built into the big white range, whirred in the silence. Timmy swallowed, rustled his comic book, pretended to wipe his nose—a throwback to a habit long outgrown, hoping to mislead her—and looked importantly at the clock. "*He* hit the car. Two times," he said.

This was spoken differently. The ugly spell was over. "Yes, he certainly did," Annette said. She was suddenly busy. "He certainly did." After a moment Timmy put down the comic book to help her. They worked easily, in silence. Eyes avoided one another. But Annette felt feverishly excited; something had been decided, strengthened. Timmy, stooping to put vegetables in the bottom of the refrigerator, felt her staring at him and peered up, his little eyebrows raised in a classic look of wonder. "You going to call Daddy?" he said.

Annette had been thinking of this but when Timmy suggested it, it was exposed for what it was—a child's idea. "That won't be necessary," she said. She folded bags noisily and righteously.

When they finished mother and son wandered without enthusiasm into the dining room, into the living room, as if they did not really want to leave the kitchen. Annette's eyes flinched at what she saw: crystal, polished wood, white walls, aqua lampshades, white curtains, sand-toned rug, detailed, newly cleaned, spreading regally across the room—surely no one ever walked on that rug! That was what *they* would say if they saw it. And the glassware off in the corner, spear-like, transparent green, a great window behind it, linking it with the green grass outside, denying a barrier, inviting in sunlight, wind, anyone's eyes approaching——Annette went to the window and pulled the draw drapes shut; that was better; she breathed gently, coaxed by the beauty of those drapes into a smile: they were white, perfectly hung, sculptured superbly in generous swelling curves. And fireproof, if it came to that. . . . Annette turned. Timmy stood before the big red swivel chair as if he were going to sit in it—he did not—and looked at her with such a queer, pinched expression, in spite of his round face, that Annette felt a sudden rush of shame. She was too easily satisfied, too easily deluded. In all directions her possessions stretched out about her, defining her, identifying her, and they were vulnerable and waiting, the dirt road led right to them; and she could be lured into smiling! That must be why Timmy looked at her so strangely. "I have something to do," she murmured, and went back to the dining room. The window there was open; she pulled it down and locked it. She went to the wall control and turned on the air conditioning. "Run, honey, and close the windows," she said. "In your room."

She went into the bedroom, closed the windows there and locked them. Outside there was nothing—smooth lawn, lawn furniture (fire-engine red) grouped casually together, as if the chairs made of tubing and spirals were having a conversation. Annette went into the bathroom, locked that window, avoided her gaze in the mirror, went, at last, into the "sewing room," which faced the road, and stood for a while staring out the window. She had never liked the color of that clay, really—it stretched up from Louisiana to Kentucky, sometimes an astonishing blood-red, pulsating with heat. Now it ran watery in the sunlight at the bend. Nothing there. Annette waited craftily. But still nothing. She felt that, as soon as she turned away, the first black spots would appear—coarse black hair—and the first splashes of color; but she could not wait. There was too much yet to do.

She found Timmy in the living room again, still not sitting in the chair. "I'll be right back, darling," she said. "Stay here. It's too hot outside for you. Put on the television—Mommy will be right back."

She got the clipping shears out of the closet and went outside, still teetering in her high heels. There was no time to waste, no time. The yellow rosebush was farthest away, but most important. She clipped roses off, a generous amount of stem. Though hurried—every few seconds she had to stare down the road—she took time to clip off some leaves as well. Then she went to the red bushes, which now exclaimed at her ignorance: she could see they were more beautiful, really, than the yellow roses. Red more beautiful than yellow; yellow looked common, not stunning enough against the house. It took her perhaps ten minutes, and even then she had to tear her eyes away from the lesser flowers, over there in the circular bed; she did not have time for them—unaccountably she was angry at them, as if they had betrayed her already, grateful to the migrant workers who were coming to tear them to pieces! Their small stupid faces nodded in the hot wind.

Timmy awaited her in the kitchen. He looked surprised at all the roses. "The big vase," she commanded. In a flurry of activity, so pleased by what she was doing that she did not notice the dozens of bleeding scratches on her hands, she laid the roses on the cupboard, clipped at leaves, arranged them, took down a slender copper vase and filled it with water, forced some roses in, abandoned it when Timmy came in with the milk-glass vase (wedding present from a remote aunt of hers). The smell of roses filled the kitchen, sweetly drugged Annette's anxiety. Beauty, beauty—it was necessary to have beauty, to possess it, to keep it around oneself! How well she understood that now.

Finished abruptly, she left the refuse on the cupboard and brought the vases into the living room. She stood back from them, peered critically . . . saw a stain on the wood of the table already; she must have spilled some water. And the roses were not arranged well, too heavy, too many flowers, an insane jumble of flowered faces, some facing each other nose to nose, some staring down toward the water in the vase in an indecent way, some at the ceiling, some at Annette herself. But there was no time to worry over them, already new chores called to her, demanded her services. What should she do next?——

The answer hit her like a blow, how could she be so stupid? The doors
were not even locked! Staggered by this, she ran to the front door,
with trembling fingers locked it. How could she have overlooked
this? Was something in her, some secret corner, conspiring with the
Mexicans down the road? She ran stumbling to the back door—that
had even been left open, it could have been seen from the road! A
few flies buzzed idly, she had no time for them. When she appeared,
panting, in the doorway she saw Timmy by the big white vase trying
to straighten the flowers. . . . "Timmy," she said sharply. "You'll
scratch yourself. Go away, go into the other room, watch television."

He turned at once but did not look at her. She watched him and
felt, then, that it was a mistake to speak that way to him—in fact, a
deliberate error, like forgetting about the doors; might not her child
be separated from her if they came, trapped in the other room? "No,
no, Timmy," she said, reaching out for him—he looked around, frightened—"no, come here. Come here." He came slowly. His eyes showed
trust; his mouth, pursed and tightened, showed wariness, fear of that
trust. Annette saw all this—had she not felt the same way about him,
wishing him dead as soon as he was born?—and flicked it aside, bent
to embrace him. "Darling, I'll take care of you. Here. Sit here. I'll
bring you something to eat."

He allowed her to help him sit at the dining-room table. He was
strangely quiet, his head bowed. There was a surface mystery about
that quietness! Annette thought, in the kitchen, I'll get through
that, I'll prove myself to him. At first cunningly, then anxiously, she
looked through the refrigerator, touching things, rearranging things,
even upsetting things—a jar of pickles—and then came back carrying some strawberry tarts, made just the day before, and the basket
of new strawberries, and some apples. "Here, darling," she said. But
Timmy hesitated; while Annette's own mouth watered painfully he
could only blink in surprise. Impatiently she said, "Here, eat it, eat
them. You love them. *Here.*" "No napkins," Timmy said fearfully.
"Never mind napkins, or a table cloth, or plates," Annette said angrily—how slow her child seemed to her, like one of those empty-faced
children she often saw along the road, country children, staring at her
red car. "Here. Eat it. Eat it." When she turned to go back to the
kitchen she saw him lifting one of the tarts slowly to his mouth.

She came back almost immediately—bringing the package of ice
cream, two spoons, a basket of raspberries, a plate of sliced chicken,
wrapped loosely in wax paper—— She was overcome by hunger. She

pulled a chair beside Timmy, who had not yet eaten—he stared gravely at her—and began to eat one of the tarts. It convulsed her mouth, so delicious was it, so sweet yet at the same time sour, tantalizing; she felt something like love for it, jealousy for it, and was already reaching for another when she caught sight of Timmy's stare. "Won't Daddy be home? Won't we have dinner?" he pleaded.

But he paused. His lips parted moistly and he stared at his mother, who smiled back at him, reassuring him, comforting him, pushing one of the tarts toward him with her polished nails. Then something clicked in his eyes. His lips damp with new saliva, he smiled at her, relieved, pleased. As if a secret ripened to bursting between them, swollen with passion, they smiled at each other. Timmy said, before biting into the tart, "*He* can't hit the car again, it's all locked up." Annette said, gesturing at him with sticky fingers, "Here, darling. Eat this. Eat. *Eat.*"

LEONARD WOLF has published poetry in *The Atlantic, Sewanee,* and *The New Yorker.* He is teaching at San Francisco State College.

Fifty-Fifty

Of love, repeat to yourself that it can only be a disaster; throw in the sponge, give up, back away—quit. Whatever you decide, you will come back to it, with or without advice, and, when you do, there she will be, waiting for you in some place she has no business to be, smiling, looking rueful, already with that expectant look in her eyes while you, who have also lived through various permutations of forgetfulness and taken vows never to see or imagine her again, give up. There's a busy destiny here that doesn't like frayed ends and therefore plaits away, braiding, braiding.

You think it's sex, the bitten lower lip, the profile of the bosom behind the translucent pane of glass where an inexpensive lamp makes a silhouette. I know. Of that and those I know all; but that's not it; not the panting, the haste, the motels, the frantic swiftness in a parked car under a wet oak tree in a corner of a public park; not even the yearning moments in a cornfield under the stars while the flashlights of private detectives moved among the broken stalks, row by row, and missed us. Not the yells of triumph or rage; not, sometimes, the silent weeping.

It has nothing to do with that. That's easy. It happens at 10.00 o'clock on any Monday morning; it happens in the dark or daylight; skinny children do it backstage in the local high school while the principal exhorts the day's assembly.

No. No. No. No. No. No. No.

We're all weary of that, and it isn't the truth. I'm talking about love, the higher cataclysm, the whole shebang.

Watch this: I say, "Put on your coat."

She is in the other room, still combing her hair, and says, "Wait a minute."

I don't need to look at that hair, thick, wavy, forever perfumed

Copyright © 1963 by Kenyon College.

with God knows what—dreadful, lovely. I turn the pages of a book and say, "Okay. But we don't want to get there late."

To which she replies, "We won't be late. Don't rush me."

Without a moment's hesitation, I say, "Who's rushing you?"

I can hear the comb, caught in the hair; the eyes are squinting a little as she looks in her mirror in that small room, too dark for comfort in the tiny squalor where she sleeps. The comb stops, and there are suddenly lines, like the staff of a musical score, waving slowly toward me. Then they turn to wires. Trouble. A living snarl of tons of wire whirling about, surrounding her at her mirror, me at my book.

I don't need to see her put the comb down. She pushes her way as she can through the wire (which has turned barbed as well), clambers into the room where I sit with the book whose title I don't know, and climbs up on the high stool beside the table she made at the Adult Education Center. She made, that is to say, by an ineptitude that wrung sweetly the hearts of instructor, neighbor on the right, neighbor on the left, principal, janitor, rodent in the cellar, cricket on the wall; in short, every creature, male, in the building. Her table was wrought out of such innocence; but, with all that help, made of plywood, rickety, and not a perfect square. She sits precariously at that table and replies to my question: "*You* are rushing me."

To which I say, "Oh, for Christ's sake, forget it. I'm not rushing you." And I reach for that book, knowing that the wires in the room are now going to stay, since one strand has just neatly wound itself around not my skull but the brain proper, the soft cerebrum, cerebellum, medulla oblongata, cortex, and whatever yielding elements there are inside that bone that wire may constrict. And there's a twinge, gentle at first, but it soon gives way to a skillful throbbing.

"That's right," she says; and it's true that her lower lip is delicious; that it does pout; that it is impossible not to think of biting it; but that is not the point. Not now. "That's right," she says. "You're not rushing me."

So I must look up from that book, lifting my head, pushing against the resistance of tons of wire as well as the fine, determined tugging of the strand inside my skull. I look up to see her, dark, small, slim, ready to go, dressed; fresh lipstick, earrings in place; the dewy look of her eyelids (applied, but nonetheless!); and I hear myself getting ready to ask, "What do you mean?" And, lo and behold, I do.

"I'm not going," she says.

And like a logical machine, having received my appropriate coin,

I spit out the appropriate gum ball, this time colored red. "Why not?"

Do you see how it was? The right thing, you might say, was to smack her. Like that: smack, bang. And then to the party or to bed: highhanded and rough. A useful way to deal with a woman. But, remember, I'm talking about love itself.

And, what's more, I did smack her once. And I did the entire prescription. It was a waste of time. She was way ahead of me, betraying the whole psychology—not laughing, but letting me know she knew what page in the book the method came from; calling the shots.

So I didn't smack her, but let her sit on her high chair at her rickety, unsquare table. First we were late to the party to which, of course, we never went. But at least, during that first interval, the party was the myth that buoyed us up; it was the goal of the conversation. If we could only make the idea of the party seem real, we might have a chance to get out of the apartment (her husband was still paying the rent . . . and that's another thing: she was helping me out because I was poor. We split the cost of our evenings, trips, motels, dinners in obscure restaurants. Fifty-fifty. My half; her half. And her half— where do you suppose it came from? He was a stickler for propriety and she was still his wife). As I say, we both thought that, if we could only get back to the idea of the party, we might have a chance. But first she had to maintain her integrity, and I, clutching the book whose title I now remembered (*Love in a Darkling Cavern*), hung onto mine. It all seemed logical.

Our words made the case out that she wouldn't be bullied, on the one hand, and that I wasn't a bully, on the other. Don't imagine that this was a spat, either. It was a reasoned analysis of each other's motivations. You've gathered from what I've already told you that we are both sensitive. She wanted me to understand what was *not* bothering her at the same time as I tried to explain, with the greatest detachment, what seemed to me to be our real motivations.

By this time, night had fallen. The lights along the bridge were turned on. It was that trembling time when they have not yet turned the harsh yellow that they become, but hesitate, a lovely amber-red; and the bay, instead of being a body of water, for half an hour announces itself as clean obsidian. Up and down the hill we could hear the prowl cars moving slowly, whining softly, mewing with their gentlest sirens, like kittens. They were looking for a poor Negro who had murdered a policeman early in the morning. "Hey, you, what are you doing there?" the cop is supposed to have said, and the Negro, doing something in the back seat of an automobile, alone, had leapt in panic from the car and driven a six-inch knife into the cop. We'd watched the helicopters searching for him all afternoon.

I suppose I should say "the poor cop," too. Why more pity for the Negro? I suppose because he was asked; he was the one intruded upon. Isn't the asker always stronger? Isn't he?

I'm sorry the cop died. We knew him—a nice boy, much like the decent folk who helped her make the table. He used, sometimes, to carry up her groceries. It was a long flight of steps from the street to her porch and she was often loaded down. You know, living alone as she did, there was something natural and even, if you like, heart-warming about all that. A kind of Greek chorus of decent men developed around her, showing up at odd times to give her a hand. They all knew about me, but a lover isn't the same as a husband, even if he pays some of the bills. So this nice cop helped her out; and the milkman; even the crazy queer next door who lived with his grandmother; and the groceryman down the hill who called me her "friend." But nobody sniggered. Love has its way of disarming comment.

Night had fallen, and it was clearly too late to get to the party. I made some sort of an attempt to phone the hostess—that is, the idea occurred to me, but by then we were up to our skulls in wire and accusations. The book became part of it all. It turned out to be a library book I had forgotten to return for her—its author a sometime friend of mine who had blown into town for a brief visit. A clever young man with lots of books under his belt, and something of a gift. Garrulous and, in his own way, brave. The women reviewers praised his understanding of their sex; the men preferred his style and called it swift, lean, alert. He traveled widely and liked to set his stories in exotic lands. He was still young and wanted to do the talking.

I rather liked him, and brought him around; though liked is a stronger word than I would use if this were fifty years ago. We got along; he was famous; I wasn't . . . there was a kind of swinging interchange between us—friendly, anxious, contemptuous, condescending, and a small bit of respect on both sides. He was rich, and when he came to town usually needed a woman. On occasion, I had done some genteel pandering for him—the usual thing: one of that new breed of employed, clever women with some ambition in the arts who read the latest books and will lie down for literate, sufficient reasons for young men much farther out on the fringes of fame than, for instance, even I was.

A sprightly, vivacious girl. We went out, the four of us, to various places where we could be aloof and bitter and amused while we waited to be rid of each other, to get back to whatever caverns, dens, shacks where they could be simple and quick and we would manage our complex affairs till dawn.

Though even for them it probably turned out not as simple as he would say. The girl came from a terribly respectable Cincinnati family and made her living as the naked swimmer in Bimbo's fishbowl. It's a nice stunt that sets the tourists off. You sit around the bar and drink and wait for the floorshow to begin; it's pleasant and wistful, when you haven't got a girl, or if you have and are not yet warm enough together; so, with your drink in your hand, you watch this mirror panorama—like looking through the portholes of a miniature Beebe diving bell. The effect *is* a little like being under water, and all of a sudden a naked girl appears, evidently swimming. Six inches from crown to toe, swimming, swimming, being very careful of her thighs, or else she breaks the law. Of course, it's all done with mirrors, and everybody except the worst of the yokels knows it. It comes on every hour, and a public intimacy grows, part shame, part bravado, a very small part lust. A roomful of peeping toms peeping also at each other. Respectable Cincinnati family or not, from end to end she looked quite good. The whole act lasts four minutes, and for a girl with ambitions in the theatre, who spent the intervals between appearances reading *Doctor Zhivago*, it was an easy way to make a living (though later the whole thing tumbled down on her head when her uncle, attending a medical convention, caught the act and wired the bad news home. They shipped her off to a psychiatrist—which is one more indication of what has happened to the idea of free will in our time). Lovely shoulders; under glass, her breasts looked better than they were.

Well, I've gone the long way around to make the point that, while the police were driving up and down our hill looking for that poor damned Negro and we were tangled in our wire maze and I was holding onto the book I had failed to take back to the library, it occurred to me at last that her sudden interest in his fiction was more than literary and less than pure. You know how a bubble can burst in the brain, and suddenly you have knowledge. But I resisted. I said to myself, "Hell, that's an unworthy suspicion." Then I remembered the Greek chorus of helpful men, and her fierce protection of her privacy. I didn't live there, you know. And I was never supposed to come without telephoning. When, on some of our angry days, I did, she just damn' well didn't let me in. I had no evidence there was anyone with her, and as things turned out I never did, then or later; still, some suspicions become facts whether they can be proved or no.

On the whole, I behaved honorably; I never taxed her. The one thing I never did was spy on her.

We continued to quarrel about the book. I said, with some violence, that my not returning it was a trivial oversight, to which she replied that it was like me to be so petty as to subject her to a daily fine of two cents out of pique with her pleasure in a writer of better (or wider—which word did she use?) reputation than my own. By this time, the room felt as if it existed on a tilted floor; tilted a full forty-five degrees, like the crazy floors in the house in San Jose that the lunatic built who was afraid to die. At the upper end, she sat on her high stool, accusing me in her hushed voice; at the lower end I sat, not quite so calmly, and replied.

At last, she said, "I'm tired. I don't want to talk anymore. It's no use."

And I said, "Come sit here. Let's not go on with this."

"That's always your way, isn't it? Put me on a couch so you can use me. It's disgusting."

But it wasn't. Sometimes the simplest touch could turn her on, and, when she was, it seemed to me that everything but that was mad. During those wild moments, each of us believed—I swear—that we could build a life on that. On that alone. Oh, the Lawrentian dreamers. The function of the orgasm is not fulfillment, but release. Do you hear? Does anyone hear?

After one of those beautiful weekends evading her husband's private detectives (fools, by the way: we weren't hiding anything. Everyone in town, including the most widely read gossip columnist, knew about us; but her husband had a New England conscience and wanted, in all things, to be thorough; as he figured it, what was generally known was not necessarily courtroom evidence) . . . The detectives, as I say, were fools, and we evaded them as a sort of game: to see if we could, to add the touch of humor that we both felt was missing in our affair. What oafs they were; eyeing us out of jealous, greasy eyes; scratching at a crotch mournfully in lonely hotel lobbies as we, clean, bathed, slept out, spent, passed them by. One knew, always, what they were imagining; both more and less than the truth. Fat men; fat men; so lonely they were available for following. After one of those beautiful weekends, as I started to say, we were driving north along the coast in her car (mine didn't have a spare tire—it was being retreaded and I'd forgot to get it back before the weekend was on us). It was late afternoon and spring, with the sun not brilliant —calm over the water and shimmering out at sea; inshore, the waves were breaking. Not angrily, but with a friendly, spent motion, curling and dissipating whitely in toward shore. From time to time, as we rounded a curve, we looked north and saw the cliffs where the land broke finally, perhaps a little brusquely, but without accusation on this sunny day. We passed rare, weatherbeaten ranchhouses; aging horses in clusters browsing among furze and heather, content and waiting to die in the ocean-and-broom-scented air. Sometimes, to the left, a few hundred yards offshore, there would rise the kind of hunk of island that looks as if it has been yanked away from the land, standing there, tall as the plateau on which we were driving, but separated now by quiet water which could, I knew, rage in the gap between. Worn with love-making and the gentle ending of the day, the car quiet, humming, the spring air flowing through the windows, bringing us the scent the horses breathed, we were quiet and, you would have thought, perfectly at peace.

And so I said of one of them, "Isn't that a fine island?"

She took her hand from mine. We were getting closer to it, and I could see three cypresses on top and the rank broom in yellow flower all along the top. "What a great place," I said.

To which she replied, "Why do you always want to own everything? Can't you just let it be? Why must you want it for yourself?"

She was so bitter that I knew she'd guessed what I hadn't, this time, said—that I imagined building a cabin on that island. Moving to it with my typewriter and my imagination; secluding myself where I could watch the ocean every morning, every night. That I wanted to be there in the winter storms when the waves came so high they pounded the windows of my invented cabin; that I had already figured out a way of getting water to the island by means of hanging pipes that would, somehow, be led to a perpetual spring on shore. That I wanted to grow old there (or in any of the scores of other such places I had had this yearning for) while I picked out of the surge of language and the sea the shape of all creation.

I felt my chest grow empty while my hands handled the wheel; we made our way around curves at forty miles an hour, and the sun slipped steadily downward. Some kind of important reply wanted to come up out of that hollow place; it should be witty or deft or scathing or cruel or like a knotted rope pulled through the heart. But a bee flew into the car and, bewildered by the glass and steel, could not find its way out. It circled, humming its minor anger round our heads. She panicked, and I stepped on the gas. The swift burst of air produced by the speed dizzied the bee or frightened it; the buzzing quickened and it flew more fiercely round and round.

"For God's sake, stop the car!" she cried as I twice veered, first right, then left.

"Don't be absurd," I answered. "Sit still. It'll fly out." I waved my hand slowly toward the bee, which merely increased its unhappy buzzing.

"Stop the car," she demanded, cowering to her side of the seat, her hands to her hair.

I said, "Just relax. There's nothing to worry about." I couldn't bring myself to obey her. There was something here; something important. The honey-laden animal held to its murmuring rage, swooping in the closed space like a tiny pursuit plane—and I could not stop the car. It had to leave as it came; it was not to shame me before her; it had to stand for the witty, the deft, the scathing, the cruel reply I had not made. An ordinary honeybee, now miles from home, trying to see the world out of its compound eyes, bumping at glass and steel and an insane dimension of speed. What must it have thought?

She bent far forward, as if she meant to be sick. Her voice came flat and low; her hands were spread over her ears and hair, her elbows meeting over her chest. "It's my car," she said. "Stop it."

And that was that. I stopped the car. I got out and so did she. In a minute, the bee also found its way out, lifted into the air, made two or three circles, and started back over the hopeless miles where, I suppose, it passed the tired detectives driving through the dusk in their rented Chevrolet, munching their cold chicken sandwiches, staring ahead in the falling dark toward love.

Past 9.00 o'clock, she was still sitting at her rickety table. Neither of us had thought to turn on a light. Our anger was going on and on, perfectly content not to be seen. Without meaning to, I'd begun to tear small corner strips from the pages of my friend's book. A shaft of moonlight, coming through her street window, fell diagonally across the room, dividing her neatly from me. The whiteness lay between us, cool, inert; it seemed to me that we would soon resemble a painting by Pieter de Hooch, though there was no checkerboard tile floor, no butter churn, no grieving picture on the wall.

There was a knock at the door, and I answered it. She only leaned against the wall; her backless stool was hard to sit on, but she wouldn't move. It was a policeman, carrying a flashlight.

"Would you folks mind turning on your porch light?" he asked. "That nigger's sure to be in one of these blocks. We're trying to cut down the places he can hide." He said no word about the obscurity in which we sat. I turned on the porch light; he thanked me and left, looking scared.

When I turned back to her, she was gone, evidently to the bedroom. I went to my corner of the couch; with the porch light on, I could now see well enough to read, and I glanced down at a page in the book my friend had written. I read, "She seduced me quite openly, almost avariciously; and, at the same time, as if she hardly noticed me. I was standing on a ladder adjusting a water bottle over the cage of a family of mice when she looked up at me, a fine glaze of impersonality across her eyes, and said, 'Come down off that ladder.' I came down and lost my virginity in a roomful of mice, behind a locked door, while in forty-seven cages hundreds of rodents rustled and tittered on their shelves.

"From then, it is not as if she taught me all I know, but for a few months, on river banks, in hayfields, behind fences, beside the stadium—everywhere, indeed, except a common bed—she emphasized the single advantage that we have in youth. On really cold nights, she taught me that it is better to love than to freeze.

"But I did not want anything from her. I hardly called her by name, and she merely gritted her teeth at the familiar moment and cried out once, after which she wanted nothing more than her delicious sleep."

It seemed to me that "it is better to love than to freeze" was a good line, but not nearly good enough to support the sudden reputation that had come to my friend recently. As for the rest, wasn't it really rather empty?

She came back into the room and resumed her seat. "Aren't you hungry?" I asked her.

"No," she said, smiling wolfishly. "Wolfish" is the right word, too. That beautiful, oval face, now touched by the light that came into the room from the porch, simply opened into a smile that had neither love nor humor in it. It came to me that she was frightened . . . triumphant and frightened.

"What have you done?" I asked.

"What do you care?" She had her hands folded in her lap, her shoulders slumped forward.

"What have you done?" I demanded.

"It isn't polite to ask a lady, but, if you must know, I've been to the bathroom." It was a wretched reply; indelicate; not like her.

"No," I said. "That's not what you've done." The secret hung between us; I was already beginning to guess—pushed along by that wolf-like smile, the hysterical contentment, the grim happiness of her folded hands.

Urgently, wearily, she whispered, "What do you care?" And, again, "What do you care? All you've done all evening is grind and grind at me. Why don't you go home and let me sleep?"

"Are you sleepy?" I said, catching the clue.

"No, but I will be."

"What does that mean?"

"Nothing. Nothing." She leaned her back and shoulders heavily against the wall, letting her eyes open to their fullest—wide, dark, at moments so plunged in melancholy I would have died to take that sorrow from her; now, so wide and glittering; expanded with her secret; joyful, and instinct with harm.

"Have you taken a sleeping pill?"

"Five," she replied.

I got to my feet. "Goddamn it. For God's sake, what are you trying to do?"

"I want you to go home," she said.

"I can't go home now," I shouted.

"Why not? You could go home and let me sleep. You could go away. You could go to a show. You could go to the party. I'm tired. I've been tired. I told you a long time ago I was tired. Go home."

"Did you really take five tablets?"

"Yes. I want to sleep."

"Come on," I said. "I'll get your coat. I'm taking you to the hospital."

"I won't go," she whispered. "No, I won't go."

I put my hand on her shoulder; that thin shoulder—I could feel the fragile collarbone under my fingers, my thumb on the delicate skin at her throat, feeling her pulse throbbing. "Come *on*," I said. "Come on."

I let her go and found her coat.

"I won't go. This is my house. Go away. Why won't you go away? Why must you sit here and torment me? Couldn't you have gone away long ago?" The words came low and secret, spoken to the darkest corners of the room.

"I can't go away. I love you."

"If you love me, you'll go away and let me sleep."

"Have you taken five sleeping tablets?"

"Do I ever lie to you?"

I answered truthfully, "Never." But she didn't need to lie; whenever she wanted to keep something from me, she simply said nothing, or ruled the question out of order. If I asked her about my friend, for instance, she would say that if I trusted her I had no right to ask; and if I didn't trust her—what was the point of our relationship? And that was true, too.

"Five?" I said, expecting God knows what reply.

"Yes. But I don't want to go to the hospital. I don't need to."

That sounded reasonable. "All right," I said. I hung her coat back up. From the couch, I telephoned the emergency department at the local hospital, where I explained to an intern that my wife had accidently taken five sleeping pills. I wanted to know what to do.

"Five isn't deadly," he said, "but you really ought to bring her in, anyhow."

"Suppose she won't come in?" It was hard to remember that the telephone was anonymous; he couldn't know her or me.

"Don't ask her, Mac. Bring her."

I shivered. "She won't come. What can I do at home?"

"My best advice is to watch her closely; but it would be better if she came in. What's the address where you are?"

I hung up, wondering if he would trace the call. She had her head in her hands and was already getting drowsy. I stood beside her and stroked her hair because she did not resist. I asked, "Will you have some black coffee?"

"No," she said.

"Why did you do it?"

Without anger, she said, "I don't know. I just got tired . . ."

"Come with me." I lifted her off the chair and crossed the ray of moonlight, taking her with me to the couch where I sat at one end,

her head in my lap. I stroked her forehead; a little later, I loosened
her clothes when I felt her beginning to relax.

For a while, she lay with her eyes open, staring across the room at
the stool from which I had carried her. I felt her body grow warm as
the sleepiness spread, and I leaned down to kiss her. "Do you think
they'll catch the boy?" she wanted to know.

I looked out across the lighted porch. The bridge lights were burning brightly and the late night traffic was sweeping back and forth. "I
don't know," I answered. "I suppose they will." I felt the stiffness, the
resentment passing out of her body as the drug took over. Again, I
bent to kiss her, and her lips parted, ever so gently, to mine. She was
already drifting away. The weight of her head and shoulders in my
lap was marvelous. I felt that we were dreaming lovers. Very carefully,
I held her head while I got up from the couch and bent to gather her
in my arms so I could cradle her completely. She whispered in my
ear, "Why do you always have to move; why can't we just be?" But
her sleep muffled the complaint, and I sat down with her in my arms.

I could see the flashlights of the policemen as they quartered the
hillside hunting for their murderer. I put my head to her cheek, to her
hair. From time to time, I put soft kisses on her lips or touched her
throat. Sometimes, I touched her body, but without desire, moving
her limbs, touching her side, her shoulders, smoothing her forehead,
holding her waist. She lay in my arms, utterly asleep. I had her and I
breathed her breath.

The moonlight crossing the coffee table caught the random pattern
of the page corners I had torn out of my friend's weak book. The
trouble was, he had insufficient needs; they could be satisfied. The
insufficiency and satisfaction crept into his book, rendering it thin. A
brief seduction in a roomful of mice; a pathetic, stage-struck girl who
kept her thighs closed not to break the law as she pretended to paddle
about in an imitation sea: his world. A world without disaster.

I had her; held her; rocked her in my arms. Toward midnight, there
were shots, but I didn't bother to turn out the light. It kept the shad-
ows from the porch till dawn.

CARSON McCULLERS is the author of many distinguished books and plays, including *The Heart Is a Lonely Hunter, Member of the Wedding, Ballad of the Sad Cafe, Square Root of Wonderful,* and *Clock Without Hands.* She is a fellow of the American Academy of Arts and Letters.

Sucker

It was always like I had a room to myself. Sucker slept in my bed with me but that didn't interfere with anything. The room was mine and I used it as I wanted to. Once I remember sawing a trap door in the floor. Last year when I was a sophomore in high school I tacked on my wall some pictures of girls from magazines and one of them was just in her underwear. My mother never bothered me because she had the younger kids to look after. And Sucker thought anything I did was always swell.

Whenever I would bring any of my friends back to my room all I had to do was just glance once at Sucker and he would get up from whatever he was busy with and maybe half smile at me, and leave without saying a word. He never brought kids back there. He's twelve, four years younger than I am, and he always knew without me even telling him that I didn't want kids that age meddling with my things.

Half the time I used to forget that Sucker isn't my brother. He's my first cousin but practically ever since I remember he's been in our family. You see his folks were killed in a wreck when he was a baby. To me and my kid sisters he was like our brother.

Sucker used to always remember and believe every word I said. That's how he got his nick-name. Once a couple of years ago I told him that if he'd jump off our garage with an umbrella it would act as a parachute and he wouldn't fall hard. He did it and busted his knee. That's just one instance. And the funny thing was that no matter how many times he got fooled he would still believe me. Not

Copyright © 1963 by Carson McCullers. By permission of Robert Lantz Ltd.

that he was dumb in other ways—it was just the way he acted with me. He would look at everything I did and quietly take it in.

There is one thing I have learned, but it makes me feel guilty and hard to figure out. If a person admires you a lot you despise him and don't care—and it is the person who doesn't notice you that you are apt to admire. This is not easy to realize. Maybelle Watts, this senior at school, acted like she was the Queen of Sheba and even humiliated me. Yet at this same time I would have done anything in the world to get her attentions. All I could think about day and night was Maybelle until I was nearly crazy. When Sucker was a little kid and on up until the time he was twelve I guess I treated him as bad as Maybelle did me.

Now that Sucker has changed so much it is a little hard to remember him as he used to be. I never imagined anything would suddenly happen that would make us both very different. I never knew that in order to get what has happened straight in my mind I would want to think back on him as he used to be and compare and try to get things settled. If I could have seen ahead maybe I would have acted different.

I never noticed him much or thought about him and when you consider how long we have had the same room together it is funny the few things I remember. He used to talk to himself a lot when he'd think he was alone—all about him fighting gangsters and being on ranches and that sort of kids' stuff. He'd get in the bathroom and stay as long as an hour and sometimes his voice would go up high and excited and you could hear him all over the house. Usually, though, he was very quiet. He didn't have many boys in the neighborhood to buddy with and his face had the look of a kid who is watching a game and waiting to be asked to play. He didn't mind wearing the sweaters and coats that I outgrew, even if the sleeves did flop down too big and make his wrists look as thin and white as a little girl's. That is how I remember him—getting a little bigger every year but still being the same. That was Sucker up until a few months ago when all this trouble began.

Maybelle was somehow mixed up in what happened so I guess I ought to start with her. Until I knew her I hadn't given much time to girls. Last fall she sat next to me in General Science class and that was when I first began to notice her. Her hair is the brightest yellow I ever saw and occasionally she will wear it set into curls with some sort of gluey stuff. Her fingernails are pointed and manicured and painted a shiny red. All during class I used to watch Maybelle, nearly all the time except when I thought she was going to look my way or when the teacher called on me. I couldn't keep my eyes off her hands, for one thing. They are very little and white except for that red stuff, and when she would turn the pages of her book she always licked her thumb and held out her little finger and turned very slowly. It is impossible to describe Maybelle. All the boys are crazy about her but she didn't even notice me. All I could do was sit and look at her in class—and sometimes it was like the whole room could hear my heart beating and I wanted to holler or light out and run for Hell.

At night, in bed, I would imagine about Maybelle. Often this would keep me from sleeping until as late as one or two o'clock. Sometimes Sucker would wake up and ask me why I couldn't get settled and I'd tell him hush his mouth. I suppose I was mean to him lots of times. I guess I wanted to ignore somebody like Maybelle did me. You could always tell by Sucker's face when his feelings were hurt. I don't remember all the ugly remarks I must have made because even when I was saying them my mind was on Maybelle.

That went on for nearly three months and then somehow she began to change. In the halls she would speak to me and every morning she copied my homework. At lunch time once I danced with her in the gym. One afternoon I got up nerve and went around to her house with a carton of cigarettes. I knew she smoked in the girls' basement and sometimes outside of school—and I didn't want to take her candy because I think that's been run into the ground. She was very nice and it seemed to me everything was going to change.

It was that night when this trouble really started. I had come into my room late and Sucker was already asleep. I felt too happy and keyed up to get in a comfortable position and I was awake thinking about Maybelle a long time. Then I dreamed about her and it seemed I kissed her. It was a surprise to wake up and see the dark. I lay still and a little while passed before I could come to and understand where I was. The house was quiet and it was a very dark night.

Sucker's voice was a shock to me. "Pete? . . ."

I didn't answer anything or even move.

"You do like me as much as if I was your own brother, don't you Pete?"

I couldn't get over the surprise of everything and it was like this was the real dream instead of the other.

"You have liked me all the time like I was your own brother, haven't you?"

"Sure," I said.

Then I got up for a few minutes. It was cold and I was glad to come back to bed. Sucker hung on to my back. He felt little and warm and I could feel his warm breathing on my shoulder.

"No matter what you did I always knew you liked me."

I was wide awake and my mind seemed mixed up in a strange way. There was this happiness about Maybelle and all that—but at the same time something about Sucker and his voice when he said these things made me take notice. Anyway I guess you understand people better when you are happy than when something is worrying you. It was like I had never really thought about Sucker until then. I felt I had always been mean to him. One night a few weeks before I had heard him crying in the dark. He said he had lost a boy's beebee gun and was scared to let anybody know. He wanted me to tell him what to do. I was sleepy and tried to make him hush and when he wouldn't I kicked at him. That was just one of the things I remembered. It seemed to me he had always been a lonesome kid. I felt bad.

There is something about a dark cold night that makes you feel close to someone you're sleeping with. When you talk together it is like you are the only people awake in the town.

"You're a swell kid, Sucker," I said.

It seemed to me suddenly that I did like him more than anybody else I knew—more than any other boy, more than my sisters, more in a certain way even than Maybelle. I felt good all over and it was like when they play sad music in the movies. I wanted to show Sucker how much I really thought of him and make up for the way I had always treated him.

We talked for a good while that night. His voice was fast and it was like he had been saving up these things to tell me for a long time. He mentioned that he was going to try to build a canoe and that the kids down the block wouldn't let him in on their football team and I don't know what all. I talked some too and it was a good feeling to think of him taking in everything I said so seriously. I even spoke of Maybelle a little, only I made out like it was her who had been running after me all this time. He asked questions about high school and so forth. His voice was excited and he kept on talking fast like he could never get the words out in time. When I went to sleep he was still talking and I could still feel his breathing on my shoulder, warm and close.

During the next couple of weeks I saw a lot of Maybelle. She acted as though she really cared for me a little. Half the time I felt so good I hardly knew what to do with myself.

But I didn't forget about Sucker. There were a lot of old things in my bureau drawer I'd been saving—boxing gloves and Tom Swift books and second rate fishing tackle. All this I turned over to him. We had some more talks together and it was really like I was knowing him for the first time. When there was a long cut on his cheek I knew he had been monkeying around with this new first razor set of mine, but I didn't say anything. His face seemed different now. He used to look timid and sort of like he was afraid of a whack over the head. That expression was gone. His face, with those wide-open eyes and his ears sticking out and his mouth never quite shut, had the look of a person who is surprised and expecting something swell.

Once I started to point him out to Maybelle and tell her he was my kid brother. It was an afternoon when a murder mystery was on at the movie. I had earned a dollar working for my Dad and I gave Sucker a quarter to go and get candy and so forth. With the rest I took Maybelle. We were sitting near the back and I saw Sucker come in. He began to stare at the screen the minute he stepped past the ticket man and he stumbled down the aisle without noticing where he was going. I started to punch Maybelle but couldn't quite make up my mind. Sucker looked a little silly—walking like a drunk with his eyes glued to the movie. He was wiping his reading glasses on his shirt tail and his knickers flopped down. He went on until he got to the first few rows where the kids usually sit. I never did punch Maybelle. But I got to thinking it was good to have both of them at the movie with the money I earned.

I guess things went on like this for about a month or six weeks. I felt so good I couldn't settle down to study or put my mind on anything. I wanted to be friendly with everybody. There were times when I just had to talk to some person. And usually that would be Sucker. He felt as good as I did. Once he said: "Pete, I am gladder that you are like my brother than anything else in the world."

Then something happened between Maybelle and me. I never have figured out just what it was. Girls like her are hard to understand. She began to act different toward me. At first I wouldn't let myself believe this and tried to think it was just my imagination. She didn't act glad to see me any more. Often she went out riding with this fellow on the football team who owns this yellow roadster. The car was the color of her hair and after school she would ride off with him, laughing and looking into his face. I couldn't think of anything to do about it and she was on my mind all day and night. When I did get a chance to go out with her she was snippy and didn't seem to notice me. This made me feel like something was the matter—I would worry about my shoes clopping too loud on the floor, or the fly of my pants, or the bumps on my chin. Sometimes when Maybelle was around, a devil would get into me and I'd hold my face stiff and call grown men by their last names without the Mister and say rough things. In the night I would wonder what made me do all this until I was too tired for sleep.

At first I was so worried I just forgot about Sucker. Then later he began to get on my nerves. He was always hanging around until I would get back from high school, always looking like he had something to say to me or wanted me to tell him. He made me a magazine rack in his Manual Training class and one week he saved his lunch money and bought me three packs of cigarettes. He couldn't seem to take it in that I had things on my mind and didn't want to fool with him. Every afternoon it would be the same—him in my room with this waiting expression on his face. Then I wouldn't say anything or I'd maybe answer him rough-like and he would finally go on out.

I can't divide that time up and say this happened one day and that the next. For one thing I was so mixed up the weeks just slid along into each other and I felt like Hell and didn't care. Nothing definite was said or done. Maybelle still rode around with this fellow in his yellow roadster and sometimes she would smile at me and sometimes not. Every afternoon I went from one place to another where I thought she would be. Either she would act almost nice and I would begin thinking how things would finally clear up and she would care for me—or else she'd behave so that if she hadn't been a girl I'd have wanted to grab her by that white little neck and choke her. The more ashamed I felt for making a fool of myself the more I ran after her.

Sucker kept getting on my nerves more and more. He would look at me as though he sort of blamed me for something, but at the same time knew that it wouldn't last long. He was growing fast and for some reason began to stutter when he talked. Sometimes he had nightmares or would throw up his breakfast. Mom got him a bottle of cod liver oil.

Then the finish came between Maybelle and me. I met her going to the drug store and asked for a date. When she said no I remarked something sarcastic. She told me she was sick and tired of my being around and that she had never cared a rap about me. She said all that. I just stood there and didn't answer anything. I walked home very slowly.

For several afternoons I stayed in my room by myself. I didn't want to go anywhere or talk to anyone. When Sucker would come in and look at me sort of funny I'd yell at him to get out. I didn't want to think of Maybelle and I sat at my desk reading *Popular Mechanics* or whittling at a toothbrush rack I was making. It seemed to me I was putting that girl out of my mind pretty well.

But you can't help what happens to you at night. That is what made things how they are now.

You see a few nights after Maybelle said those words to me I dreamed about her again. It was like that first time and I was squeezing Sucker's arm so tight I woke him up. He reached for my hand.

"Pete, what's the matter with you?"

All of a sudden I felt so mad my throat choked—at myself and the dream and Maybelle and Sucker and every single person I knew. I remembered all the times Maybelle had humiliated me and everything bad that had ever happened. It seemed to me for a second that nobody would ever like me but a sap like Sucker.

"Why is it we aren't buddies like we were before? Why—?"

"Shut your damn trap!" I threw off the cover and got up and turned on the light. He sat in the middle of the bed, his eyes blinking and scared.

There was something in me and I couldn't help myself. I don't think anybody ever gets that mad but once. Words came without me knowing what they would be. It was only afterward that I could remember each thing I said and see it all in a clear way.

"Why aren't we buddies? Because you're the dumbest slob I ever saw! Nobody cares anything about you! And just because I felt sorry for you sometimes and tried to act decent don't think I give a damn about a dumb-bunny like you!"

If I'd talked loud or hit him it wouldn't have been so bad. But my voice was slow and like I was very calm. Sucker's mouth was part way open and he looked as though he'd knocked his funny bone. His face was white and sweat came out on his forehead. He wiped it away with the back of his hand and for a minute his arm stayed raised that way as though he was holding something away from him.

"Don't you know a single thing? Haven't you ever been around at all? Why don't you get a girl friend instead of me? What kind of a sissy do you want to grow up to be anyway?"

I didn't know what was coming next. I couldn't help myself or think.

Sucker didn't move. He had on one of my pajama jackets and his neck stuck out skinny and small. His hair was damp on his forehead.

"Why do you always hang around me? Don't you know when you're not wanted?"

Afterward I could remember the change in Sucker's face. Slowly that blank look went away and he closed his mouth. His eyes got narrow and his fists shut. There had never been such a look on him before. It was like every second he was getting older. There was a hard look to his eyes you don't see usually in a kid. A drop of sweat rolled down his chin and he didn't notice. He just sat there with those eyes on me and he didn't speak and his face was hard and didn't move.

"No you don't know when you're not wanted. You're too dumb. Just like your name—a dumb Sucker."

It was like something had busted inside me. I turned off the light and sat down in the chair by the window. My legs were shaking and I was so tired I could have bawled. The room was cold and dark. I sat there for a long time and smoked a squashed cigarette I had saved. Outside the yard was black and quiet. After a while I heard Sucker lie down.

I wasn't mad any more, only tired. It seemed awful to me that I had talked like that to a kid only twelve. I couldn't take it all in. I told myself I would go over to him and try to make it up. But I just sat there in the cold until a long time had passed. I planned how I could straighten it out in the morning. Then, trying not to squeak the springs, I got back in bed.

Sucker was gone when I woke up the next day. And later when I wanted to apologize as I had planned he looked at me in this new hard way so that I couldn't say a word.

All of that was two or three months ago. Since then Sucker has grown faster than any boy I ever saw. He's almost as tall as I am and his bones have gotten heavier and bigger. He won't wear any of my

old clothes any more and has bought his first pair of long pants—
with some leather suspenders to hold them up. Those are just the
changes that are easy to see and put into words.

Our room isn't mine at all any more. He's gotten up this gang of
kids and they have a club. When they aren't digging trenches in
some vacant lot and fighting they are always in my room. On the door
there is some foolishness written in Mercurochrome saying "Woe
to the Outsider who Enters" and signed with crossed bones and their
secret initials. They have rigged up a radio and every afternoon it
blares out music. Once as I was coming in I heard a boy telling
something in a low voice about what he saw in the back of his big
brother's automobile. I could guess what I didn't hear. *That's what
her and my brother do. It's the truth—parked in the car.* For a minute
Sucker looked surprised and his face was almost like it used to be.
Then he got hard and tough again. "Sure, dumbell. We know all
that." They didn't notice me. Sucker began telling them how in two
years he was planning to be a trapper in Alaska.

But most of the time Sucker stays by himself. It is worse when
we are alone together in the room. He sprawls across the bed in
those long corduroy pants with the suspenders and just stares at me
with that hard, half sneering look. I fiddle around my desk and
can't get settled because of those eyes of his. And the thing is I
just have to study because I've gotten three bad cards this term already. If I flunk English I can't graduate next year. I don't want to
be a bum and I just have to get my mind on it. I don't care a flip for
Maybelle or any particular girl any more and it's only this thing
between Sucker and me that is the trouble now. We never speak
except when we have to before the family. I don't even want to call
him Sucker any more and unless I forget I call him by his real name,
Richard. At night I can't study with him in the room and I have to
hang around the drug store, smoking and doing nothing, with the
fellows who loaf there.

More than anything I want to be easy in my mind again. And I
miss the way Sucker and I were for a while in a funny, sad way that
before this I never would have believed. But everything is so different
that there seems to be nothing I can do to get it right. I've sometimes thought if we could have it out in a big fight that would help.
But I can't fight him because he's four years younger. And another
thing—sometimes this look in his eyes makes me almost believe that
if Sucker could he would kill me.

DANIEL CURLEY has published one volume of stories, *That Marriage Bed of Procrustes*, 1957, and two novels, *How Many Angels?*, 1958, and *A Stone Man, Yes*, 1964. He was a Guggenheim Fellow in 1958. Since 1955 he has been on the staff of the University of Illinois where he was also one of the editors of *Accent*.

Love in the Winter

Look," Ross Taylor said, when at last Grace Martin was really in his car, "instead of dropping off at the station, why don't you ride overland with me as far as Albany or Syracuse and take your train on from there?" He hesitated, appalled at the traps opening out of the simplest words. "The Berkshires will be worth seeing in all this snow, the Mohawk Trail, the Taconic Trail and all," he concluded lamely. He was glad to have got out of that corner without basing his appeal on some assumption either of his overwhelming personal magnetism or of his pathetic loneliness. (It will make the trip more pleasant for you/for me/for both of us.)

"I was hoping you'd say something like that," Grace said. Taylor had been writing the dialogue in his head for the past three days, ever since they agreed it would be convenient for Grace to drive to the station with him when he left to go back to Chicago. He had written that very speech for her, in fact, but now that he actually heard her speaking it, he felt like a vast jellyfish from his throat to his hips.

There was a lot he was supposed to say now, but he forgot it all. "Good," he said, "good." Fortunately Grace had a great many things to say about sending a telegram to excuse her change of plans, and he had to make a great many replies that didn't need thinking about.

So shaken was he, however, by the success of his opening move and even more by his audacity in making it all that he found himself unable to concentrate on the next moves in his campaign. His mind jumped from one irrelevancy to another, but kept returning to simple wonder that she was there at all.

Copyright © 1964 by The University of Colorado, Boulder, Colorado.

Why, four days ago, before he had even met her, he despised her. It wasn't enough that she was to be in the Harris' guest room so that he would have to bed down in the study. No, indeed, she had to be a dean of women on top of that, and Taylor was full of the traditional academic contempt for administrators. Of course, he hadn't had much to do with deans of women in recent years, but he remembered the breed well from his days as a young instructor jumping from hick school to hick school. Probably the one where she was dean was just like the lot of them.

His first look at her had shaken him, but he steadied himself while he took off his coat and greeted the Harrises, watching her all the while. She didn't look like a dean of women. That was hard to forgive. In fact, she didn't look like an old school chum of Jean Harris. Obviously, as a spinster dean, she had been able to take care of herself. He compared her quickly with Jean, who was iron gray and almost a nervous wreck, and with his own wife, who was now built like the Hollywood version of a Russian lady truck driver. As he moved closer, he saw that she had black hair and light eyes, a combination that never failed to move him profoundly. He was profoundly moved and despised her the more bitterly for it.

By the time the house had quieted down, however, and he lay on the couch in the study (it was really very comfortable) enjoying a last cigarette, he had so far changed his mind that he was wondering what would happen if tomorrow he found an opportunity to make her one of the vile proposals that had been running through his mind all evening from the very moment they shook hands and their eyes met and she opened with something other than the standard dean of women's gambit: "We'll get along fine—after all we're in the same game." He had been ready for that, but it didn't come, and he soon realized that she was quite incapable of it. At the same time, she was only politely interested in how his paper had gone at the Modern Languages convention that day and didn't pretend ever to have heard of the Finnesburh Fragment or any problems connected with it. She didn't even pretend to be interested. All this without leaving the least doubt that she was very much interested in him.

Before he finally fell asleep that night, he even went so far as to wonder what would happen if he had the courage then and there to pad on bare feet through the dark house and quietly try the knob of the guest room door. He told himself that he read too many dirty books. He reminded himself of the sanctity of his host's house. He reminded himself of his wife and children. He assured himself that he wasn't that kind of man. In short, he did nothing, neither that night nor the two following nights.

Each day he assured himself that he would make a move if he again caught that look that seemed to enter him like an enormous jolt of neat whiskey and explode into fire inside him. Each day he caught the look but did nothing. Well, not exactly nothing. He did check train and plane schedules and find that if she would agree to give up going by way of New York for the sake of seeing some old friends for a few hours between trains, and if she would agree to drive with him as far as Albany, they could manage a night in Albany if she would agree to that. He had it all worked out, but he didn't believe for a minute that he would ever be able to ask her.

And now it was done. They were actually driving together through the snow across Massachusetts. Of course there were still uncertainties, but if he was careful everything would lead where he wanted to go. His heart pounded at the mere idea of closing a hotel room door on himself and a strange woman. Unfortunately he could see only as far as that gesture, and he had no idea what came next. It was like a honeymoon, of course, but he had never had a honeymoon. How do people get over those first minutes alone? How long or how short is it before you can say, For God's sake, let's get to bed? Probably, since they would both know why they were there, it would work out all right, but in his imagination he remained all night with his hand on the doorknob.

With his wife he had never had to confront that problem. It had already been taken care of before they were even introduced. They had waked up in bed together after a party, very publicly compromised. In fact, it was their host's pounding on the bedroom door that awoke them. Their host and hostess had not slept well on the living room couches and were not disposed to let anyone else sleep, especially in their own bed, especially people who, no matter what éclat they had given the party, had caused all kinds of complications by locking themselves in with all the hats and coats.

During the following week, Taylor was at some pains to find out the name of the girl—his host and hostess wouldn't speak to him. But when he found her, she wouldn't speak to him either. At last she consented to a meeting in a public place. One meeting led to another. Taylor began with apology and ended with the offer of his sacred treasure. She hesitated, and Taylor's fate hung in the balance for weeks—why, she scarcely knew him—and all the while they continued to see each other in public places. Taylor was secretly horrified at what had happened, and at the same time he was secretly delighted.

In later years, however, the emotion that drove out all others was regret: regret that he had found the girl and that she had married him, thereby causing him to lose a precious secret that he might otherwise have held with warm pleasure and consolation in marriage with someone else; and regret that all the people who had been at the party had long ago drifted out of his life and there was now no one left to keep the legend alive.

Today with Grace was going to be more like the beginning of a honeymoon, for all day there would be anticipation while they drove together intimately through the snow. The words "A Night of Love" hung in the air before him as solid as if cut out of stone, as brilliant as if floodlighted on a marquee.

The snow continued to fall all day, but the roads were still good. The car was heavy, and the snow treads gave good traction even in the Berkshires. However, everything was taking longer than Taylor had planned. Never had one of those tiny New England states seemed so endless, and it was well after two o'clock when they finally stopped for lunch in Williamstown. They would still get into Albany early enough, but the sense of leisure was being eaten away, and a familiar tension was building up in the back of Taylor's neck.

As soon as they left Williamstown and began climbing the Taconic Trail, Taylor began to be on the lookout for the state line. Not the least of the incidental pleasures of the day was the knowledge that he would be violating the Mann Act. The very thought that he—Ross Taylor, for God's sake—was transporting a woman across a state line for immoral purposes in full defiance of the Federal Government and the Seventh Commandment, at the risk of his loving wife, his gratifying children, his flourishing career —that terrible thought was delicious indeed.

He knew they must be getting close to the line, and he was preparing a light speech about the Mann Act to give himself yet another *frisson* when she said suddenly, "What's that up ahead?"

Engrossed in his fantasy, he had been aware only of the immediate problems of driving, but now he saw two cars standing in the road just about where he imagined the line to be. He automatically slowed and shifted down into second so as not to lose his traction on the hill. "Looks like an accident," he said.

"Oh, I hope not," she said. "I hope no one's hurt."

By then they were close enough to see better. "No," he said, "it's not an accident. The New York plows haven't come this far, and those cars are stuck."

"Do you think we could help them?" she said.

"Not likely," he said. "I'm going to go on through, and we can leave word for the state police at the first town we come to."

"Do you think we should stop and say we'll send help?"

His neck was now so stiff he didn't expect ever to be able to move his head again. "I don't want to lose my momentum," he said, making an effort to control his temper. After all she wasn't his wife even if she did sound like a wife the way she was asking the questions he had resolved not to think about. He made a further effort. "The top of the trail is just beyond the state line. You can see it from here. Up at that bend where the wind has swept the road bare. It's downhill from there. I think we'll be all right."

"I'm sure we will."

Just hearing that was almost reward enough in itself. He had forgotten—if he ever knew—how good it is for a man to hear such things. However, he was by no means sure himself that they would get through, but he knew that their schedule was already so badly out of order that it couldn't stand much more delay.

"We'll be all right," he said again as they left behind the plowed roads and entered the rutted snow of New York State.

She said, "My mother always maintained she could tell the minute she left Massachusetts, but I never believed it until now."

He laughed because just then he was forging past the first of the stuck cars. It was a Model A and was sitting squarely on the road. It hadn't got far, and he would have thought it could be backed out without much trouble. He glanced at the driver, an old woman in a fur coat and fur cap, who smiled at him and waved him on and blew her horn in encouragement as he went past.

The second car was almost at right angles to the road with its rear end against the snow bank to the left. There was room for him to pass, but he was afraid for a minute his wheels were going to start to spin on him as he edged over off the crown of the road, but he shifted down into first and kept going.

Both his shoulders ached now, but he was very conscious of his skill in keeping his wheels under him. "It won't be long now," he said, thinking as he said it only of getting over the mountain but realizing at once that it might be considered a crude allusion. He hoped she knew he couldn't do a thing like that—yes, or she wouldn't be with him at all. Then he hit a snow drift. The car would move neither forward nor back with all his skill. "I guess that's it," he said, and immediately the tension began to be less. "We can be warm here a long time with the heater, and we have the radio if we get bored with each other's company." He flicked the radio on to demonstrate.

"Bored already?" she said.

"Nothing but football," he grunted. Being a husband for twenty years had at least taught him some arts of silence.

"Let's listen to a game for a little," she said. "I don't really feel it's New Year's unless I hear a touchdown or two."

"Any preference?"

"Rose Bowl, of course," she said. "It's more like Santa Claus." She was disappointed, however, to find that Alabama was being beaten in the Rose Bowl. "They're supposed to win," she said. "The Rose Bowl jinx."

They listened for what seemed to him like a long time. Each time he leaned forward to adjust the radio, he was conscious of her nearness, each time he lit her cigarette. The football game did not exist for him. During a time out, she said, "Do you think using the radio like this will run down the battery too much?"

"No, it's all right." He knew he had been a little curt—his wife would have noticed it anyway—so he added with some effort, "Running the motor like this is keeping the battery up." He wasn't sure about that, but he hoped so anyway.

"Perhaps we shouldn't be running the motor so much."

"There's plenty of gas," he said. "I filled it at Williamstown."

"I mean, how about carbon monoxide and all that? I don't think the school would care to have its dean of women found in a parked car on a lonely mountain road."

"It would teach the girls always to be sure a window is open a bit. You'd be a martyr for education."

She laughed, and he felt repaid for the effort, which had been considerable.

"Besides," she said, "it's not really so lonely, not with them." She gestured toward the other cars, but Taylor knew it was the nearer she meant, about twenty yards back down the slope. That car and Taylor's car were both slewed across the highway so that they were at right angles to each other. A man and a woman sat stiffly on the front seat staring through the windshield as if Taylor's car were something in a movie.

If it had not been for those spectators, Taylor would have felt obliged to consider whether this was the time to make his pass. But even so, the light was beginning to fail. The tension in his shoulders was returning. He peered up and down the trail to see if any help was in sight. "Here comes more company," he said, "and by the looks of things he won't get far."

The car he was watching made a fast run up to the unplowed road and plunged in without slackening speed. "I hope he doesn't chew us up, bulling around like that." The car got past the Model A without trouble, but immediately afterward it began to slow so that to get past the second car it had to slow down noticeably. Once it was past, the driver tramped on the gas, and his wheels began to spin. Very shortly he was squarely across the road just behind Taylor's car.

"Well," Taylor said, "this is more like it. I saw that car being worked on where we stopped for gas in Williamstown. Some college boys on their way back to school rammed a bus and smashed in their grill and radiator—Alabama, too, by the way. It looks like a bad day for Alabama all around. But now there'll be plenty of manpower to help get us out of here—according to the mechanic there are supposed to be six of them."

"You aren't going to do anything rash, are you?" Grace said.

"Good lord," he said. "Rash? What do you mean?" He would have known very well what his wife meant, and he was more than a little dismayed by the intimation that even if he was only borrowed for the night he was to be maintained in good condition.

Before she had a chance to answer, the car was surrounded by boys. Taylor rolled down the window to speak to them. "Good afternoon, sir," the nearest boy said. "We thought we'd get organized and get all four cars out of here. We'll start with the first car down the hill. That will give us a better chance to horse the others around as we come down, right? Are you with us?"

"Right," Taylor said and began to roll up his window.

"Just a minute," Grace said. She leaned across Taylor to speak out the window. The boys crowded around for a good look at her. "What my husband means," she said—Taylor was struck dumb and motionless at that, and she was leaning negligently on his knee besides, her hair brushing his cheek. "What he means is that he's with you in spirit, but the fact is that he's ruptured and can't do that sort of work no matter how much he'd like to. You see how it is."

"Sure," said one of the boys who had not spoken before.

"That's tough," said another.

"Of course," said the one who had been spokesman and whom Taylor had privately labeled Fraternity President. "Can we count on you to drive, sir, if we need you, that is, while the rest of us push?"

"Absolutely," Grace said, quickly sensing that Taylor wasn't going to reply. Taylor, in fact, had not heard the question. He was no longer aware even that he was being smothered by her perfume, her hair, her soft weight against him, a death which he had been contemplating with delight all day up to that very moment.

He was not aware of his surroundings even when she had rolled up the window and withdrawn. "I'm sorry," she said, touching his sleeve.

"That's all right," he said automatically. He also performed the gesture of patting her hand without having to return to the full unpleasantness of consciousness.

"I didn't want to do that," she said. "I knew it would hurt you—as if you needed to prove anything to those kids—"

"No, it's really all right, Betty," he said, making an effort to reassure her and turning toward her. He felt as if he had run into something in the dark when he saw that it was not actually his wife who was reading his wife's lines. He remembered vividly that he had called her by his wife's name. "That's done it," he said.

"What?" she said.

"On top of everything else, calling you by the wrong name."

"Don't think about it," she said. "In fact under the circumstances it might even be a sort of compliment, but I really don't mind anyway. I'm the one really who owes you apologies."

"No, no," he said. He had withdrawn from her as far as possible. "You did absolutely the right thing. I shouldn't have forced you to do it. It was nothing but my vanity. You were right about that."

"And men laugh at women for dressing to please other women," she said. He could tell that she would have laughed if he had been able to give her the least encouragement. "What does a thing like that matter?"

This succeeded in diverting his attention but probably not as she had intended to divert it. He wanted to ask her how she knew about that old rupture although he was aware there was only one way she could have heard of it. The whole question of what women talk about among themselves came up before him, and bitterly he faked a quotation he couldn't quite remember. "I had a gossip," he said, "and one friend more/ That if my husband had but pissed against a wall/ I must have run to tell them of it all."

"Well," she said, "is *that* the Finnesburh Fragment?"

"No," he said, "it's the Wife of Bath, who knew more about men and women than anybody. She had five husbands, you know."

"It's not very nice to have anybody know—" She broke off in some confusion. "When things begin to go wrong," she said, "they just go wrong."

"No," he said, "it will still be all right. Why, they've got one car out already and are working on the next. We'll be back in Williamstown in an hour, and if we have to stay there, why, then, we stay there and leave for Albany very early in the morning." He knew he wasn't being very realistic about it because the Model A had been no trouble at all, but now, with the second car, the boys were already floundering in the snow and showing signs of exhaustion.

"We'll see," she said. "I'd rather be in Albany tonight if possible though."

"We'll do it barring an act of God," he said.

It was very nearly dark when the boys came back to Taylor's car. "Would you mind," the Fraternity President said, "if we get into your car to rest awhile before we tackle our own car? We don't have a heater."

"By all means," Taylor said, "and, look, I've got some whiskey in the trunk. Let me get it."

"We wouldn't say no," said one of the boys who had already climbed into the back seat.

The moment Taylor stuck his head out the door, the wind whipped off his hat. Before anyone could move a step, the hat had sailed down the road, over the snow bank, and out across the valley. Taylor watched it go until it disappeared far below in the snow and dark. "Beautiful," he said. "The most pleasure I've ever had from any hat I've ever owned." His ears felt cold at once, but he thought he was behaving very well. Then he realized that none of the boys had been wearing hats all the while. "Let me get the whiskey," he said.

When he came back with the whiskey, he found the doors closed and the car full. The Rose Bowl game was on again. The Fraternity President was sitting at the wheel. "I thought," the President said, "that you might not mind holding your wife on your lap for a while."

"Oh," Taylor said, "no, of course not."

"Well, I mind," Grace said. "An old married woman like me doesn't get as many chances as all that to sit on young men's laps. You might have asked me. And so, dear, with your permission—"

"Or without it, I dare say," Taylor dared say bitterly.

"Never," she said, laughing. "Now if this gentleman will be so kind as to accommodate me—" She indicated the boy next to her on the seat.

"Speak up, clown," the Fraternity President said.

"Sure," the boy said.

"He says he is honored, madam," the President said.

"Tell him thank you," she said.

"OK," the President said.

"OK," the boy said.

"He says he is quite at your convenience."

She slid onto the boy's lap and the President slid from behind the wheel and Taylor got in out of the cold. He passed Grace the full bottle, out of courtesy, of course, but at the same time he knew he would be able to tell if she was cheating on the drink. Part of his pleasure had been based on the idea of plying her with drink. In fact, that was almost as good as the Mann Act.

She took the bottle and punished it like a man and passed it on, neglecting even the delicacy of a cough and a goddamn, to the boy on whose lap she was sitting. His face had become suddenly very red against the darkness of her coat, and when he drank, he choked and the tears stood in his eyes. He did not omit the goddamn.

The President did not drink but passed the bottle into the back seat, and when it came to him again, he urged it on Taylor as if the bottle had been his own. Taylor felt a stab of irritation and very nearly said, Goddamn it, it's *my* whiskey. But he felt ultimately that he was obliged to demonstrate—if only to himself—the superiority of his manners. He allowed the President to drink last.

"Go, Alabama," the President said as he raised the bottle on high.

"Go, Jinx," the others chorused as if they had been drilled to it.

"It's not too late," the President said. He drank. It was, in fact, much too late. Even Taylor knew it, and he never paid attention to such things as football.

"They're our boys," the others said chorally.

As the second round of drinks began, Grace gave the "Go, Alabama," and was applauded. She asked to be taught an Alabama song and learned with unconvincing difficulty a song that seemed to be mostly about corn likker and arson. At least Taylor was unconvinced although the boys were enchanted.

"Let's go, men," the President shouted, and in very short order, Taylor and Grace were alone in the car while the boys bounded through the snow yelling, "Go, go, go."

"Confess now," Taylor said. "You knew that song."

"Of course," she said. "Even my sweet little freshmen know it. They think it's very daring. We encourage them to think so."

"Apparently the boys are encouraged to think so too," he said, "but I had never heard it."

"Really?" she said. "From the way you were trying to catch my eye, I thought maybe that song was the Finnesburh Fragment."

"Now that you mention it, it is very Anglo-Saxon in mood—a getting drunk, boasting, burning down the mead hall sort of thing."

"Then what were you trying to catch my eye about?"

Taylor had to grope for a moment back to the time when all the boys were in the car. Once they were gone he had forgotten all the irritation they had caused. It infuriated him now that he was unable to cherish a manly anger, and he said with rather more heat than he intended, "I thought you were being pretty hard on the kid under you," he said.

"*I* was being hard on *him*?" she said. "That's a laugh."

"You couldn't see his face," Taylor said. "He was embarrassed. He was very uncomfortable."

"I didn't have to see his face. He was enjoying it all right."

"Christ," Taylor said, "the famous feminine intuition never knows a goddamn thing about what a man enjoys or when or how he enjoys it."

"Well, I'll tell you something," she said. "The famous feminine intuition can tell in a minute who was really being given a hard time."

"Me?" Taylor said. "Don't make me laugh. What's it to me if you want to act like a giddy freshman on her first football weekend?"

"I don't know what it is to you, but you sure are making it something."

"Look here," Taylor said. He could have gone on as far as "if you think for one minute that," hoping for some inspiration before he ran out of words, but he was saved by shouts from the boys, who were having some trouble with their own car.

Their car was stopped further down the slope now and backed into the snow bank. The boys were crowding around the back of the car and looking at something that was hidden from Taylor's car. "It looks as if they have hit something," Taylor said.

"Perhaps someone is hurt," Grace said. One of the boys was already floundering up toward them, and Taylor and Grace were both out of the car waiting when he got there.

"Let me have the whiskey," he panted. Taylor turned to get it. "An accident."

"I'll take it down," Grace said. "I know first aid. Is he badly hurt?"

"Don't know," the boy called back over his shoulder as he ran ahead of them down the trail.

They found that the car had pushed one of the boys into the snow bank and held him there so that he couldn't even move his arms. "Are you in pain?" Grace asked. The boy, who was obviously terrified, shook his head. Grace tried to pass him the bottle but couldn't reach him.

"Here," one of the boys said. He took the bottle and got into the car and, leaning out the window, held it for the imprisoned boy to drink. He drank as if he was very thirsty, and he did not cough and only added goddamn as an unconvincing afterthought.

"That's the spirit," Grace said.

"Can't you move the car away enough to get him out?" Taylor said.

"We don't know where his legs are," the President said. "We're afraid to spin the wheels."

"Quite," Taylor said to his own surprise, and he lost track of things for a minute until he realized that Americans he knew didn't get into spots like this, but Englishmen were always doing it in novels and movies.

"We're afraid he may be broken up already," the President said in a lowered voice, "but we don't want to upset him more than he is already."

"Just right," Grace said. "How're you feeling, boy?" she called.

The boy in the snow smiled wanly. One of the others called, "Old Horse is resting. He'll take a deep breath in a minute and move it away with his chest." The others laughed very loudly.

"All right," the President said. "Up on the snow bank and let's dig him out."

In ten minutes they had the boy out and were helping him to stand in the road. They were examining him as if he were something they had just unpacked from a crate that had arrived in bad condition. They moved his arms and legs and watched his face for signs of pain. There seemed to be nothing wrong with him although he could scarcely stand and didn't respond to any questions.

"Old Horse is just tired," the President said. Then in a lower voice but still loud enough for the boy to hear he said, "He's been working more than any two of the rest."

"I'll take him up to our car and get him warm," Grace said. "Come along, Horse." She took the boy's arm to lead him away, but he shook off her hand and began to follow the car, which the other boys were moving down the trail back into Massachusetts.

"I hope they come to get us out," Taylor said when he and Grace were back in the warm car.

"Of course, they will," Grace said. "What an idea."

"They're mad I didn't help," Taylor said. "And now this. They'll blame me. You'll see."

"That's all in your mind," Grace said. "Look," she said, "I'm sorry about sitting in that kid's lap. I thought I was playing the old married woman to the hilt. I thought it would amuse you. I thought you'd be as pleased with me as I was."

"I see," Taylor said. "I didn't see then, but I see now. It's really all right. I just wish I could go back over it again and laugh in the right place." He didn't feel at all like laughing as he began to understand the vast sadness of the gap between his game of the Mann Act and her game of the old married couple, but he did feel a new and very different tenderness toward her. He wondered how much of all that she knew. "I really feel as if we have been married for a long long time," he said. Then, carried away, he added what he thought for a moment might not be a lie, "I think really I was upset at the thought we hadn't been."

"Oh, Ross—" she said. She put her hand on his sleeve, but he didn't trust himself to touch her, not there, not then, not any longer.

"It's just too bad," she said.

"Please, don't touch me," he said. His hands clutched the wheel as they had all day.

She withdrew her hand but was still near him on the seat. Then he heard the boys coming up the trail. He hurriedly put his arm around her shoulders and gave her a gentle squeeze. It really was like squeezing a woman he had been married to for a long long time: they had been through a lot together and small signs meant much. When the boys began to appear out of the gloom, he put his hands back on the wheel.

"We'll laugh about this some time," she said.

Taylor was glad it was dark because he wasn't laughing then. He could feel his eyes brimming, and he was afraid the tears would start to shine down his cheeks at any minute. They didn't—not then and not on the long ride up through a corner of Vermont and down to the Albany station and not even at the station where she caught last night's train coming through six hours late—and that at least was something.

He thought about that day on every New Year's for the rest of his life and at strange moments in between, but he never once laughed about it.

JACK LUDWIG was born in Canada and is now on the faculty of the new State University Center at Stony Brook, New York. He has published a novel, *Confusions*, and short fiction in *The Atlantic Monthly, Commentary, The Noble Savage* (of which he was co-founder and co-editor), *The Quarterly Review* and *Tamarack Review* in Canada. One earlier story, "Thoreau in California" was in the O. Henry Prize Stories volume for 1961.

A Woman of Her Age

1

ONCE a week, even now, Mrs Goffman makes that chauffeur drive her slowly down from the mountain, back to St Lawrence Boulevard and Rachel Street; she doesn't want any old cronies who might still be alive spotting her in that hearse of a limousine, so she gets out a couple of blocks from the Market and walks the rest of the way, not in her Persian lamb or her warm beaver, but in that worn cloth coat she bought at Eaton's Basement years ago, the black one. Long, gaunt as a late afternoon shadow, Mrs Goffman concentrates on smiling. Otherwise she looks like a spook. At seventy-five you can feel warm, sweet, girlish even, but an old old face has trouble expressing soft feelings. Those reddish-brown eyebrows that didn't turn white with the rest of her hair, they're to blame, so bushy, so fierce, with an ironic twist that was snappy when she was a hot young radical, but now, when she's old enough to be a great-grandmother, who needs it?

'Wordsworth', her son Jimmy used to call her. In a drugstore window she sees reflected Wordsworth's broad forehead, deep-set eyes, small mouth, short chin. By God, she tells herself, this is a darned good face. Jimmy had this face. Her father had it too—who knows how far back these purplish lips go, or the dark rings under eyes, or the pale olive complexion? Moses might have had similar coloring. Her nose gives a sly twitch to call attention to itself: Wordsworth's

Copyright © 1963 by Quarterly Review of Literature.

large humped nose she has too, and it deserves the dominant spot it earned for itself on Mrs Goffman's face. She judges everything by its smell. That's why the ambassador's mansion she lives in flunks so badly—it's not only quiet as a church, it smells like a church. Six days a week her nose puts up with that dry lonely quiet smell, does what a nose is supposed to do in Westmount, breathe a little: on St Lawrence Boulevard a nose is for smelling, and Mrs Goffman doesn't miss a sniff. Families are getting ready for sabbath.

Doba, catch that goose roasting, her nose seems to say. Hey, poppy-seed cookies! *Real* stuffed fish! St Lawrence Boulevard, I love you!

2

Mitchell the 'Kosher Butcher' nodded his usual pitying nod as she walked past his full window—fresh-killed ducks and chickens hanging by their feet, cows' brains in pools, tongues like holsters, calves' feet signed by the Rabbi's indelible pencil. Mrs Goffman nodded her black-turbaned head at Mitchell but he'd already given *his* nod, and only stared back, open-mouthed, his hands pressed against his slaughter-house-looking apron. Naturally Mitchell has her pegged: doesn't he know this shopping trip is a fake, that Mrs Grosney, the cook, does Mrs Goffman's buying and cooking? Mitchell knows about the Persian lamb coat she doesn't wear to Market. Mitchell knew her dead husband well. Mitchell, like all of Montreal, knows the story of her dead son Jimmy.

When Simon-may-he-rest-in-peace was still alive the Goffmans lived down here, among people, in life. Now life was a novelty to Mrs Goffman. Six days to Westmount, one to St Lawrence and Rachel Street, what idiotic arrangement was that? Some day she'd get real tough with her son Sidney. Marry him off. Make him sell the Ambassador's mansion and lead a normal life.

Her eyebrows went into their ironic arch. You, Doba, they seemed to mock her, when could you get your kids to do anything?

3

In front of Bernstein's Kiddies' Korner a young girl pressed her lovely dark face against the window, her hand nervously rocking a

baby carriage. Black hair, heavy lips, nursing breasts, what a beauty
of a mother, Mrs Goffman thought; she could double for Jimmy's
Shirley! By rights Mrs Goffman should have a grand-daughter this
girl's age. One? A dozen!

What would it hurt if she *pretended* she had come to Kiddies' Korner to buy something or other for her grand-daughter and great-
grandchild? The thought made her feel wonderful.

'Dear,' she said, 'good morning, dear. How's baby?'

The girl nodded absently. She had eyes only for a white bunting in
the window. If she wanted pink or blue I'd know at least if my grandchild was a boy or girl, Mrs Goffman thought. In her low Russian-
sounding voice she cooed at the baby, tried to make her grand-daughter look at her.

'Dear,' she tried again, 'what do you think is nice, eh, dear?'

'That bunting,' the girl said, still not looking at her grandmother,
'but what a high price!'

'Twenty-five bucks! Highway robbery,' Mrs Goffman said in a loud
voice, thinking she'd better not ham it up too much. Her purse was
lined with dough—a few fifties, four or five twenties, a dozen tens,
fives, ones, even a two—Mrs Goffman was never too neat about
money. Every handbag was loaded this way, and what Montreal bank
didn't have Doba Goffman as an account? Money to her was like a
big soup: you cooked it in a vat but then came the problem of how
to store it. You pour in one jar, then another, then another—except
that with Sidney or Jimmy there was no end to what she had to put
in jars. The faster she stored money away the faster they brought her
more. No matter what she did to get rid of it—charities, trips to New
York every week to see shows, an opera, flights to Israel, Hawaii, buying those bozos Sulka ties at fifty bucks a crack—no matter how fast
she gave it, they stuffed her accounts, lined handbags, papered the
walls, those successes of hers, those imbeciles!

Bernstein's clerk poked his head out the door.

'Highway robbery, is that what you call it, *babbe?*' he said in a hurt
voice. 'Come inside. I'll show you my cost.'

Years ago Mrs Goffman felt offended when people called her
babbe, grandmother, but not now. She turned her head and gave the
man a mirthless smile.

'Honey,' he said to the girl, 'let your *babbe* stay out here with the
baby. You come in. I've got a real bargain for the kid.'

The girl didn't seem to hear.

'Go 'head, dear,' Mrs Goffman said warmly. 'I'll rock baby.'

The girl wheeled the carriage around and hurried towards the Market. Mrs Goffman followed quickly.

4

At the corner of Rachel and St Lawrence Mrs Goffman stopped to let a horse-drawn wagon go by. What a wonderful stink an old nag gave off! Wheels creaking was a melody to her deafish ear. Across the way was Simon's old store, the 'upstairs' they used to live in. Dimly, like an imagination, Mrs Goffman made out the 'S. Goffman and Sons' which 'J. Olin and Brother' had been painted over. Her nose sniffed at the rubber and leather smell coming from the old store. Those French perfumes Sidney gave her should only smell so nice!

Crossing the street she hurried after her grand-daughter, but, suddenly, without warning, tears gushed from Mrs Goffman's eyes, biting, salty tears mixed in with the heady fish fragrance around the Rachel Street Market stalls. Stop it, old fool, she told herself, but the tears kept running.

She pretended she was buying, dropped her eyes, rubbed a cold slimy fish with her manicured fingernails, poked open a carp's small-toothed mouth, combed its stiff freezing fins with her wrinkled hand. Next to Simon's gold wedding band was the hideous ruby Sidney gave her for her birthday last year; above them both was Jimmy's gift, a diamond-studded watch.

'*Babbe, babbe,*' a gentle voice said to her, 'why are you crying?'

She didn't have to open her eyes to know the man was new on the job: everybody on Rachel Street knew why Mrs Goffman cried.

'A Cold,' she said.

'In the eyes?' the voice said skeptically. 'Then maybe you shouldn't handle my fish?'

'Listen,' Mrs Goffman said wildly, 'give me two large carp and three nice whitefish!'

'There's an order!' the man clapped his hands together. 'Only your generation, eh, *babbe*? Big families need a full table!'

The girl with the baby wheeled up beside Mrs Goffman, hefted a small pike, looked wistful. Mrs Goffman moved over to give her grand-daughter more room.

'Mister,' she said to the fishman, 'I've got lots of time. Look after the mother with the baby first.'

The girl had turned around and was poking at the baby's blankets. The fishman grabbed at a floppy-tailed carp beating its fins on the damp wood stall.

'Today's girl,' he laughed, 'can wait longer than you, *babbe*. Your generation grinds, stuffs, cooks—just like my ma-may-she-rest-in-peace —two dozen people at *shabbes* table wasn't too much. But these kids?' He pointed at Mrs Goffman's grand-daughter. 'She'll toss a pike in a frying pan and one, two, it's *shabbes*.'

A second carp, big as a shark, fell with a splat against the first; three dancing whitefish got buried in a wad of newspapers.

'Dear,' Mrs Goffman said sweetly, 'he's ready to take your order.'

Again she didn't look up. Mrs Goffman wanted to holler—'Hey, sleeping beauty, can't you even answer when your *babbe* talks to you?'

'*Babbe*,' the fishman said, 'this parcel's too heavy. You live right around here somewheres? St Dominique maybe? I'll deliver you the fish myself.'

'I'm a strong woman,' Mrs Goffman said, holding out her arms.

'I can see, *babbe*. I only wish I should be in your shape at your age,' the man said enthusiastically. 'Have a good sabbath. Enjoy the kiddies. You deserve the best. I can tell!'

'Good-bye, dear,' Mrs Goffman said to her grand-daughter.

'Good-bye, good-bye,' the fishman answered, clapping his hands together. 'Next?'

5

The moment the fish touched her arms they seemed to revive and start swimming—twenty, thirty pounds writhing in her helpless arms! Fish? Who needed fish? When did she cook fish last! That last batch stunk up Sidney's limousine so badly he had to sell it for next to nothing!

The newspaper parcel was leaking all over her coat. Let it bust and she'd be chased by every cat in Montreal! Was she out of her mind? Seventy-five years in this world and still not able to resist the most foolish impulse!

Her arms hurt, her face turned red, her heart beat crazily. Leave it to an old Radical to act like a nut! Two blocks away is that healthy horse of a chauffeur sitting on his fanny and sunning himself. Two blocks? She'd never make it. But where could you dump this useless stuff? In the empty baby carriages scattered around St Lawrence Boulevard? She thought of letting it fall casually on the sidewalk, like a lost handkerchief. Maybe she could slip it into the empty moving van she saw across the street. Who but a woman loaded with money could afford such grandstand plays?

Fish water soaked her gloves, dribbled down her coat front: a bit of fin slipped through the dissolving newspaper, a sappy fish-eye made peek-a-boo. In a shop window Mrs Goffman caught sight of herself— a black streak, a bundle, eyebrows. Get sloppy sentimental and this is the result!

Triminiuk's. She suddenly came up with a brain-wave: Captain Triminiuk would save her! Giggling, panting, giddy, red-faced, she staggered across the street and into Triminiuk's Delicatessen.

The fish hit the counter like an explosion; the whitefish, wild as Cossacks, danced out of their covering.

'Come save an old sap, Gershon,' Mrs Goffman called to the back of the store. 'I overstocked myself with fish.'

She wiped her coat with orange wrappers, fell back, laughing helplessly, into one of Gershon's old chairs. Only Captain Triminiuk's Delicatessen still had these small round marble-top tables with wire legs and matching chairs with backs like wire carpet-beaters. The air inside was like a home-made mist—garlic pickles, pastrami, salami, sauerkraut, fresh rye bread, Triminiuk himself, who smelled like a real smokehouse.

Marching—he never walked—one-eyed Triminiuk came toward her, disapproving, as usual, everything about her. He stood at attention, his black cuff-guards up to his armpits, tieless collar buttoned at the neck, vest unbuttoned, also part of his pants. One of his eyes was almost closed, the other bright as turquoise, his moustache bristly, yellowed with tobacco.

Forty years ago, when she and Simon first met the old bluffer, he was just out of the Russian army, a cook who lost an eye from splattering fat. Since then Triminiuk, in recognition of himself, every ten years or so gave himself a promotion. Now he was a captain. Now the missing eye was a result of a sabre in the Russo-Japanese War.

'Fish?' he sniffed.

'Be a pal. Take it off my hands, Gershon,' she said flirtatiously.

'I need charity, Doba?'

'Don't play poor mouth with me, you bandit,' she laughed. 'You want to be independent, give me a tea with lemon.'

He didn't budge. Long ago she had given up trying to explain things to a stubborn old bluffer like Triminiuk. All he saw was that Doba Goffman, the hot-headed young Radical, became Mrs S. Goffman, prominent member of an Orthodox synagogue, patroness of the foolishness her sons' success brought her. Try to convince Gershon that she'd joined the Orthodoxes in protest against her sons' becoming Anglican-like Reform Jews? If those characters had stayed on St Lawrence Boulevard she would never have set foot in a synagogue. But when they climbed Westmount, bought that enormous mansion from the Ambassador, bragged about looking out on Nuns' Island, took her to Temple where the Rabbi pursed his lips in such a way that everybody should know he learned Hebrew not at home but in a University, then she, in protest, became again a Jew! Gershon should have seen the lousy Jewish-style cooking she, a Radical who had nothing to do with kitchens, forced her big-shot sons to eat—he should only know she got her Jewish recipes from *Better Homes and Gardens!*

Gershon accepted no explanations. He considered her a traitor. Worse. Maybe even a Zionist!

'My tea, captain,' Mrs Goffman said.

Triminiuk looked toward the door.

A fat woman, hair messy, hands dug deep in the ripped pockets of an old flowered housecoat, drove several kids into the store in front of her, stood for a second sighing, muttering, scratching herself under the pockets. Corns stuck out of her pink-and-aqua wedgies.

'Captain,' she said in a high nasal whine, 'my kids came to eat me up alive again. Let a mouse try to find a crumb by me, let. Herbie's wetters, Gertie's soilers, four five already, and Gertie's carrying again, you've heard about such misfortunes? They act like Westmount millionaires. You can't afford kids, don't have, I keep telling.'

Triminiuk, Mrs Goffman saw, was trying to shut the woman up.

'Lady,' he said in his military voice, 'what can I get for you?'

One of the children, about seven, a girl with black hair, black eyes, front teeth out, stared at Mrs Goffman.

'Ma,' Mrs Goffman's deafish ears heard her whisper, 'why's the old lady all in black?'

'Gimme a couple rye loaves to stop up the mouths quickly,' the woman said shrilly, 'a salami, a few slices lox—'

'Ma,' the little girl stole behind her mother's housecoat and peeked at Mrs Goffman, 'is it a witch?'

'Tammy, stop botherin',' the woman said absently, fingering the fish on the counter. 'Captain, how can you make today's kid stop carrying? It's living here with the French that makes 'em like this, hah?'

'Lady,' Triminiuk snapped, 'is this everything?'

'Ma,' the little girl tugged at her mother's sleeve, 'I'm afraid of her—'

'Let me be,' the woman whined, shoving the child at Mrs Goffman. Hard as Mrs Goffman's old face tried, it couldn't come up with a look to reassure the child.

'You're very sweet, dear,' she said softly.

The child seemed to shudder.

'What did you say?' the woman mumbled.

'She's a very sweet little girl,' Mrs Goffman said.

'Listen, you want her? She's yours, the pest. You can have these others in the bargain,' the woman said without a smile.

'Two dollars and five cents,' Triminiuk all but shouted.

'What's he getting sore for? Don't I pay in time? Here,' she threw down a dollar bill, 'payday I'll give the rest.'

'Gramma,' the smallest kid in the store said quietly, 'can each of us have a sucker?'

'I got no money for suckers,' the woman said nastily, missing with a slap she'd aimed at the kid. Tammy, the little girl, frightened, jumped toward Mrs Goffman, grew more frightened, jumped back, catching her mother's corns with her shoe.

'For godssake, pests!' the woman shouted, slapping Tammy across the cheek. 'Get out of this store!'

'Don't cry, dear,' Mrs Goffman tried to make Tammy hear.

'I'm sorry these crazy kids bothered you, lady,' the woman said as she shooed them out the door. 'With these pests gone you can have peace.'

Triminiuk went to get her her tea.

That kid Tammy was right, Mrs Goffman thought as she caught sight of herself in Triminiuk's small calendar mirror. A witch. Black. What sentimental soft-headedness made her dress this way? What right did she have to dump her mourning on St Lawrence Boulevard?

In her old age was she becoming a professional widow, a dopey eccentric? Tomorrow she'd go down to one of those fancy French shops on Sherbrooke and get gussied up in pink, violet, maybe even yellow.

Sentimentality, respectability, a tough old Radical like Mrs Goffman had been had, by America. How else did a revolutionary become a quiet-spoken tea-sipper dumb with good taste? By God, an old-fashioned St Dominique Street ma would have chased her kids out of the house with a broom, made their lives so miserable they would *have* to marry, in self-defence. And when Simon died, what stopped her from marrying again? Loyalty. Love. Now, when the time for praying was past and with the lock on the synagogue door, now she realized that love too was smaller than life. A stepfather would have been another way of getting her boys into life on their own. Jimmy had been a bachelor till forty-five, just a year before his death. Poor Sidney, still unmarried, fifty-three, a pill-swallower, complained his way from hotel to hotel crossing three continents.

Waste, Mrs Goffman thought with a sinking feeling, waste is the law of America—too much money, too much talent, even too much fish. Getting stuck with something useless like money and fish was a judgement against her and her sons.

Triminiuk came shuffling toward her, balancing a cup of tea in one hand, a glass in the other. Should she say something? I've done too much damage with silence, Mrs Goffman thought.

'Listen here, Capatanchik,' she said nastily, 'what's the big idea bringing me tea in a cup and yourself in a glass?'

'Westmount ladies drink from china cups,' the old bluffer said without batting an eye.

'Turn right around, you pirate, and get me a glass,' Mrs Goffman said, hitting her palm against the marble top. 'To hell with Westmount!'

'I got only one glass,' Triminiuk came back.

'Then it's for me,' Mrs Goffman said in triumph. 'Hand it over.'

To show he was a winner, Triminiuk poured his tea into a saucer and sipped noisy, like a roughneck.

'How's the rich son?' he asked. She couldn't tell for sure if he was being nasty.

'Sidney's fine,' she lied. One thing Sidney never was was fine, specially since without Jimmy he was a total loss in the world. He hadn't been with a woman in over a year. Women weren't Sidney's line—his hair was red and thin, his face chubby and round, his eyes watery and always blinking, his lower lip ready to blubber.

But Jimmy!

Elegant, taller than his tall mother, with her face, her colouring, dressed like a British diplomat, smooth with continental manners, chased by every woman in Montreal, and for what, what for? 'Fun,' he called it, and what came of his fun? Ashes, dust. The dopiest kid on St Dominique Street had more claim on life than her handsome successful Jimmy. He drove a Bentley, wore a white leather raincoat, a British vest with brass buttons, a Parisian necktie—what he wore Montreal copied, the gals he took out were immediately stamped with approval. 'Lover boy' the high-school year-book nicknamed him. 'Lover man' was what they called him at McGill, and 'Don Giovanni'. Women, women, hundreds upon hundreds of women, affairs without number, and what came of it all? 'Listen to me, bozos,' she had said years ago, when they'd first moved to the Ambassador's mansion, 'let's get down to life now, eh? At sixty I'm *entitled* to grandchildren. Who'll mourn me when I'm dead, our bankers?'

Mrs Goffman's eyes filled, blood rushed to her face, in anger and despair she beat her ringed hand against the marble table. Jimmy, that poor fool Jimmy, marrying at forty-five, and how, with a nineteen-year-old who'd been living with another man since sixteen!

Triminiuk put his hand on her shoulder.

'What are you aggravating yourself for?' His blind eye looked like the dead fish's.

'Gershon, the worst thing is for people to die out of their own generation.'

'If people died neatly,' Triminiuk said, raising his face from the tilted saucer, 'we'd both be long buried by now.'

A little French girl barged into the store, wiggling her hips, pushing out her breasts. Her hair was tight with nasty bobby pin curls that gave Mrs Goffman the pip, her skin was broken out, badly powdered and rouged. She chewed gum with an open mouth. Her arms, though, were lovely and slim, and her legs were shapely. Even you, you tramp, Mrs Goffman thought as she watched Triminiuk give the girl a package of Sweet Caporal, even a gum-chewing slut like you I would have taken for a daughter-in-law at the end, when I saw what the score was.

'Bye, Cap,' the girl said with a wink. Triminiuk dismissed her with a wave.

'What were you saying, Doba?'

'I was being depressed,' she reminded him with a smile, 'and you were trying to snap me out of it.'

'Why should you be depressed?' Triminiuk said after a long slurp. 'The boy died a big success. It should happen to all my granchildren, such a success.'

All his grandchildren—Gershon, big-shot atheist, lived by 'increase and multiply' the Bible's way. He *was* a success. Eight or nine kids, twenty-five thirty grandchildren. Jimmy and Sidney took 'increase and multiply' to mean mergers, expansion, deals, transactions. Hundreds of thousands Jimmy left his mother, and bonds, and buildings, and tracts of land—ashes, dust, because neither his loins nor Sidney's produced a child.

She felt the blood rush to her face again. Imbecility, America's imbecility. Jimmy galloping after success while life runs off right under his feet. Mocking, teasing. His Shirley was a born mother, gorgeous, built to bear children. Not Jimmy's, though. On Jimmy's money Shirley, the most beautiful widow in Montreal, married that childhood sweetheart of hers. For him Shirley became a mother.

'Your tea's cold, I betcha,' she heard Triminiuk's voice say gruffly.

'I'll be your guest,' said Mrs Goffman. Triminiuk gave her a searching look, nodded briskly, shuffled with a military swagger to the back of the store.

He understood everything. Sitting with Gershon was comfortable, even in silence. Their conversations were one-quarter open, three-quarters between the lines, as it used to be with Simon. But the other kind of silence, the silence that buzzed in her deafish ears in the Ambassador's mansion, that kind Mrs Goffman couldn't stand. That silence frightened her more than the loudest noise. That silence was the noise of death.

'Gershon,' she called out in spite of herself.

'Look how a *madamchikeh* can't wait for a glass of tea,' the old man scolded, but she noticed he was coming back in a big hurry.

'Gershon,' she said as he sat down, 'if we're lucky in life we *see*, if only for a split second. Life or death, there's no other issue, Gershon. Jimmy learned it too late. Not till the end could he stop for life, but he had to stop for death.'

'Doba,' Triminiuk said bluntly, 'you're beginning to sound religious.'

'What religious, when religious?' she cried out, 'in those clear moments blindness drops from us, we see and know everything!'

Twice I knew, she thought: once when Shirley's lover turned up at Jimmy's funeral in Jimmy's clothes. The other time too was at a funeral.

'So cut away my blindness,' Triminiuk said gently, poking at his inert gluey eye.

'*Touché*,' she said, hiding her face behind the tea glass. Triminiuk didn't press his advantage.

She glanced quickly at him and imagined him naked. She flushed. His face was weather-beaten, sketched over with tiny red-and-blue blood vessels, but his body would be blue-white, his back rounded, his rib-cage prominent as a starving man's. Mrs Goffman grew conscious of her own body—so long, so gaunt, so like a stranger's now the skin was dry and criss-crossed, now her breasts were flat with colour faded out of the nipples. Her nails didn't grow much, or her hair. Whatever was shrivelled in a man like Gershon was spent, whatever shrivelled on her was wasted.

Wisdom was overrated. It had little to do with life. She was wise, but powerless. When she had power she must have been stupid. Pride, shyness, loyalty to Simon's memory seemed so important years ago. Now Mrs Goffman knew she should have married even a gargoyle of a man, and had more children. But by the time she caught on to what Jimmy's and Sidney's fate was, it was too late for her to do anything for them, or herself. 'Fun,' Jimmy said, relying on his mother's Radical tolerance, sneaking beauty after beauty into the house and his bed—for what, what for? All those gorgeous Rachels, but never a fruitful Leah.

'Gershon,' Mrs Goffman suddenly said, 'blaming is for innocents. I don't blame Shirley. I don't even blame Doba Goffman.'

Shirley dressed like a Hollywood star for the funeral—a large black picture-hat, dark glasses, elbow-length black gloves, a clinging sheath dress so open down the front the gravediggers scattered dirt in all directions trying to stay in position to stare at her. Her lover wore Jimmy's black Italian silk suit. They whispered together. Shirley didn't pretend to cry. She didn't even carry a handkerchief.

Sidney, for once in his tired life, got hot, wanted to throw himself at the two of them. Mrs Goffman wouldn't let him. What was Shirley's lower-animal foolishness compared to the horrible truth—Jimmy in the ground without a child to mourn for him! Who was left, Mrs Goffman, an old woman with teeth falling out of her head?

'I get such a cold feeling,' she whispered to Triminiuk. 'We threw life aside like a rag. When we die it's an end—papa's line, Simon's line —a crime, Gershon, a crime against the whole human race.'

Triminiuk nodded stiffly, like an officer commending a subordinate.

It *was* a crime against the whole human race. Life wasn't something to be kicked aside just because you happened to have it. In crowds, on the street, Mrs Goffman felt the difference bitterly—not she alone, not Sidney alone, a whole strain in the human race was dying in them! Simon's stubborn look was finished! Her pa's bass voice. Jimmy's way of greeting you—a *hello*, his arm thrown in front of his eyes as if you were the sun and so brilliant he couldn't absorb you. Jimmy made you feel that you were morning. Even Sidney had qualities the race shouldn't lose. Character, size, shape, all human magnificence, all possibility dying, dying, dying.

Mrs Goffman thought she would pass out.

'Doba, Doba,' Triminiuk's voice sounded urgent in her ear, 'stop aggravating, I said. Look on St Lawrence. The kids are coming home from school.'

He steered her into the doorway, made her look out on the boulevard. Dabs and specks of red, green, blue danced in the distance, faint squeals and shrieks washed terror of silence away from her ears. Gershon knew his onions. Bending down—Triminiuk was the same size as Simon, a peanut—she kissed him on his wrinkled forehead. He shook her off, stood rigid at attention, nodded her away.

'Thanks for taking the fish off my hands,' she said.

'Don't do it again,' he answered gruffly.

7

Mrs Goffman concluded she would have to change her life, and immediately. She ordered her chauffeur to drive her to Fifi's, Shmifi's— a fancy French place for clothes-horses. It would be a double victory —she'd get spiffed up and stop scaring kids, she'd unload most of the money choking in her handbag.

Not all the perfumes of Paris could overcome the fish smell as Mrs Goffman entered the shop. Only her liveried chauffeur and that funeral car parked in front saved her from being tossed out on her ear. She gave the salesgirls, who sniffed usually just from snobbery, something real to sniff about!

'That coat!' she said, in a voice as military as Triminiuk's.

A salesgirl hid her nose in a useless frilly hankie and came at Mrs Goffman sideways. The coat was a Marlene Dietrich type—magenta. Mrs Goffman made a trade. The girl almost passed out.

'A Gloria Swanson hat—burn the coat, dollie, don't cling to the rag,' Mrs Goffman dismissed the salesgirl, who was greenish and crampy-looking from the fish smell. 'Get me a flapper number. And a handbag too.' With one motion she dumped all her money on the counter. The salesgirl's eyes, sick as they had been, bugged with the proper respect money always got.

'I look like a big popsicle, eh Josef?' Mrs Goffman said to her chauffeur. If kids didn't get scared to death by this number, they were still in danger of laughing themselves to death looking at her.

'Take, take,' Mrs Goffman waved the girl onward to the pile of bills on the counter. 'Put what's left in my new bag, dollie.'

Without bitterness Mrs Goffman reflected how easy it was in America to buy everything you don't want.

She left the store, salespeople bowing to her right and to her left as if she were Queen Mary, gave them a queenly wave while her nose triumphantly recorded that in the air, wistful, fleeting, elusive as Chanel Number Five, was Rachel Street Fish.

8

Josef put down her arm-rest, adjusted a small reading-light over her newspaper—Sidney's style. Headlines shimmered in front of her eyes, and the usual faces—Khrushchev the hearty liar, Dulles's sour face set permanently in a 'no', Eisenhower with that puzzled look which meant if his press secretary didn't say something fast he was a goner. What was it Jimmy said? Everybody in Eisenhower's cabinet was a millionaire except for Martin Durkin and God Almighty. The headlines recorded imbecile explosions, tests in Siberia, Nevada. Sincere falseness in Ottawa, Washington, false sincerity in Moscow. Idiots! Suckers! At least Jimmy at the end *knew*: these crumbs would never know!

'Josef, go home the long way,' she said gently. Those French put their cemeteries right in the middle of the city—gray crosses stamped on the sky, cold stone saints, wreaths of dark artificial flowers. Silence was loudest near cemeteries.

What the heck was she doing going back up there anyways? Rachel Street was like a wonderful party she couldn't stand to see end. Six more days of nothing was coming.

'Josef, drive your slowest,' she requested.

Every stage in her kids' success mocked her on these trips home. Goffman buildings, Goffman businesses. The banks their money was in. The houses they'd lived in during their climb to the top of Westmount and the Ambassador's mansion. I dragged my feet, Mrs Goffman remembered with sadness, but I didn't interfere. A young Radical became an old dishrag! Good taste left a bad taste in her mouth.

In her small vanity mirror she made a John Foster Dulles face and laughed herself back into a better humour.

9

The limousine passed the Mount Royal Hotel. Cabs lined up, people were running, some school kids tumbled out of a car and skipped giggling toward St Catherine Street. Mrs Goffman wanted to try her new outfit on a kid and see what the reaction would be. She still felt bad about frightening that young girl Tammy.

Brighten up, sister, she told herself, but the Mount Royal had done its damage already: Jimmy first saw Shirley at a Mount Royal New Year's Eve Frolic—he loved to tell about it, to begin with.

The Mount Royal was Jimmy's home ground, a perfect setting for his style. He had Sally Rossen with him that night—a Toronto deb type, gorgeous, crazy for Jimmy, hot and burning. They danced every dance, drank champagne, moved arm in arm through the ballroom, visiting parties in different rooms, Jimmy in terrific shape, gay, gallant, witty, full of life. Then he saw Shirley. Sally was out.

How his eyes lighted up when he talked about Shirley—her hair he said was like a quiet waterfall in total darkness; her black eyes with that heavy fringe of eyelashes skimmed over Jimmy; she was in white, bare shouldered, proud of her beautiful young full breasts, her sexy body, her slow slow walk. Elegant Jimmy lost his manners. Clumsy as an ox he bumped his way across the floor, leaving Sally standing

all alone. Up went Jimmy's arm in that gesture all Montreal knew—
Shirley's beauty was blinding, he couldn't look.

Shirley cut him dead.

Sucker! He should have quit! Shirley's lover said something nasty
—Jimmy heard—about 'old enough to be your father'. Shirley gig-
gled, leaned on her boy, Maxie, and left Jimmy standing just as he
had left Sally! Don Giovanni, huh? Mrs Goffman thought in her
agitation. Big shot lover? He couldn't quit.

'My dance, beautiful,' he said, almost chasing after her through
the crowd. He gave the old flourish, poured on the charm.

'My card is filled,' Shirley said coldly; they had him.

Like a crack had appeared in a great building. He didn't fall apart
then and there, where Westmount society surrounded him, where
he was familiar, where his ways could get a gentle response. Later it
started, at home, when she caught him in front of a mirror.

'Since when did you pull out grey hair, Jimmy?' she had asked.
Jimmy didn't answer.

'Grey hair makes you look distinguished.'

'Distinguished, and old,' Jimmy said with a wink.

Lines on his face from laughing, character lines which made Jimmy
the handsome guy he was, he couldn't stand them now. He wanted
to rub everything out, be as young-looking as that pimply-faced Maxie
who had the only woman who had ever denied Jimmy anything at
all. Didn't his mother see Jimmy's reaction? He started to take out
younger and younger girls—one was seventeen, not even out of high
school! A photographer told him his left side was more handsome
than his right, so the dope sat with his right side hidden, as if it had
been burned! He sent Shirley flowers, pins, necklaces, phoned her,
wired her—what a set-up for those two kids! Jimmy would spend a
fortune on Shirley, but Maxie would spend the night!

Mrs Goffman smiled to herself: in a way—if Jimmy's end wasn't
so horrible—there was justice in it. The most brilliant lawyer and
financier in Montreal getting trimmed down to his BVD's by a
couple of snot-nosed kids! Shirley had been sleeping with Maxie for
four or five years, but not till her eighth date with Jimmy did she let
him so much as peck her on the cheek. Don Giovanni?

Late one night Mrs Goffman had overheard a conversation that
made her want to ring bells and blow whistles.

'Jimmy, you, getting married?' Sidney had said—he couldn't have been more shocked if Jimmy had grown sidecurls and turned Hassidic.

'I can't get it from her any way else,' Don Giovanni admitted.

Didn't she know he was going to get trimmed? But what did she care about money by that time? Life—a child—that was at stake, not Jimmy's lousy fortune. Marry even a prostitute for all Mrs Goffman cared by then—but get married. Why, when Marie the upstairs maid got pregnant, didn't Mrs Goffman hope one of her boys had done it? To hell with Westmount's ways! She knew. She had seen the truth by then. So who has to be the knocker-up, this chauffeur Josef!

'Drive more slowly,' she said savagely, thinking how many snot-nosed kids this overgrown squash of a driver must have already brought into the world.

Josef looked back at her, startled.

'Please, I mean,' she added.

A child—she was a lunatic on the subject. After the wedding she nagged, coaxed, threatened, whined. 'Kids, go home early.' 'Shirley, maybe you're late this month, eh, dollie?' Vulgar and rude and coarse —her father's line, Simon's, that's what the stakes were! Sidney was past praying for, she herself couldn't have kids. Everything was up to Jimmy. And he wanted a child too—that was the heartbreaking thing! Jimmy knew, saw, understood everything.

Mrs Goffman felt herself suffocating in the closed car. Her ears pulsed, her heart beat fast, she felt cold all over. Weakly, falter-ingly, she rolled down the window.

If only a child *had* come out of that marriage. Suffering was a man's lot in life. Everybody suffered, but not senselessly, like Jimmy. His suffering did nothing, made nothing, was worse than death. Noises made him jump. Coffee made him nervous. He began gobbling Sidney's pills. How could a hot-looking girl turn out so cold? He was repulsive, old, a mark, a fool—his nerve went.

Every bourgeois cliché that she as a Radical had scoffed at came thudding home—*you only live once*, what was more ghastly than that realization? *You're not getting any younger*, how that mocked Jimmy! What good was Mrs Goffman to her suffering son? Could she reverse her campaign to make him want a child? Could she de-stroy what he felt for Shirley just by telling him exactly what he knew anyway—that he was a cinch, a target, a bankroll, but feeling his age and growing helpless?

Mrs Goffman began to cough, gasp, and with a great effort pushed her face close to the open window.

'Madam, what is it?' Josef said, slowing down.

'I'm alright,' she lied, 'don't stop.'

It was as if life and time couldn't hold back their revenge. Shirley sneaked ties to Maxie, money, let him put things on Jimmy's charge accounts. Flagrant, open, Jimmy was Montreal's parlour-car joke. And Mrs Doba Goffman watched and waited, hoping hoping hoping.

Shirley never did bear Jimmy a child.

10

The limousine made a sudden swoop, a turn, a halt, then began its progress up the hill. Mrs Goffman craned her head, trying to get a last look at what wasn't Westmount. Her nose behaved like a pair of opera glasses after the opera, folding itself up awaiting the next liberation. Streets were empty, windows heavily draped so you couldn't see a sign of movement. Closer to the Ambassador's house there were no sidewalks, black limousines sped out of hidden driveways. Like this one, Mrs Goffman thought, sickening.

What a terrible death! Her confident Jimmy, worrying about flat tires all the time, stopping the car a dozen times to make Josef check, or getting out himself. Nothing was ever wrong, only Jimmy's shot nerves—he was half-destroyed when he stepped into the fog on Summit Circle. A limousine crushed him against his rear bumper and finished the job! Upstairs in the Ambassador's mansion, Mrs Goffman heard the smash and Jimmy's screams—horrible, horrible!

Mrs Goffman writhed, pinned her new hat against her ears, tears streaming from her eyes. Like a tiny boy Jimmy shrieked for her, screaming, screaming, and she ran into the cold dark mist, barefoot, in her nightgown, seeing nothing, hearing nothing but silence. That silence. Death's.

She'd screamed too—slapped at Josef, called him pig, ingrate, block, crook, shirker—why didn't he get out of the car instead of Jimmy? But now, when everything was past blaming, Mrs Goffman conceded the truth: Josef had more claim to life than Jimmy, much as she loved her son, great as his success had been.

She pulled wet terrified eyes away from the limousine floor and looked out at the houses on Summit Circle.

Right here! On this spot! She closed her eyes again and waited.

11

You fake, she chided herself. A real Radical would never cry. What a way to louse up this new magenta outfit—streaming eyes, a shiny shnozzola! You'd think she'd spent her afternoon at a Yiddish tear-jerker.

As Josef turned into the driveway Mrs Goffman touched her sulking nose with a powder puff, dried her eyes, made her old face smile. When there was hope it was O.K. to despair, but now hope was gone, what was the point of it? She winked at herself.

Sidney's worried face peeked out from her heavy drapes, his wristwatch close to his bad eyes. Why depress Sidney? She'd jolly him up a little, tell him how ridiculous she looked carrying the fish, how she stunk up that ritzy dress shop good.

She shielded her eyes, sighed, smiled more broadly, seeing past Josef's shoulder Nuns' Island. It was for sale. A million bucks they wanted.

By rights, Mrs Goffman thought as she looked toward her door, they shouldn't sell it. Nuns should stay on an island.

ARTHUR CAVANAUGH was born in Woodhaven, New York, and graduated from William and Mary College. His television plays, written between 1953 and 1958, were produced on *Kraft Theatre*, *NBC Matinee Theatre*, and *Chrysler Theatre* and in England, Canada, and Australia. His first story appeared in *The Saturday Evening Post* and he has since been published in *McCall's*, *Redbook*, *Woman's Day*, and *Sign*. His first book, *My Own Back Yard* was published by Doubleday in 1962. He is currently at work on a novel to be published in 1965.

What I Wish (Oh, I Wish) I Had Said

WERE I a painter, as Aunt Tillybird had grandly hoped, I would use crayon to draw this portrait of her. I would use pale colors—citron, ocher, faint umber—and sketch her in quick, scrawling lines: the red hair (dyed), arranged in slight dishevelment; the tentative, wavering smile; the soft eyes that were uncertain, speculative, and something more (frightened? defeated?) that I could never quite define. I would sketch her seated—no, lighted on a chair, in that manner she had, like an anxious bird poised for flight. Tillybird. Her father gave her the nickname when she was a child, and she had been called by it ever since. Certainly, she never appeared offended by the name. She even used it herself. " 'Lo, there, Robbie," she would say when I answered the telephone. "This is Aunt Tillybird. How's the world treating you?" She never seemed to mind the name at all, but I wonder about it. Birds, after all, are fragile creatures, meant to be treated with gentleness, not cruelty. I, of all the family, have cause to reflect on that.

Aunt Tillybird was my mother's sister; her only relative, in fact, except for some third cousins in Yonkers, whom we children had never met. Not that we saw much of Aunt Tilly. A schoolteacher and unmarried, she lived, as we did, in Brooklyn, but in a section as far removed from ours as the sun from the earth. Aunt Tilly lived in the fashionable Heights section, in an apartment building that

Copyright © 1963 by Arthur Cavanaugh.

boasted not only a doorman, but a man to run the elevator. There wasn't, I think, a single doorman in our neighborhood, unless you counted the attendant who, after taking your ticket, opened the door for you at Loew's Gates. There weren't even any apartment buildings in our neighborhood. Just five-story tenement flats and houses—unbroken rows of them that stretched, it seemed to me, to the outer rim of the world. We lived in the Bushwick section of Brooklyn, on Warbisher Street, and I cannot remember a time when I didn't hate it. Aunt Tillybird must have hated it, too. When she came down the street to our house, she always walked with her eyes pinned ahead, her glance avoiding the squatting stoops and sagging porches. Perhaps it was partly why she didn't visit us more often. She came to the house for Christmas dinner each year, laden with gifts, and if there were a First Communion in the family or a confirmation or graduation, Aunt Tilly showed up then, too, casting herself adrift among my father's large, noisy clan, the Connertys. But that marked the extent of her visits. For us, she represented a shadowy figure in the family drama, confined mostly to the wings. She was our Aunt Tillybird, who wore perfume and displayed hair of a peculiar reddish shade and who had traveled to Europe twelve times to view the cathedrals and art museums. Very likely, if my mother hadn't got sick one winter, the pattern of the relationship would never have changed. Aunt Tillybird would never have become a part of our lives —or, at any rate, a part of mine.

I was eleven years old, that winter. All week, my mother had lain upstairs in bed with a cold. At night, I could hear her coughing— terrible, racking coughs—and the pad of my father's feet as he got up to give her medicine. Then, one night, she was carried down the stairs on a stretcher, wrapped in blankets, her head rolling back and forth. She was taken by ambulance to Saint Mary's Hospital, and for a week, the word "pneumonia" floated through the house; "pneumonia," and "crisis," and "holding her own." My sister Margaret stayed home from school to take care of us, and my father was absent from the dinner table at night, remaining at the hospital until visitors' hours were over at nine.

After two weeks, my mother was still in Saint Mary's, and some new, sharper worry had begun to pinch at my father's face. He sat at night in the kitchen with Vincent, my older brother, and talked about it. I stood outside the door and listened. "Taking more X rays,"

I heard my father say between long silences. "Calling in this special-
ist. . . . By Saturday—"

"What's this you're up to?" Margaret demanded, coming up to me.
"Okay, Robbie. Start moving."

"By Saturday, what?" Vinny asked, in the kitchen.

"Well—we'll get the verdict, son."

"*Robbie*. Up to bed."

I dawdled up the stairs, dragging my feet over the steps. "Verdict"
was a word you heard in crime movies. James Cagney was always waiting around to hear verdicts. Then, in the next scene, he'd be working
in the prison machine shop. I went up the stairs, seeing a vision of my
mother as if she were in prison. I saw her white hospital bed placed
in a cell, behind bars. By Saturday—

On Saturday, it rained. We got up early to offer Mass and Communion for my mother. "Pray hard for her," my father admonished.
After Mass, he left us on the church steps and headed for the hospital
with Vinny, who, as the eldest, had the privilege of going along.

As we went into the house, the phone was ringing. It was Aunt
Tillybird. Since my mother had been taken to Saint Mary's, she had
called the house regularly. "That you, Robbie? Don't suppose there's
any news yet. . . . Well, I'll keep in touch. Toodle-oo."

By lunchtime, Aunt Tilly had called four times.

We sat around the living room that day—Dan, Roseanne, and me.
Dan was listening to a football game on the radio. Roseanne—she
was the youngest next to me—sat sulkily on the lumpy sofa and
thumbed through a movie magazine. I sat in the Morris chair, knees
pulled up. The house was cold—in winter, it was always cold. Upstairs, Margaret was housecleaning. There would be the roar of the
vacuum cleaner, then silence, then the whooshing roar again as she
plugged in the cleaner in another room. Verdict. . . .

I got up from the Morris chair, went into the dining room, and
spread newspapers on the table. I got out the water-color set I'd pur-
chased two months before with my birthday money. Against a stack
of telephone directories, I propped a colored photograph of a New
England landscape. I would paint a picture of the scene and send it
to my mother. I would paint her a whole batch of pictures, which she
could put on the walls of her hospital room, to make it look pretty. I
dipped the brush in a saucer of water and moistened the disks of
colors. I held the brush over the drawing paper. A blob of water trickled from the brush onto the paper. I watched the wet circle widen

and seep through the paper. Verdict. Verdict. Will the prisoner please rise and— I put my head down on the table and hid my face.

Then I heard the doorbell ring.

"Eeek, look who it is!" shrilled Roseanne, peering out at the porch from the living-room window. "That's all we need today, some of that silly talk of hers."

"Aunt Tillybird!" I shouted, and ran to the front hall. There was something I'd been wanting to tell Aunt Tilly. I opened the door, and there she was.

She wore a shiny pink raincoat; in her hands she held a pink umbrella, a purse, and a wet cakebox. "Greetings, Master Robbie."

I opened my mouth to speak, but the words got twisted together, and I just stood there.

Aunt Tillybird paid no attention. Emitting little breaths of laughter, she edged into the hall, bringing with her a festive air. "How are all the lovely childees?" (She pronounced this last *"chill*-dees," in the belief, I think, that it constituted Old English.)

Margaret came down the stairs and marched toward the door, in her new capacity of hostess.

"'Lo, Margaret." Aunt Tillybird held out the cakebox. "Here you are, some goodies from that French bakery on Henry Street. *Pâtisserie, une bonne pâtisserie.* Let's hear you say it, Marg."

It was Aunt Tilly's practice, on her visits to the house, to conduct among us a running course in French, concentrating on vocabulary and gender (of which, I learned later, she had the shakiest of acquaintances).

Margaret struggled with the pronunciation, *"Ooone bun paa-teesury."* The cakebox she bore away to the kitchen contained, I knew, ladyfingers, for Aunt Tilly never brought any other form of food to the house.

I took her umbrella and raincoat.

"Thank you, Robbie. Say, you're getting tall. The famous Connerty height." A vague smile on her lips, Aunt Tilly looped her purse over her arm and patted her red hair. It was as if she had arrived for a party and found no party underway. "I take it your, umm, dad's not home yet."

"No, he isn't."

It relieved her, I sensed, to learn that my father was still at the hospital, for that meant painful discussions would not need to be launched into immediately. "Well," said Aunt Tilly, and turned to survey the living room, awash with swollen, sagging furniture, uneven tables, and tilting lamps. Blocking her entrance into the room was Dan, who lay sprawled on the floor, absorbed in the football game blaring from the radio. "What ho, there, Daniel," she greeted him, in the jocular tone she assumed with all males over the age of fifteen. Dan did not answer. And since he made no attempt to rise, she proceeded to step over him. Safe on the other side of the room, Aunt Tilly lowered herself onto the sofa, as if expecting its imminent collapse. The radio blared away. "Ah, football," she declared. "The sport of kings."

"I thought that was horse racing," Dan said.

A little laugh, a bow. "*Monsieur* is correct. Horse racing it is, to be sure. Will I ever forget the splendors of Longchamps! That's a celebrated racing track outside Paris, you know. *Champs*, you see, means fields."

Dan sprang toward the radio and turned up the volume. "Quiet, Aunt Til. I want to hear this."

Aunt Tillybird made no comment. She looked down at her purse, a smile still on her face. She clicked the round gold clasp on the purse open and shut. Then she turned to Roseanne. "Well, tell us, Roseanne, what have you been doing lately that's worthwhile?"

In truth, Aunt Tilly's inquiries were not always easy to answer. Roseanne rolled her eyes and sucked at her mouth. "Uh—well, last week I got this idea I'd be a nurse someday," she offered.

"*Très bien*," said Aunt Tillybird, and then her eyes met mine.

I stepped clumsily toward the sofa. I had been rehearsing what I wanted to say, but again the words got twisted in my mind. I blurted out, "Aunt Tillybird, you know the birthday money you sent me? I bought a water-color set with it. A water-color set," I repeated, as the sound of the front door opening struck silence into us all.

We watched as my father appeared in the front hall. Behind him, Vinny closed the door noiselessly. Margaret materialized in the dining-room doorway, wiping her hands on a dish towel. Dan quickly turned off the radio. It was time, time now to learn the verdict. I saw Aunt Tillybird's eyes fasten on my father's white, worried face as if upon a dreaded apparition.

"Damned linoleum's coming apart," my father said, kicking at the hall flooring. "Might know the weather would be rotten, too." He nodded at Aunt Tilly, noting her presence for the first time. "Good of you to come, Tilly."

"Greetings, James."

My father nodded again, then walked heavily into the dining room.

Vinny pointed at Dan, Roseanne, and me. "No horsing around, understand? How are you, Aunt Tilly?" He went into the dining room. "Drink, Dad? Maybe you'd better." Then he ducked into the kitchen.

I saw that Aunt Tilly's hands, clicking and unclicking the gold clasp of her purse, were shaking. But she got up and went into the dining room. Once there, however, resolve deserted her. She gave a nervous laugh, turned to the china closet, and clapped her hands together as if in delighted surprise. "Why," she exclaimed, "Peg's still got that darling sugar and creamer from the tea set Papa bought Mama abroad. On their wedding trip, Papa and Mama visited W*ien* —that's German for Vienna."

Roughly, my father pulled out a chair from the dining table, cutting short the guided tour. He sat down silently. Vinny came in from the kitchen with a bottle of whisky and a shot glass. He filled the glass and handed it to my father.

My father emptied the glass. He wiped his hand across his mouth. "It's bad, Til," he said. "It's bad news, I'm afraid."

Whatever he was going to say, I didn't want to hear it. I didn't want to learn the damned verdict. My father was seated in the chair nearest the kitchen door, the chair where my mother always sat. I didn't want him sitting there. It was her chair. Since the night she had gone to Saint Mary's, we had kept it vacant, ready for when she came home. Now my father was sitting in the chair as if she weren't coming home any more. I didn't want to hear what he was going to tell us about her.

"Now, James," Aunt Tilly ventured, "whatever the news, I'm sure—"

I stepped into the dining room. "You know what I was telling Aunt Tilly about?" I said to my father. "I was telling her about the water-color set I bought with her birthday money. And you know what, Dad?"

My father regarded me in blank astonishment.

Vinny said, "For God's sake, Robbie."

But I went right ahead. "You know what I'm going to do, Dad?" I rattled on. "I'm going to paint a whole bunch of pictures for Mom, so she can decorate her hospital room. See, I've got a couple already done." I went to the china-closet drawer, where I kept my drawings. "See, Dad, I copy 'em from magazines."

"What the living hell are you talking about?" he demanded. "*Drawings?*" He reached out, grabbed the drawings, and flung them onto the carpet. "Your mother's coughing blood, and you stand there prattling about pictures. Holes in her lungs, do you understand?" he shouted. "She has to go away, but you don't care about that. Oh, no, you just want to chatter about—" He stopped and looked away from me. "I'm sorry, Robbie."

"That's okay." I picked up the drawings and put them on the table. "It was nothing important," I said, and walked out of the dining room. I stood at the front door and looked out at the rain and the street. There was silence in the dining room, then voices again, as the discussion resumed. I put my hands over my ears, still not wanting to hear about my mother.

"How long will it be for?" I heard Margaret ask.

"A year, anyway. Depends. Maybe two."

I heard Aunt Tilly say, "The money will be managed. Somehow it will."

"My God, Tilly, do you know what a year at that kind of place costs?"

I pulled open the door and stepped out onto the rickety porch. The rain was hitting against the porch railing, loosening the cracked, peeling paint. I thought of the plans my father had made to paint the house in the spring. New paint job, new linoleum for the hall, new furnace, new water heater—yet nothing would ever improve it. The others—Vinny, Margaret, Dan, and Roseanne—didn't feel like this about the house. They were happy living there. They didn't mess around with stupid water-color sets and paintbrushes.

I heard a sound behind me. It was Aunt Tillybird. "Here he is," she said, "the artist viewing nature!" She held my drawings in her hand. "Mustn't worry about your mother, Robbie. We'll get her well again."

I hugged the porch post and contemplated Warbisher Street. "Some nature to view, isn't it?" I said.

"Yes," Aunt Tillybird murmured.

"The rest of the family doesn't seem to mind. I don't know why I do."

"It's because," she told me, "you're different." She looked down at the drawings. "I can't imagine why it took till today for me to recognize it. Poor eyesight, I guess."

I kept looking at the street, and in the slanting rain, I seemed to glimpse my mother coming along the cracked sidewalk, bundles of groceries in her arms. The kitchen. What a nice, cozy place it was, with her bustling around the stove, listening to you talk while she fixed supper. I felt tears on my face. I turned my head away, so that Aunt Tillybird wouldn't see.

Her hands made awkward movements. It wasn't her usual role to give comfort, and she didn't quite know how to proceed. "Say, now, Robbie," she began, after a moment. "I was thinking about something. An aspiring artist needs, you know, to become acquainted with art. He needs to visit museums and study the masters. Look, how would you like to go to the city next Saturday and tour the Metropolitan? Oh, the Rembrandts there, the El Grecos! Will you be busy next Saturday?"

I got out my handkerchief and blew my nose. "I—I don't think so," I said.

"Fine! We'll make it a date, then."

And that was how my life with Aunt Tillybird began.

"Feast yourself," Aunt Tillybird proclaimed. She drew to a halt in the gallery doorway and gestured dramatically. "Drink in the beauty of it, Robbie. Velázquez, of course." She folded her arms and studied the painting that gleamed from the wall of the room ahead. We were in a gallery on the second floor of the Metropolitan. "What *is* the title? Oh, it's famous."

I ran over to the gold-framed painting, which was of a boy dressed in a red suit. "It's named Don Manuel Osario de—something or other," I called back to Aunt Tilly. "And it's by Goya."

"Well," she said, "they're both Spanish, at least."

It was more than two years since the rainy winter Saturday. Soon after that day, my mother had been taken to Greenville Sanatorium, in Saranac, New York. I had not seen her in two years. I was thirteen now. And I was going to be a painter when I grew up.

Aunt Tilly stood beside the Goya painting and regarded the red-suited boy. "Notice the fantastic texture," she advised. "Examine the skin tones. Unique!" She consulted the clutch of museum brochures in her hand. "Shall we finish the second floor or try something else,

Robbie? The auditorium has a movie at two—a tour of the châteaux country. How's that sound?"

"Fine," I told her. "I'd like that."

"And, oh, a new Tintoretto's on display in the Recent Acquisitions Room. Why don't we head there first?"

I moved close to her. Here, in this radiant place suffused with light, Warbisher Street did not exist. Here, I could forget that my mother had gone far away from me. Forgetting was a trick I had trouble with at home. It was hard not to think about my mother there. Often at night, I would wake up calling for her. Or at supper I would look up, expecting to see her come through the swinging kitchen door. Then I would glance at the empty chair near the door and go back to eating, trying not to think about her. I tried not to think of school, too, or Warbisher Street, or the rows of houses that I hated. There was only one thing I wanted to think about: my Saturdays with Aunt Tilly.

Saturday had become like a flower, a gigantic, beautiful flower that bloomed out over the other days of the week, concealing them. Every Saturday, I would get up early, put on a fresh white shirt and my Sunday suit, and take the trolley to the tall, brick building where Aunt Tilly lived. The doorman already knew me there. He would greet me by name, and the elevator man would converse with me as he sped the car to the tenth floor.

"You're a regular escort for Miss Quinlan, aren't you?" he would say. "I don't believe your aunt's ever had a visitor till you started showing up. She's just been all alone, just living in that little apartment, coming and going all by herself."

The apartment Aunt Tilly lived in had surprised me. It consisted of one small room, with a single window that looked out on a back court. Against one wall was a studio couch covered with a paisley shawl; at night, Aunt Tilly took off the paisley shawl, and the couch became her bed. In an alcove in the corner was a pullman kitchen, hidden by a screen. Prints and reproductions covered nearly every inch of Aunt Tilly's walls. A steamer trunk pasted with travel labels stood near the window. Books were everywhere—dusty old books and old opera programs; old issues of *Art Annual*; guidebooks to museums and galleries; souvenir menus from trips to Paris and Rome and Madrid. The room was crowded, so that you couldn't move about in it very easily. It was small, Aunt Tilly's apartment, small and dark and cluttered; it gave you a surprise when you walked in the first time.

Now Aunt Tilly turned one way and then the other, surveying the museum rooms on each side of us. "Now, which is the quickest way to the main stairs?"

"If we go back through the rooms where we already were," I said, "we'll end up in that big blue room. And the main stairs are right beyond."

"Of course!" she cried. "*Exactly* the way." We turned and started back through the maze of rooms. "I believe you already know this place better than I, Robbie. I'm awfully eager to see the new Tintoretto. Those Venetian painters were so bold, such a command of color and form. Hungry yet?"

"No, I'm fine."

"We can always stop for lunch."

"But then we'll miss the movie."

Aunt Tilly stopped and looked at me. "You really like our Saturdays, don't you?" she said.

I stared up at her. Her eyes were a clear blue, like the blue in Giotto paintings. They were soft, pretty eyes, without meanness (but with something else—fear? defeat?) in them. I thought of my mother and the stretcher carrying her down the stairs, and of how far away she was. My mouth trembled. "Our Saturdays," I told Aunt Tilly, "are all I have."

Sometimes on a Saturday, especially at Christmastime, Aunt Tilly liked to stroll through the glittering department stores on Fifth Avenue, inspecting the wares. On her tours, she never made any purchases. She would pause at a counter, tempted by a bright silk scarf or a pair of French gloves. Her purse would click open, then shut again, and she would laugh. "Got to save my pennies." Afterward, we would go into a hotel—the Plaza, usually—and sit in the lobby, so that Aunt Tilly could rest her feet. She would watch the gold elevator doors glide open and the guests alight from the red-carpeted cars.

"One day, perhaps, you'll be a painter of prominence," she would say to me, "and you'll stay here."

"When I do," I would tell her, "I'll invite you to lunch with me every day. I'll have a one-man show at a big gallery, and the best painting will be a portrait of you, Aunt Tilly."

"Really, Robbie? My!"

Now and again on a Saturday, Aunt Tilly would propose still another activity. She would consult the shipping news, to learn what ships might be sailing that day. On sailing days, visitors were allowed on board the ships. "The *Normandie* leaves at three," Aunt Tilly would announce. "What say, Robbie? Shall we hop over to the pier?"

I think I liked, best of all, visiting the great, glistening liners tied up at the North River piers. Aunt Tilly and I would climb the visitors' gangplank and set out to tour the entire ship. We would inspect the lounges, the swimming pools, the cabins, the dining rooms, pushing our way through the crowds of visitors, through the smoke and babble of voices, the clinking glasses raised in farewell toasts.

Having traveled to Europe twelve times, Aunt Tilly knew a lot about ships. "There's nothing," she would declare, "to equal an ocean voyage. Shipboard life is such a restorative—and you meet such congenial people. Interesting people who *do* things."

At some point in her dissertations on shipboard life, the announcement "All visitors ashore, all visitors ashore" would issue from the loudspeaker. Aunt Tilly would give one last, lingering glance at a tea salon or a writing room, and then we would go back down the gangplank and stand at the end of the pier, among the crowds waving and shouting, and watch the ship depart. Aunt Tilly and I would stand there long after the crowds had gone, and watch the ship until there was nothing more to see than a curl of smoke far down the river. Often it was cold on the pier. Aunt Tilly would hug her arms to her body, pull up the collar of her coat, and look silently toward the curl of smoke.

I would stand next to her and think of the little one-room apartment, dark and cluttered, and the travel labels pasted to the steamer trunk. "You haven't been to Europe in a couple of years," I'd remind her. "You didn't go last year or the year before."

"No, I didn't."

"Are you making plans to go?" I would ask her. "I'll bet you'll go next summer."

Aunt Tilly would hug her coat collar to her face, wisps of red hair escaping from her hat. "We'll see, Robbie," she'd answer. "We'll see."

"Penny for your thoughts," said Aunt Tillybird, as we reached the bottom of the museum stairs and sat down on a bench.

I scuffed at the floor with my feet. "You know what I wish, Aunt Tillybird?" I said.

"What, Robbie?"

"I wish there didn't have to be anything except paintings and stat-

ues and—" I struggled for the right word—"I don't know." I kicked at
the floor. "I wish there was only Saturday and coming to the city with
you."

Aunt Tilly was silent for a moment. "I know what you mean." She
looked at the gift counter and at the people clustered in front of the
displays. "When I was young," she said, "I felt so deeply about art. I
planned to make it my career, you know. Oh, yes. I was going to be an
artist. I only started teaching school so that I could save the money
to study in Paris. But when I finally got there—"

I turned and looked at her face. Her head was tilted a little to the
side, and her eyes had a faraway expression. "What happened?" I
asked.

She shook her head, as if in amusement at her folly. "Well, I'm not
sure, exactly. I'd signed up to take a course at the Sorbonne. I was to
be in Paris the whole summer. But I—I was just too timid to attend
classes. I felt—well, what if it turned out that I couldn't paint after
all? I was afraid, I guess, that I would fail."

"You shouldn't have been afraid, Aunt Tilly," I said. "You should
have marched into those classes and painted away, and the dickens
with the rest."

"Should I have?" mused Aunt Tilly, patting my arm. "Shall we have
a look at the Tintoretto now?"

We got up from the bench and went to the Recent Acquisitions
Room. On the wall farthest from the entranceway hung the Tintoretto, brilliant with color and power.

Aunt Tillybird gazed at the painting with soft eyes. Her voice was
little and quiet. "I guess I settled for just looking," she said. "Yes, I
became just one of the onlookers."

Later, when we had left the museum and were seated in a sandwich
shop on Madison Avenue, Aunt Tilly told me that we would not be
meeting next Saturday. She was going to Saranac to visit my mother.

"Oh," I said.

Aunt Tilly pressed a spoon against the tea bag in the cup of steaming water. She removed the tea bag and stirred the amber water
slowly. "Has your father said anything yet?"

I looked up from my plate. I didn't want to know, I didn't want
to—

"Perhaps he's waiting till it's definite," Aunt Tilly went on.

I felt my heart hammering. "Till *what?*" I asked.

She regarded me across the table. "If all goes well, your mother will

be coming home soon, Robbie. We'll be bringing her home to you."
Then she said, her hand reaching out, "It's all right, Robbie. It's all
right. No one's too old to cry." . . .

My life with Aunt Tillybird did not end when my mother came
home—that is, not right away. Our Saturdays continued. It was simply that they didn't occur as frequently.

The house on Warbisher Street became transformed. It was still
—and would be forever—a derelict, squeezed-together little house in
need of patching. But now it became the place where my mother was,
the place she had left and had come back to, the place where she
could be found laughing in the kitchen, or counting sheets and pil-
lowcases in the upstairs hall.

And I was growing up. I was a freshman, then a sophomore, then
a senior in high school. I was writing stories for the school magazine,
and my name was on the masthead of the school newspaper. "Robert
F. Connerty," it read, "Assistant Editor." I had decided that I didn't,
after all, want to be a painter. I would be a writer, instead.

Saturdays found me busy with my own activities. There were as-
signments to finish for the school paper. There were parties to go to
at night. There wasn't the time, I decided, to spend a Saturday trailing around New York with Aunt Tillybird. If I wanted to go to the
city—why, I could go by myself now.

Aunt Tillybird was pleased when I told her of my resolve to become a writer. "A Balzac in the family," she declared on the phone
one night. "A Kipling in our midst."

"In the winter issue of the *Anchor*," I informed her, "I had three
selections."

"Three selections," said Aunt Tillybird. "Imagine. I guess you're
not going to turn out to be an onlooker, Robbie."

"No, sir," I told her. "Anyway, that's why I can't meet you Saturday." Aunt Tilly had phoned to invite me to a Cézanne exhibit. "I
have to go to a journalism conference that day," I told her. "I've been
chosen to represent the *Anchor* staff. So I'll be busy, you see. But
thanks for asking me, Aunt Tilly."

There was a silence on the phone, then the little laugh. "Well, we'll
try to make it another time, then. Toodle-oo for now, Robbie."

"Good-by, Aunt Tillybird," I said.

Good-by, Aunt Tillybird. . . . Good-by, Aunt Tillybird. . . .

I was twenty-seven years old the last time I saw Aunt Tillybird. I
had become a writer—or, at any rate, I had published stories in maga-

zines and been hired to work on a movie script (the studio dropped me after a month). I was living in New York and had just signed a publisher's contract for my first book. With the advance, I was planning to get married and go to Europe. It was a spring day, I remember, and John Crane, an old friend from college, had invited me to go with him to an exhibit of Piranesi drawings at the Metropolitan. The Piranesi drawings were on display in the Special Exhibits Room.

We took the elevator upstairs, started down the long corridor, and there, at the end of a corridor, was Aunt Tillybird.

I stopped, uncertain for a moment if it was she. The small figure looked even smaller; the frail shoulders were stooped; the hair was more white than red. And then I *was* sure. Of course it was Aunt Tilly.

"Aunt Tillybird," I called. The small figure continued its slow progress down the corridor. Apparently, she had not heard me. "Aunt Tillybird," I called again.

She turned slowly, and as she caught sight of me, a smile broke like sunlight across her face. "Robbie," she said. "Well, Robbie. How's the world treating you?"

I introduced John to her. How long had it been, I wondered, since I had seen her last? Not since Dan's wedding last winter—almost a year. Why hadn't I phoned her? Aunt Tilly had retired from teaching and was living on her pension. She looked old.

Birds are fragile creatures, meant to be treated with gentleness, not cruelty. Yes, I have reflected on that.

As I stood talking to Aunt Tilly in the museum corridor, I knew what I should do. John was a painter; he had just returned from Europe; he was exactly the sort of person Aunt Tilly had once treasured meeting. What I should do was invite Aunt Tilly to view the Piranesi exhibit with us, and afterward, I should take her to lunch. Instead, I said, "Well, it's been wonderful running into you, Aunt Tilly. We've got to get together soon. I wish I weren't so rushed today. I'd ask you to lunch with us, but I have to be downtown in less than an hour."

And she replied, "You'd better hurry to the Piranesi, then. You wouldn't want to miss it." Then her thin, weightless hand gripped my arm, and she raised her face for a kiss. "Good-by, Robbie dear."

"Good-by, Aunt Tillybird."

Two months later, just before I was married and left for Europe, Aunt Tilly died. The elevator man found her on the studio couch in the little one-room apartment, the paisley shawl thrown over her.

She had died in her sleep without making a sound, without telling anyone.

After the funeral, I went with my mother to the apartment to sort through Aunt Tilly's keepsakes: the dusty books, the prints and reproductions, the souvenir menus and guidebooks. In the bottom drawer of her desk, I found the water-color drawings from that long-ago day on Warbisher Street.

"Poor Aunt Tilly," I said. "She used to tell me she was just one of the onlookers. How hard it must have been, always to look on, never to do anything."

"Never to do anything?" repeated my mother, angrier than I had ever seen her. "*Never to do anything?*"

Then she told me what I should, of course, have known.

"Where did you imagine the money came from?" she asked, her face stiff with anger. "How do you think I was able to stay at Greenville? She gave me back to all of you. I'd call that doing something, wouldn't you?"

This portrait of Aunt Tilly is constructed of words only. It is nothing that can be hung on a wall or viewed in a gallery. Perhaps it does not matter, for she is not here to view it. Yet it is for her I have painted it.

I have kept her things—the books, the souvenirs, the prints. I have kept, too, the bitter memory of my last meeting with her. How I wish —will always wish—that I had said, instead of good-by, what I had never told her, as I tell her now a thousand times in my prayers. How I wish I had said, "*Aunt Tillybird, I love you.*"

MARY McCARTHY is the well-known author and critic. Widely published and read, she has had notable success with such books as *The Company She Keeps, Groves of Academe, Memories of a Catholic Girlhood, Stones of Florence* and, most recently, *The Group*.

The Hounds of Summer

THE village had an inn with thirteen rooms, running water, and a bath for general use, two boarding houses, a post office, two dark provisions stores, an open-air vegetable stand, a meat market, a bakery, a fish store, a milk store, a drygoods store, and a newsstand which sold soap flakes, toilet paper, stamps, Italian cigarettes, matches, and the provincial edition of the *Nazione* of Florence, supplemented for the summer trade by the *Corriere della Sera, La Stampa,* and *Il Giorno*. There was a pay telephone in a booth at the inn, and this *posto pubblico* was the only telephone in Porto Quaglia, except for the doctor's, so they said. Telegrams came down by bicycle from the hill town of Acquafredda, where there was a telegraph office, a *municipio,* and a police station. There was only one frigidaire, they said, in Porto Quaglia, not counting the one in the inn, and one bathroom with hot water. There was no cream to be bought in the dairy store, and the milk had to be boiled. The dentist drove over from Sarzana, the nearest market town, to pull teeth in the patient's parlor or kitchen, and in summer he brought along his bathing suit, to get double value from the trip: there were *cabine* to rent at the public beach, and a small bar selling coffee, Campari soda, *gelati* in paper cups, bottled fruit juice, and vermouth. In short, the village was poor. The villagers spoke an ugly Italian and many of them had lost most of their teeth. The older women wore dark-blue dotted cotton house dresses and had hair of that peculiar iron gray found among poor Italians and suggestive of rust and mold.

It was a fishing village, *un petit hameau de pêcheurs, un piccolo villaggio di pescatori*. That was how those who went there for their vacations found themselves describing it to their hairdressers, mani-

Copyright © 1963 by The New Yorker Magazine, Inc.

curists, pedicurists, concierges, postmen, train and air companions en
route from London, Rome, Paris, Milan. True or false?

True because Porto Quaglia was in fact populated by fishermen
whose thin brown nets like hair nets were spread out to dry in the
sun behind the whitewashed houses, and there was no other industry
in the village except for the desultory transport of marble from the
nearby mountains above Carrara, which was carried out in boats and
barges equipped with giant cranes, grappling hooks, pulleys, and
winches that appeared to spend the whole month of August toiling to
dump five or six blocks of gray stone on the waterfront and then re-
load them in a Sisyphean labor. Porto Quaglia's little harbor had
once had a fleet of sailing vessels that carried marble from Carrara as
far as Marseille, but then Carrara had built its own harbor at Marina
di Carrara, and the sons of the Porto Quaglia mariners became bar-
men on the United States and Italian Lines. At any rate, Porto Quaglia today was simply a fishing village, and yet to say so to your mani-
curist or your B.B.C. producer was a lie.

Partly because the words "*hameau de pêcheurs*," et cetera, implied
something colorful—a picturesque fishing fleet heavy with dragging
nets like dark bridal veils; orange sails, red sails, yellow sails, marked
with crescents and suns; bright-blue boats with an eye painted on the
prow pulled up on the beach; old men mending their gear. A few old
men did occasionally mend their gear but not where they could be
observed; there were no sails except the white ones of small pleasure
boats; and it was rare to see a fishing trawler, even on the horizon.
The prized local catch was *muggine*—a special kind of white mullet,
they said, that lived only in the tidal reaches of the bamboo-fringed
River Quaglia, on which the village bordered. Yet *muggine* was hardly
ever to be found in *pescheria*, which sold chiefly sole and red mullet
that were suspected of coming from somewhere else along the coast.
Fishing, such as it was, was practiced secretively as a rule. At night
sometimes you would hear a lone rowboat push off from a wooden
landing, then the plash of oars or the sound of an outboard motor.
In the dead stillness of noon, you would see a man or a boy standing
in a rowboat casting a white furled hand net into the river with a
beautiful circling, swooping motion; this net was called "the hawk"
and it struck into the glassy green water like a gauzy bird of prey.
But often the man proved to be the doctor from Carrara in white
duck trousers, who had learned the hawk in middle age; he was the
"other" doctor, married into the local hill gentry, and had a tennis

court, a telephone, a frigidaire, and at least one bath with hot water, which were never counted in the inventory, probably because *he* was not counted, out of courtesy to the indigenous doctor, who had a monopoly on the sick of Porto Quaglia. The boy in the row boat with the net was always the same boy; he cast it again and again without catching anything, giving a tranced sense of time suspended like the black cranes groping for the gray marble.

Yet the fact that Porto Quaglia did not conform to a touristic image of a fishing village was not exactly the reason for the feeling that the description was false. Had it looked like Collioure or Concarneau or Chioggia or Provincetown, there still would have been something wrong—indeed wronger. The inauthenticity of the description lay in the describers. That is, if a native of Porto Quaglia described his home as a fishing village, he would be telling the truth, but in the mouth of, say, a Milanese publisher these words became horribly fraudulent. To a local fisherman Porto Quaglia was self-evidently a fishing village, but to a Milanese publisher it was *"un piccolo villaggio di pescatori."* Those quotation marks, which sprang up around the words quite without the publisher's volition, were the source of all the trouble.

Similarly with the word "unspoiled." It was true that Porto Quaglia was not yet spoiled, comparatively speaking, yet only a very unaware summer visitor, perhaps an Englishwoman, would try saying this to a native, whose whole interest lay in having it spoiled as fast as possible. There is something suspect in a laudatory remark that cannot be made in the presence of those being lauded. "Unspoiled," moreover, had grown those quotation marks as the old women in Porto Quaglia grew tufts of iron-gray whiskers. But how else would you describe Porto Quaglia, without going into detail, except as a fishing village on the Ligurian coast that had not yet been completely spoiled by tourists?

This was the first slight embarrassment for the kind of person who came to Porto Quaglia—the difficulty of stating, in brief form, where he was going without making it sound like the kind of place that would attract someone quite different from himself—say, an editress of *Vogue* or another Milanese publisher. It was no solution to reply "I'm going to Porto Quaglia," for this led to "Where is Porto Quaglia?" and "Should I know about it?," all of which ended in a description of P. Q. as a simple fishing village on the Ligurian coast.

The only remedy, it was decided at lunch at the Buonsantis' (he was a tall bald Italian employed at UNESCO in Paris; she was small and French and translated philosophic and economic texts), would be for Porto Quaglia to be "put on the map," like Portofino or Portovenere or Port Said. But if your concierge or your hairdresser already knew about Porto Quaglia, so that the mere name produced a ready-made description like a pop-up toaster, then the reason for going there would have vanished. The reason for going there was that nobody knew about it. But of course everybody wants to go to a place no one knows about (except those in the know), though for varying motives, which is why the words "simple fishing village" have been as abused as a pinewoods in which there is now a Camping. Those who, like the Buonsantis and their guests, had been attracted to Porto Quaglia by the absence of yachts, luxury hotels, motorboats, water skiers, skin divers, golf, casinos, shops, cocktail lounges, night clubs, sports cars, and other amenities were refugees from a banal summer life, but it was impossible, they agreed, to escape from a cliché of action without being stamped with a cliché of speech, like an exit permit. The world will allow you to go to Porto Quaglia as long as it has Porto Quaglia's "number."

Fifteen people, the usual complement, were eating lunch at a long table under a trellis covered with trumpet vines in the Buonsantis' garden, which looked out onto the main street and the river, where a few masts of small boats could be seen. The garden contained a flagged terrace of varicolored marbles, a grape arbor, a sour-cherry tree, some trampled lawn, two large ornamental palms, and two Christmas trees, symmetrically planted. There was also a "fantasy" table, made of stone in the shape of a large mushroom and surrounded by little painted stone toadstools. On the balcony rail of the apartment above, facing the river, hung some striped towels and damp bathing suits. In the green midday shimmer the luncheon party, which was still peeling figs and drinking wine, resembled a scene by Renoir, the more so because they were speaking French. French was the prevailing language among the summer people at Porto Quaglia, who were known to the natives as "*i francesi*," whatever their nationality. Today the group included Mme. Buonsanti's father, the two Buonsanti children, a French engineer, his wife—a child psychologist —and their three children, a Roman editor and his wife, a Livornese professor of history on loan to Columbia University, and an American journalist and his wife, who were staying at the inn. Three bicycles, a surf mattress, and a rubber boat leaned against the wall of the house, and some beach chairs were sprawled near the table; the double doors were open into the principal room of the Buonsantis' apartment, where a great many straw hats were piled on top of the sideboard and a chessboard was set up for play on the glass-covered dining table. More "French" kept arriving and pulling up chairs. The women and girls were wearing summer cotton dresses, and the men striped jerseys with khaki shorts or long blue or white canvas trousers. They were still discussing what to call Porto Quaglia.

"You French are so frightfully analytical," said an English labor lawyer, who was opposed to what he called "blood sports" and had appeared at the end of lunch, in cleated shoes and with a sweater tied round his hips, to take the Buonsanti children on a mountain hike. "My wife and I don't find it at all embarrassing to say we're going to a fishing village. I mean, why not face facts?" He then translated his remarks into French.

"If you faced facts," said the Roman editor tartly, "you would say you were going to a summer resort."

"*Une petite station balnéaire,*" agreed Mme. Buonsanti, laughing.

"*Plage modeste,*" added her husband.

Everyone laughed, thinking of the dusty town beach where none of the "*francesi*" swam except when the sea was rough and a boat could not land at the White Rock or Raven Point or one of the many coves and grottoes farther up the coast. One reason that Porto Quaglia remained "unspoiled" was that the snobbish casual tourist saw only the *plage modeste* at the end of the village and immediately turned his Alfa Romeo around and shot off to Lerici or Forte dei Marmi. To sit in the café outside the inn and watch this happen while eating an ice-cream cone was one of the children's amusements on dull mornings when the boats had not yet come to take them bathing and the family outboard motor was "*en panne.*"

The White Rock was the chief lure and secret beauty of Porto Quaglia. Parties of bathers were taken there every morning by the fishermen in little yawls with inboard motors; informal excursions ran several times before noon from the pier in front of the inn, and regular passengers were picked up at the rickety little wooden landings along the river, off the single main street. Starting at ten o'clock, cries began to ring out from the bank as the fishing boats with little triangular colored flags in their rigging were sighted. "Pierino!" "Paolo!" "Romeo!" "*Venga, venga!*" Or "Wait, wait! I am coming. As-petti! Wait for me, Pierino!" Or "*Jean, où est Jean? Où est le mate-*

las?" "Irene, have you got the basket?" "My glasses! I forgot my glasses!" "Carlo! *Dov' è il tuo cappello?*" "*Dov' è Michel? Où est Marc?*" "*Son già partiti? Con Romeo?*" With thermos bottles of cold water, baskets of cheese and fruit, baskets and bags of bathing equipment, with surf mattresses, pails and shovels, yellow and red and white and blue inflated tubes, beach umbrellas, nets containing books and newspapers, the boats were finally packed and headed for the White Rock. Fifteen minutes later, the landing was accomplished, the older children swimming to shore and returning like a school of fish to hover alongside and seize the bags and baskets as they were lifted over the bow and offer a hand to the women in their dresses and beach gowns as they climbed down the unsteady ladder, while the men, having leapt to shore, formed a human chain along which the younger children were passed. Nearly every day someone or something fell overboard in the excitement of landing: a straw hat, a book, a pair of glasses, shoes, a middle-aged newcomer—or all of these together in one parcel. This had happened yesterday morning to the whiskered American journalist, thought by the children to resemble Uncle Sam, and François, the twelve-year-old Buonsanti boy, had jubilantly taken a picture of it with his new camera.

Starting at one o'clock, the boats reappeared at the White Rock, at Raven Point, at the various *scogli* and small pebbly beaches, to bring the bathers back for lunch. Naturally, irritations sprang up from time to time between the boatmen or between the boatmen and the passengers, who would complain that Romeo or Paolo had forgotten them and taken a party of new people in preference. But those who were left behind on the jetty would always appear at Rocca Bianca, rowed by an old man or a little boy, and some came in the old man's rowboat by preference, disapproving of the motor sailboats and the oil they spread on the water. Some of the young people came by threes and fours in rowboats rented for the summer or given them for Christmas or a birthday, and one family had an outboard motor. Sometimes the older children, in pairs or accompanied by François in his rowboat, would swim back to Porto Quaglia and arrive late and panting for lunch, or they would walk back in a party over the marble cliffs, though this was considered dangerous by their parents.

The White Rock was really a mass of rocks and cliffs of pure milk-white marble that formed a towering point jutting into the sea. Above it, on a steep mountain flank, grew ilex and pine and wild olive trees. The water around it was a pale green and exceptionally clear. If you swam way out beyond your depth you could still look down to the white marble shelving that extended along the sea floor like a vast bath for sea horses or Tritons. Along the shore it formed deep caves. The sea at this point was seldom quiet and gave the impression of washing itself, like laundry, by beating against the rock and rinsing itself as it ran in and out of the cool caves. Blue-green and violet marbles were not uncommon along this stretch of coast, but white was freakish; it was as though a vein of sculptor's marble had escaped from its mountain prison miles off in the Apuan Alps and raced underground to burst into the sea in a great release of energy, so that this marine spot was like an inchoate museum or temple or workshop haunted by glistening forebodings or polished memories of statuary—nymphs and dolphins and Venuses rising from the spray. For some reason, doubtless connected with the marble, the water here and in the nearby coves was cooler than is usual in the Mediterranean, and there were no jellyfish.

Farther along, at the beach called Raven Point and at the lonely beach called Judgment Day by the summer people, because it looked like the scene of a Tintoretto "Last Judgment," there were mussels and purple sea urchins clinging to the dark rocks. The children collected them; the men opened them with pocket knives, and the bathers shared them at midday, along with the cheese, figs, grapes, pears, peaches brought in the individual baskets, to stave off hunger, before Pierino or Romeo or Paolo came to take everyone home for a two-o'clock lunch. Like a backdrop to this watery, summery scene bobbing with small craft and bright swimming tubes, the Carrara mountains came into view as the boats rounded into Porto Quaglia's harbor—pale brown, like canvas, in the blue distance, patched with what appeared to be snow fields, streaked with crevasses and awesome glaciers, all made of white marble—a realm of Titans, Michelangelo Land. In the intermediate distance, in the green-forested hills above the Quaglia, were belfried Tuscan hill towns that caught the gold of the afternoon sun in their medieval clocks, towers, and ramparts. It was like an illustrated history lesson: the children's eyes travelled thoughtfully from the remote white fissures of the quarries, which had been opened in Roman times, down to picture-book Castelnuovo, where Dante had stayed, down to the stone artillery nests, so near you could almost touch them, that the Germans had made in the last war.

Except on Sundays, when trippers came from Sarzana and Acquafredda, the "French" usually had the White Rock to themselves, and the strangers, principally English, who from time to time "discovered" Rocca Bianca while staying at the inn or in a *pensione*, were adopted by the "French," offered fruit and cheese, the loan of a child's pail or surf mattress, invited to play chess in the evenings or join in political discussions in the café outside the inn. The English, henceforth known as "*francesi*" to the boatmen and shopkeepers, reciprocated with ice creams, lifts to Sarzana or Marina di Massa for shopping, invitations to drive to Lucca or Pisa. Sometimes, when the "French" went to Raven Point or Judgment Day, a smart motorboat with water skis would come whizzing up from Lerici, disgorging Roman writers, society women, publishers, who were staying at the Hotel Doria or the Hotel Byron or the Hotel Shelley e delle Palme. A different world, as different as the blue Lerici waters from the green waters of Porto Quaglia, a world of palms, villas, and esplanades, but this world too was accommodated. Joint dinners were arranged at a mountain inn known for its *prosciutto* and sheep cheese or else in the port of Lerici, where the guests would eat *spaghetti alle vongole* or plates of *datteri*, those brown polished date-shaped mussels that grew only on the soft stone of Portovenere, where they were said to burrow holes like cliff swallows. Or the Roman writers and publishers would come to dinner at the inn at Porto Quaglia, telephoning ahead of time to the *posto pubblico* to order *muggine ai ferri* and to recommend that the waiters wear jackets. But the boy waiters in the inn at Porto Quaglia did not have jackets; the only smartening up they could do was to roll down their shirtsleeves and take the pencil from behind their ear. "*Un piccolo villaggio di pescatori*," the host at dinner would explain to the troop he had brought with him, bestowing a tender, fatherly smile on the café where the "French" were playing chess as if nothing had happened.

There was no fear that these Romans would "discover" Porto Quaglia, for they believed they already knew it, like the inside of their pocket. Still, word was getting around, as Mike, the American journalist, was saying to Hélène Buonsanti, lowering his voice slightly, as though passing on a piece of confidential information.

"*Qu'est-ce qu'il dit, maman?*" said Laure, the fourteen-year-old Buonsanti girl alertly. All the children were on the *qui vive* for any threat to their summer home, and they understood by instinct when it was being talked about, even in a foreign tongue.

Mme. Buonsanti's father, Dr. Bernheim, shook his gray head and checked his granddaughter with his eyes, which were generally half closed, as if inattentive, like the ear of a confessor. His lids now dropped again, and his hand cradled his chin, but the tilt of his head betrayed the fact that he was following closely what the American said.

"Yep," continued Mike, "the word's getting around, I'm afraid, Hélène." He coughed and moved his chair closer to his little hostess, still talking under his breath, but since he was in the habit of raising his voice when speaking English to a foreigner, the effect was of an arresting stage whisper. Everyone at the table turned to listen. "I read about it in New York," he shouted, sotto-voce. "Last winter. In *Harper's Bazaar*. A highbrow fashion magazine. They said Porto Quaglia was where the French left-wing intellectuals went for the summer."

"How stupid!" said Hélène Buonsanti coldly. "The French left-wing intellectuals! *Ecoute, Arturo. Figure-toi.*"

"*Mais c'est vrai, maman!*" said Laure. "*C'est vrai, maman,*" said François, grinning. "*C'est vrai, n'est-ce pas, Catherine?*" He turned his bright, demure black eyes to the engineer's oldest daughter, who was fifteen and humorless.

"*Tais-toi, François!*" flashed his mother. The children made fun of spectacled Catherine, because in her *lycée* she had organized a circle of *Filles des Obscurs Intellectuels de Gauche*. "*C'est dégoutant,*" Hélène burst out, banging her fist on the table.

"Why does it make her so mad?" demanded Mike, of the table at large. "Why does it make your daughter so mad?" he added, shouting at the doctor.

Hélène calmed herself. "It is the same as 'fishing village,'" she explained in her slow English. "It is true when the children say that we here are intellectuals of the left. But if someone says it in a fashion magazine it is a silly lie."

Arturo Buonsanti was laughing. "*Mais c'est merveilleux!*" he cried. "Eh, Hélène? Next summer when your hairdresser asks you where you are going for your vacation, you can answer that naturally you are going where the French intellectuals of the left go."

"*Et les juifs, et les juifs, papa!*" chanted Laure, jumping up from her place and putting her arms around her father's neck. A few days before, someone had noticed that the greater part of the summer people were either Jewish, half Jewish, a quarter Jewish, or, like Arturo Buonsanti, married to someone Jewish. This *trouvaille* still enchanted the children, like a meadow full of four-leaf clovers. "*Pauvre papa,*" murmured Laure, hugging him. "*Tu n'es pas juif; mais moi, je le suis!*"

Arturo Buonsanti was chuckling. "*Modeste station balnéaire, très frequentée par les juifs.*"

"Oh, I say," protested the British lawyer, "that would be liable to misinterpretation, wouldn't it?"

"Gives the wrong picture, I agree," said Mike. "Sort of a Miami Beach." He laughed nervously. Both he and the Englishman were embarrassed by the children's freedom with the "racial" topic, which their parents seemed positively to encourage, like premature talk about sex. Mike, in particular, had an uneasy notion that he was being led on by this permissive atmosphere into making what might sound (to Jews) like an anti-Semitic remark. The other day at the café, for instance, they had teased him without mercy because he had refused to believe that everyone present was Jewish. "But you don't *look* Jewish, any of you."

"*Il cherche le nez,*" François had murmured, watching the American stare at each face in turn.

"Hey!" Mike had retorted. "*Vous avez tort, mon garçon. J'aime les juifs.* I'm not Jewish, but my wife is. Aren't you, darling?" The children had burst into giggles. They loved to tease Mike, because he was good-humored, said "*vous*" to them, and was exactly like their idea of an American. Even Catherine had asked him gravely whether all Americans ate with their feet on the table—she had seen it in the films. So that now, when Catherine and her cronies passed him eating breakfast at the café, he would quickly put his feet on the table and, for good measure, his spoon in his coffee cup, to the amazement of the waiters, whom he tried to include in the joke with a series of broad winks. The result of this charade was that Elisabeth, another American, who lived above the Buonsantis, was asked by the innkeeper whether all Americans ate with their feet on the table.

Mike's wife failed to find the story amusing. She was irritated by these nonchalant and observant children, whom she had overheard chiming "Don't you think so, darling?" in what she uncomfortably recognized as her husband's voice. It was obvious, she told Mike, that these European children had been indoctrinated with anti-Americanism. Their good manners offended her too—always "*Bonjour, Monsieur,*" "*Bonjour, Madame,*" instead of "Hi, Mike," "Hi, Irene," the way she was used to in America. She was touchy about being American and touchy about being Jewish. She had a rather large nose, which she was touchy about too. "That little boy," she said, "was making fun of my beak." She could speak quite coarsely when she wished to. "*Il cherche le nez.*"

Mike shook his head. "No, no," he said. "He was riding me. As a matter of fact, honey, when he caught me I *was* looking for the nose. I have to admit it."

Irene resented Porto Quaglia. She was sorry she had ever saved that clipping from *Harper's Bazaar*. It was not a *real* fishing village; there were no real intellectuals, like Sartre or Françoise Sagan; there was nothing to buy; and though they had been here only a short time, she was pressing Mike to go to Ischia. "I like it here," Mike kept repeating, but Irene's dissatisfaction was slowly convincing him; like an echo, he too began to criticize the *pensione* at the inn: spaghetti twice a day and fish with too many bones in it.

"*Vous n'aimez pas la nourriture italienne*," Hélène Buonsanti said kindly to Irene. She meant, Irene retorted, that Americans only liked steak and fried potatoes. "*Mais non*," Hélène protested, determined to make peace. "*Le steak et les frites sont tout à fait français.*"

Mike interposed that no one liked Italian cooking better than he and Irene, but why couldn't they get real filet of sole at the inn? "*Without bones*," he emphasized. Hélène had had her cook fillet the soles for lunch, over the objections of Arturo, who said that they would be flavorless. Mike was a popular figure, and everyone saw regretfully what was happening. To please his wife, he would soon have to leave Porto Quaglia, and he was foxily seeking a reason for leaving without regrets. Yet no one at the table was prepared for the undercurrent of antagonism that had made itself felt, like a sudden cold tug, just now, at the end of lunch, when he began playing with the notion that Porto Quaglia's days were numbered. "Yes, Hélène," he went on easily, "it's just a question of time, I'm afraid. *Une question de temps.* Irene and I went exploring this morning. We got a boy to row us across to that big beach on the other side of the river."

A look of understanding passed along the table. "*Lo spiaggione*," whispered a pretty girl to a young architect from Turin. "*Parla dello spiaggione.*" "*La grande plage, grand-papa*," said Laure to Dr. Bernheim. "*Oui, mon enfant. J'ai compris*," said the doctor, nodding sadly.

"*Quelle horreur!*" said Mike. "Wasn't it, darling? *Ruinée, eh, Arturo? Kaput!*"

The host, who resembled a sage because of his prematurely bald

head, knitted his brows and agreed. "*J'ai raison, eh?*" said Mike, looking around him. No one dissented. Until the previous year they had
been in the habit of going across the Quaglia and walking half a mile
down a path through a thicket of bamboo to *lo spiaggione*—a big wild
sandy beach on the other side, on the open Mediterranean, where
there were rollers to ride and where the children could build sand
castles. This had been a regular alternate to the White Rock. But the
tide of humanity coming up the coast from Viareggio, with its flot-
sam of night clubs, cheap hotels, neon-lit seafood restaurants, had
finally overtaken Punta Sabbia, as the settlement across the river was
called, and a Camping that had been planted there two years ago was
literally the last straw. The *grande plage* was now covered with straw
huts, bamboo huts, loose straw, tents, candy wrappers, ice-cream car-
tons, rusty cans, broken bottles, old automobile tires, watermelon
rinds, not to mention the lengthening row of *cabine* and rented umbrellas; to reach the water in many places it was necessary to pick
one's way through refuse and human bodies as in a game of stepping
stones. The advent of the campers, moreover, had created a serious
sanitary problem, and the refuse had bred flies and mosquitoes. This
summer only the children had been across to the big beach; the
grownups did not speak of it any more, as if it were someone who
had died in a horrible way or lived on upstairs in a special room like
an insane relation in the last century. The *grande plage*, which had
been an essential feature of the Porto Quaglia agenda, like the yearly
boat trip to Portovenere or the climb up Monte Morello, was stead-
fastly ignored. No one cared even to remember the indignant meetings of the summer before last, when they had tried to save *lo spiaggione*: the open letter to the mayor of Acquafredda protesting the
sanitary conditions on the other side of the river, the manifesto to
the Belle Arti at La Spezia calling attention to the despoilment of the
bamboo and the *pineta*, the photographs of Before and After they
had sent to *Il Mondo* and *Italia Nostra*. The ruin of the *spiaggione*
was accepted, and there were those who, last summer, had claimed
to see a virtue in the necessity, pointing out that what had happened
on the other side would be a lesson to the elements in Porto Quaglia
that wanted to see it "developed." Mass tourism, they declared, could
not be stopped; the hope was to divert it, and Punta Sabbia ought
to be welcomed as a human garbage dump, where all the undesirables
collected in one place, without any compulsion being exercised but
according to a kind of natural zoning law. This summer, though,

these arguments, once half persuasive, had been put away regretfully, like last year's faded bathing suits and rusted bathing caps; they did not seem to fit any more.

"*Mais c'est tout à fait différent!*" said the Roman editor sharply, breaking the gloomy silence that had fallen on the table. "The *spiaggione* is sand, good for pitching tents. Here we are on rock and stones."

"'It can't happen here,' eh?" said Mike.

"But, Francesco, what about the new Camping at the *bivio?*" gently put in the editor's wife. This was a very small Camping, of only a few tents, at the fork two miles away where the road from Sarzana divided, the main branch going south toward Carrara and a long spur following the river to Porto Quaglia, where it ended.

"It is at the *bivio*," her husband said impatiently. "They do not come here to swim; they go to Punta Sabbia." And he went on to reiterate his theory that Porto Quaglia could not be "developed" because it was not on a through road. "People looking for pleasure don't like to be at a dead end. They are afraid of being bottled up. They are restless. Everyone today is restless—especially the Italians." This theory, which he had been propounding for five years with increasing conviction, served as usual to pacify the doubters; his disgust with the tendency of modern life, familiar to readers of his editorials, made him all the more credible as a forecaster—an optimist they would not have relied on. In the same way, the whole community, including the children, trusted him as a weather prophet because he distrusted the weather.

Just then, down the marble walk under the grape arbor, came the Irish poet Frank O'Hare. He was a big pale deep-chested man with a fringe of gray hair, the night owl of Porto Quaglia; he rented a house from a fisherman, never swam or sunned, and was seldom seen in daylight, though he was generally dressed only in bathing trunks, as he was now. To see him saunter down the walk in broad afternoon was a sign of trouble, as though an evening bat had flitted across the palm trees; if he came by day, it was to "have a word" with Dr. Bernheim, and everyone now jumped to the conclusion that his pregnant wife or one of his five children must be "under the weather" again. But he wore a large smile and carried a chessboard. "I've come for a game with Arturo," he explained, shaking hands all around and accepting a glass of whiskey, which Hélène had run into the house to procure. O'Hare was the chess champion of Porto Quaglia—a title he held from having beaten Hélène's father three out of five at the end of the previous summer. This was only his second year at Porto Quaglia; he spoke no French and hardly a word of Italian, but he was extremely sociable and knew all the gossip of the village, which he picked up at the "pub" over a glass of beer (he did not drink wine) and from his private sources among the fishermen and maids. "Have ye heard the news?" he said now, and at once everyone guessed that this was the reason for his visit. "The Germans have discovered Porto Quaglia."

A long cry of dismay went up in the garden. O'Hare raised a hand to hush it. This morning, he went on, folding his arms, he had gone into Sarzana to get some medicine for Sean, whose foot was infected again ("I'd like a word with you later, if I may, Doctor." "*Papa—*" "*Oui, ma fille, j'ai compris*"), and while he was there he had stopped in at the travel agency, where they sold the bus tickets, to pass the time of day. There he had found a young German pair inquiring for a purse the girl had left on a bus from La Spezia; the long and short of it was that he had acted as translator for them (the boy had a little English) and had asked them, by the bye, what they were doing in Sarzana. They told him that a tourist bureau in Frankfurt had recommended Porto Quaglia.

"*Oh, là là!*" said Arturo Buonsanti. "*Oh, là là!*" said the engineer. "*Oh, là là!*" cried all the children.

"*Qu'est-ce qui se passe?*" called a woman's voice with an American accent from the balcony above.

"*C'est les allemands, Elisabeth!*" shouted the children. "*Ils sont à Sarzana. Ils ont découvert Porto Quaglia.*" A shriek answered.

The Buonsantis' cook, Anna, rushed out from the kitchen. "*Cosa, signora? Cosa?*"

"*I tedeschi, Anna,*" said Hélène. "*Son arrivati qui.*"

Anna shielded her eyes and peered out to the street, along the green tunnel of the arbor. "*Dove? Dove sono, professore?*" She turned to Arturo. "*All' albergo?*"

Arturo reassured her. "*Non è vero, Anna. Almeno è un po' esagerato.*" But he too, behind his smile, was very much taken aback. "*Oh, là là!*" he repeated to himself.

Down the outside staircase trooped the families who rented the second-story apartments—Mme. Brée, wakened from her after-lunch nap, was wearing a frilly cotton dressing gown, and her children's hair was tousled. Fat Margherita from the house next door, who took boarders, appeared in a parting of the hedge; from the house behind, young Dr. Livio, from Rome, came buttoning his white shirt. Little Anne, the engineer's youngest, hopped on a bicycle to go tell her friend Suzanne down the street. O'Hare stood clasping an oar and embroidering the tale for the group clustered around him while Hélène and Elisabeth, the American, acted as interpreters.

"You'd think it was an air-raid alarm," said Mike, guffawing.

"They were here in these hills," replied the professor of history, chidingly. He nodded his head at the green hills behind the house. "In '44. Fighting the Partisans, who were hiding in the woods on Monte Morello. Anna remembers."

"That was a tragedy," said the Roman editor. "This is farce."

Mike's wife interrupted. "Those people in Sarzana—were they West Germans or East Germans?" "West, of course," said the editor irritably. "They are from Frankfurt." "I don't think we should be prejudiced against the West Germans," declared Irene in a virtuous tone.

"I quite agree," said the British lawyer. "I bear no prejudice against the present generation of Germans—West or East. I loathe prejudice of any kind. As I loathe blood sports. That's the thing I hold against your lamented compatriot, Hemingway—" "Sh-h-h," Mike said to him. "I want to hear this."

"They won't be coming here after all," O'Hare was saying. "They'll wait for the purse to turn up and then go on to Pisa."

The lawyer frowned suspiciously, hearing a note of mischief in the poet's bland tone. "What did you tell them about Porto Quaglia?"

O'Hare grinned. "Well, I painted the picture a bit black, you might say. They asked about the bathing, and of course I was bound to tell them that I'd been here a month and hadn't had a bathe yet. Not so much as a sunbathe." A gleeful laugh rang out. The Irishman's white torso and limbs were not a testimonial to Porto Quaglia as a summer resort, and the others began to joke about posting him at the *bivio* as a deterrent, like a quarantine sign.

"Very funny," said the editor tartly. "It would be very amusing no doubt to see O'Hare turning back the Huns. A Ste.-Geneviève at the gates of Paris—perhaps our poet can be canonized. But it is not a joke, what he has told us. Porto Quaglia is on a tourist map of Italy published in Germany as a vacation guide!"

The poet nodded. "I saw it. With my own two eyes. Porto Quaglia is there, big as life, with a star."

"But how?" cried the pretty girl, who was the daughter of the history professor. "It is not even on the Esso map. How did the Germans find out about it?"

"They have their ways," said her father darkly, at which everyone burst out laughing.

"*Ils ont leurs espions!*" cried the children delightedly.

And now it was remembered that a pair of fat middle-aged blond strangers had been seen one day the previous summer on the marble rocks at Rocca Bianca, but though they had been heard to speak German, they had been given the benefit of the doubt, for they might have been refugees. And only a few weeks before, Anna the cook had brought the news that Germans had been reported in the new Camping at the *bivio*. But two possible Germans on the rocks, two more in a Camping had not been seen as significant; now these isolated cases suddenly "made sense," like the first seemingly unrelated deaths in what would prove to be the outbreak of an epidemic. There had always (that is, for several years) been Germans across the river, which the poet had one night fancifully compared to the Rhine, with the Germans on one side and the French on the other. But now, it seemed, scouts had crossed the frontier, and an invasion was beginning against which Porto Quaglia was defenseless. The French would be mowed down as by a Panzer division. The local inconveniences that had protected Porto Quaglia from prosperous Italians and Americans would make no difference to the Germans, who never seemed to take baths while travelling and were not particular about iced drinks. Porto Quaglia, in fact, would yield without a murmur to the German soul, which vacationed with quotation marks in its rucksack ready to fasten around "*ein kleines Fischerdorf.*"

"*Ja, ja, wunderschön!*" savagely mimicked François in his cracking voice, hoarse as a crow's from the onset of puberty.

The grownups nodded. They agreed that it was just a question of time till the dread signs "*Zimmer*" would be posted outside the homes of the simple fisherfolk of Porto Quaglia. "*Zimmer und Frühstück,*" "*Lebensmittel*"—they had seen these signs move up the coast, as though the Angel of Death had passed by marking the villages, one by one, for liquidation.

Mike's wife spoke up. "I think you're setting your kids a very bad example. You should teach them to judge Germans as individuals." Hélène whirled around. "Do they come here as individuals or as a mass? With a map from headquarters like an army? Do you meet German tourists as individuals or in busloads?"

"*Écoute, Hélène,*" chided her husband. "*Frank vient de rencontrer deux individus à Sarzana.*"

"The first swallows, though," observed O'Hare. "We've got them in Killarney—all the old Nazi boyos. The new landed gentry. Hitler's chief of protocol. They've closed off the beaches to the Irish poor."

"*Tu vois?*" exclaimed Hélène.

"*Franchement, je les déteste,*" said the engineer's wife calmly. "If Germans come here, I will not come back."

"Do you mean that seriously?" asked Mike. "You mean if one German comes here you won't come back? Supposing Mayor Brandt comes here next year for his vacation?"

"*Soyez sérieux, Mike,*" interposed Arturo. "Mayor Brandt is not the question. *Vous le savez bien. Nous parlons du touriste moyen.* The ordinary tourist."

"Let them go to Pisa!" burst out Hélène. "Let them go to Florence! *Là il y a l'histoire, les monuments! L'histoire, les monuments appartiennent à tout le monde.* To everybody. *Mais Porto Quaglia nous appartient à nous.*"

"So it belongs to you. How interesting," said the British lawyer in a courtroom manner. "I should think it belonged to the fishing people."

"It belongs to the fishing people first," said Hélène. "Next it belongs to us." "By what right?" said the lawyer. "By the right of use," said Hélène. "Is that not a right in English law? We have been coming here now for ten years; our children have grown up here. We have rights here; we belong here. Why should Germans come and push us aside? As they do always in queues. I have seen them in Paris. Because I am small, they try to push me aside."

"You should see them in Killarney," eagerly put in the poet, and everyone began to recount some personal experience of German effrontery.

The lawyer raised his voice. "And if the fishing people want their trade? Will you forbid Pierino or Romeo to take them to Rocca Bianca? Perhaps you'd like to institute some racial laws here to prevent that?" "Hear, hear!" said Irene.

Hélène raised her small tanned face anxiously to her tall husband. "*Aide-moi, Arturo.*"

"*Il a raison, Hélène,*" Arturo said mildly. "*Sur le plan légal.*"

"Hell," said Mike suddenly. "Can't Hélène say what she thinks about German tourists without being attacked as a racist? I'm on her side. Lafayette, we are here!" He laughed at his own weak joke to break the tension.

Spots of color appeared in the Englishman's cheeks; he and Mike were not congenial, having already had disputes about prizefights and the execution of Caryl Chessman. "And what about the Americans?" he said to Hélène in a trembling voice. "Personally, if we must speak in these terms, I prefer the Germans to the Americans."

"No!" said Hélène, with violence. "The Americans do not come where they are not wanted. They are more sensitive, even the worst. They go where there are other Americans. To Harry's Bar."

"What they do as tourists doesn't interest me," retorted the lawyer. "Unlike you, Mme. Buonsanti, I try to think politically. On that level, I can assure you, the Americans are not wanted in Europe. I can't speak for the keepers of public houses, but I can promise you that the English people don't want the sensitive Americans with their nuclear toys. Nor the Scots, nor the French, nor the Italians, nor even the Germans—if their governments consulted them. 'Go home, Yankee,' is what the Europeans really feel. Try talking to the fishing people here. If your American friends"—he glanced around him— "were sensitive, they'd clear out. No wonder the Germans are welcomed by the plain folk. At least there are no German military bases outside Germany!"

Irene was the first to speak. "You can thank the Americans for that!" "I prefer to thank the Russians," said the lawyer.

"You are so rude," said Hélène, wheeling on him, "that I would think you were probably a German. You look like a German." Her blazing eyes surveyed his mountain-climbing costume. "I do not believe you are an Englishman."

"Ma fille," said her father warningly. "Calme-toi." And he rose, small and peaceable in his open-throated tan sports shirt, to put his arm around her and lead her to a chair. As he did so, they all saw the blue tattoo, like a laundry mark, on his plump sunburned forearm: his number at Auschwitz. Everyone drew a sharp breath. Nearly all of them had at least glimpsed it before—on the White Rock, while the doctor lay sunning, at table, during a chess session. But generally they tried not to look at it, even the smaller children, out of courtesy to the doctor, as if it were a deformity, and the doctor himself made this easier by his habitual meditative posture, chin sunk, arms folded on his lap. Now they stared at the number, at the lawyer, at Hélène.

"Here," said the Irish poet suddenly to the children, reaching into the pocket of his bathing trunks. "Go get yourselves ice creams." He treated children to ice creams with the same absent abandon that he treated or tried to treat grownups to drinks. "Have a whiskey" or "Have an ice cream" was his customary greeting, according to age. But the children this time refused to budge; instead, the lawyer turned, picked up his stick, and marched down the walk without speaking.

At once Hélène was remorseful. "*J'ai trop bu à déjeuner,*" she confessed.

O'Hare and Arturo began to play chess at one end of the table, while the doctor watched; he had learned the game in Auschwitz. The children lingered round the table, as if feeling cheated at the way the discussion had been terminated by the unexpected appearance of Dr. Bernheim's "number," like a card produced from his sleeve. Everyone was silent, pursuing his own train of thought.

"*Tu l'as fait exprès, Maurice,*" Arturo declared suddenly to his father-in-law, looking up from the board with a chuckle. "He did it on purpose, O'Hare."

"What?" said the poet.

"Showing his number. To help his daughter."

The old man indicated a chess move with a silent finger. "*Peut-être,*" he said imperturbably.

"You know, *maman,*" exclaimed Laure, raising her head, "I think you were right. I think he *is* a German."

"*Mais oui, mais oui!*" shouted François, his eyes sparkling. "*Maman a parfaitement raison!*" And the little boy assured them that the Englishman had paled when the word "spy" was mentioned. "*C'est lui, j'en suis sûr, qui a dénoncé Porto Quaglia aux allemands. Il a pâli, comme ça.*" He gave a wild start, shuddered, and tried to make his small brown face blanch. The other children watched this performance agog. The adults, impressed for a minute by the boy's conviction, quickly regained their balance. "*Mais non, mais non!*" they cried soothingly.

"It's just that he doesn't like Americans, François," Mike explained. "You can understand that, can't you?" And he made a funny face. "He thinks they eat with their atom bombs on the table."

"What are you trying to cover up?" demanded Irene. "François is old enough to know that that man's a Communist!"

The "French" protruded their lower lips and doubtfully shrugged their brows; Arturo glanced up from the chessboard. *"Je ne crois pas,"* he said soberly.

"La Voix de la Raison a parlé," announced the editor, clapping his friend on the shoulder.

"Mais en tout cas ce n'est pas une injure," mildly pursued Arturo. And the others began to argue as to whether it was an insult to call a person a Communist.

"Anyway, he's not a Communist, honey," said Mike, intervening. "It's not that simple. He's an overexcited unilateral disarmer." "But why should that make him pro-German?" someone demanded. *"Mais il n'était pas pro-allemand,"* objected someone else.

The Irishman had been concentrating on the chessboard, ignoring the conversation. He captured a rook with his knight. "I'll tell ye what it is," he said abruptly, tilting back in his chair. "This fellow is a German who passed for English during the war years in England to keep on the good side of his neighbors. Get him to show ye his passport. I'll wager he was born in Hamburg."

"C'est plutôt un juif allemand qui s'est fait anglais," murmured the doctor. *"Mais tu es fou, papa!"* cried Hélène.

"Favole!" said the editor. "You are telling each other fairy stories. The truth is simple. This Englishman would like to be unprejudiced, but he is not, unfortunately. Hélène would like to be prejudiced, but she is not, fortunately." He rose to leave. "Meanwhile," he added, with a grimace, "the real Germans are advancing." Mike and Irene rose too.

Irene approached Hélène. "I'm sorry I attacked you about the Germans coming here. I forgot about your father."

Hélène started to reply hotly, *"Ce n'est pas à cause de mon père,"* but then she gave it up, realizing that she could not explain in English to Irene what she felt toward these new Germans, and that if she were able to explain it in French, Irene would not understand. *"Merci,"* she said simply, instead.

The summer, after this, was not the same. The only immediate consequence was that for a few days Hélène and the English lawyer stopped speaking when they met. But Hélène would not allow this to continue, for it would have ended in the creation of factions. There had never been factions in Porto Quaglia, and Hélène, therefore, when the time came, invited the lawyer and his family as usual to François' birthday party—the great social event of the season, for which cakes were baked in Parma and sent over the mountains by bus. The English accepted, and the quarrel was patched up.

The party was just like the parties of other years, except that it was too much like them—too defiant of change. The littlest girls dressed up in costumes representing, this year, the great sirens—the Queen of Sheba, Cleopatra, the Lorelei, Brigitte Bardot—and were made up by one of the painters; François shinned up a palm tree; everyone came, old and young, maids and nurses. As usual, the first goodbyes of the season were said, for François' party was in the middle of August—after that, traditionally, the first departures took place. Yet the fact was these gay promises—"See you next year," "All' anno prossimo," "À bientôt"—were tinged this year with uncertainty, wan like the flickering light of the Chinese lanterns hung from the trumpet vines and fir trees. Everyone looked at everyone else, wondering which would be the defector, which family would send postcards next year with "auguri" for François and love to everyone from Provence or Elba.

From the day of O'Hare's discovery, the "French" had been living in a state of apprehension, which they tried not to show to each other. The blue buses that came nearly every hour from Sarzana and La Spezia were covertly watched, and no one went into Sarzana without casting a supervisory glance over the main square, to note what strangers were about. At the sound of an unfamiliar horn along the road, walkers would stop to listen anxiously, expecting a big German tourist bus to appear around the next curve. The yearly expedition to Portovenere, which included a swim from the boat in a blue grotto and lunch outdoors on an island under a tree with a swing, was repeatedly postponed on various excuses, as though the "French" were afraid to leave Porto Quaglia unguarded, lest they come back and find it violated. None of these actions was planned; no one watched on purpose stationed in the café. It was just that now automatically even the chess players glanced up at the sound of a car or a bus braking, whereas before nobody had paid any attention unless waiting for a friend or a package. The effect of the alert was most noticeable on the children, who roamed about the village in bands, were reluctant to go blackberrying on Monte Morello, and swam in expeditionary forces beyond Raven Point to reconnoitre the coves and grottoes. As if enlisted by this esprit de corps, Mike and his wife had stayed on.

The only person not privately on the watch for Germans was their herald, O'Hare, who again was invisible in the daytime and was said to be writing a verse play on Marlowe and the School of Night. And at night peace returned to Porto Quaglia. Just before dusk the old ladies, mothers of the Italians among the "French," appeared on the road, walking with sticks, in pairs or leaning on the arm of a servant or a daughter-in-law. The emergence of *le mamme*, white-haired, talcum-dusted, woolly-shawled, like soft, powdery moths heading for the café, was the sign that traffic had stilled and Porto Quaglia was safe for the night; the buses had stopped running, and few cars passed. Across the river, the last rays of the sun, already hidden from the village behind Monte Morello, touched the windows of the golden hill towns, which sparkled and beaconed like fireflies or as though they had been turned into quartz or mica embedded in the green hills. After this, O'Hare, the owl, cruised into the café.

At night Mamma Nature took possession of Porto Quaglia. After supper the children thronged up and down the waterfront picking out the stars, which seemed very near and bright. Sometimes the poet would join them in front of the café and teach them the English names—a game that caused much laughter, incredulity, and wonder. To think that what little Anne's star book called the Great She Bear was known as the Big Dipper to the English, and La Chaise was Cassiopeia's Chair.

"There's Orion's Belt, Frankie," O'Hare would say to François.

"*Ah oui, c'est Le Bâton de Jacob.*"

"Jacob's Rod, is it?"

"*Mais non, c'est Les Trois Rois!*"

"*Mais si,*" Catherine would speak up. "*Le Bâton de Jacob et Les Trois Rois sont la même constellation, n'est-ce pas, Monsieur O'Hare?*"

"Here's a good one," the poet would interject. "Do ye know what the English call Sirius? Orion's Hound." This pleased the children in the same way as penetrating the foreign disguises of the pieces on their fathers' chessboard: was it true, they would ask the poet, that the English called the *fou* the "bishop"? And the Italians called him "*l'alfiere.*" The chessboard had its own constellations, said the Irishman, and the fixed moves of the pieces were like the fixed courses of the stars; it was a very old game—as old as the hills.

When the children had gone to bed, the moonlit village was still, except for the faint sound of dance music coming from across the river, from the restaurant Il Pilota, near the house of Romeo, the boatman. The honky-tonk sound floating across the river seemed bathed in frontier innocence, and the menace of Punta Sabbia, just beyond, was reduced to the melody of an old jazz tune. In former years the "French" would have themselves rowed across on a Friday or a Saturday to dance, but now no one went, not even the young people, but the music still continued, as old as the hills itself, as if nothing had changed.

In the daytime this illusion could not be maintained. The sighting of the Germans in Sarzana had served to call attention to a fact that had been half escaping notice: the White Rock was filling up with bathers. Each day there were new ones. Arriving in their boats, the "French" would discern dark figures, tiny in the distance in the white glare of the cliff, which made them look like people in an overexposed photograph; disembarking, the "French" would often find their places preempted: Dr. Bernheim's special shady corner under an overhanging cliff, François' lookout post on the highest rock, Hélène's hollow. Another umbrella would be standing in the crevice where the engineer's wife had always planted hers; in the cave where they were in the habit of changing they would find a fat man asleep or a couple embracing. Romeo, Pierino, and Paolo were continually chugging back and forth with strangers aboard whom they deposited—strangers from no one knew where, since they were not staying at the inn or at either of the two boarding houses. And as if this were not enough, new motorboats and even small cruisers began appearing from the other direction and discharging passengers.

All these people, materializing seemingly from thin air, behaved as if they belonged here, as if they had "always" been coming to the White Rock, which they treated in cursory fashion, like a row of *cabine* with showers. They did not exclaim over the beauty of the spot but at once put on diving masks and flippers and began to swim. Or launched their children in tubes and themselves on surf mattresses. Or slung cameras round their necks and started photographing— "action" shots of a group splashing each other in the water. This matter-of-fact behavior and the way they ignored the "French," who outnumbered them, gave the August mornings the quality of a dream sequence. It was as if the "French" collectively had become invisible; the others crossed by them, climbed over them, talked past them, as if they were not there at all in reality but were only figments of their own imagination. If they spoke, they felt they would be inaudible, like someone trying to shout in a dream, and in fact they became remarkably silent. Only their eyes spoke. Some of the strangers, who for the most part were extremely ugly, brought food with them and ate lunch at midday, scattering grape skins and peach pits and salami rind and crusts of bread on the marble and throwing empty Chinotto bottles into the sea. Large horseflies appeared on the White Rock. On the green water there was an iridescent film of gasoline.

These strangers varied from day to day, but they did not have a marked individuality; rather, they seemed a species whose children, summoned in raucous authoritarian voices, were all named "Umberto" or "Massimo." "They will go away after Ferragosto," the editor prophesied, but the fifteenth of August passed and the shriek "Umberto!" "Massimo!" was still heard on the White Rock like the perpetual crying of gulls.

And one day, at last, Germans came; Romeo had brought them from the Camping at Punta Sabbia. First there were two, then four, then a whole boatload, many of them middle-aged—the men old enough to have been in the S.S. or, to judge them more charitably, to have manned those very pillboxes just around the point that had cowed the area with their artillery till the Americans took Viareggio. Yet now that they were here, in the too too solid flesh, the "French" banished these memories, just as they tried not to look at the number on Dr. Bernheim's arm. In actuality, the Germans from the Camping, it was admitted, were no worse than the invaders who had preceded them; the invaders were all "Germans," in the sense of a foreign species with the power of rapid multiplication, as the invaded were all "French."

But as if to illustrate the complexity of the subject, Irene was accosted one morning toward the end of the month by an Italian crone, the grandmother of some Umberto or Massimo and their little sister (never summoned) Marisa or Silvana. "*Sprechen Sie Deutsch?*" said the old woman, seizing Irene by the skirt of her beach gown as she tried to pass on the rocks. And when Irene refused angrily to answer her, she continued to gabble at her in German, eager, no doubt, said the editor, to renew conversations she had enjoyed in the old times with the Nazis. Soon afterward Hélène had a similar wounding experience in the post office when she went to buy stamps. "*Francobolli, per favore,*" she said, pushing her postcards through the window and starting to make a remark about the weather.

"*Per la Germania?*" interrupted the employee. "*Deutschland?*"

Hélène was outraged. The woman had not even troubled to *look* at the postcards. Or at her. They were for France, Hélène pointed out. She was not German; she was the Signora Buonsanti. But the employee, who was new, it seemed, did not recognize her. *"Cento lire,"* she said, counting out stamps for the postcards and handing them back for Hélène to lick.

"A près dix ans c'est un peu fort," declared Hélène, seating herself with a thump in the café.

Arturo gave his genial laugh. *"Comme c'est beau!"* he said. *"Per loro adesso siamo tutti quanti tedeschi."*

Seriously, put in the professor's pretty daughter, this must mean that there were Germans actually in the village.

O'Hare got up from a chess game at the next table. "Haven't you heard?" he said. "They're at the Pensione La Perla. Have a whiskey."

The following morning, the Germans from La Perla were in the boat that came to fetch the group from the Buonsantis' landing. The "French" behaved politely, helping the Germans land their equipment as they helped everyone else, and the English lawyer, already sunning, was particularly assiduous in holding the boat's painter to steady it for the fat women's descent. But Laure, usually coöperative, refused to lend a hand.

"Mais qu'est-ce que tu as, ma petite?" chided her father. Laure would not reply and sat stubbornly at the water's edge, brooding and casting dark looks at the Englishman, who was chatting in German with the newcomers. Finally, when the others were in swimming, she explained.

In the boat she had seen the Germans staring pointedly at the number on Dr. Bernheim's arm. And to bear her out, that morning they all noticed still other Germans, from the Camping, eying the number too, passing and repassing the old man as he sat reading a volume of Stendhal, and actually stopping to get a better view. If Dr. Bernheim was aware of this, he gave no definite sign, but after his second dip he moved his place farther along the rocks, and before the boats came he asked François to row him back—he had taken too much sun.

"Mais c'est inouï!" burst out Hélène, when her father was gone. *"Que mon père ne puisse pas se montrer en public, à cause des allemands! C'est eux qui auraient dû se cacher!"*

No one could say she exaggerated; it was the Germans, not her father, who had something to be ashamed of, but it was the Germans who were making it impossible for him to appear in public. Because

of the Germans ought he to wear a long-sleeved shirt? Or Cover-
mark, as Mike sarcastically proposed?

This was the turning point. The next day, despite the children's
protests, the "French" set out for Judgment Day Beach. The White
Rock had been abandoned to the enemy.

Judgment Day Beach, like Raven Point, though pleasant for an ex-
cursion was not really a substitute for the White Rock. It was a pebbly beach, and the sharp stones hurt the tender feet of the younger
children, who were not quite consoled by the stone collections made
for them. Moreover, there was no shade—no protective cliffs, no
cool caves. The small children sat in their straw hats in a row and
demanded to know when Romeo was coming back for them. This
was another difficulty. On calm days the boatmen did not like to go
to Judgment Day; it was farther than the White Rock, but the price
per head, fixed early in the summer, was the same. The advantage to
the boatmen was that it was easier to land there, but when the sea
was quiet this did not matter, and the boatmen, with the trade they
now had, did not care to make the longer trip simply for the "francesi." Hence, every morning Pierino or Paolo or Romeo, pretending
not to have understood the wishes of the "French," would try to
take them to the Rocca Bianca, as if as a matter of course.

"No, Paolo, niente Rocca Bianca," some strong will among the
passengers would have to interpose. "C'è troppa gente. All'altra
spiaggia." Paolo, muttering, would yield, and they would sail past the
marble rocks, as though past a siren, watching the British lawyer and
his wife, who had declined to join in the exodus (they had met some
lovely couples among the new folk at Rocca Bianca), wave to them
cheerily from the marshmallowy cliffs. The boatmen showed their
dissatisfaction by arriving late to pick up the "francesi" at lunchtime, with the excuse that they had first to pick up the various parties
at the White Rock. Sometimes it was three o'clock before the boats
returned to Porto Quaglia, and as they neared the landing, the
Buonsantis would see tall Anna standing there, her hand shading her
eyes, waiting to make sure they were aboard before putting on the
spaghetti. Lunch, with a spoiled roast, would be served at three-fif-
teen. Those who were in pensione at the inn would find the day's
specialty "finito" or sitting in tepid grease. Anna was cross; the waiters in the inn were cross; the lesser family cooks up and down the
main street were cross. The "French" were being punished by the

boatmen, and this punishment, like some Biblical malediction, spread over the whole village.

Only the old man with the rowboat and his grandson remained faithful to the "French," but it was a long row to Judgment Day, and the boat could not go back and forth many times in a morning. Soon another old man, with Garibaldi mustaches and an ancient dinghy, turned up at the pier; then a third, an octogenarian with a rakishly worn sailor's cap, a cheroot, and a leaky outboard motor. But this created further bad blood with the "regular" boatmen, who would sometimes decline to take a group they had seen patronizing the old men and the boy. In short, the balance of Nature at Porto Quaglia was upset. Some days it would happen that most of the "French" did not go to swim at all. After a family dispute, the sulking children would take their bathing suits and walk down to the *plage modeste* at the end of the village, while their parents sat at home fuming and declaring that they might as well be in Paris, Rome, or London. One morning the Brées and the Livios quietly crossed to Punta Sabbia—on the theory that the "Germans" encamped there had all gone to the Rocca Bianca. But this attempted "castling," as Arturo Buonsanti called it, did not work out either. The position was deadlocked: the "French," having surrendered Rocca Bianca, refused to be returned there under duress; the boatmen continued to lay siege to them by the device of marooning them at Judgment Day Beach. The Milanese publisher took to going late and bringing a cold lunch; Elisabeth, the American, brought steaks one day for twenty and cooked them on the beach. But the absence of shade at Judgment Day, as well as the absence of wood, discouraged these solutions.

By September, the "French" were talking of buying outboard motors for the children's rowboats; the engineer went to look at a sailboat that was for sale across the river. "Make yourselves independent of the boatmen," Mike counselled. But if every family had a boat, what then? Who was to promise them that next year the "Germans" would not push on to Judgment Day?

"You could sell them your boats," said Mike shrewdly, waggling his beard. But the "French" were cold to this idea and cold to the idea of acquiring shore property—another notion Mike broached. Though he was receiving cables telling him to get back to work from his editor nearly every day (with a two-hundred-lire delivery charge), he lingered, feeling it his duty as an American to exercise his ingenuity on a problem that the "French" by themselves could not solve.

"Why don't you get together and buy the Rocca Bianca?" he said to Hélène one morning as they were swimming. Far off to the right, they could see the white point jutting into the sea; from here it was evident that the marble there had once been quarried—slices had been taken off. This in fact was what had suddenly given him the idea.

"It is public property," said Hélène. "The shore belongs to the *comune*."

"Are you sure?" he said. "If the shore belongs to the *comune*, how come all the bathing establishments across the river?"

"They are concessions. Leased from the *comune* by business interests." But the Belle Arti, Hélène went on, would not permit anybody to lease a landmark like the White Rock. And they would be right.

She and Mike began to argue heatedly. He bet her that by bribery or influence the "French" could lease the White Rock and post it with "No Trespassing" signs. "Supposing you all got together"—he counted —"there must be at least twelve families of you, and some pretty important people, by Italian standards. You could fix the Belle Arti and the mayor—" "No," said Hélène.

"What do you mean 'no'? Assuming you could, for the sake of argument—" "No," said Hélène.

Mike took a few short exasperated strokes toward shore. Then he turned back. "I'll bet you," he said patiently, "that within ten years —no, five—somebody buys that whole cliff, leases the Rocca Bianca for ninety years, and builds a hotel. With a bar and a terrace."

"And dressing rooms cut into the rock," concurred Hélène. "And showers and toilets for *signore* and *signori*. And a night club over the water—why not? They would make a road and sell off plots of land for villas and *villini*. After that, a shopping center. It will happen. You are right. *Arturo pense la même chose.*"

Mike's jaw dropped. He swallowed water. "Well, then," he said, spluttering, "if you see it coming so clearly, why don't you get in there first?" "Preventive war," commented Hélène.

Mike ignored this. "Between you, you could raise the money for the necessary bribes."

"It would not be cheap."

Mike floated. "You'd buy the land above of course, too. You'd have to, to protect yourselves. And if you had the land, you'd build—the whole group of you. Why pay rent in Porto Quaglia? Say twelve houses." He narrowed his eyes, thinking. "You could build twelve houses in those trees if you kept them inconspicuous. In good taste. Blending with the landscape. Leaving green areas. You'd form a syndicate—incorporate. Get a good modern architect from Milan. Use native building materials."

"*C'est-à-dire le marbre*," said Hélène.

"Why, yes!" Mike ejaculated. "Yes. Come to think of it, you'd have a free marble supply. That'd be something to leave Laure and François. A marble house. How about it, Hélène?" If he could have nudged her in the water, he would have done so. "Don't laugh. I'm serious. They laughed at Columbus. How about it?"

"*Non, merci*," she answered, striking out for shore. "What do you mean, '*non, merci*'?" he called after her.

Hélène swung around in the water. Seeing the American's plaintive expression, she was angry. "*J'ai dit non*," she said. "*Mon père n'a pas été cinq ans à Auschwitz pour devenir propriétaire d'une villa en marbre sur la côte ligurienne.*" "I can't understand you," yelled Mike. "You're talking too fast." "I said my father has not spent five years in Auschwitz to become the owner of a marble villa in Italy."

"I don't see the connection," called Mike.

"We are plain people," shouted Hélène. "What do you call it—wandering Jews."

Mike reflected for a minute. "I don't get it," he said. "Are you against owning property?"

"Yes," shouted Hélène, though this was not the truth—she was against being the kind of person who would preempt a natural marvel like some common piece of shore property, but she did not know how to express this in English, least of all to Mike, whose relentless American logic made it impossible, she said to herself, to have a reasonable conversation with him. Moreover, she had never known how to answer the insane argument that one ought to do something bad because if one did not someone else would do it instead. She struck out for shore again.

"You French have no vision!" Mike's voice roared after her indignantly. He backstroked a few moments, to cool off, not sure himself whether he had been joking about the marble villas and she had taken him seriously, in which case he would have a right to feel injured, or whether he had been serious and would have a right to feel injured at not having been taken seriously enough.

On the shingle they found another argument going on—one party asserting that the source of beauty was in Nature and the other claiming that Nature was simply a sentimental name for tradition, the way things had "always" been. A fishing boat, Elisabeth had said, belonged to Nature, while a smart motorboat did not. But Arturo begged to differ. A fishing boat on the horizon appeared to be a part of Nature because it had "always" been there, like the sun in the sky, or the mountains, or the stars. But the stars in fact had changed; the Pole Star of the ancients was no longer the Pole Star of today. A horse or a pair of oxen in a field were viewed as a part of Nature, but when there were no horses or oxen there would be another Nature, and a tractor, to Laure's children, would be an intrinsic part of it. For that, said the painter, you would need a new Millet; it was the artists who decided what was Nature and what was not. Why then, said Elisabeth, could you paint a good picture of a carriage, while an Alfa Romeo could "sit" only for advertisements? What about a plastic dish, said a woman's voice. The engineer said there was no inherent reason that plastics should be uglier than marble; it was a question of good design. No, said the editor; plastics offered no resistance to the manufacturer, which made them inferior to marble. "Inherently," he added tartly, skipping a stone across the water.

The discussion veered to the White Rock. It had not "always" been there, said Mike. "*Si!*" objected Hélène.

"No," said Mike. "Some acquisitive group around Dante's time must have formed a corporation to exploit the marble there. Originally, the whole point must have been green, covered with trees, like the rest of these slopes. Then somebody struck marble. The White Rock is the end result of man's tampering with Nature. If he'd left Nature alone, there'd be no White Rock."

"*Il justifie le capitalisme,*" observed Laure in her still childish voice.

"*Il justifie le progrès,*" said François sombrely, with a malign look at the American. "*Et tu es contre le progrès?*" asked his father, smiling. "*Mais naturellement,*" retorted François. "*Moi aussi,*" said Laure. "*Moi non,*" said Catherine.

"*Regarde-moi ça, papa!*" bitterly exclaimed Hélène. "*Mes enfants sont devenus conservateurs, grace aux allemands.*"

It was a fact, as already had been noticed, that the coming of the "Germans" was bringing out the worst in the community.

The doctor looked up from his Stendhal. She would not, he said tranquilly, want them to take all their views from books. They must learn from what they saw around them.

"From Nature's book, eh?" quoted Mike, with a loud laugh, clapping the old man on the shoulder.

And from what they heard, the doctor added in a lowered voice to his daughter: children, like old people, were afraid of any suggestion of change; one had to be careful how one spoke of it to them—let them see more and hear less. He looked at his watch. "*Viens, mon fils*," he said to his grandson. "*C'est l'heure.*"

It was too early, objected the others, but the old man insisted that François should take him and the younger children home. Mike and Arturo pushed the rowboat off.

"*Regarde, mon fils*," said the doctor, as the boat rounded into the harbor.

The boy at the oars briefly raised his eyes to the marble mountains in the distance.

"*Elles sont belles, les montagnes?*"

"*Oui*," admitted François.

"*Pourquoi?*" said his grandfather.

All the children gazed at the white-capped peaks.

"*Parce que le marbre ressemble à la neige*," the boy answered promptly. But it was a cheat, he added in his hoarse, angry voice. "*C'est truqué, quoi. C'est de la fausse neige. Et cela ne justifie pas le progrès.*"

Perhaps not, the old man replied serenely, but it justified snow. This afternoon, he continued, hopping out of the boat and holding the painter for his grandson, they would all go to see the quarries.

The youngest children looked doubtful. "*Elles sont loin, les carrières.*"

Not too far, said the doctor; they would start right after lunch.

It was the first time the "French" had visited the marble quarries, though for several years a sign, "*Visitate le cave di marmo*," had been urging them to do so, on the road from Viareggio. This sign, in fact, which recently had begun reiterating its message in German, had killed their interest in the trip. But now several cars filled with "French" followed the doctor in his old Peugeot. The last car in the procession was the poet's battered Austin station wagon; having got wind of the expedition, he had brought his wife, a stroller, and four of his children—the baby had been left at home.

The first stop was at one of the quarries advertised on the road from Carrara. It was a "commercial" quarry; near the entrance was a stand selling Coca-Cola and beer and another selling marble souvenirs. Around the souvenir stand were German tourists in a group; a tourist bus stood waiting, and the cars parked along the highway were all marked with a big "D" for Deutschland. The quarry, which was not very deep, was no longer worked, and the principal attraction was a train track on which carts carrying blocks of marble shuttled back and forth. This was not the real thing, Mike protested.

"*Bien sûr,*" said the doctor, but it would amuse the younger children. The real quarries lay beyond, high in the mountains; the doctor had telephoned the doctor from Carrara, who had suggested the itinerary. After the "play" quarry, they would leave the tourist area and visit the mills where the marble was cut.

The mills lay along a stream that had turned white with marble dust; they made an atrocious noise, cutting the marble into slices with big iron blades—the small children were frightened. They wanted to go back and see the little train again.

The adults glanced at each other. The poor mountain villages that straggled out from the mills were extremely dusty; everyone began to cough. The mills themselves were dismal; the water from the stream used in the cutting process splashed over the ground, creating a gray mud. The streets of the villages were caked with gray mud; there were no trees, and the air was cold and wintry, for the mountains cut off the afternoon sun.

"*Ça suffit, papa!*" exclaimed Hélène, but the doctor would not heed her, leading them from village to village, mill to mill, consulting from time to time a slip of paper. They ought to see everything, he said. In each mill, he asked questions, which Arturo translated, while the others paced restively about, the Irishman pushing the stroller; the doctor wanted to know the details of the cutting mechanism, the incidence of silicosis among the mill workers—were there many tuberculars?

"*Tu es en vacances, papa!*" irritably cried Hélène. "Yes, Doctor," said the poet. "Take it easy; you're on holiday."

Finally the cars left the melancholy mills and proceeded farther into the mountains along a narrow winding road, past chambers of smooth gray marble cut into the hillsides and heaps of marble gravel. Suddenly the doctor braked, and the "French" for the first time saw, right before their eyes, the snow fissures and gleaming glaciers they had known for so many years from across the river. These in fact were marble slides—avalanches of quite ordinary-looking stones that had tumbled down the mountainsides. Seen close up, they were not even white but a pale leaden gray in some places and a pale urinous yellow in others. Dr. Bernheim glanced at his slip of paper, and the cars continued upward till they arrived at a narrow bridge across a chasm; here a worker stopped them. They were at Fantiscritti, the last name on the doctor's list. It was the end of the road. Because of the dangerous marble slides, cars were not permitted to go any farther; if the *francesi* wanted to visit the quarries beyond, they would have to go on foot.

Arturo took the slip of paper from his father-in-law. *"Mais tu t'es trompé, Maurice,"* he said. *"Sûrement."* This was the conviction of everyone—that the doctor had come to the wrong place.

Looking about them, they were conscious of a fearful disappointment. The spot on which they stood, surrounded by marble slides, looking into a chasm of rubble at the bottom of which ran a dirty *torrente*, was at the farthest extreme from what they had imagined. The scenery around them, far from being alpine, was a Cyclopean desert or monstrous manufactured wilderness that resembled, more than anything else, a set for some early super-colossal film, before the day of sound or color. The absence of sun in this pocket of the mountain combined with the bleaching light diffused by the monochrome stony gravel to suggest an interior, artificially lit and yet without shadow. There was no sign of a quarry or of a village—only a sort of frontier hut with a bus placard posted on it, around which some workers were loitering. Added to this, it was dusty; everyone was thirsty.

As they stood there, uncertain, a boy approached them and offered to accompany them to the nearest quarry, which he said was two kilometres off. They were in the right place, he assured Arturo and the editor. The quarries up there—he nodded toward the farthest mountain—were very old; Michelangelo had worked there before the birth of Christ, and slaves had carved pictures of Roman soliders on the walls, which was why the place was called Fantiscritti.

The "French" smiled dubiously at each other and looked at their watches: to go or not to go and see for themselves? Looking up at the towering mountains, the younger children refused; they were afraid of the avalanches. Finally it was decided that the men should go ahead with the older children, while the women could stay behind with the younger ones. "I'll take Seanie in the stroller if you like," said the poet, speaking of his six-year-old, but the boy guide protested this arrangement and Sean was left behind with his mother.

The women walked across the bridge in the direction in which the others were vanishing up a mountain track; as they chatted, Sean slipped away from them and began to sidle down a sort of path that led to the half-dry *torrente*. Suddenly the women heard cries in a dialect they did not understand; a worker came running very fast across the bridge to warn them. What the boy was doing was dangerous. At any moment he might dislodge a stone and start a slide that would bury him.

But he seemed not to hear the workers' cries or his pregnant mother's pleas to come back, and Hélène started to run down after him. "No, *signora, no!*" the workers shouted. A few stones began falling, like flour from a sifter, in her wake. She hesitated, saw the peril for the boy in her rashness, and turned back.

Then they simply waited, holding their breath, watching the child wave to them from the abyss; in the end, he returned coolly, unconscious of his danger, carrying with him a purple flower he had picked on the edge of the stream.

This nerve-racking episode confirmed the sinister impression made by the lonely spot. A bus came and collected the workers from the other side of the bridge, turned around, and started down the mountain. There was not another human being to be seen; they had not passed a single car on the way up; the women and children were alone.

"I don't like it here," "I want a drink of water," "I want to go home," the children whimpered, looking at the family cars, driverless, like a group of widows, on the other side of the chasm. Sean's older sister, Brigid, profited from the occasion by trying to imitate her brother's exploit; she was hauled back at once and spanked, with the approval of the child psychologist. Time passed; from the changing of the light, the women assumed that somewhere the sun had set. It grew colder, and the children were shivering in their summer clothes. The mothers fought down their hysteria, offering each other various explanations of why their husbands were so long in coming back. When the men and the older children at last returned from the quarry, they found their families huddled, terrified, in the automobiles, with the heaters turned on.

It had not been so different from the tourist quarry, they reported —another chamber cut into the wall of the mountain. The deep quarries, where they cut the white marble, were higher up; the workers walked an hour and a half every morning to get to them.

"Did you see the soldiers?" demanded the little children.

No, they had not seen the soldiers; the old Roman quarry had been closed a long time ago and the *fanti*, the foreman had said, were in the museum in Carrara.

"*On peut visiter, maman?*" said the children, coming to life.

But again they were told no; another day perhaps—at this hour the museum would be shut.

So instead, though it was dark and nearly their suppertime when they reached the bottom of the mountains, they all had ice-cream cones at the marble counter of a *gelateria* in Carrara, and the older children and the fathers heard about Sean's adventure.

"*Qu'est-ce que tu es venu chercher ici, papa?*" Hélène said thoughtfully to her father on the way home.

"*Rien,*" equably replied Dr. Bernheim. "*Une petite distraction.*"

Hélène shook her head. It was not just for amusement, she told her husband, that her father had brought them here. He wanted to tell them something. She knew her father, she said.

That night Arturo did not play chess. He and Hélène stood on the pier listening to the music coming from across the river. She was pensive, still thinking of the "scenery" they had visited, which on close view was an industrial landscape—a big gray outdoor mill. It was ugly, she said, turning to Arturo with a question in her voice. "*Très laid,*" her husband agreed.

She remembered the sallow marble slides and shivered. "*François a eu raison. C'est de la fausse neige. Comme dans le théâtre. Nous l'aimons parce que nous aimons la vraie neige.*" But everything here, she went on, was slightly false. The "French" were not French; the "Germans" were Italians; the "Jews" were a little of everything. The "Englishman" was maybe a German. Or a Jew, according to her father. The "fishermen" were businessmen. Everything was in quotation marks. Even François' "birthday." His real birthday, which they had all forgotten, was today. She sighed heavily. "*C'est moi, tu le sais, qui l'a faussée.*"

She was the one, alas, who had done it; she had moved his birthday ahead, two years ago, so that it would fall in the middle of the month before the first departures. And now other families had followed suit, so that every child's birthday celebrated by the summer people of Porto Quaglia was a false birthday. She gave a guilty, skittish little laugh. All was false, she repeated despondently—theatrical snow or the snow in a souvenir paperweight.

Arturo listened. "*Ce qui est vrai, Hélène, c'est le travail.*" The work of the fishermen, the work of the miners in that fearful dust. It was work that joined man to Nature. Not vacations, despite what people thought.

"*J'aime les vacances. Je déteste le travail,*" Hélène flung out. And it was true that she loved vacations and was already hating the day they would pack up and leave for the winter's work. After a pause, she asked in a different voice, diffident and stealthily curious, "*Et comment c'était, dans la carrière?*"

Bad, Arturo answered; the work conditions were hard. Every other day, according to the workers, a miner lost a thumb, an arm, a leg. "*C'est pas joli,*" he added, grimacing. The work was unhealthy and badly paid; the less-skilled miners got a thousand lire a day.

"*Mille lire!*"

Arturo nodded. François, he said, had been very much struck by that; Laure too. There were many strikes, and many of the miners were Anarchists. "*C'est drôle que c'est la première fois que nous y sommes allés.*"

Yes, agreed Hélène; it *was* funny that they had never gone there before, in all their years at Porto Quaglia. "*Les 'intellectuels de gauche'!*" she burst out after a minute. Another set of quotation marks, another cheat. Good, she went on bitterly, it was finished. They would not come back to Porto Quaglia another summer. She refused to live another summer with such trite illusions and echoes. "'*Ah, comme elles sont belles, les montagnes de marbre!' 'Que j'adore la Nature!'*" Mimicking her own voice, she stamped her foot on the pier.

But it was the same everywhere, replied Arturo, smiling. All the desirable vacation spots were like that. All vacationers "adored" the poverty of the natives. "*Surtout les âmes sensibles.*"

"*C'est vrai,*" muttered Hélène.

Why not be honest, said Arturo. If they never came back to Porto Quaglia, what would be the reason? "*Je ne sais pas,*" said Hélène.

The true reason, declared her husband, was very simple: "*les vacances payées.*" When they had first come to Porto Quaglia, only a few —professional people, artists, and salaried intellectuals like themselves —had a month off in the summer and a car or the price of railroad tickets to take them far from home. Now the many had it, especially the Germans. It was the "higher standard of living"—he quoted the words in English—of the European workers and small employees that had put Porto Quaglia on the map. The vacations of the masses were necessarily mass-produced. There was no escape from the "Germans" except for the very rich. Next summer the same problem would present itself. What would Hélène say when her *coiffeur* asked her where she was going for her holidays?

"*Il faut avoir une réponse, Hélène. C'est une question très importante. Tout le monde a le droit de savoir.*" The whole world had a right to an answer—the concierge, the grocer, the mailman, her editor at Gallimard. What was she going to tell them? An undiscovered Greek island? A woodcutters' hamlet in the Alps? A hotel in Turkey? A cliff on the Dalmatian coast? "*Un château en Espagne?*"

Hélène did not respond to her husband's raillery. There were Germans everywhere, she agreed morosely. "*Bon, donc. Au travail.*" She leaned her head against his chest. "*Mais comme j'aimais Porto Quaglia!*" Hearing the past tense of the verb that meant love, Arturo stared stiffly ahead of him into the dark.

"*Oui, c'était beau,*" he said.

WARREN MILLER was born in Stowe, Pennsylvania, and now lives in New York. He is the author of several novels, among them *The Cool World, Flush Times, The Way We Live Now,* and in 1964, *The Siege of Harlem.*

Chaos, Disorder and the Late Show

I AM a certified public accountant and a rational man. More exactly, and putting things in their proper order, I am a rational man first and an accountant second. I insist on order; I like the symbols of order—a blunt, hardy plus sign or a forthright minus delights me. I make lists, I am always punctual, I wear a hat. Maltz believes this has caused my hairline to recede. Maltz is one of my associates at the office. He married too young and he regrets it.

In fact, there is no scientific foundation for his view that wearing a hat causes the hairline to recede. Such things are largely a matter of heredity, although my father has a luxuriant head of hair. But what of my grandfathers? I have no doubt that one of them accounts for my high forehead. Talent, I believe I have read somewhere, often skips a generation or jumps from uncle to nephew. Studies have been made. Naturally there are exceptions. But it provides one with the beginning of an explanation. The notion of having been an adopted child is a fancy I have never indulged. I have never doubted that my parents are my true parents. But I sometimes suspect they think I am not their true son.

Let me say just this about my father: He is a high-school history teacher, and every summer for twenty-five years he has had a three-month vacation. Not once has he ever put this time to any real use. He could have been a counselor at a camp, taught the summer session, clerked at a department store or . . . any number of things. I recall that he spent one entire summer lying on the sofa, reading. Some years he goes to the beach. Once he went to Mexico. His income is, to be sure, adequate, but I am certain that one major illness would wipe out his savings. I have tried to speak to him about pre-planning; he listens, but he does not seem to hear.

Copyright © 1963 by The Curtis Publishing Company.

My mother—I think this one example will suffice—my mother believes that Leslie Howard, who was a Hollywood actor killed in the war, is still alive. My father merely smiles when she speaks of Leslie Howard—I believe he actually enjoys it—but I have brought home almanacs and circled references in *Harper's* and other magazines attesting to the fact that Leslie Howard is, in fact and in truth, dead. Definitive proof.

Not that I care; not that I care very deeply. It is a harmless-enough delusion; but it is sloppy. I believe that the world tends naturally to chaos and that we all have to make our daily—even hourly—contribution toward order. My parents, in my opinion, are unwilling to shoulder their share of this responsibility.

I have, once or twice, discussed the matter with Maltz, whose wife has proved to be unreliable in some ways and who has a sympathy in matters of this kind. Maltz agrees that my father is mistaken in his indulgent attitude; on the other hand, he believes it would, perhaps, be better psychologically if I ignored my mother's pitiful little delusion—as he called it.

But it is like a pebble in my shoe or loose hair under my shirt collar. Chaos and disorder in the world, in the natural scheme of things, is bad enough; one does not want to have to put up with it at home too. The subways are dirty and unreliable; the crosstown buses are not properly spaced; clerks in stores never know where their stock is.

The extent of the breakdown is incredible. Every year at this time I rent an empty store on upper Broadway and help people with their income-tax returns. These people keep no records! They have no receipts! They lose their canceled checks! They guess! The year just past is, to them, a fast-fading and already incomplete collection of snapshots. It was full of medical and business expenses and deductions for entertaining, yet they remember nothing. Believe me, the chaos of subways and crosstown buses and our traffic problems is as nothing compared to the disorder in the heads of *people*. Every year I am struck with this anew.

This extra-time work continues for three months and becomes more intense as deadline time draws near. It is amazing how many people wait until the last possible moment. Often I am there until nearly midnight.

At the beginning of March I hire Maltz and pay him by the head. He is not as fast as I would like, but he is reliable and, because of his wife and her extravagances, he needs the money. "It would embarrass me," he says, "if I had to tell you how much she spends every week on magazines alone."

Poor guy.

I live with my parents. The store I rent is near their apartment, a matter of three blocks, walking distance. It is a neighborhood of small shops and large supermarkets which once were movie houses; their marquees now advertise turkeys and hams. Maltz occasionally will walk me to my door.

That night, the night of the incident, it was snowing. It had been snowing all day. No one had cleaned his sidewalk, and it made walking treacherous. I almost slipped twice.

"Isn't there a city ordinance about people cleaning their sidewalks? Isn't it mandatory?" I asked.

Maltz said, "There is such an ordinance, Norman, but it is more honored in the breach than in the practice."

The sadness of his marriage has given Maltz a kind of wisdom. The next time he slipped I took his arm, and I thought, Here is a man who might one day be my friend. The loneliness of the mismated is a terrible thing to see. It touches me. I believe I understand it. At the door of my building I said good night and I watched for a moment as Maltz proceeded reluctantly toward home.

The elevator was out of order again. When a breakdown occurs, tenants must use the freight elevator at the rear of the lobby. I had to ring for it three times and wait more than five minutes; then I had to ride up with two open garbage cans. It was not very pleasant. The elevator man said, "How's business, Mr. Whitehead?"

"Very good, thank you, Oscar," I said.

"I'll be in to see you real soon, Mr. Whitehead."

I nodded. I knew he'd wait, as he did last year, until the last possible moment. I tried to shrug it off. It's no good trying to carry the next man's share on your own shoulders, I told myself. Forget it, I thought.

Because I had come up in the freight elevator, I therefore entered our apartment by way of the kitchen. I took off my rubbers and carried them in with me, my briefcase in the other hand. As a result the door slammed shut, since I had no free hand to close it slowly.

"Is it you?" my mother called.

She was at the kitchen table having her midnight cup of tea; she said it calmed her and made sleeping easier to have tea before bed. I have tried to explain to her that tea has a higher percentage of caffeine than coffee, but she continues to drink it.

She was smiling.

"What is it?" I said.

"Mr. Know-it-all, come here and I would like to show you something."

She had a newspaper on the table. I did not move. "What is it?" I asked.

"Come here and I will show you, Norman," she said, still smiling.

At this point my father shouted something unintelligible from their bedroom.

"What did you say, dear? What?"

"Bette Davis on the late show. *Dark Victory!*"

My mother put her hand to her heart. "I remember the day I saw it," she said. "At the Rivoli, with Millie Brandon." She sat there, staring at nothing; she had forgotten all about me.

"What was it you wanted, Mother?" I said.

"Twenty-five cents if you got there before noon, would you believe it," she said.

I looked at the newspaper. I was astonished to see that she had brought such a newspaper into the house. There it was, beside her teacup, one of those weekly papers that always has headlines such as: Mother Poisons Her Five Babies or Tab Hunter Says "I Am Lonely." The inside pages, I have been told, are devoted to racing news.

"Mr. Know-it-all," she said and began to smile again.

"What are you doing with *that* paper, Mother?"

"Millie called me this afternoon and I ran out and bought it. Look!" she cried, and with an all-too-typical dramatic flourish she unfolded it and showed me the front page. The headline read: Leslie Howard Still Alive.

"So much for your almanacs and your definitive proof," she said. "Now what have you got to say, my dear?"

"Two minutes, dear," my father called in to her. "Commercial on now."

"Coming," she called back.

"Mother," I said, "you know very well what kind of paper this is."

"Why should they pick this subject?" she said, tapping the headline with her fingernail. "Why should they pick this particular subject right out of the blue? I would like to ask you that."

"Did you read the article itself, Mother? Is there one iota of hard fact in it?"

"There are facts, and there are facts, my dear boy."

I was very patient with her. "Mother," I said, "he is dead. It is well known that he is dead. He went down at sea in a transport plane. . . ."

"First of all, Mr. Smart One, it was not a transport. It was a Spitfire. He always flew Spitfires. He and David Niven."

"Well, then, Mother, just tell me this," I said. "If he's alive, where is he? Where is he?"

"It's starting, dear," my father called.

"The loveliest man who ever walked this earth," she said.

"I have never had the pleasure of seeing him, Mother."

"Steel-rimmed glasses. A pipe. Tweed jackets."

"Well, where is he, Mother?"

"So gentle. Gentle, yet dashing. If everybody was like Leslie Howard, wouldn't this be one beautiful world. Oh, what a beautiful world it would be!"

"Under no circumstances would I trust that particular newspaper," I said.

"This newspaper, my dear boy, is like every other newspaper. It is sometimes right."

I put my rubbers under the sink.

"The year you were born I saw him in *Intermezzo*, Ingrid Bergman's first American movie. Produced by Selznick, who was then still married, I believe, to Louis B. Mayer's daughter Irene." She sipped her tea and looked at the headline. She said, "These days they don't even name boys Leslie anymore. *Girls* are now named Leslie. Before the war people had such lovely names. Leslie, Cary, Myrna, Fay, Claudette. What has happened?"

She looked at me as if it were all my fault. "*I* don't know what's happened, Mother," I said, perhaps a little testily.

"It's your world, my dear; therefore you should know," she said. "Nowadays they even name them after the days of the week."

"I have named no one after any day of the week, Mother," I said, but she was not listening.

"You could always find a parking place. People were polite. Self-service was unheard of. Frozen food was something to be avoided at all costs."

"I can put no confidence at all in that particular newspaper," I said. "Absolutely none."

"Then I am sorry for you and I pity you," she said in a manner that I thought entirely uncalled for.

"Why? Why should you be sorry for me and pity me?" I asked.

I waited for her to answer, but she went back to sipping her tea and reading the headline.

"I have a good job," I said, "and I am doing the work I like."

"Nevertheless, Norman, I feel sorry for you."

I had not even taken off my overcoat, and I was forced to put up with an attack of this nature! I was struck by the unfairness of it. I said, "You *know* what a silly newspaper that is, Mother. What is the matter with you? You know he is dead. I know you know it. Everybody knows that he is dead."

She banged down her cup. "He is not!" she said. "He is not dead! He is not!"

"What's going on in there?" my father called.

"He is alive!"

"Then where is he?" I demanded, and I raised my voice, too; I admit that I raised my voice. "Where is he?"

"Oh," she said as if she were completely disgusted with me. "Oh, Mr. Born Too Late, I'll tell you where he is," she said, getting up from her chair, the newspaper in her hand. And she began to hit me on the head with it. She hit me on the head with it. Every time she mentioned a name she hit me. "I'll tell you where he is, I'll tell you where he is. He is with Carole Lombard and Glenn Miller and Will Rogers and Franklin . . ."

I ran out of the room. Why argue? She has a harmless delusion. From now on I will try to ignore her when she gets on this particular subject. Maltz may be right about this. I hung up my coat. Fortunately it is only when I stand at my closet door that I can hear the sound of their television set, which often goes on until three in the morning. Once I shut that door, however, my room is perfectly silent.

Magazines Consulted

ANTE — Echo Press, P.O. Box 29915, Los Angeles 29, California

ARARAT — Armenian General Benevolent Union of America, Inc., 250 Fifth Avenue, New York 1, New York

THE ANTIOCH REVIEW — 212 Xenia Avenue, Yellow Springs, Ohio

THE ARIZONA QUARTERLY — University of Arizona, Tucson, Arizona

THE ATLANTIC MONTHLY — 8 Arlington Street, Boston 16, Massachusetts

AUDIT — Box 92, Hayes Hall, University of Buffalo, Buffalo 14, New York

CARLETON MISCELLANY — Carleton College, Northfield, Minnesota

THE CAROLINA QUARTERLY — Box 1117, Chapel Hill, North Carolina

THE CHELSEA REVIEW — Box 247, Old Chelsea Station, New York 11, New York

CHICAGO REVIEW — University of Chicago, Chicago 37, Illinois

THE COLORADO QUARTERLY — Hellums 118, University of Colorado, Boulder, Colorado

COMMENTARY — 165 East 56th Street, New York 22, New York

CONTACT — Box 755, Sausalito, California

COSMOPOLITAN — 57th Street and Eighth Avenue, New York 19, New York

DECEMBER — P.O. Box 274, Western Springs, Illinois

ENCOUNTER — 25 Haymarket, London, S.W. 1, England

EPOCH — 159 Goldwin Smith Hall, Cornell University, Ithaca, New York

ESQUIRE — 488 Madison Avenue, New York 22, New York

EVERGREEN REVIEW — 64 University Place, New York 3, New York

FANTASY AND SCIENCE FICTION — 347 East 53rd Street, New York 22, New York

FORUM — Ball State Teachers College, Muncie, Indiana

FOUR QUARTERS — La Salle College, Philadelphia 41, Pennsylvania

GENERATION — THE INTER-ARTS MAGAZINE — University of Michigan, 420 Maynard, Ann Arbor, Michigan

GENESIS WEST — 711 Concord Way, Burlingame, California

(GQ) GENTLEMEN'S QUARTERLY — 488 Madison Avenue, New York 22, New York

THE GEORGIA REVIEW — University of Georgia, Athens, Georgia

GOOD HOUSEKEEPING — 57th Street and Eighth Avenue, New York 19, New York

HARPER'S BAZAAR — 572 Madison Avenue, New York 22, New York

HARPER'S MAGAZINE — 49 East 33rd Street, New York 16, New York

THE HUDSON REVIEW — 65 East 55th Street, New York 22, New York

THE KENYON REVIEW — Kenyon College, Gambier, Ohio

LADIES HOME JOURNAL — 666 Fifth Avenue, New York 22, New York

THE LITERARY REVIEW — Fairleigh Dickinson University, Teaneck, New Jersey

MADEMOISELLE — 420 Lexington Avenue, New York 17, New York

MAINSTREAM — 832 Broadway, New York 3, New York

THE MASSACHUSETTS REVIEW — University of Massachusetts, Amherst, Massachusetts

MC CALL'S — 230 Park Avenue, New York 17, New York

MIDSTREAM — 515 Park Avenue, New York 22, New York

MINNESOTA REVIEW — Box 4068, University Station, Minneapolis, Minnesota

MOTIVE — The Methodist Student Movement, Methodist Board of Education, P.O. Box 871, Nashville, Tennessee

MUTINY — Box 278, Northport, New York

NEW MEXICO QUARTERLY — University of New Mexico Press, Marron Hall, Albuquerque, New Mexico

NEW WORLD WRITING — % J. B. Lippincott Company, 521 Fifth Avenue, New York 17, New York

THE NEW YORKER — 25 West 43rd Street, New York 36, New York

NIMROD — University of Tulsa, Tulsa, Oklahoma

NORTHWEST REVIEW — Erb Memorial Student Union, University of Oregon, Eugene, Oregon

PARALLAX — Box 519, Carbondale, Illinois

THE PARIS REVIEW — 45-39 171 Place, Flushing 58, New York

PARTISAN REVIEW — Rutgers University, New Brunswick, New Jersey

PERSPECTIVE — Washington University Post Office, St. Louis 5, Missouri

PLAYBOY — 232 East Ohio Street, Chicago 11, Illinois

PRAIRIE SCHOONER — Andrews Hall, University of Nebraska, Lincoln 8, Nebraska

QUARTERLY REVIEW OF LITERATURE — Box 287, Bard College, Annandale-on-Hudson, New York

QUARTET — Purdue University, Lafayette, Indiana

REDBOOK — Published by McCall Corp., 230 Park Avenue, New York 17, New York

REFLECTIONS — THE FREE SOUTH REVIEW — 102 Mallette Street, Chapel Hill, North Carolina

THE REPORTER — 660 Madison Avenue, New York 21, New York

SAN FRANCISCO REVIEW — Box 671, San Francisco, California

THE SATURDAY EVENING POST — 666 Fifth Avenue, New York 19, New York

SEQUOIA — Box 2167, Stanford University, Stanford, California
SEWANEE REVIEW — University of the South, Sewanee, Tennessee
SHENANDOAH — Box 722, Lexington, Virginia
SOUTHWEST REVIEW — Southern Methodist University Press, Dallas 22, Texas
STORY — 207 East 84th Street, New York 28, New York
STUDIES ON THE LEFT — P.O. Box 33, Planetarium Station, New York 24, New York
TEXAS QUARTERLY — Box 7527, University of Texas, Austin 12, Texas
THE TRANSATLANTIC REVIEW — Box 3348, Grand Central P.O., New York 17, New York
THE UNIVERSITY OF KANSAS CITY REVIEW — University of Kansas City, 51st and Rockhill Road, Kansas City, Missouri
THE VIRGINIA QUARTERLY REVIEW — University of Virginia, 1 West Range, Charlottesville, Virginia
VOGUE — 420 Lexington Avenue, New York 17, New York
WESTERN HUMANITIES REVIEW — Bldg. 41, University of Utah, Salt Lake City 12, Utah
WOMAN'S DAY — 67 West 44th Street, New York 36, New York
THE YALE REVIEW — 92-A Yale Station, New Haven, Connecticut